I0653313

The Visitor Comes for Good:

The Complete Visitor Saga

Visitor #1–#7

by

K.D. West

Copyright © 2017, Stillpoint Digital Press
stillpointdigital.com

Published by Stillpoint/Eros

All rights reserved

This is a work of fiction. Any resemblance to actual people,
places or events is purely coincidental.

Warning: This work contains explicit descriptions of
fictional sexual activity provided for the reader's enjoyment.
It is not intended as sexual or medical advice. Readers
should educate themselves and take all proper precautions
(including condoms) before engaging in any acts depicted
herein.

All sexual encounters in this work occur between —
and among — consenting adults aged 18 and above.

ISBN: 978-1-938808-40-1

K.D. West's Friendly Ménage tales:

Stillpoint/Eros

stillpointeros.com

Contents

The Visitor 3

The Visitor Comes Home 21

The Visitor Comes Again 35

The Visitor Goes to Work 45

The Visitor Entertains 59

The Visitor Takes a Trip 101

The Visitor Has Company 141

Goddess: The Visitor's Wedding 195

About K.D. West 199

The Visitor Comes for Good

The Visitor

Lea didn't usually masturbate in airplane bathrooms, because, after all, they're bathrooms. On airplanes.

But half of the way through the long flight across the country to Atlanta, she found herself in the tiny, tinny cubicle with one foot up on the wall and the other in the sink, with her fingers buried to the second knuckle in her pussy.

Thinking of Sean, her best friend's older brother.

Sean the firefighter of the broad shoulders and the narrow hips. Sean of the gentle Southern drawl, the polite tone, the blue eyes, and the wicked, square-jawed smile.

Sean, who she had always wanted to wrap her arms and legs around, but never managed to do more than flirt with a bit.

Sean. Who had found out that she was interviewing for the job in Atlanta and had, with smooth, apparently subtext-less Southern hospitality, invited her to save the cost of a hotel room and stay with him. Well, on the sofa of the apartment he shared. But still. Just a door away... *Oooo, Sean.*

She wanted him. She had always wanted him, since she was a college sophomore and his sister Kirsten's roomie. She wanted his strong arms around her. Wanted his big hands pulling her pelvis *tight* against his. Wanted to feel what she knew would be his big, thick cock spreading... *Ooo...!*

With a shudder of pleasure and relief that she knew was only temporary, she came, swallowing as best she could the groan that wanted to explode from her gut.

Carefully, quickly, Lea lowered her legs, pulled up her panties, pulled down her skirt and smoothed it as best she could, washed her hands, and opened the bathroom door.

A woman just a few years older than Lea stood in the narrow galley glaring daggers at her. Her elbow-high child was doing a dance that made unmistakably clear just how long they'd had to wait.

"Sorry," Lea murmured. "Thanks."

"Yaw're welcome," the mother grumbled in a thick-as-honey accent that made Lea feel anything but welcome as the woman and her child pushed past.

Even so, hearing that Southern sound got Lea thinking of Sean again, of his arms and chest and ass and mouth... and got her wondering just how long the mom and kid were going to take, because, *oh*, she could have started all over, airplane bathroom or no.

The plane finally landed and Lea picked up the beat-up old Civic she'd rented. Sean had told her that he'd have loved to pick her up, but he wasn't going to be getting off duty until about the time Lea landed, and since she was going to need a car the next day anyway to get to the interview, she drove herself north from the airport — around the city and into Cobb County, where Sean and the other firefighter shared a place, where she'd be sleeping on their couch.

Well, she thought *let's not lie*: Lea hoped that she *wouldn't* be sleeping on their couch. She hoped very much that she would at last be sharing Sean's bed. She knew that she should have been thinking about the interview, but hey — there are lots of jobs. There was only one Sean, and she'd lusted after him for far too long.

Well. She *was* thinking about the job interview. It was for the position of assistant business manager of a mid-sized professional theater — her chance finally to work somewhere other than the glorified community theaters she'd been slaving at since graduation. She was excited by the opportunity.

But Sean....

Her thoughts less on the road than they should have been, she followed her phone's directions around the city, past dozens of malls, hotels, and office buildings mostly bearing the name *Peachtree Whatever*, and out into the gently rolling hills and lush greenery of the Atlanta suburbs. "Exit the highway," said her phone, and she exited. "Turn left," it intoned, and she turned left.

She wondered if she could give her GPS voice a Southern accent. *Tuhn leyeft, honey*. That thought made Lea smile.

She reached the complex, parked, and followed Sean's very clear directions to his second-floor apartment. Fighting down the images of Sean's broad chest — and narrow hips — that had driven her to the airplane lavatory, she knocked on the door.

A muffled voice called out, "C'me in! It's unlocked."

She opened the door and was assaulted simultaneously by the delicious smells of something sweet baking and something frying, as well as by the vision of the tall, tapered figure at the stove.

Him. Cooking. Looking like every masturbatory fantasy Lea had ever had about him, only better. Except fully dressed, but *food*. *Shit*.

"Sorry I couldn't come to the door," he said in that sweet Georgia drawl. He finished flipping something in the pan. "I'm up to my elbows in fried chicken. Hope you like — "

Lea threw her arms around him from behind and took joy in squeezing his chest hard. "I love it! Thank you so much for having me."

"Uh. Welcome." He stiffened before relaxing and turning in her grasp. "Nice to meet you, too, miss."

Lea looked up at the eyes smiling down at her. Brown. At the dimpled chin. *Not Sean. Oh, SHIT.* She released the man — he had to be Sean's roomie — and stammered, "I'm so, so… I, uh…"

"Naw, miss, don't be sorry, that was a nice hello, no doubt!" The roommate put down his tongs and smiled at her. He held out his enormous hand. "I'm Andrew. You must be Lea."

She shook his hand and nodded, still speechless.

His grin grew. "Really, don't feel bad. It happens more often than you'd think — the captain mixes us up so much he's taken to just calling us the Twins."

"Huh," Lea grunted. She was feeling the ghost of that muscled chest on her fingers.

"There you are, Lea!" Another Southern voice called from the other side of the apartment. She turned: it was Sean, no doubt this time. Blue eyes. Square jaw. Nothing on but a towel around his waist. *Oh. Shitty shit-shit.* He ran his hand through his short, wet hair. "Sorry, I was just taking a shower, I didn't want you to have to smell me like the hog I am."

"Huh," Lea repeated.

Sean smiled warmly. "I see you met Andy. I hope, Andy," he said, his voice lowering in mock threat, "that you've conducted yourself like a gentleman toward this young lady."

"I wasn't the one came out half-naked," joked Andy.

Lea found her voice. "Besides, I was the one molesting *him*."

Sean raised his eyebrow, that supremely wicked grin on display.

"Yeah," laughed Andy, "lucky me! She thought I was *you*. Couldn't see your ugly face 'cause I was dealing with supper."

"*My* ugly face!"

"Anyhow," Andy laughed, "why didn't you tell me our visitor was such a bombshell? Begging your pardon, Miss Lea."

Lea felt Sean's eyes flash to hers, saw the smile turn from wicked to evil. "Didn't want you getting ideas, Andy."

Lea couldn't think of anything to say to that.

"Ideas, huh?" Andy snorted and turned back to the stove. "You go get some pants on, boy, and we'll have some supper and then we can talk about who's getting *ideas*."

Now Sean's grin turned sunny again; he waved and turned, and Lea was treated to the sight of his retreating, naked, rippling back and his tight, towel-clad ass as they made their way down the hall.

I'm getting ideas, Lea thought, and then tried very hard not to think any more.

Dinner — *supper* — was of course fried chicken, with, of course, corn on the cob and amazing peach pie. "You've now hit all of the high points of Georgia cuisine," Sean joked.

"Hey!" said Andy, "we haven't even got to grits and boiled peanuts!"

Making a face, Sean said, "What a shame."

"You call yourself a Georgia boy?" said Andy. "You're all city, Sean, admit it."

"You have to be from the country to be a Georgian?" Sean raised an eyebrow.

"Naturally," Andy replied. "Q.E.D."

Trying not to get totally lost in enjoying their banter (*flirtation?*), Lea said, "Sounds like something my mom always used to say: if you live in New York, you're Jewish. If you're Jewish living outside New York, you're *goyisch*. Um, gentile."

"Me," said Sean, "I have always considered myself a citizen of the world."

Andy laughed, "Yeah, listen to the cosmopolitan here. Visit's his sister off in California, and he comes back talking about *artichokes* and pizza with all kinds of fancy stuff on it, and *sushi*."

"I didn't know you liked sushi, Sean!" To be honest, Lea couldn't remember Sean ever eating a meal that he didn't seem to enjoy.

"Oh," Sean said, he eyes holding hers once more, "I *love* sushi." His tone barely changed, and his expression seemed to hold exactly the same open, welcoming grin, but there was something about the way he said it that made Lea's middle flutter as she imagined him kneeling between her legs. Imagined the feeling of his tongue… He winked.

He's flirting with me, Lea reveled. Oh, god, yes, he's flirting with me.

Andy laughed again and popped open another beer for Lea. "Now see, *me*, I like my fish too, but I like it as the first course, not the main dish."

Lea's eyes snapped to Andy's and she saw that he too had a lazy, sexy smile on, and that — yes — she hadn't imagined the sexual undertones this time either. *Playing games, gentlemen?* She took a swig of her cold beer and twirled the drumstick bone she'd been fiddling with. "Well," she said, letting her voice grow raspy, "I like my meat red, generally. Love to chew on a rib, for instance. Nice, long, hard rib, dripping juices down my chin…" She ran her tongue up the length of the bone. "*Mmm.*" When both men's jaws dropped, she couldn't help it: she laughed.

Sean and Andy were both turning bright red, but they too laughed, long and hard.

"Mind," Lea finally managed to say, waving the bone, "this chicken really was fabulous."

"Thank you," Andy said with a smile and mock bow.

They proceeded to drink and talk. And drink some more. Beer. And then some bourbon. And then some more.

And Lea was flirting with two fantastically hot firemen, and they were both flirting back, and she felt absolutely fucking fabulous.

And just at the point that Lea was ready to pull her shirt off and yell, *COME TO MAMA!* to them both, Sean — or maybe it was Andy — stood up and reminded Lea that she had an interview in the morning. And then Andy — or maybe it was Sean — walked remarkably steadily over to the couch, pulled it out, and began to make up Lea's bed.

And the other helped.

For a brief moment, watching the two burly boys arranging her pillows and smoothing her sheets with an almost military precision, Lea indulged in an image of both of them stripping off their t-shirts, dropping their jeans and joining her....

But then both stepped away, wished her a good night, and sauntered together back toward where their bedrooms were. Each seemed to be trying to make sure that the other was leaving the room first, but eventually they left side by side, their shoulders barely clearing the hallway walls.

Well, shit.

As Lea slipped off her skirt, her shirt, her bra, and the panties that she'd been wanting to shed since she entered the apartment, she stood there, horny, naked, and more than a little drunk. *I could sneak into Sean's bed,* she thought. *He wouldn't kick me out, I know it. Or Andy's. Or...*

She shook her head. No. They'd made the sensible choice. She sat down and started to look for her pajamas....

But the air was warm and thick.

And she was tired. And light-headed.

And so she slipped, pajama-less, under the covers in the foldout bed, dreaming that the fingers stroking her clit and teasing her nipples belonged to two very large, very strong, very different sets of hands.

Lea's dream was very, very pleasant. In it, someone... Or perhaps more than one someone... Well. In either case, licking of her foot was involved, by a tongue or tongues unknown. *Mmm.*

Her eyes fluttered open.

It wasn't a dream.

A tongue was in fact running up Lea's instep, sending a flare to her crotch that caused her to writhe on her belly and groan. *Mmm.*

"Hey, Lea." The voice was soft and male and Southern. "Thought you might want some company."

Between the pleasant suddenness of her wakening and the alcohol that was still in her system, Lea could only manage a throaty "Uh-huh." She spread her legs wide, her foot pulling the sheet aside and uncovering her lower body.

"Mmm," whispered the voice. "I like peach pie just fine, but this was what I wanted for dessert."

"Uh... huh!"

Without warning the tongue had slid all of the way up her inner thigh and licked the entire length of her pussy, sending Lea's smoldering arousal into full flame.

"Shh." He chuckled. "Don't want to wake no one. 'Cept you, 'course."

Lea wanted to say something smart, but a whimper was the best she could do. Her pelvis arched up of its own accord.

Whichever of the men he was, he was clearly a gentleman. He took the invitation graciously and dove in. His tongue and lips began to tease and pleasure her lips and clit. His nose tickled her asshole, the hot breath sending what was already an indescribable sensation truly transcendent.

"Hnnnh!"

"Shh," he said again, this time against her clit.

Trembling, Lea stuffed her face into the pillow, screaming into it as he pleasured her with his tongue, his lips, his nose. When his fingers slid up under her belly and began to massage her breasts, she lost all sense of what was happening and where — her body was one nerve, pulsing, *now*.

Usually, Lea liked long, slow bouts of foreplay, liked kissing and touching and feeling a man slowly meander his way to going down on her. There was something wonderfully romantic about watching a head wandering down her belly and between her thighs. Nose bobbing as he lapped at her. Eyes open and smoldering or closed and abandoned as he pleasured her.

But this? Having her face shoved into the pillow, her ass up in the air, and that *mouth*.... Even if Lea had been on her back, even if it had been less than pitch black, she didn't think that she'd have been able to see straight anyway.

Thick, strong fingers pulled and teased remarkably gently at her nipples, causing her to scream on into the pillow as wide, fine lips sucked her sizzling clit against a fluttering tongue. *Cleft chin, or square?* she found herself wondering for a moment, though of course his chin was down between her spread thighs where she couldn't tell. But then an electric spark began to shoot from her clit up her spine, joining with the arcs of pleasure fired by those amazing fingers in flaring up to her brain and shutting down all thought quite effectively.

Thunder rumbled. At first, Lea thought it was her imagination, part of the monumental orgasm that set her aflame. Then, as the explosion subsided, she realized that not all of the lightning was inside of her. There was a storm outside, the kind that rarely visited Lea's home state.

Her visitor was kissing his way from her right cheek of her ass across the dimple at the base of her spine to the left cheek.

"Fuck me," moaned Lea into the pillow. "*Fuckmefuckme.*"

"Yes, ma'am," said the deep voice. "Always give a lady what she asks for, that's what I was always taught." She heard him fishing for something, heard the distinctive crinkle of a foil condom package being opened, a rubber being rolled down over a hard cock. A wide hand ran over her ass, her back, sending a tremor through Lea. . "Like this, or — ?"

Fuck. Me. She reached back between her legs, found a hard, long, latex-encased penis, and pulled it toward her.

"Yes, ma'am," he said, a quaver of desire in his voice that made Lea feel incredibly sexy and incredibly hot and that made her want him inside of her *right now*.

Again: Lea usually preferred to face her lover — whether in straight mission-ary position or with a leg or two over his shoulders — for a couple of reasons. First of all, she liked being able to see the effect she had on a man, could be in itself an incredible turn on. Second, she liked the feeling of the cock plowing the front wall of her pussy. Lea had discovered her G-spot long before she'd ever heard the term, had discovered that, unlike most of her girlfriends, she could have a very satisfying orgasm just from being fucked (so long as her lover was big enough and lasted long enough).

Just now, however, she didn't mind being banged from behind, her face still stuffed into her pillow.

As this cock head pressed into Lea's pussy, however, she gasped in surprise, feeling it surge along the front wall of her vagina: this cock, unlike any she'd ever had inside of her, curved *down*.

It was perfect.

It made her *scream*. If there was thunder and lightning rolling on, Lea couldn't have seen or heard, because the cock that was now pounding hard into her sent her nerves roaring, her blood screaming.

Orgasm, which hadn't ever quite left her, came howling back, playing hide-and-seek with her consciousness as her visitor slammed into her, one massive paw pulling her hips back against him as the other reached around and found...

Found her clit, and...

Oh, FUCK.

Was she dreaming again? Was it all just one enormous, wet blurry wet....

Lea's fingers reached down her belly between her legs. No cock.

No cock, but fabulously tender. Wet.

Had she hallucinated it? Or had she passed out, drunk and spent on whiskey and sex?

Blearily she turned over, looking for...

Lightning flashed, revealing a broad-shouldered silhouette. "Fuck," he said. "You are so fucking beautiful."

So are you, Lea tried to say, but couldn't be sure that any intelligible sound had passed her lips. She reached up, her slick fingers finding a muscled chest, caressing a tiny, jewel-hard nipple.

"*Shit.*" He hissed, and leaned forward, his lips finding hers as the retreating storm finally rumbled its own approval.

The flame inside of Lea, barely banked, flared back to light. Not quite so urgent as before, but no less strong, and so she pulled his body to hers, burying herself in him, running her finger along his ribs, the muscles of his back, feeling that hard cock, un-rubbered now, straining and leaking against the outside of her thigh.

Yet he seemed in no hurry this time, and so Lea was able to indulge and kiss and explore.

Her fingers counted the vertebrae down to the taut swell of his ass, the concave plane of his hips.

His fingers flowed slowly, reverentially over her flesh: her hips, her belly. Down? Please?

Well, no: as they kissed, as their tongues danced, those amazing, enormous, shockingly *delicate* fingers explored upward, skirting the outside of one aching breast, defining the line of her collar bone, of her throat, her earlobe....

How was it that a light touch against her ear could make goose pimples erupt all of the way down to her knees? She moaned into his mouth; desire clutched her again, throbbing through her. She wanted him inside of her — wanted him *so much* — and yet...

And yet the passion of their last fuck and the languor of this session had left her without will, without a muscle in her body. She was his, to take at whatever pace it pleased him, and *oooohhh*, it pleased him to take his sweet, sweet, Georgia-peach time, and it pleased her to be taken so.

Lea had lost her virginity during the summer before her senior year of high school. She and Sam had been dating for two years at that point, and had done just about everything that could be done with fingers and mouths, and so Lea hadn't been shocked at Sam's urgency or his hair trigger. Not shocked, but disappointed. They'd eventually worked out how to make sure that she got her fair share out of their sessions: it had usually involved lots of kissing and caressing, ending with his head between her thighs. He hadn't been exactly patient, but he had at least tried, the sweetie. Of the dozen or so lovers she'd had since, the more successful had usually followed a similar formula: petting her until she was worked up, getting her off with their tongues, then pumping into her until *they* got off. When she was really lucky, the man lasted long enough and was properly endowed — neither too well nor not well enough — so that the pressure of his cock against her G-spot and his pelvis against her clit got her off again before he exploded.

None of them had ever managed to set her alight without actually touching her crotch.

Her new lover was getting dangerously close. All with a slow, gentle touch that spread over her like honey on fire.

He broke their kiss, and Lea whimpered. And yet when the lips began a voyage along her chin to her ear, tongue flowing lightly around the lobe and *in* before continuing down her neck even as those amazing fingers began to outline the curves of her breasts, she found that she couldn't complain.

He kissed on down, licking at the hollow of her throat and at her chest, at the top of one swelling, aching breast, even as his fingers traced the bottom of her rib cage, the lines of the abs she never thought she had, the tightly trimmed bush of her pubes.

And at the same bright, shining moment, his lips closed around her right nipple as one of his hands caressed the other and the other hand slid over her pussy lips, stroking her vibrating clit.

Even in the moment, Lea was disappointed that she couldn't have enjoyed that slow, fabulous journey for longer. Even in the moment, Lea knew that she felt so fucking *good*.

Clenching her jaw, pressing her mouth against the top of his head, she screamed once again, her thighs clamping around his hand as a slow-motion tidal wave of an orgasm sloshed up through her and back down, leaving her limp and quivering.

She collapsed, her head flopping back, her legs falling apart, her eyes falling closed and her mouth falling wide open.

Holy fucking shit. Fuck. Oh, fuck.

How long had they been at it? Ten minutes? An hour? Long enough for the storm to have wandered away. Long enough for her to have come three times, each as hard as she could ever remember coming. *And I don't even know which...*

He kissed her breast lightly, his fingers still on the other nipple, his other hand still gently cupping her pussy. "God," he groaned, "you're so fucking *wet*."

"For *you*," she rasped. "You... fuck? *Please*."

"Oh, God, *yes*," he hissed, and Lea once again heard the sound of a hand fumbling in a pocket, of a foil packet being ripped.

This time she wanted to help roll the latex down over that magnificent erection, but her arms were boneless. She heard him grunt as he finished putting on the condom — next time, she'd have to invest in an IUD or a diaphragm or any fucking thing so they wouldn't have to *wait....*

Lea started to roll on her belly again, but he stopped her. "Naw," he sighed. "Wanna see you."

And so, half-conscious, she lay back as he slid between her legs, placing himself at her entrance. "Ready?" he grunted.

Lea nodded, or thought she did.

Whichever, he pressed himself in, filling Lea with airless, dark flame. *"Fuck!"*

"Yup." Lea grinned. Felt her entire body grin.

As he slowly pressed in, stretching her wide once again, he leaned down and kissed her — no teasing this time, just lips on lips. Closing the circuit.

In close embrace, in full contact from nose to knee, they began to fuck. *Fuck indeed!*

Well, to be completely honest, she was still as limp as a rag doll. He was doing the fucking, slowly, with agonizing tenderness that was just as intoxicating as the wild abandon from earlier. She could feel flare of his cock pressing along the ripples of her vaginal walls, could feel...

Fuck.

As they fucked — as he fucked her — his hands continued to explore, to enrapture. She could feel him stoking the flickering flame of her arousal, could feel it building, but so, so slowly that it made her want to weep, even as it made her want to sing.

John, with whom she'd lived for almost a year before moving back in with Kirsten, had gotten off on tying Lea up, teasing her. *Edging*, he called it: keeping her on the verge of coming for as long as he could before finally giving her release — but only when she was begging for it. She'd gone along with this game because it felt fucking *good*, but it had turned out to be one of a number of clues that he was a controlling asshole. A pleasant clue, but still.

This slow, slow fuck didn't feel like Lea's lover was trying to control her. It simply felt as if he was *in control*, savoring the delight with her, as if they were sharing a particularly fabulous meal.

"You… feel so fucking… *good*," he moaned into Lea's mouth.

Once again, "Yup" was all that Lea could reply. Or possibly "Yum."

She could feel a slick layer of sweat beginning to form between them, could feel his nipples, small and tight, dragging against hers, could feel the blood build up around her G-spot as the fabulous, wonderful, unbelievable cock massaged it, gently but mercilessly. Could feel arousal expanding her infinitely outward

"*Legs*," she panted, "*up….*"

He understood, apparently, because he slid his hands down under her knees and lifted them as he arched backward and pressed her calves upward with his square shoulders. Opening her to him. All without stopping his thrusts.

The change in angle absolutely scrambled what was left of Lea's brain, as her body clearly had clearly known that it would. The fuck was the only thing that existed in the world. It was a universal fuck. A metaphysical fuck.

He was speeding up — minutely, but noticeably, he pistoned into her more quickly, more forcefully. Lea wanted to beg him not to come too soon, to wait for the avalanche that was bearing down on her to sweep her away.

But her lips wouldn't form words.

His thrusts began to become less and less measured, more and more frantic, and Lea almost wept, because it felt so *fucking good*, but she was *so close* and…

And as her demon lover gave one last gigantic, spastic thrust, he reached between them and pushed his wide thumb firmly but gently against her clit, pressing it against the base of his cock, and…

And the avalanche carried her off in a flood of white pleasure, and if she were never to wake again, she considered it a fair trade. *Aloha. Shalom. Arrivaderci. Sayonara.*

To her surprise, however, she didn't die.

"Oh, gawd, oh, gawd," her lover gasped, his chest heaving against hers. Her legs were bent nearly flat against her torso, a level of flexibility she'd never quite managed in yoga, but was reveling in now, because she could *feel* his cock still within her, still pulsing. Which caused her to contract around him. Which made them both call out to a higher power.

Carefully, still buried in her, he released her legs. With as much regret as relief, she lowered them, squeezing his softening erection out of her body, which made both of them moan at the loss.

Lea became aware that her back, her ass, her legs — they were all burning. She was going to be sore as all fuck the next day.

But it was worth it.

They lay there, still entangled, as their breaths and pulses slowed. They kissed again. No frenzy. Just touching.

She must have fallen asleep at some point, because she startled to find him tucking her under the covers.

"Shh," he said, and placed a feather-light kiss on her forehead. "You get some sleep, now, you hear?"

"'Night," she rasped.

But he was gone.

One last distant rumble of thunder shook the night.

And all was darkness.

When Lea's phone started crowing at her to wake up and greet the bright new day while the sky was still dark — while it was still the middle of the night back on the West Coast — she slapped at it with a groan. *Fucking…*

Fucking.

Thunder. And a mouth on my foot. And a nose against my asshole. And a cock screwing me into the pillow. Fingers like feathers of fire. A slow, full-body fuck for the ages.

Fucking…

Must have been a dream, right?

Lea shifted, trying to shake the cobwebs from her brain, and her body screamed at her that it had been no dream. She was sore from knees to nose, but it was a fabulous sore, not like anything she'd ever endured after a run or a yoga class.

Trying to sort out just what had happened from the swirling mass of over-amped sensory impressions, Lea rolled (somewhat tenderly) to the side of the pull-out mattress. *Amazing you're still standing.* She patted the sofa-sleeper on the arm-rest. *Well done!*

Grabbing toiletries and her bathrobe, she made her way to the bathroom.

Which was right between the two firemen's bedrooms.

Which one was it? She couldn't decide whether she wanted her phantom lover to have been the man she'd had a crush on since she was nineteen or the stranger she'd just met.

Either way, they were both snoring, clearly sound asleep.

One of them had truly earned it, that was for sure.

Smiling — still moving gingerly — she went into the bathroom, closed the door somewhat regretfully, and took a long, hot shower that almost returned her body to her.

When she wrapped herself in her robe and stepped out of the steamy bathroom, she was greeted by two very solemn looking, bare-chested boys.

"Morning, Miss Lea," Andy said, while Sean simply turned "Lea" into an eight-syllable twelve-bar-blues of a mumble.

"Good morning, gentlemen!" she chirped, thinking, One of you was the best fuck I have ever had in my life, and I have no idea which of you it was.

"What do y'all want for breakfast?" mumbled Andy.

Sean muttered back, "You made supper, Andy. I'll take care of this one."

Each of them had his eyes on her, but even so, both of them seemed more aware of each other than of her.

Oh, god, she groaned inwardly, *they're both trying to mark their territory.* And while the idea held a certain amount of abstract fascination, she had absolutely no interest in being fought over or peed on. "It seems to me, gentlemen," she said, aiming for sweet-and-unassailable, "that it's your day off, and you've already provided me with a lovely meal and a lovely bed." She looked to see if either of them took that any way but literally, but their expressions remained stony. "It would be my pleasure to cook breakfast. *Y'all* go sit, and I'll cook."

When they tried to object, she reached out and grabbed each by the chest hair, twisting just enough to get their attention.

Their eyes bugged out and their jaws dropped, but they consented to sit together at the table.

Lea chatted away, pulling eggs and sausages out of the fridge — remarkably clean for a pair of guys, but hey, firemen know about hygiene, right? She had the sausages frying and was whipping the eggs when the sun broke through the clouds that were the only evidence of the previous night's storm. "Man," she sighed, taking in the golden light that washed over the small woods behind the apartment, feeling the warmth on her gloriously weary body, "will you look at that. Just gorgeous."

She hadn't really said it for their benefit, and so she hadn't *really* expected them to answer, but still, she was surprised when all she heard from behind her was a quiet choking sound.

Both of them were staring at her, jaws dropped, eyes wide.

Oh. Fuck. Silk robe. She started to try to make her silhouette a bit more modest, but then thought, *What the fuck, why not?* Standing there, knowing that they could see the outline of her body very clearly, she repeated. "Gorgeous. Don't you think?"

"Yes, ma'am," they both answered, making Lea laugh.

As the sausage sizzled away in the pan and the eggs cooked, she thought, Look as much as you want, gentlemen. One of you owns all of this already. *And then a thought occurred to her that made her blush and grin:* And if I can figure out who it was, maybe I'll give all of it to the other one tonight!

When she brought the breakfast to the table, both men kept their eyes glued to their food.

More's the pity, sighed Lea, as they ate in silence.

When they were done, Lea started to clear, but Sean stopped her. "Naw, you cooked, we'll clean."

"You should get ready for your interview," said Andy, very seriously.

And so Lea left them to it, grabbing her garment bag and retreating back to the bathroom.

In the bathroom, she took stock. No more thinking about hunky firefighters, *she scolded herself.* Time to go get yourself a job.

When she came out, hair tamed (more or less), makeup sparingly applied, battle armor on, ready to take on the world, the two men were still in the kitchen, which was indeed now clean. They still didn't seem to have anything to say to each other. They were standing, arms crossed, leaning against the counter.

"You look lovely, Lea," said Sean, which made her middle go soft.

"Gorgeous," added Andy, making it go warm.

"Thanks, boys." She took a deep breath, trying to focus on the interview, and not on their muscular torsos. "Wish me luck."

"Good luck," they said in unison, and away she went.

The interview went far better than Lea had even hoped. She hit it off immediately with the business manager, a sardonic, middle-aged Canadian with the unlikely name of Sassy ("It's Sally actually, but they started calling me Saskatchewan, which they then shortened, and it's kind of stuck.") By late morning, they were swapping war stories, and Sassy dragged Lea out of her office to show her through the entire building, introducing Lea to staff as they went — an army of fundraisers, marketers, and box office staff, then backstage to meet technicians and the wardrobe department, and finally into a rehearsal — a set designer was showing the cast what the stage was going to look like, so it must have been a read-through. When the cast took an Equity break, Sassy buttonholed Bob, the artistic director of the theater, and asked him to join her and Lea for a late lunch at the barbecue joint across the street.

Trying not to think too much about the fact that she was now having lunch with the senior management of a theater that Lea would kill to work at, she gnawed away at her pork ribs.

"I think this is how we keep Sassy here," said Bob with a broad smile.

"It's true," said Sassy, smirking. "Every time I want to head back to the great white north, someone drops a take-out bag of ribs on my desk, and I know I can't leave."

"We have our ways," Bob chuckled.

As they bantered on, Lea felt the sauce from the rib she was chewing on dribbling onto her chin, and she couldn't help but remember teasing Sean and Andy with just that image the previous night, couldn't help but remember their stunned expressions. Couldn't help but remember what happened after the lights went out.

"Well, something's got you smiling," Sassy said.

"It's the barbecue," said Lea as she dabbed at her chin. "I can see why you can't leave it behind."

They all laughed.

They offered her the job before she'd even finished eating, and she accepted on the spot. The pay wasn't great, and she'd have to leave California and her best friend, but the opportunity was too good to pass up.

"Are you going to need help finding a place to stay?" asked Sassy, clearing their sauce-soaked baskets.

"I… think I may have one lined up." This brought an even broader grin to Lea's face than before.

She called back to the apartment. One of them — she thought it was Andy — picked up, and before he could say more than "Hello," she shouted, "I got the job! Dinner tonight's on me!"

"Well, congratulations!" said whichever of the men was on the phone.

And before he could say anything more, she hung up and did a dance, right there in the restaurant.

When she walked back up the stairs to the apartment a couple of hours later, she had in one hand an enormous bag full of barbecue chicken from the same joint she'd had lunch at, with orders of fried okra and corn bread. In the other hand, she swung a bottle of Maker's Mark, with which she knocked against the door.

Just like the day before, a muffled voice called out, "C'me in! It's unlocked."

"Can't!" she called back. "Hands full!"

"Hold on," said a slightly closer voice, and the door swung open, revealing Sean, who was still wearing nothing but low-slung pajama bottoms.

Andy was sitting at the kitchen table, identically dressed.

"Haven't you guys even gotten dressed all day?" Lea laughed and gave Sean a sound kiss on the lips.

He looked astonished, but Andy scowled.

"None of that!" burbled Lea, dancing into the kitchen and giving him an equally sound smooch. That seemed to cheer him up. "Tonight, we're celebrating!" She held up the barbecue and the bourbon.

They were happy to go along with this plan, and were soon all stuffed and pleasantly buzzed. Between the warmth, the Southern humidity, the food, and the alcohol, Lea was getting sweaty, but she couldn't have cared less. She was hoping to get a whole lot sweatier. *Now which of you was my mystery man last night,* she found herself wondering as she took off her jacket and tossed it in the general direction of the pullout. *And am I going to get him to fuck me again, or am I going to try out the other one. Or…*

She looked back at the two men, whiskey-wild thoughts bouncing through her head.

They were both staring at her. At her chest. Both licking their lips.

When she looked down, she saw that sweat had made her white silk blouse all but translucent. The lace bra showed clearly through. She grinned at them. "Well, gentlemen, like what you see?"

They both looked back up at her, hunger and shock plain on their faces.

Lea stood and walked around to their side of the table, unbuttoning her blouse as she went. "I have a confession to make, guys."

"Oh?" said Sean with a gulp, his eyes following her fingers' journey down from button to button.

Andy's eyes were still on Lea's tits.

"Uh-huh. I had a visitor in my bed last night."

Both men turned bright red and looked down at their feet.

Aha! Gotcha! "I got fucked good. And hard. And long."

They both gulped.

"Now, it was dark last night, and so I couldn't see just who this mystery lover was, and so all today, I've been trying to figure out." She knelt between them. "Was it you, Andy?" She touched him on the knee and tried not to laugh when he jumped. "Or you, Sean?" She ran her fingers up the inside of his thigh and he let out a choking sound.

"And as we were eating that wonderful barbecue tonight, I've remembered something. Do you want me to tell you what it was?" She slid her hand slowly up their thighs, so that all they could do was nod. "Well, I'm sure as firefighters you must have to study a *lot* about anatomy and such."

They nodded again.

She trailed her fingertips up onto their bellies. That stopped them. "Know what a G-spot is, boys?"

Again they both nodded.

"What *good* boys you are. Well, the G-spot is located at the front wall of a woman's *puuuuussssy.*" She drew the word out, trailing her fingers down the tops of their outside legs. "Now last night, I was sleeping on my belly when my lover woke me and, *oooh,* that was how he fucked me, and, *oooooo,* that long. Hard. Cock." Her fingers circled back up the insides of their legs. Sweat dripped from Sean's nose and Andy's cleft chin. "It *stimmmm*-ulated my G-spot — remember, on the front of my body, and — " She gave a low moan. "It felt *soooo* good. It made me come *soooo* hard!"

Her fingers reached their crotches; she pushed underneath, cupping their balls, which jumped in her hands, evoking gasps as they spread their legs to give her easier access. *Such good boys.*

"And then," she sighed, feeling her own crotch beginning to overflow at the bounty before her, "I got fucked again. On my back this time." One of them gasped. "And it was slow. And sweet. And aaaaaagonizingly good, and he did it again, his cock making that little spot in my *pussy* feel... *Mmm....* I came again, so hard I passed out."

She looked up at them as she juggled their testicles. Their eyes were closed, their jaws slack. "Now, gentlemen, do you know what I've realized?"

They shook their heads.

"Oh, now, gentlemen, I think you have. I think you have figured out what it took me *alllllllll* day to work out." She began to run her hands up the fronts of the pajamas. *Oh, yes. I got it. I win!* "Open your eyes please."

They both did, each gazing at her hand pressing against his crotch.

"Now, gentlemen, for this demonstration to work, you shouldn't be looking at your *own* equipment. Look at your roommate's."

Sean's gaze shifted smoothly to Andy's lap. Andy's locked pleadingly onto Lea's.

"Now, now, Andy, if you're a good boy, you know you'll get a reward, don't you?"

"Uh-huh," he gasped, sounding in fact very young. Very eager to please. And very horny. He pulled his eyes away from hers and looked down at where the tip of Sean's cock was pushing above the waistband of his pajama pants.

"Here's what I realized, gentlemen." Now she stroked their growing erections, urging them on. "I realized that I came twice from having my G-spot *stimulated*." She slid each hand up to where each cock had now pushed out of the pajamas; she circled the tips with her fingers. "Once on my belly. And once on my back. And what does this tell us, gentlemen?"

"Both of us," sighed Sean, eyes half lidded but still locked on Andy's cock. "We both — *aah!*"

She had wrapped her hand around that long cock, which was now poking him in the belly button, and begun to stroke it.

He moaned and threw his head back, no longer able to watch.

As she continued to stroke him, she teased the uncircumcised head of Andy's, which was pushing away from his body as if desperate for more. "Do you see how good boys are rewarded, Andy?"

"Uh-huh." His eyes were still glued on the spectacle of Lea's hand milking Sean's long, freckled erection.

"Now," Lea pouted, "what I really want is one of these beautiful cocks in my *mouth*." She let loose a sigh. "But *then* I wouldn't be able to do as good a job with the other, and that wouldn't be any fun, would it?"

"Nuh-uh," they both grunted.

"I know! I'll suck the first one of you that helps me jerk the other off!"

Sean started to lift his hand, but — as Lea had guessed — Andy's shot out faster, grabbing Sean's erection at the base while she was at the head.

Andy's hand slid up to meet Lea's, and then, together, they traveled down again. *Well, fuck, good thing you're so long, Sean!* she thought as they began to stroke him.

Sean screamed, and Lea felt a splash of pre-cum spill over her knuckles.

"What a *good* boy you are, Andy! If you help me just a *little more*... Look, Sean! Look at both our hands on your beautiful, long cock."

Seemingly against his will, Sean's eyes pushed themselves back open. "Aww...

Fuck."

In unison, Lea and Andy sped up; Andy seemed to be as proficient and energetic at jacking off as he was at fucking, because Sean soon started thrusting into their hands. His cockhead was slick, and dark, dark red.

Suddenly, he stopped, held his breath, and...*"FUCK!"*

A rope of thick, white cum spewed over Lea's hand, landing in a long rivulet that started at one of Sean's nipples and ran down nearly to his navel.

Grinning up at him, Lea ran a finger through the cum and brought it to her lips. She licked it off. *"Mmm."*

"Lea," Andy whimpered.

"Don't worry, sweet boy. I'm going to give your reward now, don't you worry." Turning toward Andy, she worked to free his cock from the flannels that were holding it back; it was pushing out toward her like a dog pulling at its leash.

The PJs didn't want to let it go.

Finally, he pushed the offending pants down to his knees.

"Thanks, Andy," purred Lea, grasping his cock in both hands and bending forward to kiss the head.

"Damn," he gasped. "Good gawd *damn.*"

Slowly, carefully — trying to think through how having a cock that curved down your throat was going to be different — she slowly sucked him in, and he continued to cuss a blue streak.

She discovered that actually, for such a big cock, Andy's was relatively easy to take into her mouth, because of the reverse curve. She was just beginning to give herself over fully to giving him a blow job that would repay the mind-blowing fuck that he'd treated her to the night before when a hand began to slide up the inside of her thigh — from the back.

"Aw, sweetheart," whispered Sean into her ear. "You have no idea how fucking hot you look, that pretty mouth stretched around his big ol' thang."

She moaned, mouth full of *thang*, incredibly nimble fingers exploring her crotch.

"What reward'll you give *me*, Lea," Sean whispered on, his other hand gliding just over her belly, her breasts, "if I help you suck this country boy off."

Releasing the dick in question from her mouth but not her hands, she groaned, "Anything you fucking want."

"Anything?"

"Yup." Not wanting to lose herself in those blue eyes, in the feeling of those strong, gentle fingers on her flesh, or the thought of that cock... She went back to sucking on Andy's equally lovely pound of flesh.

"What I want, Lea," said Sean, fingers scintillating as he leaned forward with her and gave one of Andy's heavy balls a slow lick. "What I've wanted since I met you seven years ago..." He sucked the testicle into his mouth and released it, causing Andy to howl and a dollop of bitter pre-cum to splash into Lea's mouth. "What I want, baby, is *you*." He ran his tongue up the length of Andy's erection until his mouth met hers; together they devoured Andy, whose fingers tangled in both heads of hair.

And as they kissed around Andy's cock — a kiss that Lea too had been dreaming about for seven years, though she'd never anticipated the swelling cock head pressing between and through their lips — Sean moved Lea's panties smoothly to the side, slipped his once-more hard cock smoothly into her, and for a moment — just one endless, timeless moment — the whole fucking world was absolutely fucking *perfect*.

Six months later, and it was football season, and so Lea knew where she'd find them — where she *hoped* she'd find them — after she'd finished house-managing the Sunday matinee: watching the game, sitting at the edge of the pullout they all now shared.

Well, *Sean* was sitting.

Andy was kneeling between Sean's thighs sucking at his roommate's long, gorgeous, spotted dick.

Fuck, thought Lea, *how the fuck did I get so lucky?* "So, Sean, you win a bet, or lose one?"

Her lover's eyes were half-closed from the pleasure that their other lover was giving him. "Won it. Idiot thought the Falcon's'd score on the last drive."

"Never bet against the San Francisco team, Andy, don't you know that?" laughed Lea, dropping her clothes to the floor and sliding up behind Andy, taking his semi-hard cock in hand, working to make sure that there was nothing *semi* about it. Once it was fully erect, she sidled her way between them.

Andy moaned, and Sean's cock popped free; Lea licked at it even as Andy moved behind her and pushed that wonderful inverted *thang* of his into her weeping pussy. "*Holy fuck*," she cried into Sean's cock head. Panting, she said, "Now, I hope you boys left some for me?"

They both gasped, "Yes, *ma'am*."

Swallowing Sean as Andy began to plow her from behind, she thought, *What good boys you are!*

And then thought became unimportant, because the whole fucking world was absolutely fucking *perfect* once more.

As it absolutely fucking always should fucking be.

The Visitor Comes Home

Lea was back in an airplane bathroom; her legs were down this time, and her panties were up; she was done using the facilities, and masturbation was the last thing on her mind — and the last thing that her body could handle.

Sean and Andy had made very sure that she'd had *all* that she could handle over the last three days. And nights.

Well, *more* than she could handle, which she wouldn't have thought possible. She wouldn't be walking straight for days. Probably wouldn't be able to touch herself for weeks. Well. Till the next day, anyway. Well. Okay. Until that night. If she were careful.

Not that she would be complaining any time soon.

But what she wasn't sure how to handle was how to explain any or all of this to her best friend and roommate, Kirsten — Sean's sister. Lea couldn't think of a good way to approach the fact that not only had Lea finally, *finally* bedded Kirsten's older brother, whom Lea'd crushed on and lusted after since the two women were still in college, but that they'd frolicked with *Sean's* roommate. Who, like Sean, was a tall, broad-shouldered, Southern firefighter. A wet dream on legs.

And that was quite outside the difficulty of letting Lea's best friend know that she would be leaving San Francisco at the end of the month, leaving Kirsten without a roommate.

It was overwhelming to feel so excited and *satisfied* at the same time as Lea felt nervous and *sore*.

The bell rang and the captain's voice rang out. "We've got some turbulence ahead. Please take your seats and buckle your seat belts. We'll try to keep this as smooth and as entertaining as possible."

Thanks, thought Lea. *Will you come home with me?*

When Lea texted *Landed!* from the airport and didn't get a text back, she figured that Kirsten was at work; the Union Square store looked askance at pulling out your phone on the sales floor. Still, it would have been nice.

So Lea sent the same text to Sean and Andy and was gratified to receive *great miss u* from Andy and *WHEN ARE YOU COMING BACK????* from Sean. She was grinning from her head to her aching hamstrings as she boarded the BART train and texted back *Can't wait to come back there and burn down the REST of Dixie!*

Her two Georgia boys informed her that would never happen, not even if she brought Sherman and his whole army.

She informed them — as her bus approached her stop — that the only army she planned on encountering when she came back to Atlanta was the two of them, and she had every hope that the South would rise again. And again.

Which they solemnly promised her it would.

Backpack on her back, Lea was giggling — *giggling!* — as she made her way up to her floor, fished out her keys, and threw open the door to the crowded one-bedroom that she shared with Kirsten.

The apartment was small. Lea and Kirsten had learned to deal with this. They'd lived together before, were (mostly) compatible and (mostly) in sync, and so they'd learned how to avoid being walked in on — or being the one who walked in.

Obviously, the lesson hadn't stuck, because the sight that greeted Lea upon returning from her odyssey was her best friend, head thrown back in ecstasy, her blonde mane trailing along the length of the kitchen table, her legs wrapped over a pair of very fine, very feminine shoulders.

"*SORRY!*" shouted Lea before her brain could point out to her that she could simply have closed the door and come back later.

Kirsten's blue eyes — the same ridiculous, washed-denim blue as her brother's — flew open, as did Kirsten's mouth. The woman who was pleasuring Kirsten looked up into Kirsten's face, and then spun around on her knees and screamed, covering her body and bolting through the door to the apartment's miniscule bathroom, which she shut with a bang.

Kirsten and Lea stared at each other.

"I... I..." spluttered Kirsten.

"Sorry, I'll come back, oh, god, I'm so sorry!"

"No, Lea, wait," soft, long, Georgia vowels called out.

Head whirling, Lea turned to the front door, took a breath and closed it. "You, um, want to put some clothes on?"

Behind Lea, Kirsten chuckled. "Kinda late for that."

Lea turned and tried to return her friend's grin. Given how awkward Kirsten's smile looked and how brightly Kirsten was blushing from head to mid-thigh, Lea figured she was doing a pretty good job of approximating it.

"Um," Kirsten began, then shook her head and chuckled. "Thought you were coming back tomorrow."

"Nope."

"Guess not."

The friends both laughed, and Lea felt her heart begin to descend from her throat when she made out a quiet, sustained sniffle from the bathroom.

Kirsten grimaced and went over to the bathroom door. "Hey, Gianna, sweety? You want your clothes?"

"Please." The voice from behind the door was very small and very moist.

Lea picked up the skirt, top, and undies at her feet that looked nothing like anything she'd ever seen Kirsten wear and raised an eyebrow at her friend.

Kirsten shrugged and took the clothes, turning to the bathroom door and knocking. "Here y'are, sweetie." She passed the clothes through.

Lea found herself staring at her friend's naked back, at the freckles that were so much like the ones she'd been staring at — licking — just that morning. She shook her head, trying to clear it.

The bathroom door opened. Gianna turned out to be a very petite woman. She shuffled out, her eyes downcast.

Kirsten turned to Lea, tits high, as if they were meeting at a formal ball. "Gianna, I've told you about my friend Lea. Lea…" Kirsten's eyes widened slightly. "This is my… my girlfriend Gianna."

Lea and Gianna both glanced at Kirsten before looking at each other.

"Nice to meet you," said Lea.

"Pleasure," said Gianna, almost managing a smile before her dark skin darkened several shades. "Call me, K. Bye," she murmured to Kirsten, kissing the blonde on the lips very briefly before disappearing out the door.

Lea finally dropped her backpack to the floor.

"Welcome home?" Kirsten flashed a dazzling, off-center smile.

"Thanks. Kirsten? Girlfriend?"

"Uh, yeah." The blush that had begun finally to recede on Kirsten's fair skin came roaring back.

"I mean," Lea said, "that's great, but… Wow. Since when?"

"'Bout a month." When she noticed Lea's shocked expression, Kirsten shrugged. "Well, honey, you've been a bit pre-occupied with the whole job search. And… Anyway. Yeah."

"So, girls?"

"Yup."

"Did you just —?"

"Oh, gawd, no. She's not the first or anything."

"*Really?*"

Blushing fully now, Kirsten turned and walked into their kitchen. "Um, naw. Remember Billy?"

"The guy with the thing for handcuffs?"

"Yeah, but, see, um, more of a Billie-with-an-i-e than a Billy-with-a-y." Kirsten grabbed a bottle of Pinot Gris out of the fridge and poured two large water glasses full.

"Oh." Fuck. That had been… Just after college! No wonder Kirsten had never brought him — her — over. "Why didn't you ever *say* anything?"

Kirsten's shoulder's slumped. "Some of us don't come from liberal San Fran families, sweetie." She handed Lea one glass of wine and sipped at the other.

"Kirsten…"

"Yeah, well, see, also, see, I mean I've always liked guys too, but see, I've known I've liked girls a long time, only I didn't actually think that was anything I could, you know, do something about until college."

"So? You could have told me!"

Kirsten favored Lea with a miserable smirk. "Sweetie. You're my best friend. And that's why I couldn't."

Lea just stared at Kirsten.

"Gawd, Lea, don't..." Kirsten looked away, took a drink, and put down the glass. "I couldn't tell you, sweetie, 'cause, you know, besides being my roommate and my BFF and all that shit, you have a cute fucking ass and I had a huge fucking crush on you that confused the shit out of me, okay?"

"Uh. Okay?" Lea tried to consider whether any of this upset her or weirded her out. Nope. Well, it did make Kirsten's whole obsession with helping Lea choose her underwear seem a bit less benign. But other than that... nope.

"And I still love you, but no, not like *that*. I mean, I figured out real quick you were just about the straightest girl on God's green earth, so I haven't been lusting after you all these years, which I didn't want you to have to think about, which is another reason why I didn't tell you, okay?"

Lea clicked her glass to her friend's. "Okay, K. I got it. I'm sorry."

Kirsten laughed. "*Sorry?* What the hell for?"

"That you didn't feel like you could just tell me."

"Aw, honey, I probably should have long ago. I mean, I guess I knew you wouldn't mind, I just..." She shrugged again.

"Hey, no prob." Lea frowned. "I'd give you a hug, but that seems like it would be sending the wrong signal."

Kirsten gave a sad smirk and shook her head. "Yeah. How 'bout I get some clothes on?"

"If you think it would help." A laugh fought its way up Lea's throat. "Thought you said it was too late?"

"Yeah, well, your damn city is cold, and anyway, I'm feeling kinda stupid standing here butt-naked." She walked around the table and picked up her dress.

"So. Gianna? Seems... nice."

For the first time that Lea could remember, Kirsten turned away as she got dressed. "She is, a real sweetie."

"Hope I didn't scare her off."

"Me too. Actually, that's another thing I probably shoulda talked to you about before now." Kirsten turned around, fully dressed but uncharacteristically timid.

Lea walked over and gave her a hug — fuck sending the wrong message. "Talked to me about what?"

"Well, see..." After a moment's hesitation, Kirsten hugged her back. "See, we've gotten kinda serious, the last few weeks, and, see, she's got this nice little place on Leavenworth, just a few blocks from the store, and, um..."

Lea backed up and looked at her friend, whose expression had gone from humiliated to thoroughly miserable. "What? You… You want to move in with her?"

"Um. Yeah?" Kirsten's brows bowed down. "But see, I didn't want to leave you having to pay for this place on your own, so — "

Lea laughed and hugged her friend, so that some of the wine poured down Lea's back. "And here I was worried about having to tell *you!*"

"Tell…?" Then Kirsten gasped. "Oh! Sweetie! You got the job?"

"Yup!"

"That's so great! Hey! Congratulations!" Now Kirsten gave Lea a real hug. "Wow! Can't wait to tell Sean!"

"Um. He already knows."

Kirsten pulled back from her friend and peered into her face. "Oh?" Kristen began to grin.

Now it was Lea's turn to blush.

Kirsten gave a whoop and hugged Lea again. "Are you telling me you and Big Bro finally got off y'all's asses and got *lucky?*"

"Oh, boy, yeah." Lea knew that she was turning bright red, but she too was laughing; it was hard not to laugh with Kirsten — or with her brother, for that matter.

"Thank *gawd!*" Kirsten gave Lea another squeeze and went to refill her wine, most of which she'd now spilled. "If I had to listen to the two of y'all *lust* after each other any more — " Kirsten turned back and shot Lea a supremely wicked grin. "So? Was it good? Did y'all fuck each other's brains out? I mean, I don't want details, this is my brother and all, but *still*. Dish, girl!"

"Um. Yeah. God. Kirsten!" That morning, in the back of Andy's Yukon, Sean licking Lea's pussy while Andy suckled on her nipples… They had made her feel exactly as if she had just had not one but two amazing men pleasure her in every way imaginable for three whole days and nights. Which in fact she had. Lea could barely bend her own brain about what had happened. She couldn't even begin to think how to tell her best friend, who happened to be one of her lovers' sister. She figured that nothing that she could say would come anywhere near to the truth.

"Wow," laughed Kirsten. "I always thought Big Bro was the mushy, romantic type. Didn't figure he'd fuck you speechless!"

"Had help," Lea muttered.

She hadn't meant to say it out loud, and so she was shocked when her friend blinked at her. "Say *what?*"

"Uh." Lea hid behind her glass of wine.

"No, no, no, Miss Lea, you don't get to drop a little bomb like that and then play *peek-a-boo!*" Kirsten squinted through Lea's Pinot Gris. "Now, did you say what I *thought* you said?"

Lea sighed.

She'd figured that — if the arrangement continued, as it showed every sign of doing — she was going to have to tell Kirsten eventually. She just hadn't planned on blurting it out quite so soon. "What did you think I said?"

Kirsten made a face that was even more contorted viewed through the glass. "Sounded like maybe you and Sean had some *company.*"

Lea just nodded.

"Well, damn! What did...?" Kirsten gasped, reached out, and moved Lea's glass to the side. "Please tell me it was Andrew."

Again, all that Lea could do was nod.

"Holy fuck." Beyond that statement, Kirsten was speechless — a rare occurrence. After a moment she recovered. "I mean, those big country boys don't usually do a *thang* for me, but he is a beautiful piece of man-flesh, sure enough."

"Tell me about it," sighed Lea.

"No, honey, *you* tell *me!*" Kirsten laughed, then shook her head and held up her hand. "I mean, naw, bleh, don't. Don't wanna hear about it if Sean was... I mean, are we talking, you know, *both* of them?"

"Uh-huh."

"At the same time?"

"Well," Lea said, fidgeting, "first night it was one, then the other." She shivered, remembering the two mind-scrambling fucks, remembering the thunder. "But after I got the job..."

"Holy fuck," Kirsten said again, looking properly stunned. She bit her lip. "Um. Did Sean and Andrew...?" She pointed her index fingers at each other, sloshing some more wine.

"I think I'm going to let *Sean* tell you about that." Lea took a deep breath and a sip of wine. "And you can tell him about Gianna."

"Wow. Uh. Yeah." Kirsten drank from her glass, and shook her head again. "There's a conversation our mama won't ever want to hear about. And here I always thought Sean was the good one in the family."

"Oh," laughed Lea, "I think you're both wonderful."

As it turned out Lea *hadn't* scared Gianna off. Though the petite brunette seemed very calm when she picked Kirsten up to go to dinner, however, Gianna still couldn't look Lea in the face.

"You sure you don't want to join us, Lea?" Kirsten asked for the third time.

"No, I think I've interrupted you two enough for today," answered Lea, and after a moment all three women laughed. Even Gianna.

After they had left, Lea sighed and shuffled her way over to the fridge. Three heads of lettuce — the red leaf badly wilted, but the romaine and the butter lettuce still looking good — her choice of eight kinds of hummus, and a few leftover falafel. No pita, but some whole-grain tortilla — instant dinner.

As she pulled her plate together and moved over to the table — aware only after she already eaten most of her meal that she'd sat at the spot where Gianna had been dining on Kirsten earlier that day — she sighed, knowing she was going to miss California's food. *But Atlanta's a big city,* she reasoned, *I'm sure I can get good food.* Then she giggled as she thought, *And I sure know I can find some great meat there!*

After eating Lea retired to the bedroom she had shared with Kirsten since breaking up with John the Control Freak a bit over a year before. She started to watch *30 Rock*, but found that she kept glancing over at her roomie's bed. Would it be any different sharing a room with Kirsten now that Lea knew that her friend liked girls — had had a crush on Lea herself? Well, that had been years before. Kirsten was obviously fine with it. And they'd made (and so far kept) an agreement when they'd roomed together in college: no bringing anyone else into the bedroom without giving the other a chance to clear out.

Lea had just started to wonder whether she should look for another place to spend the night so Kirsten and Gianna could have some privacy, when Lea's phone chirped. A text from Kirsten read, *Spending the night at G's. OK?*

Smiling, Lea texted back, *Great. Have a nice sleepover. ;-)*

LOL! ILU! came back the response almost instantly.

As she was putting her phone back down, ready to dive back into the ever-entertaining travails of Liz Lemon, Lea's phone chirped again.

It was from Sean this time: *Hey, miss you. Both of us do.*

Lea's chest filled with warmth. She answered, *I miss you both too.*

Sean: Wanna see us?

Lea: ?

Sean: Video chat. On the computer. Andy wants to be able to see too, for some reason.

Lea laughed, imagining the two burly boys fighting over the little phone. She flipped open her laptop. *Okay. Tell me when.*

Now? And he gave a link.

Lea entered it into her browser. The feed loaded… "Holy shit."

Two broad-chested, naked male bodies greeted her, visible from the neck down, so she wasn't immediately sure which was which. They were sitting on the edge of the pullout, knees spread, each stroking the other's cock.

Yes. The one on the right had a cock that curved away from his body: Andy.

"Holy fuck," she repeated.

"Nice to see you too," one of them murmured – over the tiny laptop speakers, she thought it was Sean, but wasn't certain.

"Guess you guys couldn't wait."

"Told you we missed you," said the other one, accent a bit heavier, so that had to be Andy.

"Uh-huh." Lea could feel warmth spread through her middle, could feel her still-sore pussy moistening and her nipples reaching out through her blouse toward the screen. "So… Tell me, boys, what part of me did you miss?" And before they could answer, she began to unbutton her top.

Stripping had always seemed like a silly exercise to Lea. She was a practical girl: the whole taking-clothes-off thing just got in the way on the way from fore-play to *play*. But men, she knew, were visual souls — and her boys, clearly, were men. As Lea slowly opened the front of her sensible blouse, their stroking slowed, and they visibly leaned forward.

Besides, this was the best they could give each other until next month.

Once the last button was undone, she slid a finger all of the way back up her torso. "Did you miss my neck?"

"Yes, ma'am," said one. "Uh-huh," said the other.

Taking the collar, Lea pulled the blouse away from one side. "My shoulders?"

This time, they both just grunted their assent.

Lea pouted down at her own flesh. "Someone clearly misses it — they left teeth marks there."

There was a hiss from the speakers.

Lea slid the other shoulder free. "No marks there though. Guess you don't miss this one as much."

"Nuh-uh," groaned one of the boys.

"Miss that one too," said the other. "Lots."

"Mmm." Lea slid the bra strap on that side down. "You sure?"

"Yes," they groaned together. Their hands had begun moving minutely more quickly.

"You sure you miss my left as much as you miss my right?" Down slipped the other bra strap.

"Oh, fuck yes," said one.

"Huh" was all the other could manage.

Lea let the blouse slide off of her, down to the bed. "What else have you missed?"

"Uh…"

She held the bra up with one hand and trailed the other downward. "My bel-ly? I see some marks there too — you must miss that."

"Damn."

"Yeah."

Grinning, she turned away from the screen. "Tell me, did you leave any marks on my back?" And before they could even grunt, she added, "Oh! But you can't see the whole back. Here." She popped her bra open and let it join the top on her comforter. "Miss my back?"

"You know we did."

"Love… bites."

Lea wriggled, pretending to try to look over her shoulder. "Ooo, really? I wonder whose?"

"Pro'lly both," one of them grunted.

"I sure hope so," she said. "But have you checked my *whole* back?"

"Uh…."

She got up on her knees. "How about... down here?" She pushed her jeans down an inch.

"Um."

"Don't... see nothing."

"Oh, what a shame." She popped the button on the jeans and slid them another inch down. "How about... here?"

"Um, maybe."

"Can't quite, um, see."

"Well, we wouldn't want to have that." She bent forward, wriggling the jeans and panties down so that her whole ass was pointing at the screen.

"Sweet Jesus."

"Fuck."

Lea couldn't help it. She laughed. "Guess you do miss this part. Don't think either of you took full... possession, though."

Groans answered her, and the sound of each pounding the other's cock.

Stepping out of the jeans, she bent all of the way forward. "This part, though?" She reached between her legs and gently stroked herself. "This part? Oh, guys, you sure as hell took possession of this part of me."

Whimpering.

"This part of me? It misses you both too. Sooooo much..." Gingerly, she slid a finger in, and was amazed that it felt so good. "You guys fucked my lights out, but my poor little pussy is still weeping for more." Another finger. Lea hissed; it stung a bit, but honestly, it was true. She wanted it. God help her: she wanted *them*. She peered back between her legs and saw them stroking each other on her little laptop screen — another wet dream come to life.

Andy was rocking his hips, thrusting into Sean's hand. Lea could tell that he was close.

Apparently, so could Sean. Disengaging Andy's hand from his own erection, Sean knelt to the floor, staring first at Lea — Lea's bottom, spread for both of them to see, Lea's fingers thrusting slowly in and out — and then staring up at Andy. Sean kissed Andy's slick cockhead. "You can think about think about fucking that sweet poon there," he rumbled, "an' come in my mouth. If you'll let me come in yours." He gave Andy's cock a lick, from balls to head.

Andy gasped. Though he'd seemed to be okay touching Sean's rod, he'd been much less comfortable letting any part of his body other than his hand touch Sean anywhere — certainly not his mouth, and certainly not Sean's cock.

Lea wanted to be patient and kind, wanted not to force Andy to do something he clearly wasn't totally comfortable doing. But the sight of Sean on his knees between their lover's legs, licking his way up their lover's cock — it left Lea with no patience. No kindness. "Oh, Andy," she moaned, sliding her fingers in and out, arching her ass, "want you in me *so bad...*"

Sean's mouth reached the top of that long prick, and stayed there.

"*GAWD,*" cried Andy, all restraint breaking, as he began to thrust into his friend's mouth. "Gawd, fuck, *fine, SHIT,* you can stick that *thang* in my mouth, *FUCK,* just, just let…"

Sean showed that he had been paying close attention when he'd been helping her suck Andy off. Smoothly, Sean took an astonishing amount of that long *thang* of Andy's down his throat.

"God," moaned Lea, "so fucking beautiful." Her thumb was trembling as it stroked her clit. "Fuck me, Andy."

And fuck her he did — fucking Sean's face as he grimaced at her, her cunt, at the fingers stretching it….

"Oh, fuck, fuck, fuck me, Andy, fuck me…!"

Andy screamed and arched, thrusting hard. Once. Twice. Then he collapsed back onto the bed. "Aw, fuck. Fuck."

Sean came coughing up, wiping his face. "Well, damn, boy, you just about broke my spine from the inside!"

"Aw, fuck…" Andy was still lying back, his cock leaning drunkenly down over his thigh.

Sean slid up next to Andy, and for a terrible, scintillating moment Lea was sure that Sean, the mushy romantic as Kirsten had said, was about to kiss his roommate. But after a second, Sean just reached down and gave Andy's softening cock a squeeze. "Andy-boy, you don't have to — "

Andy's hand shot out and grabbed Sean's, which was still hard.

Sean gulped, and Lea gasped in sympathy.

"Y'all both sucked me off how many times, last few days?" rasped Andy, stroking his friend's prick. "I mean, mean, if you can take *me* in y'all's mouths, shouldn't ought to be no big deal to take *this* little ol' thang in mine, right?"

"*Little?*" Sean scowled, and (upside down as she was) Lea couldn't tell if he were kidding or not.

But Andy didn't volley back. Instead he rolled on his stomach and held Sean's cock steady before him. He stared at it as if it were a stick of dynamite, liable to go off at any second. He leaned forward, face stony, and gave the head a kiss.

Sean pushed up on his elbows; his eyes darted between Andy, who had backed up and was now licking his lips, and over Andy's back at Lea, who was trying to assuage the fire in her loins as gingerly as she could.

Andy opened his mouth wide, as if he were about to begin a hot-dog eating competition — which, in a way, he was — but Lea had enough brain left to whimper, "Teeth."

Andy blinked up at Lea, and then back down. "Oh. Right." He carefully covered his teeth with his lips, closed his eyes, and took the tip of Sean's cock in his mouth.

It wasn't an expert blowjob, but Lea could remember her own first attempt, and gave Andy an A for diving right in.

Sean looked stunned. He still couldn't seem to figure out where to look: at Lea's open cunt on the computer screen, or at his friend's open mouth, bobbing up and down on his cock.

Lea decided that he deserved a bit of torture as well. "Feel good, Sean?"

His eyes flashed up to the webcam and locked on hers.

Lea flexed her ass, grinding on her own hand. "Looks so fucking hot, Andy sucking you off. Don't you think so, Sean?"

Sean growled. Scowled. But his eyes flashed down.

Lea grinned, astonished to feel an orgasm beginning to build up in her tired pussy. "Wish I was there... *Mmm...* Wish I was there to help Andy... Or... Or I could... *Mmmm...* Could suck on him while he.... *Hnh...!* While he, um, sucked on you, and.... Is he, uh, *god,* is Andy getting hard again, Sean?"

Eyes smoldering, Sean slipped his hand under Andy, grabbing something that made Andy lift his pelvis up, revealing that, yes, he was hard again, and yes, what Sean had grabbed hold of and was once more stroking was that gorgeous cock of Andy's.

"Oh, *fuck,* Sean, god... And you could use that amazing mouth of yours on *this...*" She arched her pelvis again, opening herself to him, thrilled and terrified to find herself sliding another finger in; she could feel the muscles protest, could feel them exult. "God, Sean, Andy, want you so much, *want...!*" She began to buck against one hand as she sucked the other into her mouth, seeking *fullness,* seeking completion such as only those two had ever given her...

Sean screamed. Her name, maybe. Or maybe the Supreme Being's. Or hell, maybe Andy's.

Lea couldn't tell, because to her own great and wonderful shock, she came, hard, squeezing tight the three fingers in her snatch, screaming into the fingers in her mouth.

Once she had returned to her body, Lea curled her knees to her belly and rolled onto her side, staring at the screen.

Her two boys were there, slick with sweat. Andy had come still dribbling down his chin, but he was hard in Sean's hand. Each was slack-jawed. Each was staring back at her.

Lea felt tears overflow — something she'd promised herself she wouldn't let happen. "Miss you both so much."

"Love you," they both murmured to her together, and Lea surrendered herself to the tears.

That night, they could barely say anything else to each other than to agree to talk again the next night. "Can't do it like this," mumbled Andy.

Sean added, "We're at the firehouse the next three nights."

"Oh," sighed Lea — sorry, even as her body was relieved.

The next night, they chatted briefly, both men looking very businesslike in their Atlanta FD t-shirts. The laptop was on Andy's knees, and so it felt as if

Lea were looking up at them. It made her feel oddly small. It made her feel... oddly safe.

"Anyone else there with you guys?" Lea asked.

Andy's eyes flashed up, over the top of the computer, while Sean simply nodded.

"Oh, shoot," Lea pouted.

They both grinned sadly at her.

"Hey," said Sean, "Sis and I had... a really interesting conversation earlier tonight."

Kirsten was once again over at Gianna's. Lea grinned, relieved that the siblings had in fact not made her bring it up. "Did she tell you who *she's* moving in with?"

Sean scratched his head. "Uh. Yeah."

Andy looked at him quizzically.

Lea laughed. "Put it to you this way, Andy, their mama is going to have lot easier time swallowing her boy sharing a girl with you than her *girl* being with a —"

" — with a, yeah," Sean broke in, and whispered into Andy's ear.

Andy's eyes got very wide.

Lea laughed. "Yup! Kirsten told me that conversation was one your mother would probably be better off never hearing about."

"Well, she had that just about right."

"Hey." Lea felt her mischievous side rising. "I know there's other guys there, but they can't see the screen, can they?"

Both boys shook their heads.

"Good," said Lea, and lifted her shirt over her head.

Their twin stunned expressions was all the payment she wished for... that night.

Two nights before it was time for Lea to fly back to them, Lea got on their now-nightly chat full of excitement. She'd shipped boxes of belongings to their place — her place soon — had put in her last day at the tiny theater she'd managed to keep from folding, and had helped Kirsten finish moving into Gianna's. She had the bare apartment to herself, had nothing to do tomorrow but pack and see a few friends, and tonight her boys were home — the next night they were on duty.

She looked forward to a long, leisurely video threeway, their last, thank god, for a long time, because, really, she was ready to have them both take her again. And again.

She anticipated them being naked, as they had been every other night when they were at their apartment. Had anticipated watching them sucking each other off. Maybe, a secret, very adolescent part of her hoped, she could encourage one of them to let the other fuck him if she offered her own ass as a reward. The thought of taking one of those very sizable cocks up her backside was more than a little terrifying, but….

When she got online at the appointed time, however, both boys were sitting, still fully clothed in their fire department duds. Both very serious. Each holding a piece of paper.

"Guys?" Lea asked, nervous at their unaccounted solemnity. "Everything okay?"

They nodded, still grim-faced. Andy held up his piece of paper. "Got the results of our physicals back."

"Oh?" What the hell?

"Look in your inbox," said Sean, and that serious face suddenly had a spark of something smoldering beneath it.

Nervous, Lea opened her email. There was a message from Sean with two PDFs attached. She double-clicked on them.

At the bottom of each was the blood screening. Sean was O+. Andy was A+. Both had good cholesterol; Andy's HDL was marginally higher. Neither tested positive for any of several cancer markers.

Each had tested negative for HIV, HPV, genital herpes, syphilis, gonorrhea, and any one of a number of other communicable diseases.

They were clean.

Not certain why they were sharing this with her, she looked up at them. "Guys?"

They were both staring back at her. Andy's gaze too was full of banked flame now. "Wanted you to know," he said, "that you didn't need to worry."

"We'll still wear rubbers and all when we're, you know," Sean's face darkened, "fucking. But…"

"You don't need to worry," repeated Andy.

A thick gobbet of emotion stopped Lea's throat for a moment. "What about… you guys… worrying about *me*?"

"We trust you," said Andy.

"Also," added Sean, that wicked smile of his creeping in, "I know from Sis that you hadn't had, uh, intimate contact before us with anyone over the last two years except for John the Controlling Asshole. And he always wore rubbers 'cause — "

" — because he didn't want any Little Johns running around without his permission," finished Lea, trying but failing to match his smile. "Uh, guys?"

"Darlin'?"

"Baby?"

"I renewed my prescription for, um, The Pill."

Sean's eyebrows raised. "So…"

Andy licked his lips. "So…"

Love and desire swept through Lea. "So. Gentlemen. Next time I see you in the flesh, I am *soo* going to be able to feel both of you go off inside me. At the same time."

"Well…" Sean murmured.

"Golly," gulped Andy.

And each began to pull his t-shirt over his head as Lea unzipped the hoodie that was all that she was wearing tonight.

I'm going home! she sighed to herself, and then groaned as her two gorgeous, sweet men each pulled the other's pants off and began to stroke the other hard.

The Visitor Comes Again

Lea had just lowered her skirt and stood up when the captain came on the intercom and said, "Ladies and gentlemen, they've cleared the runway, and so we are now descending into Hartsfield-Jackson Atlanta International Airport. Please take your seats."

Out in the cabin, there was cheering — there had been threats of diverting to Miami.

In the bathroom, Lea was having a panic attack.

Fuckity-fuck-fuck. What was she *doing*?

Well, she thought, as she made her way back to her seat, she was moving to Atlanta for her new job, which started in just a week's time. The job she'd been dreaming of, at a theater she was overjoyed to be working at. She was going to have a *staff*, for fuck's sake! She wasn't going to *be* the whole staff — and the janitor, and the concessions-stand dishwasher, and…

And she was moving into her new apartment. Moving in with Sean. And Andy. Sean and Andy.

Thinking of Sean and Andy — her two boys, her two *men* — who, damn it, wouldn't be able to see her until tomorrow because they were, damn it, *working* — got her middle moving again, but this time it wasn't anxiety. She was thinking of the feeling of two cocks in her hands. Of one of them in her cunt while the other filled her mouth. Of Sean helping her suck Andy dry. Of the two of them whispering, "Love you," over the video chats that had been her life-line to them over the past few weeks.

Of the fact that she was *moving in* with two men whom she'd only really gotten to know over three days of bacchanalian orgy — well, and two weeks of passionate (if wistful) video-fucking.

She'd lived with men before. Roommates. Boyfriends.

But two of them *at once?* One she'd known for years, but how well? He was her best friend's brother, but really? What did she know about Sean?

And *Andy?* What did she know about him at all?

Well. That he came from Smoky Mountains. That he liked boiled peanuts. That his cock bent away from his body, and he could make her come *so* hard.... That he made really good fried chicken.

It wasn't a whole hell of a lot.

She had her key in her purse. They'd made up the big sofa-sleeper for her use — and theirs, once they were off duty.

They were good guys. Good boys.

But she was going to have to make her way through — of all things — a snow-bound Atlanta, and then she was going to spend her first night in the apartment alone. Which shouldn't feel shitty — Lea liked being alone — but it did. Feel shitty.

The downside of living with two firefighters was definitely going to be that they had twenty-four hour shifts.

The upside, she knew, was that they only had two of them a week. Which left them the rest of the week to make Lea feel like a very, very natural woman indeed, thank you, Carole King.

Still, *thought Lea with an internal pout,* couldn't they have managed to have today off?

"Your boyfriend meeting you in Atlanta?" asked the grey-haired black woman in the floral print dress sitting in the window seat.

Not feeling like it was worth the trouble of explaining the complicated mess she was walking into, Lea just nodded.

"Thought so," tittered the woman. "I've seen *that* look before!" She graced Lea with a a self-satisfied smile. And before Lea could say anything, she turned back to her copy of *Fifty Shades.*

Fuckity-fuck-fuck.

As they descended into Atlanta, Lea found that *fifty shades of grey* was about right: the city, which had been verdant the last time she'd flown in just a few weeks before, was now monochromatic. Flat.

The lady next to Lea seemed to be just as disconcerted. "Why, will you look at that? If it's global *warming* what the hell is Atlanta doing looking like *that?*"

Lea decided not to get into a debate about climate change — it didn't seem like anything good would come from that. "Do you have someone picking you up?" she asked.

"Oh, yes, bless you, my oldest boy will be there. He's got a big ol' four-by-four pickup." She patted Lea on the knee with a mahogany hand. "He's a fireman."

Lea fought back a wave of irrational panic. She *knew* this lady wasn't one of the ladies she'd one day have to explain just how she'd contributed to her beautiful, upstanding son's downfall. She'd met Sean's mother, who was as fair and freckled as her children, and Andy was if anything paler. It seemed un-likely that he would have an African American mom. Still... "I... I'm seeing a fireman." *I am,* thought Lea with a guilty, swallowed giggle, *TWO of them!* "Midtown."

"Oh, how nice! My boy's down in East Point." The woman's hand flapped against Lea's knee again. "I'm sure they know each other!"

Lea tried to keep the nascent panic out of her smile. "I'm sure they do." *Oh, God,* Lea thought once more, *what am I **doing?***

The plane touched down smoothly, though Lea's stomach still lurched — more from the fact that she was already close to throwing up than anything. The other passengers cheered.

Lea sat back and closed her eyes.

"Well, honey," burbled Lea's seatmate, "here we are!"

"Here we are," Lea agreed, voice thin even to her own ears.

As they shuffled up the big metal tube to the terminal, Lea could see her breath. *Weird,* she thought, and *How the fuck I'm I going to get to the apartment?* She had a rental car waiting for her, but there was sure to be ice, the car was almost certainly not going to have chains, and Lea wasn't exactly used to driving in winter conditions. For the four hundred and thirty-second time, Lea found herself wishing that even one of her boys had been able to pick her up. They both drove four-wheel drive cars, but beside that, Lea just wanted to *see* them. She felt pathetic.

"Well, now," said Lea's former neighbor, "you'll have someone to warm you right up soon enough." The woman laughed. "You give that fireman of yours a big squeeze for me, you hear?"

Lea nodded, trying to smile. She found herself trembling, and the cold had almost nothing to do with it.

As they entered the terminal, the woman patted Lea on the shoulder and strode off through the sea of disgruntled passengers, her copy of *50 Shades of Grey* held proudly to her chest.

Lea stepped out of the flow of traffic and closed her eyes, leaning against one of the glass walls that looked out at the plane she had just left. *It will be all right. I'll get to the apartment okay. I'll survive one more night with no one to keep me warm. And then tomorrow...*

"Excuse me, miss," said a low, gruff voice. A heavy hand touched Lea's forearm, which was clutching her purse to her chest. "Would you mind coming with us?"

Lea's eyes flew open. The hand on her arm was gloved — heavy, industrial gloves — and attached to an arm clad in a heavy, buff-colored coat marked *Atlanta Fire & Rescue.* Blinking, she followed the arm...

It was attached to Andy. Andy, in his full turnout gear — coat, overalls, helmet.

And behind him, Sean.

Both of them somber-faced, but each with a joyously evil glint in his eye.

Lea started to squeal, to leap at them both, to see if she could rap her arms and legs around both of them at once — to hell with people watching — but Andy's hand held her fast. "I… I thought you were working!"

"We are," answered Sean. His posture said *On duty*, but his eyes promised pleasure, a promise that Lea's body immediately began urging her to collect on. "Obviously."

"We managed to *volunteer* for an extra shift out here at the airport," Andy added quietly, and then said more loudly. "We just need you to identify something for us, miss, if you'd just follow us."

"Identify?"

"Yes, miss." Andy winked, and gestured down the terminal — not in the direction of baggage claim, but toward one of the thousands of non-descript doors that you never notice as you wander through an airport.

Andy led and Lea followed; she could hear Sean taking up the rear — an image that set *all* sorts of nasty thoughts going in Lea's nasty, nasty mind. Andy used a key to open the door and waved the other two through into a small stairwell.

As soon as the door *clicked* shut, Lea turned and leapt, grabbing both men's collars, wrapped her legs around both of them — as best she could, since even without these heavy coats on they were not exactly small guys — and proceeded to kiss them both soundly. Two big hands reached under her butt, each holding up one cheek, each pulling her tight.

After a few minutes — not long enough, *never* long enough — Andy backed away from her neck and Sean backed away from her ear. "Guess you did miss us," chuckled Sean.

She glared at him and then grinned. "What do *you* think?"

"I think," Sean murmured, "that we missed the fuck out of you too, begging your pardon."

Her grin grew. She pushed her hand down between the two men, feeling their erections pressing together through the heavy overalls. "So, gentlemen. You had something you wanted me to *identify*."

Sean hissed.

Andy grunted through gritted teeth, "Not here. Security cameras all over."

"Oh?" Lea pushed her hand down again and wriggled against them. "You don't think the TSA would want to watch me take both of you in my mouth at the same — ?"

Sean stopped that mouth with a hair-curling kiss. He turned and pressed her up against the cold concrete wall, and Lea was just as happy that it was cold, because she wasn't sure that that Sean's heat wouldn't have vaporized her.

She heard a loud *thwack!* Sean broke the kiss and snarled at Andy, "Hey! Keep your hands to yourself!"

Andy smirked at them both, panting steam into the stairwell. "Come on, you two. Let's take this somewhere a bit more private."

Somewhere a bit more private turned out to be a ready room for the AFRD's airport battalion. "There's one in each terminal," Sean said as they made their way through an endless maze of corridors. "This one happens to be assigned just for us for today."

"How... convenient." Lea was walking between the two men, her arms hooked through their arms. She'd never been more conscious of just how much bigger than she they were. "A nice coincidence that you happened to be housed in the terminal where my flight landed."

"Isn't it?" Andy chuckled. "We may owe a few favors."

"Oh." Lea looked from one to the other. "Well, I hope that it was worth the trouble. I mean, doing all of that *just* so that you could see me when I got in..." She was teasing them, but in all honesty she truly was deeply touched.

"It was our pleasure," said Sean.

"We couldn't wait to see you," said Andy.

Two maintenance workers sauntered past in the opposite direction, paying them no notice.

"Well, then," Lea sighed, "I suppose I'll just have to do my best to make sure that it was all worth your while."

"Er," said Andy.

"Huh," said Sean.

Lea just smiled and pulled their arms closer.

After what seemed like hours of meandering aimlessly through a labyrinth of anonymous corridors, they stopped at a door that looked exactly like several hundred other doors that they'd passed, except that this one bore a placard reading *AFRD BATT 7.*

As Andy pulled out the key, Lea asked, "BATT 7?"

"Battalion 7. That's the airport battalion," Sean answered.

"Wow. A whole other battalion. You guys *do* owe some favors." Lea grinned at him in a way that she hoped promised *just* how much she was going to make it worth their while.

Such good boys!

Sean grinned back, and it was his most wicked, pulse-quickening grin. "You have no idea."

A not-very-nice thought occurred to Lea. "You didn't promise anyone... *me*, did you?"

Sean's face fell, and Andy, who had just opened the door, turned around looking if anything even more abashed. "Lea! We wouldn't!"

She shivered, suddenly feeling the cold of the concrete floor flood up through her.

Sean led her through the open door; Andy closed the door.

Lea found suddenly that she couldn't look them in the face. She was staring at the battered, red industrial carpet.

Sean knelt so that he was looking up into her eyes. "Lea. It isn't like that. Honest."

"You think we'd *share* you?" Andy knelt beside Sean. "Like we'd share a truck or a hound?"

"You're pretty comfortable sharing me with each other," Lea joked — though it was a pathetic attempt even to her own ears.

"It ain't like that at all," said Andy, looking deadly serious. "It's not *sharing*, it's... I mean..." He reached a hand to her hip.

Sean took her other hip and, in fact, it felt as if they had rooted her back to the ground. "This is how we *get* to be with you, Lea-honey. And all," he added quietly, blinking at Andy, who blinked back.

"Lucky me." She was smiling, but she could feel that she was on the edge of tears. *Why?* "Sorry." She reached out and ran fingers through two heads of fine, blond hair. She was glad that they'd hung up their helmets — she could see them hanging on hooks by the door. Her boys in their gear, looking incredibly sexy... It was wonderful, but she was glad to be able to see their faces.

"What've you got to be sorry about?" Andy's hand drifted up to her ribs, sending predictable but unpredicted sparks to her nipples.

Sean leaned forward and kissed the point of Lea's hipbone, and that sent sparks further south.

Astonished to find the cold vacuum that had threatened to consume her filling with heat, Lea gasped, blinking at them both.

Their matching serious expressions of earnestness melted to smiles. Andy let his hand slide up along the bottom of her breast to where the nipple was now threatening to burst through the fabric, while Sean went back to kissing her hip, his eyes still raised to hers, his hand drifting up the inside of her knee....

"Lock... door?" Lea managed to splutter.

"Already locked," Andy said as his fingers began lightly to tease her nipple through the damned bra and the damned sweater and...

"And nobody else's coming in here until midnight," mumbled Sean into her skirt as *his* fingers slid up beneath the hem, blazing a path of glory up the inside of her thigh.

"Oh," sighed Lea, feeling as if it were a miracle that she was still standing, "Great..."

At that moment, Sean's fingers brushed along the length of her pussy through her panties, Andy pinched her nipple between his thumb and forefinger, and — not coincidentally — brought Lea herself to her knees.

Sean gave her a lazy smirk. "Nice of you to join us, Miss Lea."

She couldn't think of any response in that moment other than to stroke their coat-clad chests.

"I think we might be a mite overdressed for this next bit," Andy chuckled.

"Let me undress you both. I've always wanted..." Running her hands down to their crotches, she felt suddenly shy. Overwhelmed.

"Wanted to jump a fireman in his gear?" asked Andy, a smirk still coloring his voice. His fingers continued to tantalize her breasts.

Lea nodded, pushing their coats off their near shoulders.

"Sorry we can't do this with you on a truck," said Sean.

"Fuck the truck," panted Lea, pulling the heavy coats down so that they slid off of the men's arms and onto the floor behind them. She pulled the near suspenders off, then pushed the far ones. Her fingers trailed down their chests — both vibrating at her her touch — and came to rest on waistbands of their thick trousers. She couldn't see any fly or buttons. "Huh. Am I supposed to *tear* these off?"

"Uh," gasped Andy.

"Velcro," grunted Sean.

"Oohhh." Letting her fingers slide across the fronts of the pants — which were growing visibly tighter — Lea found the closed-away flaps. "Don't want to let go of either of you," Lea sighed. "So how am I going to open these pants? *Stop.*"

Each of the boys had begun to reach for his own fly, but Lea wanted no help. Grinning at them both, she leaned forward and gave the lump at the front of Sean's pants a gentle bite.

Sean sounded as if he might be choking.

But Andy was the less patient of her two men, Lea knew that, and so she turned toward his crotch, grabbed the waistband, and ripped the Velcro flap loose with her teeth. Gazing up into his eyes, she found his zipper with her teeth and pulled it slowly down over her lover's burgeoning erection.

All the while, she kept a firm grasp on the tented front of Sean's trousers.

"Fuck. Lea." Andy's molasses-dark eyes were half-lidded, smoldering.

Her gaze still locked on Andy's, Lea bit his boxers — being careful not to bite *him* (not too hard, at least) — and pulled them and the pants down to his knees on the floor. She kissed her way back up, grabbed his cock, and gave the head a long lick and a kiss.

Andy groaned gratifyingly.

Sean whimpered, and so Lea gave Andy's cock another quick lick, and then turned to her other lover and repeated the entire procedure, her hand stroking Andy's cock to keep it from feeling jealous.

"You want me to suck you?" Lea felt incredibly hot, incredibly powerful — two beautiful hard-ons in her hands, two beautiful mean nodding eagerly at her. "But who first?" she said with a pout — and then a thought came back to her — an incredibly nasty thought from earlier — and she went with it, not wanting to give them or her the room to get nervous: she pulled the two of them so that their balls were pressed together, their cocks a single spear of flesh in her hands. "Mmm," she said, and opened wide, taking both of them into her mouth at once.

Both men began to swear, and that heat, that power, flared even brighter inside of Lea.

She was amazed at how well their cocks fit together — Andy's reverse curve matching Sean's more typical one perfectly. The feeling of those two thick cock pressing over her tongue and into her throat was intoxicating — but almost too much. She backed off of them, just to make sure could still breathe.

Each of her men had grasped the other. Their heads were on each other's shoulder, their eyes closed. It was, Lea thought, the most sublime thing she had ever seen.

As Lea readied herself to take them back into her mouth, Sean began to rock his hips, pressing his cock through her grasp and along Andy's erection.

Andy gasped, "Damn!" He began to rock in opposition to Sean's thrusts.

If Lea had thought that her excitement couldn't grow any further, she'd been wrong. "That... feel good, guys?"

"Fuck, yes," murmured Sean. Pre-cum was spilling from the tip of his cock onto Andy's and onto Lea's hands.

"It's called —" She licked to the two erections into her mouth again. "— frotting."

"Huh," grunted Sean.

"Say what?" muttered Andy, one hand in Lea's hair, the other pulling Sean closer.

"*Frotting.*" A term she'd learned from fanfiction. All those years of reading Gundam Wing and Harry Potter slash had paid off after all! "Two girls rubbing their pussies together, it's called *tribbing.*"

Sean just repeated, "Huh."

Andy, however, opened his eyes again. "T-tribbing?"

"Uh-huh."

"Damn."

Lea took them both into her mouth again, evoking a pair of deep moans before she pulled off again and looked up. "You guys happy? 'Cause I'm pretty fucking happy."

Sean sighed, "Happy, yeah, but..."

"But... we'd kinda like to both wanna be..." Andy hissed as Lea sucked them both in again.

Sean continued, "Inside. You. *Please.*"

"Well," she laughed, "since you ask so politely, how can I refuse!" Letting go of Andy, she moved Sean back a bit, bent down and took him into her mouth.

Andy did as she knew he would: he moved behind her, flipped her skirt up, and gave her pussy a searing kiss.

Lea groaned around Sean's cock, and both men laughed. "Yeah," Andy said, kissing his way up her bottom, "she's got a lot to say when it's her at the receiving end!"

Lea was about to pull off Sean, turn around, and give Andy a piece of what was left her mind when Andy thrust into her, and she didn't have any pieces to spare.

Perfect. There was something about being with Sean and Andy that was just *perfect.* Didn't matter who was filling her mouth and who her pussy, or how well she knew them, or if both were in her hands or between her breasts or...

Sean reached down and cupped Lea's still-covered breasts, which were swaying wildly to Andy's thrusts. His fingers closed around her nipples and...

Mr. Sanderson, her senior-year Composition teacher had spent an entire class period once talking about how some adjectives can't be modified. *A bit pregnant. Really unique.*

More perfect — Mr. Sanderson had pointed up at the poster with the preamble of the US Constitution when he said that.

But Lea now felt she had reason to disagree. Before had been *perfect*. Now was *more perfect*. And then Andy's hands slipped around her hip and closed and her clit and...

Most perfect.

———

Sean and Andy were lying on the floor, each with his head at the other's knees. Lea was draped across them, her top and bra up under her armpits, her skirt around her waist. *Take that, 50 Shades Lady! Bet you didn't see* this *coming!*

Lea giggled moistly and then blinked. "Oh. Fuck. My luggage."

Both men laughed, literally rocking Lea's world. Andy snorted, "Knew we forgot something!"

Before Lea could jump up, Sean slid his hand — which had been resting on her thigh — up to her snatch, stilling her quite effectively. "Told you, Lea. We needed you to identify something."

Blinking, Lea looked at Sean and then at Andy, who laughed again and pointed over by the door. Her well-traveled back-pack and duffel bag were right there. "Oh. Thanks." She grabbed two semi-hard cocks and squeezed them, getting two rumbling groans for her trouble. "And thanks for meeting me."

"We couldn't stay away," said Andy.

Sean added, "And we didn't want you to have to drive with the roads like this." He stroked her hair. "If you don't mind, we get off shift at midnight."

"Mind? Hell, no!"

"Lea," said Sean, his fingertip running along her earlobe, the line of her chin, "You seemed a mite antsy. Is this really okay?"

She was going to answer *Are you fucking kidding?* But she recognized that it was a real question and deserved a real answer. "Yeah. Yeah. It's just..." She kissed Sean's hand and then turned and pulled Andy's to her lips. "I think this all scares me a bit. I mean, I barely know you guys, but this just feels so... *right*. You know?"

"Yeah," Andy said, as both men let their fingers explore her collarbones, her ribs. "Yeah, I reckon we sure as hell know."

"Indeed we do," said Sean. His fingers grazed the bottom of Lea's right breast so that she could *just* feel it. "And we know that worrying about it won't get us nowhere. Now what do y'all both say," he continued in his low, rolling drawl, "about seeing just how *right* we can keep this feeling before Andy and me have to get back out there in the cold?"

Andy and Lea both concurred that Sean's was a mighty good plan.

Perfect, even.

The Visitor Goes to Work

Lea's phone went off, crooning U2 at her.

First day of work.

Meeting with her boss, Sassy.

Meeting with Bob, the theater's artistic director.

Meeting with the box office staff and training on the ticket software with Zach, the theater's resident computer guy.

Tour with Gus, the tech director.

Lea needed to pee.

Heart racing, adrenaline singing through her veins, Lea leapt out of bed to go to the bathroom.

Well. She tried to leap.

Something heavy was holding her down.

Two somethings, in fact: Sean and Andy, whose legs and massive arms wrapped Lea in a cocoon that would have been incredibly sweet if she didn't need to get up and get ready for her first day on the job.

Also, she still needed to pee. "Guys?"

As Bono continued his ode to the glory of the day, Lea's boys snored on.

"Sean? Andy?" Wriggling, Lea realized that her hands were at each of their crotches. What a surprise. She squeezed two well-worn, well-earned morning hard-ons evoking two somnolent groans. "Boys. Get off of me or I'll fry these up for breakfast."

Andy's head shot up. "Uh. 'Morning."

Sean's face rolled off of Lea's right tit. "Hey."

Anxious as she was, Lea couldn't help but smile down at the shit-ton of male gorgeousness that she had somehow managed to snag for herself. "Hey, yourself. I need to get up."

Now Sean sat up. "Right. First day at the theater." He pronounced it as a three-syllable word: *the-AY-tuh*.

"Uh-huh. And as much as I'd love to stay and play — "

"No," both men said, and like the firemen they were sprang out of the bed, treating her to the sight of her shit-ton of pulchritude standing naked and cum-stained on either side of her bed, and making Lea briefly wonder if she *really* needed to be on time for her first day of work....

"We'll start some breakfast," Sean said, pulling on the pajama pants they somehow always put on but somehow never kept on.

Andy reached out to Lea. "You take a shower." When he pulled her up out of bed, momentum carried her body against his, and the feeling tempted Lea to stay.... He gently propelled her toward the bathroom. "You go. I'd say make yourself prettier, but t'ain't possible."

She beamed at him. "Flatterer."

From the kitchen, Sean called, "No, ma'am. Just the facts, ma'am."

"Uh-huh," said Lea with a very non-Southern smirk. "I've got my eye on you two. Don't think I don't."

"No, ma'am," answered Sean, his smile very Southern, and very wicked.

Standing under the spray, Lea contemplated the fact that tonight would be her first night alone in the apartment. Both of her boys would be back to the firehouse tonight, and that knowledge filled her with anticipated ache, even as it filled her with a bit of relief. Since Andy and Sean had met her at the airport three nights before, it felt as if most of her waking time had been spent in a fog of sexual satiation. One, the other, or both of the boys always seemed to be ready and raring to go, and that was hardly something Lea was going to complain about. Even so, Lea had lost count of the orgasms they'd brought her too, and she hadn't even tried to count the number of times they'd come on or inside of her. Her pussy. Her mouth. Between her tits...

The previous night, when she'd needed to catch her breath, on each other: frotting — grinding their cocks together, each grabbing the other's ass, pulling the other close, Sean on top, Andy with his head pressed against Sean's sweaty shoulder, his eyes locked on Lea's as he bucked against his friend and spurted up against Sean's flat stomach, setting Sean off....

It was just about the sexiest thing that Lea had ever seen, and was the closest she'd ever come to understanding her friend Kirsten's fascination with gay porn.

As the shower poured down on her, Lea felt her nipples hardening, felt the hot water streaming between her labia. *Oh, god....*

Sliding into the corner of the shower stall, trying not to think about time, Lea rubbed her hands over her wet body. She let her fingers trail down between her legs, and hissed as they encountered her pussy — satiated, yes; tired, perhaps; but still ready for more....

"You need a hand there, Miss Lea?"

Through the steam-fogged glass door, Lea could see that Andy and Sean were standing at the door of the bathroom. "Huh," grunted Lea. Bulges in their low-slung pajama pants made it obvious that they were having as hard a time as Lea was *not* thinking about about the last few days. "Uh-huh," she groaned. *"Please."*

They dropped trou — *why did they ever bother putting them on?* — and stepped into the shower. The brief flash of cool air that they'd let in was immediately replaced by the heat of their bodies pressing against hers. "Rolls in the oven," mumbled Andy, huge hands flowing over Lea's belly and hips. He leaned down and sucked Lea's right nipple into his mouth, eliciting a spark of pleasure and a small scream.

Sean stopped her mouth — gently, always gently — and began to slowly kiss his way across her cheek to her chin. Up her chin tortuously to her ear. He pulled on her earlobe with his lips, let it slide by the smallest possible degrees out of his mouth, and then whispered, "What you thinking about, Lea? What got you all hot and — " He let his fingers join Andy's sliding along the slick out lips of her pussy. " — ready for us?"

Whimpering, Lea tried to spread her legs, to open to them, but their massive thighs pressed against hers, and so she settled for letting each run his hand in the crease between either thigh and her pussy. It made Lea wonder why she hadn't ever tried masturbating two-handed.

Would she ever need to masturbate ever again? "Thinking... of you," she groaned as Sean began to apply his amazingly talented, *slow* mouth to her free breast. She reached down, taking two wet hardons into fingers that she could barely control. "Rubbing... 'gainst each other. *Fuck!*"

Sean had finally sucked her left nipple between his teeth.

Into right breast, Andy murmured, "Wouldn't you rather have us rubbin' 'gainst you?"

"Um..." Honestly, Lea had no ability to say what she'd *rather* have, but yes: that sounded very nice indeed. "Uh-huh...."

Grinning, Sean slid up Lea's body and turned her toward him. Andy pressed up against her back and reached around her, pulling Sean's ass, so that Sean's cock slid up along Lea's belly.

Sean pulled Andy close as well, and his cock slid against the length of her spine, his balls spreading her butt cheeks. Both men began to kiss and nibble at her neck, her cheeks, and to grind aganist her.

Fuckity-fuck-fuck.

They were fucking *through* Lea. Lea *was* the fuck. Her entire body felt like one enormous erogenous zone.

Each began to grunt ferally into one of Lea's ears.

FUCK....

But...

But as exciting as it was — and it was — Lea was aware of her own pussy weeping with need, the greedy thing, adding more moisture to the wet shower. "Um..." She found one leg sliding up onto Sean's hip.

Without any further prompting, Sean's hands slid to Lea's ass and lifted her, so that his cock was grinding against her clit and Andy's was sliding up the crack of her ass. "Damn," he grunted.

"Uh-huh," Lea sighed as the two erections sparked all sorts of fascinating sensations in her lower body.

"Damn," echoed Andy.

The two of them continued their steady rhythm. Lea hardly had do a thing other than enjoy herself and try not to pass out.

After a few minutes she felt the rhythm shift, speeding up. "Uh, Lea, honey?" moaned Sean. "Can I... inside you?"

"Please!"

In rhythm, he lifted her, then lowered her onto his cock.

Lea and Sean both swore in some Stone Age language that bore no particular resemblance to English. The feeling of Sean's sweet erection stroking her g-spot as Andy pushed against her pelvis, made her clit grind into Sean's pubic bone...

"Um, Lea? Baby?" Andy whined.

Lea threw back her head and kissed him. "Huh?"

Andy slowed, his expression pained. "Could I maybe...?"

"Oh. Sure. After Sean. I'd... *HNGH*... love... that." Sean had latched onto one of Lea's nipples again.

"Um, yeah, me too, um..." Andy panted, grinding against Lea's ass as Sean thrust up into her cunt. "Uh, maybe...?" He slipped one hand free and steadied his cock, lining it up with Lea's backside.

"*Woah!*" gasped Lea, her buttocks clenching around his head, her body stiffening, her cunt contracting so that Sean screamed his orgasm into her chest, and they all nearly toppled over.

"Sorry!" moaned Andy as Sean slid slowly to the shower floor, Lea on top of him. "I didn't — !"

"No, no, no, it's okay, I mean," panted Lea as she felt Sean pulsing inside of her as she lay on his chest, "I mean maybe we can do that, can talk about that, but, um, not right now, okay?"

"Okay." Andy sounded about five years old.

Sean slid his cock out of Lea, making her gasp again. "Don't worry, Andy. I think sweet Miss Lea here still needs some help gettin' off, and seems to me she's got a very sweet, very hot hole to file."

Lea tilted her pelvis so that Andy could see her pussy, washed by the shower spray, dripping Sean's spray, open to him.

"O-okay." Andy knelt behind Lea, between Sean's thighs, and buried his reverse-curved cock in her, and it was his turn to join her in screaming that Paleolithic war cry.

As Andy began to pound her from behind (and from his whimpers, he was clearly close, which was probably why he'd been so eager to stick his *thang* up her ass, the poor dear, and *oooo*, she was *sooo* close too), Sean's fingers slipped down Lea's belly and through her bush, finding her clit, and...

And...

As the mist cleared, Lea was first aware of *wet*. Wet Sean against her belly. Wet Andy gushing wet inside of her. Wet her. Wet air. Wet tile.

Tears. Water.

Wet.

"Think those rolls are done, Andy-boy?" asked Sean, reaching beneath Lea's overflowing pussy and squeezing his friend's balls, releasing more *wet* inside of Lea.

"Aw, *fuck yeah*," groaned Andy.

"Then let's go get this girl fed and off to her new job."

"Fuck yeah," panted Lea with a slack grin. "I'm definitely ready now."

Lea's first day was a whirlwind. Sassy, Lea's sardonic, Canada-born boss, was overjoyed to have a fulltime assistant for the first time in years, and showed Lea off around the office like a new baby. The theater was in the middle of producing one season and mounting its subscription drive for the next one, and so between the main office, the shop, and the box office, there were well over a hundred new faces and new names for Lea to learn. After her last job, where she and the artistic director had comprised the entire fulltime staff, the flood of new people and energy overwhelmed Lea, even as it thrilled her.

Everyone seemed incredibly friendly. She got five different offers of places to stay, and was asked out on three dates — two very different men and one woman — the office manager, Jaimie, who reminded Lea strongly of Sean's sister, Kirsten. It was quite nice to be able to say that she was all taken care of in both regards.

Nicer to be able to say it while she could still feel the remnants of Andy and Sean's passion inside of her.

After watching a few rounds of this, Sassy got an incredibly knowing, wicked look on her face. As they ate lunch in Lea's tiny new office (barbecued ribs, of course, which Sassy claimed was her main reason for staying in Atlanta), Sassy waited until Lea's mouth was full and shot her a sly grin. "So. Boyfriend? Girlfriend?"

"Um," said Lea, trying to swallow, trying to think how to answer. "It's... complicated."

Sassy's eyebrows shot up. "Is it, really? Well, well, well. It's always the quiet ones."

Lea knew she was turning the color of the barbecue sauce, so she didn't even try to answer, letting Sassy chuckle to her heart's content.

As they finished up their lunch, Sassy said, "Complicated is what we do best, of course, but if it becomes *too* complicated, don't feel shy about letting me know, eh?"

"Thanks," said Lea, trying to match Sassy's no-nonsense tone. "I think for now it's just complicated enough."

"Lucky you." Sassy's grin widened. "So, after your last meeting, I'd love to take you out to dinner with Bob." The artistic director of the theater. "Won't be stepping on any plans?"

"No," said Lea. "I'm on my own this evening anyway."

"Oh?" Sassy raised her eyebrow again, but apparently decided to move on. "Well, you've got a training session in the box office with Zach. He's sweet, but watch his hands."

"Okay," said Lea, thinking, *I'd rather watch Sean and Andy's hands, stroking each other...* Smiling, she shook her head, and then remembered her last meeting of the day. "No problem. Do I need to worry about Gus?"

"Oh, no." Sassy gave what was for her a soft, warm smile. "Gus is a sweetheart. You won't have any trouble with him."

"Great." Lea gathered up the napkins and sauce-soaked bags. "Well, let me strap on my armor and go get trained by Zach."

Zach turned out to be no problem. Lea short-circuited any potential ass-grabbing when she breezed into the box office and asked if he knew where Sean and Andy's firehouse was. "My boyfriend works there," she sighed, "and I'd love to drop in by surprise when I get off work tonight."

Politely Southern as most of the staff, Zach pulled up a map and showed Lea that the firehouse was only a half mile from the theater — which Lea already knew. After Lea had gone on about how wonderful her boyfriend was — and he was, whichever of them she happened to mean — she thanked Zach fulsomely.

He smiled back, a nervous, thin-lipped smile, and proceeded to teach Lea the intricacies of the box-office software.

Zach never touched her.

As Lea walked through the door that led backstage to the domain of Gus, the theater's tech director and senior designer, Lea texted the boys: *Miss me?*

Like crazy, came back Andy's immediate answer.

Think we're both addicted, added Sean.

Lea shivered and smiled. Me too. Hey, I'm having dinner with my bosses tonight. Any chance I can swing by and visit after?

After a minute or so, Sean's answer came back: Afraid that's probably not a good idea. We kind of pushed our luck swapping shifts to meet you out at the airport. Another time?

With a sigh, Lea sent them a frownie face, and then texted, *I'll be so lonely in that big pullout without both of you.*

She got two frownie faces in return. *See you tomorrow,* they both answered.

"Ah, Lea, how nice to meet you." Gus was grey-haired and small — pixyish, even — and though he was easily the oldest person working at the theater, his eyes and smile were bright and he was bouncing on the balls of his feet as he approached. "Sally's said such wonderful things about you."

"Glad to hear it!" Lea laughed. "You're the first person I've met here who doesn't call her Sassy."

"Oh, well..." He blinked at Lea. "My wife was named Sally, you know. My late wife."

"Oh." Lea felt all of the heat that had flooded into her middle as she texted Sean and Andy turn cold. "I'm so sorry."

"Oh, no need," Gus said with a bright, sad smile. "It's been four years, though there are days when it feels as if it was only yesterday. But we had a wonderful life together. Here. I'll show you." He led her into the bowels of the shop area behind the main stage; a group of artists were painting an elaborate starscape on what looked like an old barn door. "Look's gorgeous," said Gus, and the crew looked up. "Everyone, this is our new assistant business manager, Lea."

Lea waved. "The box office staff have already dubbed me *Mini-Sassy*," she laughed

The painters waved and introduced themselves; Lea despaired of remembering any more names, and then Gus tugged on her sleeve. "Come on," he said, "let me bring you up to my aerie." He led Lea up a steep staircase — almost more of a ladder — up to a room that was easily sixty feet above the shop floor.

"Whew!" Lea said when they reached the top. "No wonder you have so much energy! You climb that all of the time?"

"Oh, yes," Gus said, blinking, as if it had never occurred to him that it might be a difficult climb. "I suppose that's why I don't get too many visitors." He flashed his bright smile and ushered Lea in.

The office was easily three times the size of Lea's, but it didn't feel it. It was crammed with set models, blue prints, a wide-format printer, three work tables overflowing with sketches, swatches, paint chips and random pieces of hardware. And the walls were invisible, covered by dozens of brightly colored paintings. A number were of dogs and sailboats, but a number were amazing, impressionistic portraits of actors and...

"Here's my Sally," said Gus, that sad smile resurfacing. Behind what seemed to be his desk — it was difficult to tell, given the glaciers of beautiful bric-a-brac piled on top — hung eight different paintings that featured a beautiful redheaded woman. Well, it was difficult to tell what she *looked* like, but the paintings made it very clear how the painter had *felt* about her. "We were married over forty years," Gus sighed, "and she was as beautiful when I lost her — " He pointed to the portrait furthest to the right, which showed her red hair shot with white. " — as she was when I met her." He pointed at the painting at the opposite end, where her hair seemed to be almost a fire.

"Wow," said Lea, breath truly taken away. She gazed at the other paintings, each stunning, and noticed in three or four another figure: a tall, dark-haired man. "That's not *you*, is it? Do you have a son?"

"Hmm?" Gus followed Lea's gaze. "Oh. No. We didn't have children. That's Frank." Gus's eyebrows bunched, which looked almost unnatural on his face. "He was our friend. Good friend. Well, he was our boarder."

"Boarder?"

"Yes. He lived with us for nearly a quarter century, if you can believe that." Gus sighed. "We lost him nearly a decade ago."

"Oh, Gus, I'm so sorry." Lea felt as if she were walking through a minefield and tripping every last one.

"No, no, don't be, my dear." Gus's eyes were sparkling again, and his mouth was back in its usual bright smile. "One of the things about reaching my age — I'm seventy-eight — is that one loses people. Careless, I know, but it can't be helped! And in the mean time, I've known more than my share of love and laughter, and I've still got work that I enjoy, and a building full of young, creative people keeping me alive. I haven't any complaints!"

When Lea met up with Bob and Sassy, she was still laughing. "You told me Gus was a sweetheart, Sassy, but *wow!*"

"He's something, eh?" said Sassy with a wink. "I'm convinced he'll be here, running up and down to his office and giggling like a little gnome long after I'm dead and gone."

"Yeah," laughed Bob. "His crew believes he lives on paint fumes. They call him the Painter of Dorian Grey."

They all laughed at that, and the artistic director continued, "Mind, he's a brilliant designer. As much the reason this theater is still standing as anyone. I don't know how the heck we'd ever get by without him. Which, I hope and trust, we won't have to any time soon!"

"Here, here," Sassy agreed. "Now, Lea, let's get out of this building so we can show you that there is in fact food in Atlanta aside from fried chicken and barbecue. I know we're a little further away from the ocean than you're used to, but there's a seafood place just a few blocks away that makes some of the best sushi you'll find in the South. And while we ply you with seafood and sake, you can give us your impressions of the theater."

The meal was long. The conversation was fascinating. The sake flowed freely.

And the sushi was definitely fabulous.

I know Sean would love this place; wonder if I could get Andy here? Lea imagined their hulking forms in the beautiful, quiet restaurant. She imagined them nibbling at the sushi.

She imagined them under the table, nibbling at *her*, and she blushed.

When she arrived back at the apartment, it was almost eleven, and she was dead on her feet. Happy, but exhausted. She was almost glad that she would be able to fall into bed alone and simply go to sleep.

Almost.

There was a package in front of the door. Addressed to her.

Intrigued, Lea picked it up and let herself in.

The apartment was neat as a proverbial pin. There were roses on the table. A note that read *We can't keep you warm with our bodies tonight, but we hope our love can help at least a little.* They'd both signed it.

It made Lea's middle go soft and her eyes overflow, and she felt like such a *girl*, but what the fuck: she *was* a girl, proud to be one, and she had more than her share of masculinity at her beck and call (if not tonight) — and they'd been incredibly sweet.

Suddenly, she missed them terribly, even though she knew their purpose in leaving the flowers and the note had been quite the opposite.

She threw herself down into one of the chairs — usually Andy's chair — only then remembering the package.

It was from a store that sounded vaguely familiar, one in San Francisco, but not one that Kirsten had ever worked at, Lea was pretty sure. She couldn't think why it seemed familiar.

Using her keys to cut the packing tape (and trying to ignore the voice of her father telling her not to use her keys that way), Lea opened the box and pulled out the invoice, which included a note from Kirsten:

A housewarming present for my best friend, K.

Intrigued, she pulled out the newsprint that had been used as packing material — reminding herself to ask the boys where to find a recycling center. In the box were three smaller boxes and a tangle of nylon, plastic, and fabric that, as Lea pulled it out, looked like some bizarre combination of sports gear and lingerie. *What the fuck, Kirsten?*

She lay aside the whatever-it-was, and pulled out the smallest of the three boxes. It contained what looked like nothing more than a plastic plumb bob, about three inches long, with a strawberry-shaped head. It was colored bright purple.

Alarmed now, Lea grabbed the largest box, having some sense of what it would contain — and it did.

A penis. Not quite as long as Sean's or Andy's, but a very nice size, to Lea's eye. Made out of silicone.

It too was bright purple. And had what looked like a handle at the back end.

Lea had her phone out and had hit her friend's number before she could even think to breathe.

"Hey, Leelee!" Kirsten's voice was warm, and bright, and welcome. "You get my package, sweetie?"

"*Holy fuck, Kirsten!*" Lea gasped. "What the fuck am I supposed to *do* with this?"

"Well, now, Lea, sugar," laughed Kirsten, "I am quite sure that you could figure out something to do with it all on your lonesome. But I kinda figured that with all of that boyflesh around you, there might be some fun uses you could put it too!"

"*Kirsten!*" Lea felt about thirteen, felt about as humiliated as she had when she figured out why the boys sometimes walked with their notebooks in front of their crotches. "I mean, thanks a lot, but I've got to tell you, I may be alone tonight, so I'm sure it will be great, thanks, but I've got two very nice penises already — your *brother's* being one! — so I don't see how having yet another phallus to stick inside of me is going to do me a whole lot of good!"

Kirsten cackled. "Oh, I know it'll do you a *whole* lotta good!" She laughed again and then said, "But Lea sweetie, that isn't just for you, you know!"

"Isn't just...?" Lea puzzled at the floppy plastic thing. "It's a dildo, for fuck's sake. I know what a dildo is."

Again Kirsten laughed maniacly. "And what do you think that doodad at the bottom is for?"

Lea grabbed it. "I don't know, a handle?" When Kirsten snorted, Lea growled, "*Kirsten!*"

"Heh! Okay. Okay. Well, did you try on the harness?"

"What, the nylon thing? I'm supposed to *wear* it?"

"Definitely," Kirsten said with a giggle, and before Lea could bark at her again, Kirsten asked, "You in pants or a dress, or what?"

Lea blinked, disconcerted. "Dress. It was my first day."

"Perfect. So slip that nylon thingee on like it was undies. You can slip off what you got or not, whatever."

Perplexed, Lea did as she was told; letting her panties fall to the floor, she stepped into what she could now clearly see were loops for her legs. "Okay."

"Really? Damn, I didn't think it would be that easy."

"Kirsten."

"Sorry. Yeah. So it's not all the way up, is it?"

"Nope." Lea had pulled it to just above her knees.

"Perfect. Now, see at the front, there's a kind of plastic ring, goes right over where your bush would be? Take the dong and slide it through there."

Lea did — and comprehension began to dawn. But still... "But... where will the handle go?"

Kirsten snorted again, but swallowed it. "Sorry! But that's not a handle."

"Not a...?" Lea pulled the harness up the rest of the way, trying to see how the whole thing would work.

As soon as she had pulled it the whole way up, the purple hard-on sprang proudly in front of her, and the protuberance that she'd taken for a handle pushed up against her entrance. *"Oh!"* As soon as Lea's body began to react to the pressure, it slid in. *"OH!"*

"It's called a double dildo, sweetie. A strap-on." Kirsten sounded very pleased with herself. "You ever wonder what it would feel like to fuck your guy, to have a cock? Well, now you have one!"

As the smaller end of the dildo pushed up into Lea's pussy, a nub at the front began pressing against her clit. Grasping the purple phallus with her free hand, she rocked her hips and felt the nub moving against her, the smaller phallus moving within her. "Oh..." she sighed.

"Uh-huh," said Kirsten. "Told you. Feel good?"

"Um. Yeah." Lea and Kirsten had talked about sex a lot, had even discussed vibrators a few times, but they'd never actually talked while *doing it* and Lea was feeling more than a bit uncomfortable — all the more so since she knew that Kirsten was even more bisexual than her brother Sean and had had a crush on Lea. "But, um, what am... How...?"

"Well, me," Kirsten said, all but purring now, "I like to do Gianna with it, right?"

"Sure, but — "

"But , see, there's *ways* to use it with a guy too. You see the butt plug?"

"Huh?"

"Thang looks like a big ol' strawberry? And there should be a bottle of lube in there, and a DVD."

Lea stared at the plumb bob. *Butt plug?* Still more than a little distracted by the feeling of the dildo inside of her, she searched the box; indeed, there was a small bottle of lube and a DVD. *"Guide to... Pegging?"*

"Yup. Peggin'. Trust me on this. Guys like gettin' it almost as much as they like givin' it." Now Kirsten was definitely purring. "God, what I wouldn't give to see you take big ol' Andy up the ass."

"Huh."

"But Lea, sweetie?"

"Huh?"

"I don't want to know what you and my brother get up to, okay?"

"Uh... 'Kay."

"Now, tell me, sweetie! How was your first day?"

Lea gave Kirsten the full rundown — though her mind was definitely occupied.

After her best-friend-forever hung up ("Gotta go use *my* srap-on on my girl-friend!"), Leah watched the video.

She was with Kirsten on this one. *Lea* wanted to see herself fuck Andy's sweet ass. And Sean's.

After the video was over, she brought all of her new toys into the bathroom, still wearing her harness and dildo, which she couldn't bring herself to take off.

She opened the lube and spread some over the butt plug, and then put a dollop on her finger and distributed it gently to the inside of her anus. Her *asshole*.

And then she slid the butt plug gently in.

She had tried anal sex with a couple of her boyfriends — well, they had tried it with *her*. It sure hadn't been her idea.

It hadn't been a whole lot of fun. But then neither of them had known what the fuck they were doing. John the Controlling Asshole had considered lube to be a sign of decadence. There wasn't any burning feeling now. Just a feeling of fullness, of *nastiness,* like saying forbidden words when she was a kid or touching her first boyfriend Sam's cock.

And feeling both of her lower openings spread, even as her clit was beginning to vibrate against the little nub... *Lordy-lord-lord.*

Lea stared at the purple penis in the mirror, holding up the front of her dress. What was it that was so fucking sexy about it?

But it was.

Having poured a little more lube onto her hand, she grabbed the dildo and began to rock her hips, thrusting the faux cock through her fingers — just *practicing,* to see what it would feel like.

It felt... weird. Good. Weird. The little dildo inside of her created a really nice sense of friction and of pressure. She was aware of her butt being spread every time she thust forward through her fist and clenched her ass cheeks — still, it didn't hurt at all, it felt good, but... weird.

The closest thing Lea could think of was the time that John had taken her out to dinner with a mini-egg vibe inside of her, and the control on his keychain.

Only this time, she was in control.

Did it feel like this for the boys when they jerked off? Well, she thought, it almost certainly felt even better. That being the case, she couldn't believe that they could manage to keep their hands off of themselves at all.

Her boys...

Watching through the mirror as her purple cock thrust through her slick fingers, Lea could feel her nerves beginning to catch fire — the little mini-dildo inside of her was rubbing her g-spot, the nub was rubbing her clit, and the butt plug in her ass and the dildo in her hand had her feeling *so* fucking sexy....

Her boys. Standing almost right here. Watching her in the shower. Getting hard. Rubbing themselves. Fucking *through* her. *Oh. Oh. Ooooohhh....*

The orgasm wasn't titanic, but it shook her — nipples buzzing, vaginal muscles, ass muscles, legs quivering spastically.

She collapsed, panting, against the counter.

Without even thinking, Lea took out her phone. She snapped one picture of the dildo in the mirror, her legs spread, the silicone glistening. Then she turned around and lifted the the back of her dress and took a picture of the little purple hexagon spreading the cheeks of her ass.

She texted the pictures to Sean and Andy and waited.

A minute later, Andy texted back, *WTF?*

Sean texted, *Video chat?*

You someplace private? Lea asked, knowing they were on duty.

Privateish.

Okay. I'll go get my laptop. Text when you're ready.

Okay.

Lea considered taking the strap-on off and removing the butt plug, but no — visual aids were always good for educational presentations. And they'd clearly gotten the boys' attention. And so she walked out into the living room, the silicone dick wobbling in front of her, her ass muscles squeezing around the plug, feeling incredibly silly and incredibly sexy, both a the same time.

She set up her laptop on her bed and knelt, waiting for Sean and Andy to get online.

She didn't have to wait long.

"Hey, Lea." They were crowded together in a small, dark space.

"Hello, boys. Where the hell are you?"

"Um. Cab of the ladder truck," said Andy sheepishly.

Sean gave an embarrassed smirk. "Biggest closed space we could find away from the bunks."

Before Lea could answer, Andy said, "But hey, how was your first day?"

"Oh! Great!" And Lea told them about her day from beginning to end, only vaguely aware that she was stroking the dildo in her hand or rocking against the one in her pussy.

She didn't tell them about Gus's paintings. It seemed... personal.

They *ooo*'d and *aaah*'d in all of the right places, promised to beat up Zach if she wanted, and then, when she was done, fell silent.

After a moment, Andy said, "So. Lea."

"Hmm?"

His expression was serious. "What the ever-loving *fuck* were those pictures you sent?"

"Didn't you like them?"

Sean answered, "Well, Lea, sweetheart, *like* isn't quite the word. *Nearly had to perform CPR on each other* is closer to it."

"Mmm," purred Lea. "Would have liked to see that."

"Uh-huh," Sean answered. "So...?"

"Well," Lea answered, aware that her voice was a bit higher than usual, "I got some toys for us to play with and I just wanted to show you." She thought that mentioning that she'd gotten them from *Kirsten* probably wouldn't make her brother very comfortable.

"Toys?" gulped Andy.

"Uh-huh." She got up on her knees so that they could see the dildo and the harness. "This lovely strap-on, and — " She turned around and lifted her dress. " — this lovely butt plug. And a video that taught me *all sorts* of interesting things that we could do with them. And I've been playing with them all by myself tonight, which is nice, but I thought, perhaps, we could play with them together."

Sean licked his lips. "Uh-huh."

Andy seemed to be sweating. "To... Together?" Andy jumped and caught his breath, and Lea was pretty sure that Sean had grabbed Andy's crotch.

Lea sighed. "Yeah. Together. See, the thing is, Andy, you asked if I would take you up my ass this morning, and, you know, I want to, because the idea of both of you inside of me at the same time is fucking amazing, but it's also kind of scary, you know? But I do want to give you that, because I love you both so much."

Both men gulped but nodded. "Love you too."

Lea felt heat spread through her whole body, and knew that it wasn't a blush of embarrassment or shame. "So, here's my bargain: if you want me to take it up the ass, I would love to, but you have to agree to take it up the ass as well."

"Jesus, baby," said Sean.

"Let *you* take us up the, um, ass," asked Andy, eyes wide, "or take, you know...?"

Sean glanced at his friend. His lover. "Andy?"

Andy's fair skin darkened and he looked down. "Or take, you know... each other?"

"Oh," said Sean.

"Oh, Andy, baby," gasped Lea. "That's... That's up to the two of you." Pulling her dress over her head, Lea smiled. "Now, if you'd like, I can show you some of the things we can do with these toys. Would you like that?"

"Oh, yeah," said Andy, face still dark.

"Please," added Sean, grinning.

And Lea did.

And they did like it.

And so did she. She took pleasure in the knowledge of a job well done.

The Visitor Entertains

Lea had never really been one to watch the news. She'd always read the newspapers for work — mostly the entertainment section for the reviews, and occasionally the sports. But by her second month in Atlanta, she had learned to tune into the five o'clock local broadcast — at least on the days when Andy and Sean were on duty.

She had also programmed an alert that would pop up on her phone whenever the words *Atlanta, Downtown*, and either *fire* or *fatality* appeared in a bulletin. Because when they did, the odds were good that her boys would be coming home sore of body and heart, and full of need.

The need expressed itself differently in each of them. Sean needed to touch and be touched. Andy needed to be inside of her. *NOW.*

And so on the evenings when Lea was able to be at the apartment when they came home, she would wear a bathrobe with nothing on beneath. Sean would come and kiss Lea and caress her and hiss at her caresses, while Andy would unzip, flip up the back of her robe and, after rubbing his cock head against her labia a few times to make sure that her juices were flowing, thrust in, *hard*.

Sometimes they would fuck just like that — standing in the middle of the room. Sometimes they would end up in a pile on the floor: a Lea sandwich.

And once Andy had come, which, if it didn't set her off, usually got Lea herself pretty fucking close, he would slide out and Sean would slide in, and all of their fear and sorrow and love would pour into her, and she would give them light. Respite. Surcease. Reassurance that they were alive and she was alive, and life was not all flame and tangled metal, but also joy and love and heavy doses of physical pleasure and all of the wonderful things that went with them.

She wouldn't have admitted it, but Lea was relieved that Sean and Andy were gone at least two nights a week. In the first place, it gave her poor, lucky body a chance to recover — each of the boys had at least as much stamina and desire as even the most energetic of her former lovers, and between them, they made sure that her body was ravaged. Every night.

A body wasn't really meant to take so much of that kind of pleasure. Not that Lea was ever going to complain.

The other reason that she didn't mind their being gone (even as she missed them) was that it made their homecomings so *amazing….*

That particular Saturday, she actually saw them on the big flat-screen while she was finishing preparations for dinner. It was between a story about the dearth of striped bass in northern Georgia's rivers and another on the debate about the fares for the new downtown streetcar (on which Lea's boss Sassy had already bought an ad reading *Desire,* with a picture from the theater's current production of the Williams classic).

The story, which lasted all of fifteen seconds, was about a six-car pile-up earlier that afternoon at the tangled cloverleaf that connected I-85 to Highway 10. The anchor reported blithely that the accident had been caused by a texting driver, and that Atlanta Fire and Rescue had transported four people to the hospital, where two were listed in critical condition, but that three people had died at the scene, including a two-year-old girl.

The video showed firefighters using the jaws of life to peel the roof off of one of the cars; it was crumpled like a beer can. As one of the firefighters reached through the hole, the one who had been handling the pneumatic cutter turned toward the camera. She'd have recognized that dimpled chin anywhere: Andy. The other firefight turned and shouted something. Square jaw. Eyes that were blue even through the face mask. Sean.

They looked grim.

They'd be headed home now — showered off, but still smelling of the ghosts of smoke and gasoline and adrenaline.

Pursing her lips, Lea picked up her phone and texted them: *Just saw you on TV. The accident. Okay?*

She'd expected a reply from Andy, because Sean usually drove them home. Instead, it was Sean who answered: *No. Not really OK. Bad day at the office.*

No kidding, thought Lea. It was always hard for the boys whenever they couldn't save someone. But a little girl? She texted back: *So sorry. ETA?*

Traffic sucks, came the answer. *Half hour?*

I'll be waiting, Lea answered. *Can I take your minds off your troubles? PLEASE.*

Then, a few seconds later, *Andy says fuck yes.*

Well then, I will give you the heroes' welcome you deserve.

A pause and then: *Not heroes. Not today.*

Yes you were. Yes you are. You are my heroes every day.

Sean didn't respond to that.

Damnity-damn-damn, she thought.

Lea found herself looking around. Considering.

Lasagna in the oven. A salad for Lea and Sean ready in the fridge; green beans boiled to hell the way that Andy liked them warming on the stove. Three glasses of good rye whiskey on the counter.

But their hunger wouldn't turn to their stomachs for a while.

She texted one last time: I promise, I will help make you feel much better. I have a surprise for you.

With a nod, Lea downed her shot — to give her courage — dropped her robe to the floor, and went to prepare.

When she saw the big SUV pull up in the parking lot, Lea — aided by a second healthy shot of rye — fought down rising panic and walked over to the table. "Please don't break tonight," she pleaded.

The sturdy if beaten-up oak table didn't look concerned.

And so she took two of the sets of handcuffs that she'd had since her days with her power-game asshole ex John, but that she hadn't yet used with Sean and Andy. Before she could have second — or eighteenth — thoughts, she spread her legs and locked her ankles to the legs of the table that were closest to the door. When she heard their muted voices coming down the walkway outside their apartment, she leaned across the table and bound each of her wrists with one of the other cuffs to the top of one of the far legs.

And she waited. Her naked ass pointed straight at the door, the bright purple butt plug that she'd inserted probably making her look like some very weird cyclops.

Too late to back down now, *she thought. And then,* Oh, fuck. I hope none of the neighbors is walking by when they open the door.

Their voices grew louder, though they still sounded less energetic than usual. They were talking about the Hawks. That was a good sign, at least.

The sound of the key turning in the door sent Lea's heart up toward her tonsils. *Oh, god. This is such a bad idea. What if they don't want to? What if they DO?*

But as she had already told herself, she was in no position to turn back now. Well. To turn *front.*

The door opened. Andy's voice rolled out in a flat drawl, "Hey, Lea, we're…"

Silence.

Lea heard two loud thunks. She hoped it was their duffles hitting the floor, that they hadn't both passed out and left her chained to the table where she couldn't do any of them any good. She was reassured when Sean gasped, "Holy *fuck.*"

Silence.

"Um, guys, I'm glad this rendered you speechless, but would you mind coming in and closing the door? You are both welcome to look as much as you want — and touch, and anything else that you'd like to do. But I'd rather not have my naked bottom on display for all of Cobb County to see."

That broke the spell. The door slammed shut and suddenly her boys — her men — were around and against her. Sean, as she'd guessed, was leaning over the top of the table, kissing her, stroking her back, her arms, her neck.

Andy, to her surprise but to her great pleasure, knelt behind Lea and began to kiss the taut backs of her thighs, her butt cheeks, and finally, emphatically, her pussy, which was already moist with anticipation.

Lea groaned into Sean's mouth, her body pulling against her restraints, even though the last thing she wanted was to disengage Andy's wonderful lips, his lightning tongue, from her pussy.

And Sean's fingers began to glide slowly down her sides, counting her exposed ribs before brushing feather-light along the sides of first one breast and then the other....

Her image of this whole encounter had been about getting *them* off — about clearing the angst and sorrow from their hearts and simply giving them pleasure. Instead, Lea found herself submerged — as she so often did — in her lovers' very different rhythms, their very different approaches to pleasuring *her.*

And as Andy lapped at her, Sean's hands found Lea's nipples, revealed as she'd arched back under their ministrations. *Everyone needs to feel this way,* thought the small part of her brain that was at all clear. And then the typhoon of sensation blew out even that little bit of clarity, and all that Lea knew was that it felt *good.* And everyone else could find this feeling on their own.

Submerged as she was in the feeling, Lea forgot about the handcuffs. Forgot about the table. Forgot about the butt plug — except when Andy's nose occasionally brushed it and it sent a *different* tremor of sensation rippling through her. As far as her body was concerned, she might have been on a bed of rose petals or...

Andy kissed his way up her butt cheeks, alternating left and right, and then licked up the length of her spine, and suddenly Lea was very aware of her restraints. She heard him unzip his jeans and had just enough time for the thought of him replacing the plastic plumb bob in her ass with that long erection of his — just enough time for the whole of her body to break into goose pimples — when he pushed into her pussy instead, and the typhoon swept her away again.

Lea was spread-eagle over the edge of the table, and as Andy began to fuck her, her pubic bone was pressed firmly against the wood, and so his downward-facing dick stroked along the front of her vagina even more firmly than usual. She screamed.

Sean's lips pressed against Lea's ear, and he murmured, "Too hard, baby?"

"No," groaned Lea, "no, god, no." And she screamed again.

"Huh," chuckled Sean, finally releasing her nipples, which now bounced against the table top. "Then I think, if you don't mind, I'm going to go down the other end and lend the two of y'all a hand."

Andy continued to fuck her with everything he had — he was now holding onto the sides of the table so his thrusts didn't push it and Lea away. It wasn't surprising, then, that Lea forgot entirely about what Sean had said, until she felt two big hand push in from between Andy's thighs. She could feel him let Andy's balls slide over one even as the other found the hood of her clit and began to stroke it and squeeze it against Andy's thrusting cock.

"Aw, *shit!*" Andy shouted, and Lea felt him push even deeper into her.

Neither of her boys had anything like a quick trigger; unlike some of her former boyfriends, Andy and Sean were both quite capable of fucking her until she turned to jelly. Not even jelly.

If either of them was more likely to be thrown by a *surprise*, however, it was Andy, as he was currently demonstrating. Evidently, having Sean grab his balls while Andy was plowing Lea was just enough to make Andy pop his cork, which he proceeded to do, pushing into her hard enough that, even though he was holding the table down, he moved them both a foot or two toward the sink. He bellowed, and a flood of his come spilled into and — quickly — out of her, around his shaft. "Aw… *shit,*" he repeated, panting into the back of Lea's neck.

Once they'd lain there for a moment, both sweating and gasping for air, both dripping onto the table and floor, Sean gave a laconic chuckle. "Sorry, Andy-boy." He patted something — probably Andy's ass, because Lea felt the cock planted deep inside of her twitch, felt more liquid spill from her cunt lips.

"Sorry," grunted Andy. "Like hell."

"Hey," Sean said, laughing, "you didn't exactly seem to mind! Not my fault that Lea's sweet pussy feels so good all it took to set you off was a little *squeeze.*"

Sean must have squeezed Andy's balls again, because Andy groaned, arched back, and poured more of himself into her. His cock, rapidly diminishing, began to slide out of Lea, and her attempts to *keep it,* to squeeze it hard so that it would stay inside of her, only pushed him the rest of the way out, to both of their loud disappointment.

"Damn you, Sean." Andy stumbled around the table and sat in a chair at the edge of Lea's sight. He may have been grumbling, but as he let his head fall back, she could see a small grin on his face.

Sean chuckled again. "Uh-huh. Damn me." Suddenly his hands, cool and rough, brushed against the heated flesh of Lea's ass. "Hey, baby."

"Hey," panted Lea, "baby." Now that Andy had departed, she could feel all of that spunk flowing down her left thigh, cooling as it dribbled.

She heard Sean drop his jeans to the floor — he must have kicked his boots off at some point — and felt him come up behind her, not *quite* touching. Lea tried to push back, to capture that beautiful erection that she knew was just behind her. But of course, she couldn't. She gave a quick moan of frustration.

Sean, standing right behind her, hissed.

"Well, Sean," said Andy — he was the one chuckling now. "You gonna leave our beautiful Miss Lea hanging like that?"

"No, sir," said Sean, and with a smooth, steady stroke, filled the space that Andy had just vacated.

Lea moaned again, but there was no frustration in the sound this time: only satisfaction and sensual delight.

As Sean began to fuck her — slowly, sensuously, making Lea's nerves sing — Andy got up and went over to where the whiskey glasses sat on the counter. He downed one tumbler, and then walked the other over to Sean.

Without stopping his gentle, overwhelming thrusting, Lea heard him toss back the shot. She felt it hit bottom, felt as his whole body shuddered — making her shudder as well. Sean leaned down and kissed her ear, the smell of the liquor wafting from his mouth to Lea's nostrils, intoxicating. His belly pressed against the butt plug, pushing it further into her.

"Baby," he whispered, "if you're ready to seal that bargain you made with us, I am. You can fuck my ass any old way you want, if you'll just let me fuck yours."

"Please!" Lea screamed. She'd meant to whisper it, to match him, but somehow…

"Huh," answered Sean.

There was a *thunk* on the table as, right next to Lea's head, Andy dropped the bottle of lube, the condoms, and the strap-on that she had laid out beside the whiskey on the counter.

"Thanks, Andy," said Lea and Sean together.

"Y'all… 're welcome." There was a catch in Andy's voice.

"Turn you on, boy?" asked Sean, continuing to fuck Lea even as he picked up the lube. "Which part? Me fucking her sweet ass — " He reached between them and turned the butt plug just the *tiniest bit*, but enough that it sent lightning through Lea. " — or is it her doin' *me*?"

Andy's answer was monosyllabic and indecipherable. He went back over to the chair and sat. His cock raised its head drunkenly from his lap.

Sean leaned forward, pressing himself deep into Lea and biting her earlobe. "You ready? 'Cause if I keep thinking about this, I'm going to go off where I don't do either of us any good."

"Ready," whispered Lea, as goose pimples marched up and down her flesh. She arched her neck back; Sean took the hint and kissed her, letting his tongue snake between her lips and touch hers, even as his cock squeezed up into her, touching her cervix and setting her aflame.

Nonsensically, the voice of her high school physics teacher, Ms. Lighty, droned into Lea's head, talking about electrical current and how when you closed a circuit…

Sean's tongue and cock both retreated, and the circuit was broken, though the flame was by no means doused. He backed up until the tip of him just barely spread Lea's labia open. With one set of long fingers, Sean circled both of their sexes, pressing her lips gently against his head. With the other hand, he turned the plastic in Lea's rear end and pulled gently.

Lea had not herself been at all gentle in inserting the plug; she'd been aware that she needed to get it in as long before her men arrived as possible. She'd practiced with it often enough — they all had, on her, on each of the boys — that she knew to use plenty of lubricant, that she knew how to relax into the pressure. But mostly, she'd just shoved the thing in.

Removing it, however, Sean was his slow, irresistible self, and the sensation as the thick part of the butt plug stretched her, and then her anus squeezed out the long, tapered head, could only be described as *exquisite*. Finally he withdrew it, and Lea lay, panting, quivering on the table, asshole open and slick, pussy open and flowing, and she had never wanted anything more in her whole life.

Well. Almost anything.

No. *Anything.*

That was a surprise.

So was the sensation sparked by the feeling of Sean pressing against the over-heated flesh of her sphincter.

A few of Lea's boyfriends had been into anal sex — Asshole John, of course, but also Kirby, her first experiment with anal, who argued that they might as well take advantage of his small endowment. She hadn't exactly enjoyed any of the experiences — John had made it actively unpleasant by insisting that they use no lubricant other than her natural juices — and so, knowing that her boys would enjoy it, Lea had hoped, at best, that she wouldn't hate it, given Andy and Sean's heft.

She didn't hate it.

She *really* didn't hate it.

Lea could hear as Sean smoothed a rubber down over his hard-on and then drizzled a hefty dollop of lube over his already-slick erection. "Okay?" His voice sounded strained.

Lea nodded and tried, against her body's loudly screaming instincts, to relax. *Like yoga. Just like yoga.*

Only not.

Sean leaned forward, trying to press in without pushing too hard, but his cock head slipped up the crack of her ass. "Oops." He put one knee up on the table to give himself a better angle, lined himself up again, and gently but insistently pushed.

"AH!" shouted Lea, aflame once more as she felt that cock head, which could do such amazing things to the inside of her vagina, slid smoothly a few inches into her ass.

Sean immediately stopped. "*Okay?*" he asked through gritted teeth.

"Great," sighed Lea, and she was surprised to find that, yes: she was. It was. Great. Fabulous.

Much of the discomfort that had accompanied her earlier experiences with anal sex, Lea realized — to the extent that she was thinking at all — had been the result of the fact that she had not, in fact, been *ready*. Even though she'd known what was coming (more or less), and even though Kirby, at least, had squirted KY on his lovely little prick, every time a man had pressed himself into Lea's rear entrance before, he had simply lined himself up and *pushed*, and Lea had found herself feeling....

Well. *Violated*, if she were to be honest.

For John, that had probably been the point, but Kirby and the couple of others she'd done this with would almost certainly have been devastated to hear that she had felt that way.

This was no violation. This was *sex*. Whether it was the fact that she and the boys had been talking about this for a month and a half, or the fact that Kirsten's house-warming gift had both planted the idea and educated Lea and her lovers in how to do this, or the fact that she had let butt plug help her relax and get ready — whatever the reason, the feeling of Sean lowering himself, inch by inch, into her, spreading the cheeks of her ass, sliding through that ring of muscle, felt…

Well, yeah. *Sexy.* Nasty. Exciting.

"Oh. God. Lea. Baby," Sean gasped as he leaned over her, his head resting now against her shoulder, his right knee up against her waist, his other leg pressing against the back of her chained one.

Lea could feel the tickle as his balls came to rest against her open, buzzing cunt. A sense of fullness, of heat, of just how deeply he was buried in her overwhelmed Lea. A sound ejected itself from her throat. Pleasure? Something. Ecstasy.

Answering her in kind, Sean began to withdraw, and then to slide back in. The amount of lube he'd added to what was already on the condom, in addition to the generous amount that she'd slathered onto the butt plug before inserting it, made the action smooth and frictionless, and so it felt amazing. Not the same feeling as having him fill her cunt definitely — *darker,* in a way that had nothing to do with *where* he was fucking her.

Where he was fucking her. He was fucking her ass. Sean was fucking her ass, Lea's ass, Lea cuffed to the table, and *god…!*

As Sean continued his steady, deliberate strokes and the heat poured from Lea's ass down into her pussy, she locked eyes with Andy, still sitting in the chair.

His eyes were half closed, his face dark, and his cock, no longer even the slightest bit soft, seemed to strain against the hand that fisted it. "Feel good?"

Lea just nodded, her tongue beyond her control. Through a clenched jaw, Sean grunted, *"Fuck yeah!"*

Andy shot them a tight grin and stood, still stroking his hard-on. "Think I'll give the two of y'all a hand. Or something."

Lea and Sean both grunted as he walked behind them — god alone knew *what* he had in mind, but Lea had too little brain-space to spare for any speculation, and it sounded as if Sean was just as lost in the feeling of their fuck as she was.

And so it came as an absolute surprise — though it probably shouldn't have — when Lea felt Andy's long tongue lap once again against her open, overflowing slit, running from her clitoris and along her spread labia, up toward the place where Sean's cock was now spreading her open, and the contrast in the two feelings was so… *so,* that every muscle in Lea's body contracted involuntarily — her legs and arms pulling *hard* against their bonds, her ass clamping down on Sean's cock, forcing him to stop and evoking a strangled gasp.

Chuckling against her pussy, Andy said, "Hey, Sean-boy, not my fault that Sweet Miss Lea's tight ass feels so fucking good that you nearly get set off by a little *squeeze!"* He licked again, starting once more at Lea's clit, but this time continuing onto Sean's cock, his balls.

Sean swore, saying words that would no doubt have gotten his mouth washed out with soap by his kindergarten teacher mother, but after leaning against her back for a moment, he growled and continued his strokes, maybe a bit less steadily, but no more quickly.

Andy laughed, and began to apply himself to torturing his lovers with his tongue. It was the sweetest torture imaginable and in all honesty Lea never wanted it to stop. Why would she?

And so as she felt Sean slowly begin to pick up steam, his thrusts coming jerkier, Lea found herself emitting a keening whine as she chased the feeling of Andy's tongue against her clit even as Sean's now-pounding cock pushed her in another direction entirely. *"Wait,"* she muttered into the table as her lips slipped over the wood, *"wait, wait, oh, god, wait..."*

Sean let out a low growl, and as he thrust deep and hard into her, Andy's mouth closed around Lea's clit, and sucked it in, and just like that, the deep, *dark* flame that flared out from where Sean was planted in her merged with the lightning sparked by Andy's mouth, and Ms. Lighty's voice whispered once again in Lea's mind: *A circuit closes, the current flows, and the filament...*

Ignites.

The first thing that Lea became aware of, once the impossible light receded, was Sean's breath, wet, hot, and gasping, against the back of neck — of her own hair, damp with her sweat and his, spilling over her face and onto the table.

Oh, and the swell of Sean's cock, still pulsing inside of her ass.

Andy's lips kissed Lea's labia, drawing a gasp from Lea, sending another ripple of orgasm through her, and her sphincter squeezed tight around Sean, and he screamed, pressing deep into her again, evoking an open-throated bellow from Lea herself.

Gasping again, Lea was shocked to see Andy leaning down to her, now kissing her mouth. "Hey, baby," he murmured.

"Huh!" was the only answer she could give.

Andy glanced up — at Sean, evidently, because Sean suddenly leaned forward and for a moment, Lea was certain they were going to kiss, but Andy suddenly flinched to the side, and Sean's lips met Andy's cheek.

After a moment, during which both Sean and Lea caught their breaths, Sean withdrew gingerly from her bottom. "Got the key so we can unlock you?" he laughed breathlessly, or are we going to eat dinner off your back?"

Smiling almost sleepily, Lea raised the key — which she'd been clutching desperately in her palm. She was almost sorry to be released from her voluntary bondage.

Ah, well, she thought, *I can always go back there again.* As she stood up on shaky legs, her muscles screamed. *Maybe not tonight, though.*

As they ate dinner at the very table that they'd just thoroughly debauched — and which had held up just fine, thank you very much — Lea smiled, even as she shifted gingerly in her seat.

The shadow of the day had passed from her men. She had given them heroes' welcomes indeed, and they sat, smiling, grinning at her as they ate.

They wouldn't allow her to help serve, clear, or clean. "You were already the main course," Sean joked. "You shouldn't have to do *anything*."

And so she sat, enjoying watching them move, enjoying even the feeling of her protesting muscles, because *man*, if you couldn't enjoy *that*, you didn't deserve a body at all.

After the meal had been cleared away and all of the dishes cleaned and stacked, Andy splashed another two or three fingers worth of whiskey into each of the three tumblers and carried them back to the table.

Once they had drunk a silent toast to each other, Lea grinned at her lovers. The heat from the sex and the heat from the liquor had her feeling *good*, *languid*, and she could almost see herself being able to play some more. Soon.

"What you smiling at, Lea-honey?" asked Andy with a smirk.

"You two," she sighed. "What else?"

"Lucky us," laughed Sean.

"Lucky me!" giggled Lea, and raised her glass.

They all drank to *that*.

"So," Lea sighed, "you guys up for the trip to the *the-ay-tuh* tomorrow?" She pronounced it as they would: a three-syllable word.

"The *what?*" Andy blinked.

Sean shook his head as if to clear it, and then nodded. "Oh, yeah. 'Course. Taking my mama to that *Streetcar* play."

"Yup! I'm looking forward to showing you where I work!"

They glanced at each other, laughed, and then grinned at Lea.

"What?"

Andy laughed again, "Well, was gonna be a secret, but..."

With a snort, Sean cut in, "But we want to make sure you're actually there."

"There?"

"Well, see," Andy jumped in, "we volunteered. To do the fire marshal inspection on Monday."

"So we wondered," said Sean, "if maybe you'd be the person to give us the tour."

"Oh." Monday. When the theater was dark, and most of the staff took what was essentially their weekend. "Uh. Yeah. I'm sure I can arrange that."

"Good," they both said with matching smirks. Sean's foot brushed against hers. "So we'll get to see the the-ay-tuh with my mama tomorrow." He exaggerated the Southern pronunciation. "But we kinda hoped you could give us the *real* behind-the-scenes tour on Monday.

Holy fuck, Lea thought. *What in god's name do you two have in mind?* "Hope you don't get me fired!"

"Oh, Lea, no," Andy said, more serious than serious, "we wouldn't that."

"Naw," agreed Sean. "We want you to be be able to give us the tour every month. Gotta make sure the theater's up to code, after all."

"Oh." Lea gave a mock-somber nod. "Yes. We've gotta make sure of that."

Afterward, they lay together on the pullout bed that somehow never got folded away and watched a basketball game. The Hawks were losing, and so somewhere around the third quarter, Lea simply reached into their boxers — they'd never put their pants back on — and began stroking them. Even though their focus remained on the game, she knew she had their attention. "Guys? You up to play some more?"

"Always," answered Sean, his eyes heavy-lidded in a manner that might have made her think he was falling asleep if she didn't know from experience just how much flame that look hid.

Andy simply turned away from the TV and looked at her.

"What you got in mind, Lea-baby?" Sean sighed, his cock gaining length under her fingers. "You want to try that strap-on tonight?"

Andy took a breath. Looking at Sean as she was, she couldn't tell if it was a gasp of surprise at Sean's question, or at the movement of her hand up and down his burgeoning flesh.

"Up to you, Sean," Lea answered, no more willing to push than he had been.

His washed-denim eyes met hers, and he nodded. It warmed Lea's stomach to see that, in fact, he was nervous. The sweet boy.

"Here," said Andy, dropping the strap-on, lube, and condoms again, this time in Lea's lap.

She stared down at them. Clearly Andy had been prepared, firefighter that he was.

"Guess you do wanna see this bit," Sean chuckled nervously, his eyes on the purple phallus that lay on Lea's thigh.

"Wouldn't you?" Andy said. "Wanna see what it looks like. Wanna see how it feels."

Sean chuckled again, his voice even higher.

"And you, Sean?" Lea squeezed his cock. "Do you want to see how it feels?"

Sean's eyes rounded, his focus entirely on Lea. He didn't answer her in words; he simply leaned forward and kissed her.

For a moment, Lea just lost herself in the heat of his kiss. Andy was a wonderful kisser, there was no doubt about it, but Sean... Sean kissed her as if there was nothing else going on in the whole universe but the kiss.

Tonight, however, something else was going to happen. Something that they'd been talking about and playing with the idea of for weeks, but that had never happened before.

Once the kiss found a breathing point, Lea backed up, her eyes still on Sean's, and ran her hand down his chest. She pulled up the bottom of his t-shirt. "Let's take this off, and why don't you lie down. On your belly."

"Yes, ma'am." Sean's voice was husky with desire. With fear?

Lea began to pull the shirt up, and found Andy's fingers helping. Andy winked at her.

Once the shirt was off, Sean took a deep breath, released it, and lay on his belly on the big pull-out bed.

"Want to help me give Sean a back rub, Andy, to help him relax?"

Andy nodded, and together they massaged Sean's muscular back — not a massage to get deep into the muscles and work out the knots, but a light one, to help Sean relax. Let go.

They'd done this much before, and so when Andy and Lea began to tug his boxers down, Sean didn't object, but simply raised his hips.

They kept rubbing, stroking, down Sean's legs — the soles of his feet. Sean purred contentedly, his head resting on his crossed arms. "Mmm. It's okay," he murmured. "You can… go ahead."

Trying to keep herself relaxed, Lea reached over with one hand and picked up the bottle of lube, careful to keep her other hand on Sean's calf. She lifted the bottle, offering it to Andy, but Andy shook his head. He'd never been comfortable enough to play with Sean's ass; with Lea a bit, sure, but not with Sean. Smiling, she leaned over and gave him a kiss.

And then she opened the lube and squirted a healthy dollop onto her finger.

Though the rest of him seemed to remain relaxed, Sean's tight butt bunched.

"Shh," Lea said. "Andy, could you keep working on his feet?"

Nodding, Andy did, and Sean once again let his muscles go.

Lea slid up Sean's side, letting her un-gooped hand float along the planes of his back, finding his neck. When he seemed all but melting into the bed, Lea whispered, "I'm going to touch that beautiful ass of yours. Okay?"

He nodded, eyes closed.

Lea ran her un-lubed hand down Sean's back and over the butt that she so loved to squeeze. Well. One of the *two* butts that she so loved to squeeze, and got to squeeze on a regular basis, lucky girl that she was.

She massaged one cheek and then the other, and Sean's breath quickened slightly, he didn't tense up. Reaching down with the hand with the lubricated finger, she parted the cheeks gently, revealing the puckered hole that lay between them.

Andy moved Sean's legs a bit further apart, giving Lea more access, allowing Sean a bit more comfort, and no doubt allowing himself a better view.

She lowered her slick index finger, letting the fingertip come to rest on Sean's anus. Sean's breath hitched, and Lea was surprised to find her own ass pulse in sympathy; it knew *just* what was coming. She ran the pad of her finger in a tiny circle around the opening, and Sean released a pleasure-filled sigh.

Lea had never been so glad that she was a nail-biter; the video that they'd watched together had talked about ways of dealing with long nails, but that was never a problem for Lea. After stroking his asshole for a minute or two, Lea asked, "What do you think, Sean? May I?"

Now it was *his* turn to groan, *"Please."*

Grinning, Lea pressed her finger in — just to the first knuckle, just enough to feel the ring of muscle squeezing her finger. The couple of times they'd done this much before, she'd found the pressure a bit scary — she didn't want to hurt him. But now, for some reason, she found it incredibly exciting; the feeling of his ass squeezing her finger sent sparks to all sorts of interesting places.

She pushed down a bit more, wiggling her finger a bit as she did, and Sean let loose a full, deep groan that she could feeling buzzing around her finger.

"Looks like that feels a lot better than when the doctor does it," said Andy. Lea would have thought it was a joke, since Andy knew exactly how it felt, but he didn't seem to be smiling.

"Does," Sean answered. He *did* seem to be smiling.

"Glad," said Lea, grinning herself, and pushing just a bit deeper. With her free hand, she cupped Sean's balls and squeezed them lightly, evoking another groan.

When she'd released his testicles, Sean sighed, "In. Just... *Ahh.*"

Lea smiled as she felt what she now knew was Sean's prostate swell as she gave it a minute *come hither* stroke with her finger, which was now buried past the second knuckle.

Both boys liked this bit. A lot. And Lea liked it too — that with the smallest of movements in the most unlikely of places, she could bring them such pleasure. It was also more than nice that the movement she used on them was the same as the movement that she used on herself to stimulate her G-spot. Once she'd pointed *that* out to them, Andy and Sean's already impressive repertoire of ways to make Lea come had become truly and literally breathtaking.

Andy watched, apparently transfixed, stroking himself almost absentmindedly.

As Lea carefully tickled Sean's P-spot, as the boys had taken to calling it, Sean continued to give small sounds of contentment. A few minutes in, the sounds were becoming louder, and Sean began to push against the pressure, lifting his hips slightly.

Lea began to reach beneath his hip to stroke Sean's cock, but she found Andy's hand already there. "Jinx," she giggled, and began to help Andy stroke their lover's semi-hard penis — Lea from the side, Andy straddling one of Sean's legs and reaching up past Sean's balls. Though neither of the guys seemed to be able to achieve a full erection when she had her finger inside of them, both insisted that the feeling of being stroked was every bit as intense.

Though his upper body remained just as relaxed, Sean pulled his knees up underneath him, lifting his ass and making it easier for Lea and Andy to play with his cock, which was streaming pre-cum onto their hands. Sean's pale skin was turning redder as his excitement grew, and Lea contented herself simply to —

Sean reached between his legs to still her hand and Andy's. Before Lea could ask if there was anything wrong, he said, his voice low with lust, "Think I'm ready." His blue eyes stared over his shoulder, looking somehow darker than usual.

"You sure?"

He nodded, and then groaned as Lea withdrew her finger from his ass.

"Don't want the butt plug?" Andy asked, running his hands absentmindedly over Sean's balls, his thighs.

"Nope. Ready. Now."

"Okay," Lea found herself saying — mouthing, since her heart was now in her throat. She grabbed the dildo and harness and pulled them up her legs, marveling at the buzz of anticipation in her fingertips.

Shifting up onto her knees, she handed the bottle of lube to Andy. "Help get me ready."

Andy's eyes flashed as he took the lube with one hand and reached out to Lea's pussy with the other. "And here I thought you were *always* ready."

Staring at them over his shoulder through half-closed eyes, Sean chuckled.

"When you two are around, definitely," Lea answered, and then gasped as Andy's fingers squeezed her labia. "Doesn't... *huh*... Doesn't mean I don't like a helping *hand...*" She gasped again as one of those fingers slid between those lips and into her.

With his other hand, Andy slathered lubricant over the thick portion of the strap-on that was going inside of her, then leaned over and kissed her.

She found herself giving in to the kiss, to the feeling of Andy's hand — but then Sean cleared his throat and murmured, "I think she's ready, Andy."

Lea and Andy enjoyed one last breath, and then parted. Still staring into his deep, brown eyes, she pulled the thick back end of the dildo into her pussy, feeling the rippled surface sliding up into her, and she gasped again.

Andy tightened the harness straps and stroked the purple phallus that now protruded from Lea's *mons.* "Damn," he muttered, stretching the word out for what seemed like days. He lifted the condom packet to Lea's lips; she bit on the corner and he tore the packet open, pulled out the rubber, and then rolled it over Lea's *faux* cock. His hands trembled.

After kissing him again quickly — grinding her erection against his — Lea ran her hand up Sean's leg back to his ass and stroked it. "So. Sean. How do you want me to, um, fuck you? On your belly like this?"

"No. I want to see you." Even with his eyes half closed, his gaze burned.

"Okay." Lea felt a lump rise in her throat again, and wasn't sure why. Well, she could think of dozens of reasons why, but she really didn't feel like sorting through them in the moment. "Um. In the video, remember — ?"

Sean rolled and slid until his legs were off the bed. He remembered. As Lea shuffled off the bed, her dildo wobbling disconcertingly, he handed her a pillow.

To kneel on, Lea realized. "Thanks." Her eyes never leaving Sean's, her hand trailing down his body to his hip, Lea positioned herself between his thighs. She'd been *here* before — just never for *this*. Leaning down, she kissed the head of his cock — an activity that had grown quite familiar in the past few months, if no less exciting.

As Sean closed his eyes in pleasure, Lea slid her still-slick index finger back between the cheeks of his ass and stroked his asshole.

He groaned and lifted his legs to her shoulders, which Lea took as an invitation: she pressed her fingertip back into him, and he groaned again — louder this time. His ass opened to her more easily this time, and quickly Lea's finger was buried inside of his ass and she was playing with his prostate. He started to reach for his erection, but Andy beat him to it, giving Sean a long stroke that made Sean's ass contract. Sean gasped, "No fair. Teaming up."

"Aw, poor boy," Andy said; a joke again, but Andy looked grimly serious.

Taking in the pleasure that she and Andy were giving Sean now, Lea asked, "Sean, are you sure — ?"

Sean's eyes opened, full of blue fire. "Fuck my ass, Lea, baby. Fuck my ass."

"O-okay." Lea slowly slid her finger out of Sean, eliciting a hiss, and used the slippery hand to line up with his asshole, which was still open. She placed the purple head of the dildo against the opening and took a deep breath. "You want it, Sean?"

He nodded, gulping.

"Ask for it. Ask me again."

"Fuck me, Lea. Please, fuck my — *ah!*"

She pushed into him — just an inch or so, just enough that the bulbous head was fully planted inside of Sean. She watched his eyes cross before they closed, and Lea found every nerve ending in her body thrumming.

Andy stroked Sean's cock again, causing their lover's ass to tighten around the invasion, but then Sean fell back onto the bed, releasing his hamstrings and glutes, and whispered, *"More."*

And so Lea leaned over him a little, kissing Andy as she did, and then pushed her pelvis just a *bit*, sliding the dildo another finger's width or so into Sean, causing him to pant, *"Fuck!"*

That's the idea, thought Lea with a smile, excitement replacing nerves. She could feel the movement of the silicone inside of her, and she knew that this was going to be *fun*. Letting his legs fall around her hips, she leaned further over Sean, pushing the dildo deeper, and felt her belly press against the head of Sean's cock, which Andy was still holding, felt liquid spilling against her skin. She rocked her hips back minutely and then thrust forward again; Sean rewarded her with a high-pitched moan and more pre-cum on her stomach. She'd hit his prostate. *Will it feel good if I press past there?*

Only one way to find out: she leaned close to Sean, the tingling tips of her breasts brushing his panting chest, and pressed deeper into him.

The gasp this time was lower, and Sean's eyes flew back open. "Jesus. God. Lea." He lifted up on his elbows and kissed her.

It felt *so fucking good* to be there, planted in him as he had so often been planted in her, and she tried to rock her hips back and then forward again. She managed it, fucking him for a few strokes, each pushing a gasp from Sean.

It felt fabulous, her nipples bouncing against his chest, the pressure of his ass causing the part of the dildo inside of Lea to press against her G-spot. But it wasn't exactly *easy*. Well, it wasn't easy at all. *How the fuck do they do this for so long?* she mused. Leaning back, she lifted his legs back to her shoulders until it was his calves her breasts were pressed against. She found it easier to thrust this way, using her thighs and butt muscles to push into Sean.

Andy began stroking Sean's cock again, which was only semi-erect, but was streaming clear pre-cum as Lea stimulated the gland that produced it. "Feel good, boy?" His voice was low and husky, his eyes on Sean's face.

Sean, however, remained completely focussed on Lea. "You... *huh!* You have no... idea." Now his gaze shifted to his friend's. "God. Andy. Feels so fucking good, feels..." He gasped as Andy's strokes and Lea's found a rhythm, Lea's thrusts pressing Sean's cock up through Andy's fingers.

Holy fuck, Lea thought, aware that her own juices were now flowing freely over the dildo inside of her. *I'm fucking Sean. I AM FUCKING Sean!*

She'd had so many fantasies over the years about what it would be like to have sex with this gorgeous man, her best friend's brother. *All* kinds of fantasies she'd had back in the days before they'd ever actually fucked — fucking on his fire truck, fucking center-stage at the theater with a packed house watching, him tied up like one of the old paintings of St. Sebastian, only instead of him being pierced with arrows, he was piercing *her...*

Never this.

Thank you, Kirsten. Not that you're ever going to want to hear about me fucking your brother up the ass with the strap-on you gave me. Or that he's ever going to want me to tell you.

But thank you anyway.

Reaching out, Lea caressed Andy's butt for good measure. *What the hell! My ass is theirs, theirs are* mine!

Andy gave a gurgle and squeezed Sean's glistening cock, making their lover scream out once more to a higher power. To several. Of whom Lea was very pleased to find herself one.

"You feeling good, Sean?" She kissed his ankle and licked it.

Letting his head loll to one side — but keeping his eyes locked on hers — Sean laughed breathlessly. "What... the fuck... d'you *think?*" He started blinking, staring at his own cock in disbelief. "Aw, Andy, Lea, fuck, *fuck! FUCK ME, BABY, FUCK!*" he threw back his head and screamed, his face reddening as it so often did when he came — but instead of a geyser of pearly cum erupting from his cock head, more clear pre-cum spilled onto Andy's hand. "Aw, god, damn, what the — ?"

"You want me to stop, Sean?" Lea asked, but he shook his head vehemently.

Adding his own hand to Andy's, Sean began smoothing the slick liquid over his shaft. As Lea began to fuck him again, he laughed, groaned, and laughed again. "I just... Andy, when you were a kid, you ever beat off?"

Squeezing the semi-hard cock of his friend and lover, Andy chuckled. "Like, every chance I could."

"Yeah, yeah, I... *hnh!* I meant, like before you were all... Before you could really... I just... Coming just now, that felt so... I remember fuckin' my hand in bed, didn't even have hair down there or nothin'... *Hnh!* And... coming like that, just clear, no... And doing it again and... *Hnnh...*"

"Damn," sighed Andy. "Yeah. I kinda remember that. Remember doin' it till I felt like I had a bruise inside my..." He flashed a smile at both his lovers. "Damn. That was my P-spot, wasn't it?"

"Yup," said Lea, fondling his bum some more. "I reckon so."

"Think I can get you to come some more, Sean-boy?"

"Please."

Grinning, Andy leaned down and sucked down Sean's cock.

Sean closed his eyes, sighing as Lea's thrusts pushed his cock up into Andy's mouth, and then sidled underneath Andy, returning the favor.

And that was the image that etched itself into Lea's brain: her shit-ton of male pulchritude locked in a sixty-nine while she lovingly buggered Sean's ass. A 697? A 169? Whatever.

It was beautiful.

And even as her thighs and hips began to tell her that they were going to have words with her later, Lea's pussy told them to shut up; it was beginning to feel very, very nice.

And then Sean managed to lower his feet so that his toes squeezed and pulled at Lea's nipples (*holy fuck — the man must be part gorilla*) and she began to feel even nicer. Oozing pleasure, she began to let her hands run over her lovers' bodies, feeling their muscles bunching as they pleasured each other, as they pleasured her.

And her still-lubed finger found Andy's ass and slid in.

Ms. Lighty began to drone about circuits and filaments, and Lea didn't give a damn: she had better things to think about. The six-ninety-seven or whatever the fuck it was began to buck and groan like the single creature it had become, and Lea, Sean, and Andy where all lost.

Simultaneous orgasm is a remarkably imprecise term, especially when one is trying to describe an event or events sparked in the midst of such a timeless, out-of-body experience. Lea couldn't have said what led to what, who came first, who came last — the distinctions had no meaning.

But they all came. Even Lea, who didn't expect it at all, sensitive as her G-spot was. Even Sean, who had her strap-on filling him, and whose toes squeezed *hard* on Lea's nipples. And definitely Andy, whose ass clamped down on Lea's finger as he poured himself down Sean's throat.

They came. They came together.

Come together, right now…. under me.

As they lay in bed that night, glorying in the afterglow, Lea considered the possibility — not for the first time — that she was the luckiest woman on the face of the earth.

"Hawks lost," she murmured as they turned off the television and got under the covers.

"Fuck 'em," said Andy.

To which Sean added, "We won." And he turned off the light and spooned up behind her, wrapping his arms over her and Andy, his now-sleepy cock nuzzling between the cheeks that it had so thoroughly fucked earlier that evening — and Lea knew that *lucky* only began to describe it.

As they approached the theater the next day, Lea had her arms hooked through each of her boys' elbow, and the feeling of well-being still oozed from her every pore. Who cared about the aches in her muscles? Who gave a shit about the funny look their downstairs neighbor Lorelle had shot them as they walked by the laundry room on the way to leaving.

Life was as close to perfect as this imperfect life could provide.

Sean and Kirsten's mother stood waving at them from the theater entrance, her white hair gleaming in the afternoon light.

"Hey, Mrs. O'Connell!" Lea called, releasing Sean so that he could give his mom a kiss on the cheek, and then releasing Andy so that she could receive an embrace of her own from the older woman.

"Violet, please, Lea, I've told you." Violet gave Lea a squeeze and then turned to Andy. "Andrew, you're looking lovely as ever."

"You just say that because he looks like your son," Lea laughed, and laughed again as both men blushed.

"Perhaps," chuckled Sean's mom, "but I can see in your eye that *you* know that it's true."

Now it was Lea's turn to blush. "You caught me."

"Oh, Lea, honey, I'd have to be *blind* not to see it." Violet patted her son with a carefully manicured hand. "Just as I'd have to be blind not to see how this big old softie of mine appreciates how lovely *you* are." She peered at Andy. "And this big old country boy as well." She cast a cagey look at Lea that Lea had no idea how to interpret.

"Hey, Mama," Sean said, clearly trying to change the subject, "Kirsten call this morning?"

"Oh, yes." Violet went along with the course shift with a wink at Lea. "I think she misses her best friend here, though. It sounds as if your sister is having a hard time with her new roommate."

"Really?" Lea felt her face fall. "Oh, that's too bad."

Violet shrugged. "Or maybe it's boy trouble. She was pretty vague. My Kirsten can be closed-mouthed when she wants to be."

Nodding, Lea shot a glance to Sean, who was frowning. Not like she's going to tell her mother that her roomie Gianna *is* her boyfriend. Well. Girlfriend. Damn. I like Gianna. Hope things are okay.

"In any case, she sent her love to all of you, and says she wishes she could watch the show with us."

"Oh, yes," Lea said, smiling as brightly as she could, "she'd love this show — I know you guys will too. Come on, let's go in."

At the box office, and then in the lobby, Lea found herself introducing the O'Connells and Andy to the theater staff, and was surprised at how uncomfortable she was feeling. Some of the guys looked at her lovers as if trying to figure out which one to punch. A number of the women — and a couple of the men — looked at the two men hungrily and then stared appraisingly at Lea.

As the house manager, Jack (who had practically salivated at the sight of Lea's boyfriends) rang the gong that encouraged the audience to take their seats, Lea's boss Sassy came up with the theater's technical director, Gus. They made a funny pair: Sassy all squares, iron-haired, with a dead-pan expression, and Gus with his fly-away grey hair, bright eyes and pixy-ish build. Lea introduced them to her companions.

For once, there was no competitive heat aimed either at Lea or at her boys. "Nice to meet you," Sassy said. Turning to Andy and Sean she gave a grin so minute that Lea knew that only she would recognize it. "Lea has spoken very highly of you both."

"As well she should!" burbled Gus, bouncing on his toes.

"Agreed," laughed Violet, patting each of the boys on the arm.

"I think I recognize you, Mrs. O'Connell," Gus chirped. "Are you a subscriber?"

"Well, no, though Miss Lea has rectified that situation for next year. I believe... Is your wife's name Sally?"

Gus smiled his brilliant, heart-breaking smile. "Late wife, yes."

"I'm so sorry to hear that," said Violet, looking truly devastated.

"Yes," Gus agreed, his smile scarcely dimming. "It was terribly sad. But I like to remember the pleasure we had together." As Violet nodded sadly, Gus's eyes sparkled and he said, "Ah! Yes, now I remember. We knew you from the Fitzpatricks'."

Again Violet nodded, smile a bit brighter now with nostalgia. She seemed about to ask something when Jack rang the gong again. "Well, we should be getting in. Wouldn't want to miss the *Streetcar* now would we?" She shook Gus's hand and Sassy's.

"Pleasure to meet you, Mrs. O'Connell," said Sassy — and again, Lea knew that only she picked up on the emphasis that the laconic Canadian put on the first word. *What the hell, Sassy?*

"Lovely to see you again, Violet." Gus leaned down and kissed Violet's hand. "Enjoy the show." With Sassy, he wandered off to watch from the stage manager's booth at the back of the theater.

As they walked to their seats, Sean was staring at his mother with a look of amused bewilderment. "Was that old guy *flirting* with you?"

Violet shot her son a look of dignified authority that had no doubt command-ed her kindergarten classes for decades. "That *old guy* is a very lovely man. We used to meet for bridge, but honestly, no one cared about the cards, thank good-ness. The Fitzpatricks had a knack for inviting the nicest, most *interesting* people. Gus was simply being friendly and courteous."

"Uh-huh," said Sean, clearly unconvinced.

From Lea's other side, Andy waggled his eyebrows at Sean and mouthed *Flirt-ing*. And Lea couldn't help but agree with him. *What the hell, Gus?*

As they walked Sean and Andy from the theater to their firehouse, the two men argued over whether Tennessee Williams wanted the audience to hate Stan-ley or Blanche more. Violet and Lea settled for occasionally interjecting, but most-ly observed in amused silence.

"Stanley is a…. a *wife-beater* for goodness sake, Andy," said Sean, noticeably swallowing his expletives for his mother's sake. "And he *rapes* his wife's sister!"

Andy waved the broad-palmed hand with which he'd stroked the man he was arguing with the night before. "Which is just awful, definitely, but Blanche is, like, this huge black hole that comes and sits in his house and treats him and his wife like dirt."

"She's *crazy*, Andy. I mean, yeah, she's nasty to him sometimes, but I feel sorry for her."

"You would," Violet laughed. "My knight-in-shining-armor son."

Sean ducked his head.

Walking arm in arm with Sean's mom, Lea chuckled too. "And what about Stella?"

Both men turned back from where they were striding ahead of the women, their broad foreheads creased. "What *about* Stella?" Andy asked.

"Yeah, I mean, she's stuck with these other two. She's got a baby coming and all. What's she supposed to do?" said Sean.

Lea shrugged. "Well, yeah, fine, but she chooses Stanley over Blanche. She turns her back on her sister. She has to have at least guessed what happened the night the baby was born. Stanley and Blanche are who they are, and they're poison to each other, but Stella? She *chooses* how she wants things to be."

Both men pondered this, scowling.

Violet mused, "Well, it's not like either choice is exactly an attractive one. And a new mother in those days wouldn't have had an easy time walking away from her husband. You could argue that the choice was made for her."

Sean grunted, his eyes flicking to his mother's face. Sean and Kirsten almost never talked about their father, who'd disappeared when Kirsten was very young. He'd sent money regularly, and the couple had never divorced, but as far as Lea knew Violet hadn't seen her husband in a quarter-century. Kirsten and Sean definitely hadn't.

"Well," Lea said, trying to break the sudden cooling of the mood, "I think that's the point of the play. Each of the three main characters is sympathetic. Each of them is awful. It's one of the reasons I love this production so much — so often the play is about the Stanley and the Blanche, and you almost forget about Stella. This is like watching a threeway… um, car crash." That wasn't the simile that had actually popped into Lea's head, but she was going to be damned if she was going to reveal the depths of her depravity to Violet just yet. Well, hopefully, she'd never have to.

They walked up to the fire station. As every time Lea had come here, a group of the other firefighters was working on one of the trucks. This time they all stopped to razz Andy and Sean. "Hey! Look! The Twins brought dates!"

"Yeah," said the one woman in the group, "Andy's date is a knockout. The young one's pretty cute too."

Lea laughed and stuck her tongue out at the woman, while Violet blushed.

"Seeya tomorrow," Andy said, staring at Lea with a glum expression.

Sean was more cheerful. "Bye, Mama. Don't have too much fun without us, Lea." He squeezed her hand.

Then both men walked into the station, and Lea was aware that the eyes of all of the people on the truck including the woman — what was her name again? — were locked on Lea. Measuring her. Challenging her. "Hope you guys have a quiet night," she said, and waved.

They all waved back, and Lea and Violet walked another three blocks in silence to the restaurant where Sean's mother had insisted on taking Lea, "to repay you for the lovely tickets."

"You don't have to repay me, Violet," Lea said as the server seated them. "The tickets were comps, and it was my pleasure."

"Now, Lea, honey, the pleasure was ours. Let me buy you dinner; that pleasure will be mine, all right?" Violet's eyes, the same pale blue as her children's, sparkled.

"All right," laughed Lea, unable to refuse the eyes, just as she was unable to refuse Sean or Kirsten's.

They chatted about work as they looked over the menu. Violet had been trying to retire since Lea and Kirsten's graduation, but the district kept begging her to stay on — she was much beloved. She told Kirsten how odd it was to be teaching her students' children. Lea laughed, and told her how weird it was to go from being one of two full-time employees at a theater where most of the performers were younger than she was to one of nearly a hundred members of the artistic and business staff, of whom she found herself to be one of the youngest.

When their chicken Caesars were delivered to the table, the conversation slowed. At one point, Lea looked up to find Violet peering at her with a small smile on her lips. Lea couldn't help herself; she ducked her head and looked back down at her salad.

That didn't deter the older woman: "You've told me about your work, Lea, and I've seen for myself what a lovely place it is, but tell me, how is the living situation?"

Lea found herself turning bright red and choking on a croûton.

Laughing, Violet handed her a glass of water. "Oh, don't worry, dear. I knew what was going to happen the minute Kirsten told me you were moving in."

"You... you did?" Suddenly, Lea's stomach felt very full, and not in a good way.

Again, Violet laughed. "Well, of course! Kirsten and I have been expecting you and Sean to come together for years."

Not trusting herself to say anything that wouldn't make things worse, Lea simply nodded.

Reach across the table and taking Lea's hand, Violet took on a more somber tone. "My boy is such a romantic — I knew he wasn't ever going to push things, and so I was glad that circumstances... encouraged you together." Violet gave Lea's hand a squeeze. "But you have to tell me one thing, Lea, honey."

"W-what?"

"I saw the way that Andrew was looking at you. Please tell me that you and Sean are being sensitive to him. I know he looks like a big old country boy, but I suspect he's every bit as much a softie as my son."

Oh, Lea thought, *you have no idea how hard — or how soft — he can be.* When she was able, she said, "No, no, we're all really... careful. The boys both know how I feel about them." Well, that much was true.

"And how do you feel about my son, Miss Lea?" When Lea's face fell, Violet chuckled and added, "I know the answer, sweetheart, I just want to hear it."

"I love him."

Violet patted Lea's hand. "And I hope that he has told you how he feels about you."

"Oh. Yes." Also how he feels about Andy. And Andy's told me, and... *"Yes."*

"I'm so glad." The older woman's gaze became misty, focussed somewhere other than the restaurant, and Lea knew that she was thinking about the past. "Love is such a complicated business, isn't it?"

Lea couldn't help but concur wholeheartedly with that statement.

───────────────

By the time that Lea finished walking from the bus stop to the apartment building, her heart had finally descended from her throat. The rest of the dinner had been nice enough, but all that had been going through Lea's mind had been been the image of thrusting her dildo into Sean's ass and her finger into Andy's while they sucked each other off.

Not something you want to be thinking about while having dinner with one of your lovers' mothers.

As Lea came to the bottom of the stairs, looking forward to nothing but some wine, some stupid television, and maybe a chat with Kirsten, a lumpy silhouette greeted her from the open laundry room door. "Hey, there."

Startled, Lea turned and watched the shadow resolve itself into Lorelle, the downstairs neighbor. She was carry her sleeping four-month-old on her shoulder. "Hey, Lorelle," Lea whispered back.

"Oh, you don't need to whisper or nothing," Lorelle said. "Once Peanut is out, it's hard as hell to wake her."

"Oh."

"Mind, last night, *someone* woke her up real good." Lorelle said this last with a smirk.

"Oh." *Fuckity-fuck-fuck.* Shame lit Lea's face like a beacon. "Oh, Lorelle, oh, god, I am *so* —"

"Naw, honey, don't, please, I mean, good *gawd!*" Lorelle, whose skin was usually the color of weak tea, darkened to something closer to coffee. "I mean, last night... You know Freddy's been on night shift last month or so, right?"

Lea shrugged. She and Lorelle had had perhaps four conversations, all while folding laundry.

"Well, and he hasn't... Um. Since Peanut was born, he's kinda scared to look at me, okay? Which was just fine with me for a while, but honest, um...."

Lea blinked at Lorelle, who was probably a couple of years younger than Lea herself, but like all new mothers, hadn't slept in months, and so looked a decade older; it seemed weird that she was acting so —

"See, even before, when Freddy and I moved in, okay? Those two men of yours, I mean, *gawdamn!* A woman'd have to be, like, a statue or something not to..."

Lea blinked some more.

Lorelle closed her eyes and took a deep breath. The baby shifted on her shoulder. "See... Even... When Nola here was, you know, *conceived,* I may have been in bed with my husband, who I love and all, but I was thinking about what it would be like to be in bed with those two boys of yours. Okay?" Lorelle's eyes flew open. "And this was before you moved in or anything, okay? This was last year and all, so..."

Lea found herself giggling. "No. Lorelle. It's okay. If I didn't get to climb into bed with them myself, I'd be thinking the same thing."

"Oh. Yeah." Lorelle shot her an embarrassed smile. "I guess. I wanted to say... Lea, honey, you're my hero, okay? I mean, I'm a happily married woman and all, but when I hear y'all get up to stuff, just, you know, I want you to know..."

Lorelle's skin was now so dark that it was almost indistinguishable from her hair. "Well. I'm, um, cheering you on. Okay?"

Lea laughed, not knowing what else to do. "Okay. Thanks? I'm still sorry we woke Nola."

Lorelle laughed along. "Oh, don't be. That... I mean, I wasn't *exactly* sure what y'all were getting up to last night, but *gawdamn*, that was the sexiest sounding shit I *ever* heard. Helped *me* sleep real good, let me tell you."

They laughed together, and Nola wriggled on her mother's shoulder.

"And, listen, um, I don't know if you and your boys have anything planned for Wednesday night?"

"Not that I know of. We're all home."

"Oh. Good. Well, I was kinda thinking... It's Freddy's night off, and maybe y'all might... inspire him a bit?"

"You mean...?"

"Uh-huh."

"Oh. Okay." Lea dissolved into giggles again, because it seemed called for. This was, without a doubt, the weirdest conversation she'd ever had. Which was saying something when Kirsten was your best friend.

Again they laughed, and Lorelle hugged Lea, and wished her a good, *quiet* night.

But as Lea made her way into her peaceful, empty apartment, all she could think was, *Great. Now I get to think about our* audience *every time we fuck.*

Lea called Kirsten and shared the story, figuring her friend would at least see the absurdity of the situation, but Kirsten only chuckled politely. "Hey, K?" Lea asked. "What's wrong?"

And so Kirsten launched into a long, sniffly discussion of the state of her relationship with Gianna — how they hadn't really spent much time together recently, how they hadn't had sex in weeks, and, finally, about how Gianna's old boyfriend had been coming around and making noises about wanting to get married.

"Oh, fuck," said Lea.

"Yeah. And she isn't telling him to fuck off, which sort of leaves me hanging, you know?"

"Yeah."

"And when I tried to talk to her about it last night, her big answer was maybe we could try a threesome. Like y'all."

"Oh." Lea tried to think about that. "Well —"

"And yeah, honey, it seems to be working so well for y'all, and I'm so happy for you and Sean, but I kinda don't think it would be that way here — I think it would be about the two of them getting off, and me along for the ride, which would suck. Also, he's really short, and he has bad breath."

"Oh, Kirsten. I'm so sorry."

"Yeah, well, like I said, it sucks. And I think she's at his place now, which sucks more."

"Oh, K." And the two of them wept over the phone as they'd done together dozens of times over the years, until Kirsten was finally ran out of steam and laugh, "So Lea, honey, tell me about this young mother-of-the-year whose down jilling off to the sound of my best friend, my brother and their lover making the beast with three backs?"

That made Lea laugh too. "Oh, well, it's not poor Lorelle's fault. I guess we got kind of... carried away last night."

"Uh-huh." Kirsten's voice made it very clear that she'd be asking for details if one of the participants weren't related to her.

"And it's your fault."

"Mine?"

"Uh-huh. We finally put your housewarming gift to, uh, full use last night."

"Oh." It sounded as if Kirsten were the one blushing for once. "Um. And?"

"And we all had a very nice and, apparently, a very *loud* time."

"Damn."

"So thank you, Kirsten, for the lovely strap-on. I promise that it will be well used."

At that Kirsten cackled, sounding much more like herself, and Lea smiled as they went on to have a much more normal conversation. Normal for *them*, anyway.

The next day, the theater was very quiet. The box office was closed, it was the Equity day off, so there weren't any rehearsals, and the shop was closed, since *Streetcar* was the last show of the year — though Lea was sure that Gus was up in his aerie of an office, doing whatever it was that he did up there. The bookkeeper Chris was toiling away in his cubby. The telemarketing manager, Dave, had his feet up on his desk and — as always — a phone attached to his ear. The development director, Alice, seemed to have fallen asleep (she, like Lorelle, was a new mom). And the office manager, Jaimie, was restocking the supply cabinet and flirting with everything that moved, including Lea. But only in a half-hearted, Monday-afternoon kind of way.

Sassy actually asked Lea to be the liaison with the fire marshal before Lea had thought to bring it up. (*Marshals,* Lea thought.) She said it with her usual flat voice, but there was something about the look in her eye that made Lea uneasy.

In any case, by 4:00, most of the staff had shuffled off early to beat the traffic. And so when Andy and Sean strode into the office, Sassy and Jaimie were the only ones left.

"Good afternoon, gentlemen," Sassy said, striding forward to shake their hands. "Nice to see you again. Since you already know my assistant Lea, I think I'm going to let her show you about, if that's okay."

"That'll be just fine, ma'am," said Andy with a nod.

I bet it'll just fine, Lea thought, looking at her two boys in their blue uniform shirts. *Just fine.*

Behind Sassy, Jaimie was all but drooling.

"Come on, Jaimie," Sassy said, grabbing Jaimie by the elbow and all but drag-ging her to the door. "Let's let the gentlemen do their inspection unmolested. I'll buy you a beer. Do you know why American beer is like making love in a canoe…?"

Once the door had closed behind them, Lea turned back to her boys, ready to pounce; they were still all business, however.

"We do have to do the inspection," Andy said apologetically. He was turned slightly away from her.

Lea lifted her hand to his chin and turned him toward her. He was sporting a black eye. "Andy? Was there… an accident?"

He looked to Sean, who shrugged. Sean said, "He was in a fight."

"A fight?" she asked Sean. "What about?"

It was Andy who answered. "It was Miller. He was…"

As Andy fizzled out, Sean picked up. "The guys were giving us shit 'cause of you. Which of us you were dating, and like that. Just shit. And Miller starts in saying, 'Well, why would they be dating her, they're dating each other,' and that gets a big old laugh, ha-ha, very funny, 'cause they have no idea, right? But he won't let it alone. All last night, keeps on calling us 'the Faggot Twins.' And…" Sean looked to Andy.

Andy grimaced. "We were coming back from a call this morning — false alarm — and he starts in on which of us likes taking it up the ass. And no one's laughing any more, but he isn't stopping, so I told him to shut the fuck up." Sean put his arm around Andy's shoulder, but Andy shrugged it off. "So we're back at the station now, and Miller sort of smirks at me and says it must be Sean, and I'm getting protective of my *girlfriend*. So I punched the fucker."

"Miller's an asshole." Sean embraced Andy again, and this time Andy let him. Sean continued, "It was a stupid-ass fight, like most stupid-ass fights. the two of them punching and wrassling, and Andy's got Miller in a head-lock when Joanie dumped a pitcher of ice water over them, which broke that up."

Joanie. Right. That's the woman firefighter's name.

Andy sighed and rested his head on Sean's shoulder. "Then the captain came in a gave both of us a tongue-lashing that still has my ears ringing, told us both that if he heard so much as a squeak out of either of us for the rest of the day we'd be home without pay for the rest of the month. And that was that."

Lea hugged Andy from the side not taken up by Sean. "I'm so sorry."

"Naw. The thing is," Andy muttered, "it wasn't that he was calling us *queer*, 'cause guess what? Whatever we are, it ain't whatever *straight* is. Not that it's any of their gawdamn business. It was just he was so *nasty*. And when he started on Sean… It was like, I don't know, like if he'd started in on your being Jewish or something; who the fuck is he to throw that sort of shit around?"

Sean patted Andy's back. "Yeah, well, the rest of the guys knew he was just being an asshole. I mean, he's been on Joanie all year, saying she's a dyke, which

I'm pretty sure she's not, but it doesn't matter, 'cause what fucking difference does it make? He's fucking married."

Andy gave a short, bitter laugh. "Yeah, well, Joanie's tougher than me, that's for damn sure. She just keeps telling him to shove it."

Lea kissed the back of his thick neck. "But she doesn't have a girlfriend working right there with her." She laughed, and both boys looked at her. "Did you hear what your mother called you yesterday, Sean?" He shook his head. "Her 'knight-in-shining-armor son.' You're another one, Andy. You were protecting Seans's honor. Such a good boy!" She gave his butt a squeeze, which caused him to jump, and made Sean snicker. "You okay?"

Andy shot her a smirk, but nodded. "More embarrassed that I lost my cool than anything. Haven't been in an actual fist fight since I was, like, fifteen."

"Well, it's about time then," Sean joked, and he too patted Andy's butt, which made Andy's eyes go wide. "Come on, let's get the inspection started. I'm looking forward to getting it done with."

And so Lea led them around the theater: first the offices, obviously, since that's where they were, and then the lobby and the rehearsal studios, and then the back stage area. Sean and Andy kept checking the smoke detectors and the fire extinguishers, looked at the entrances and exits — including the few windows — to make sure that nothing was blocking them. In one of the studios they pointed out that a stack of set flats were blocking one of the exits; it was to a costume storage closet, but there was a fire escape from that room, so the doorways needed to remain unblocked. They pointed out a couple of doors that had been "ragged open," strips of fabric wrapped around the handles to make the doors open and close silently. This might make for better shows, but it would allow a fire to spread more quickly, since the doors were never fully shut.

Lea took notes on her tablet, creating a shared to-do list that would get the appropriate members of the staff to take care of each of the problems.

When they walked back into the shop, the men's eyes widened. "Damn," Andy said. "This is, like, my daddy's idea of heaven."

Lea laughed, looking around at the huge collection of power tools, neatly stored lumber and hardware, racks of painted flats, and even the shell of an old Chevy that had been used for a production of *Grease* a few years earlier.

"What's up there?" Sean asked, pointing at Gus's office, some sixty feet or so above the shop floor.

"Oh, that's the tech director's lair. You guys met him yesterday — Gus, he knew your mom, Sean."

"Oh. Right. We should probably check up there."

The drapes in the window glowed. "I think he's up there. Come on. I'll introduce you guys. He's a sweetheart. If he weren't 78, you guys would have competition, I'm telling you."

They climbed up the steep stairs to the office. "He's 78 and he's up and down these all day?" Sean asked.

Laughing, Lea nodded. "Yup. He's something." She knocked on the office door, and Gus's voice bubbled back. "Come in!"

Lea opened the door and followed her two firefighters through.

Gus was at one of the three drafting tables, working on sketches for God knew what. "Good morning, gentlemen!"

Lea smiled. "It's four, Gus. Everyone else is long gone. You should go home."

Gus blinked up at the hand-painted clock that was barely visible on his wall, surrounded as it was by set designs and paintings. "Four? Oh. My. So it is. Well, it's always lovely to see you, Lea. And it's nice to see your two friends as well. I've been thinking about your mother, Mr. O'Connell."

"My...?" Sean frowned.

"Oh, yes, you see, she and my Sally were very close for a while." He smiled his bright, sad smile and pointed at the purple-inked sketches on his drafting table. "I'm thinking of making another painting of Sally, you see."

Lea looked back over Gus's desk, where there was a line of paintings of Gus's late wife, her hair fading from flame red to snow white, and then peered at the abstract sketches on the drawing board.

"There's Sally, you see," Gus said, pointing to what Lea now recognized as the central human figure in the image before pointing at two other shapes, "and here's Violet O'Connell, and our friend Frank. This was at one of the Fitzpatricks's parties, about fifteen, twenty years ago." He ran his hand over the drawing, his smile saddening. "It doesn't feel so very long ago. These two are gone —" He pointed at the central figure and the one to her right. "— but seeing your mother again yesterday, Mr. O'Connell, it brought back some really lovely memories."

"I'm glad," said Sean.

"Well!" Gus said. "Given your uniforms, I assume you're not here to listen to me reminisce. Any problems with the shop?"

"No, sir," Andy said. "Do you have a second exit from this office?"

Gus showed them the exit to the fire escape — which in spite of having a lit EXIT sign was almost invisible because of all of the paintings and bric-a-brac around it, and let them check his smoke alarm. "Is this your last stop of the day?"

"No, sir," Sean said. "We still have to look through the theater auditorium."

"Well, much as I've enjoyed having you here, please, don't let me keep you." He waved to them from his drawing board, already immersed back in his new painting.

Lea, Andy, and Sean walked down to the shop, the boys shaking their heads. "Well, he's definitely what Mama'd call a *character*," Sean chuckled. "Nice guy. A little funny that he's putting my mama in a painting, though."

"Oh, I think it's because when they met yesterday, it reminded him of happy times with his wife. He was gaga about her, obviously."

"Not as gaga as we are about you," Sean answered, running his fingers through her hair.

"Oh, gawd, you're gonna get all mushy, aren't you?" grumbled Andy.

Lea turned to him. "It's all right, Andy. We're gaga about you too."

He blushed and muttered some more, but smiled even so.

They inspected the stage, Sean and Andy admiring the height of the fly system overhead, where scenery was lifted during shows. It wasn't Lea's favorite part of the theater, not by a long shot. She wasn't fond of heights. She wasn't *afraid* of them, exactly; she just had a healthy respect for them and avoided them whenever possible.

"So were you ever an actress, Miss Lea?"

"Yeah, in school a bit." Holding their hands, she walked them through the auditorium, its green EXIT lights all proudly on display. "Found out I liked being behind the scenes more, so I started directing, stage managing, that sort of thing."

"Stage managing?" Andy asked.

"Yeah. Stage manager is in charge of every aspect of the performance; makes sure the actors are in place, calls all of the cues, makes sure that any problems are dealt with invisibly."

"Kind of like a dispatcher," Sean said.

"Yeah, but roll the captain in with that and you've got a better idea of how central the job is. The old joke is that directors speak only to God, but that the stage manager *is* God. I'll prove it to you. Come on — I've been saving my favorite room for last."

She led them up a narrow staircase that ran from the stage-right wings up behind the wall of the auditorium. The lighting was dim — though the safety lighting limned every stair — and the carpet was thick. No sound- or light-bleed coming from here.

Lea opened the door to the booth, and as always felt as if she were entering a magical realm. The theater's tech booth was beautiful — a thick-paneled floor-to-ceiling glass wall at the front that gave a full view of the stage and the house, state-of-the-art sound and light boards, and between them, the stage manager's throne. But honestly, she'd loved every literal hole-in-the-wall booth she'd ever been in. There was something special about them — apart from the actors, above the audience, *private*.

And she'd always wanted to have sex in a booth, but there'd never been the right time.

Only now she'd found the right time.

"So, you said you'd prove the stage manager was God?" Sean said, shaking Lea out her reverie. She blinked at him and saw that he and Andy both had their serious, sexy faces on.

"God. Right." She turned away from them and walked toward the stage manager's station, pulling off her jacket and letting it fall to the carpeted floor. She began to undo her blouse, flashing one boob at them but stopping before continuing the strip tease because they were both standing there, completely naked. *How the fuck…?* By the time her chin had picked itself back up off of the floor, she had realized, *Right. I've fallen in love with a pair of firemen. Dress quick, undress quick.*

"God?" Sean reached out and started stroking Andy's cock; Andy returned the favor.

"Um. God." *God!* Lea moved backward and ended up falling back into the SM's chair, not able to look away from the spectacle before her — no matter that it was one she got to see all of the time. Reaching out to steady herself, she grabbed the first thing that came to hand: the mic. *Right.* "See this?" When both men nodded solemnly, she asked, "Do you know what it's called?"

They shook their heads.

Smiling, she pushed the big captain's chair back far enough that she could see the console and them at the same time. She turned on the PA system, grabbed the mic, clicked the trigger so that the red light showed, and spoke into it: "Ladies and gentlemen, your attention, please." Her voice rumbled from speakers all over the building — not just in the auditorium but backstage, in the lobby, and even up in the offices. Echoes rumbled through the building. "There's a fire in the booth. Could all members of Atlanta Fire & Rescue please report immediately to put it out?" Sean grinned, Andy scowled, and Lea laughed. "God mic! Ergo, the person who sits here is…"

"God," they said together.

Before putting the mic back, Lea said, "This has been a drill. No additional assistance is necessary. Thank you, and — "

Then they were on her, and all thoughts of the mic — or God, or anything — went right out of her head.

Sean was kissing her chin, her neck, her ear, in that unbelievably distracting way that he had, all while undoing the rest of the buttons to her blouse.

Andy undid the zipper of her skirt and had it, her panties and her stockings down in a heartbeat, her shoes off, and there she was, naked before them as they were naked before her, and as much as she had fantasized about fucking in a stage manager's booth thousands of times, it had never been anything compared to this.

Lea fell into the sensation of her two lovers loving her, and was amazed that they could have her so excited so quickly. Or maybe not — she'd been waiting for this all day. Since the previous, lonely night. Since the end of their epic fuck the night before. If she were really honest with herself, she'd never really stopped wanting to feel them touching her, *adoring* her, as they were doing at that very moment.

From experience she knew that each of them was more than capable of bringing her incredible pleasure on his own. But from the first time that they'd all made love together, there had been something, something magical, about the way that they could make her feel together. It wasn't just the sexual part — though, *holy fuck*, that was beyond unbelievable — but also because she could feel them loving her, and trusting her, could feel their love and trust for each other, and it felt a bit like standing in the middle of the sun.

Then Sean's tongue found Lea's ear as Andy's found her clit, and honestly, the sexual part really would have been enough. Really.

She'd asked them a week or two before whether having two lovers pleasuring them short-circuited their nervous systems the way it did hers.

Andy, whom she and Sean had just finished sucking off, had simply laughed and said, "Hell, yeah!"

Sean had wiped Andy's jism off of his chin thoughtfully and had answered, "I think sex with even one of you guys starts me at short-circuited. By the time you're both involved, *all* the damned wiring is blown out."

Yeah, *Lea mused as her pelvis bucked against Andy's mouth and her chest against Sean's,* that sounds about right. I don't need an electrician, I need the fire brigade, and what the hell! They're right here!

Lea found that she was saying things, saying them pretty loudly, but had no clear concept of what she was saying. Their names, maybe. The seventy-two names of God. The capitals of all fifty states.

Love. That word featured in there a lot. Which made sense. To the extent that Lea had any sense left at all.

She was coming. Stupid word, *coming. Arriving* seemed more like it. Or *exploding.* Was there a word that meant both?

If there were, it would have described what she was doing. Again, very loudly.

It was only as their mouths began to disengage and the experience began to recede that she became aware of how *good* she felt.

Sean kissed his way back up to her mouth. "Hi," he murmured into her lips.

"Hi," she gasped.

Andy removed his finger from her, triggering another round of ecstasy. "God, you're beautiful."

Stroking Sean's cock, Lea laughed, "Which one of us?"

Lea could feel Andy bury his face in her belly, which was still trembling, so that she felt rather than heard him say, "Both."

The only answer she could think to give was, "I love you." And then into Sean's lips. "I love you." And before Sean could say anything mushy, she stood on shaky legs, pushed him into the chair, and then knelt between his thighs, and began to pleasure him with her lips, her tongue, her teeth.

If he could torture her, then she'd show *him* how it felt.

Somehow, Lea didn't think Sean would mind.

She felt Andy moving up behind her, unusually tentative. His hands found her pussy again, which welcomed them, and Lea wasn't surprised when one thumb meandered up the crack of her ass and circled her asshole. She murmured into Sean's shaft, "Either, Andy. It's up to you." She lavished Sean's rod with a long lick from balls to head, bringing a loud groan, and then looked back at her other lover, who was staring down at her backside like a kid at a candy shop window. "Really, Andy. I'm all yours." She gave Sean's cock head a lollipop lick. "And all yours too, Sean."

Andy's voice came dangerously close to a whimper. "We don't have the, um, strap-on."

"No," Lea answered between sucks. "But I trust you. I know you're good for it." He gulped. "The lube and condoms are in my jacket."

He shot her a nervous smile. "Brought some too."

"What a boy scout you are!" Lea took one of Sean's balls into her mouth ("Oh, Lea, *Baaaaby!*"). Releasing it, she wiggled her butt against Andy's fingers. "I'll give you anything you ask for."

"Anything?" When Lea nodded before swallowing as much of Sean's erection as she could, he whispered, "Can I fuck your ass, Lea?"

"Mm-mmm" she agreed, mouth full and focussed on pleasuring Sean as *slowly* as she could.

Behind her she heard the tearing of foil, the ripple of latex being smoothed over flesh, and the *slurp* of lube against her own backside.

She pulled off, eliciting a gasp from Sean. "Try to go as slow as you can, okay? I haven't been able to use the butt plug or anything today."

Andy nodded, and concentrated on helping Lea relax the muscles of her ass. He applied himself to the job with a real attention to detail. And he used his cock to keep her pussy from getting too envious.

Before this month, Lea had never experienced having a guy playing with her butt as *sexy*. Some of her boyfriends had really gotten off on it, and so that had been fun. But having Andy tease her asshole, gently relaxing it, pushing ever-so-slowly into it, all while she continued to lick languorously at Sean's cock — sexy was sure as hell the word for *that*. Having *Andy's* cock moving just as slowly inside of her definitely added to the general sense of sexy, sexy sex.

Eventually — if she'd had to guess, Lea would have said it had taken twenty or thirty minutes, all while Sean moaned to Lea's mouthly ministrations — Andy had patiently worked two fingers into her. Combined with the feeling of his cock filling her cunt, it didn't just feel sexy — if felt gloriously, wonderously, nastily *fabulous*.

Lea found that she was simply moaning incoherently into Sean's thigh. He ran his fingers through her hair. "You ready for him, Lea-honey?"

She nodded and then hissed as Andy withdrew his cock from her cunt and then slipped his fingers slowly from her ass. She knelt, gasping, Sean stroking her head like a frightened dog's.

She could hear Andy once again lubing his cock, could feel him sliding up behind her. He leaned over and kissed each of her butt cheeks reverently, and then blew gently on the still-open hole between them.

She shuddered — maybe a small orgasm? hard to tell, but whatever was going on, she moaned into Sean's hip as sensation sloshed through her.

Then she felt the tapered tip of Andy's cock sliding against her asshole, and suddenly everything was very still.

He pushed in as gently as he could, and the thick head pressed open her anus.

Andy was just a bit thicker than Sean — not enough that it had ever made any difference before, but she could definitely feel it now, and it took her breath away. That wasn't at all a bad thing, but as he began to push in, she realized that between that and the reversed curve of Andy's cock, this position wasn't going to be anywhere nearly as fun. "Andy, sweety," she gasped.

He grunted back, stopping his insistent thrust.

"Can I... pull a Sean, here?" She licked Sean's balls, which were right in front of her. "I'd... kind of like to see you."

She could almost hear Andy's teeth grinding as he tried to stop doing what his body clearly so wanted him to do. "Sure... baby." He pulled out — he was only a couple of inches in, but as soon as he had, Lea knew she'd made the right choice. Andy's voice came in pants: "How. You want. To do. This?"

Sean stroked Lea's hair. "Maybe you on top, Lea? So Andy here can just relax and enjoy?"

Also, Lea realized, so she could stay in control. "Um. Yeah. Let's try that, if it's okay with you, Andy?"

"Lea," Andy said, running his hand down her back and over her butt, "I am happy to do whatever you want, however you want."

Turning around on her knees, she kissed him. "Then lie back. Let me do the work."

"Okay," he sighed, and lay back on the thick plush carpet. "We don't have to —"

She straddled his waist on her knees. "I'm going to take that beautiful cock of yours up my ass, Andy, and there isn't a thing you can do about it." When his eyes grew huge, she laughed, then leaned forward and kissed him, letting her body flow against his. As they melted into each other, Lea felt Sean's hand gently stroke her back, felt Sean insinuate the length of Andy's rod between the cheeks of Lea's ass — not thrusting in, just up between the cheeks, but it still felt fabulously intimate and fabulously nasty, especially because it was their partner doing it, not Lea or Andy.

Andy groaned into Lea's mouth and then gasped when she flexed her butt cheeks, squeezing the length of him, pushing him against Sean's hand.

"Feel good, baby?" she asked, her lips still pressed to Andy's. She didn't mind that the answer he gave was incoherent. She could feel Andy trying to hold back from thrusting. "Want to try?" He nodded against her mouth, and so she kissed him again and sat up. "Sean, baby, I'm going to lift up; could you do the honors?"

"My pleasure," said their lover.

And so Lea lifted herself up — just high enough that she could feel the tip of Andy's erection piercing her cheeks. "You ready, guys?"

Andy nodded, eyes enormous, and Sean simply answered, "Ready."

And so, trusting Sean to hold Andy steady, willing herself to relax, she backed down onto Andy's cock. "Just stay still, Andy, let me move, okay?"

He nodded again.

Closing her eyes, she worked to relax her muscles — the muscles in her butt, the ones in her legs — and let gravity lower her onto Andy's waiting penis. Held firmly by Sean, Andy's erection once again spread the ring of muscles in her anus. Once again it slid through — but this time, it went smoothly, as if filling a space where it was meant to fit. Inch by inch she let her own weight bring him up into her.

After a time, she felt Andy's pubic hair against her open cunt, and she opened her eyes. "Hi."

"Hi," Andy said. She could see that he was working hard at not moving. His expression was transported, full of wonder. "I... I've always wanted —"

Lea lifted back up, Sean's fist continuing to hold Andy's prick steady, and she grinned as Andy's eyes closed and he lost the power of speech. "Wanted to fuck my ass?"

He gave a quick pant of a laugh. "Yeah. Yours. Gorgeous. *Tight*. But... *Any...!*" He groaned as she began to lower herself again.

"Anyone's?" Sean asked.

Continuing to groan, Andy nodded. "Never... Never wanted t'ask... 'cause... *Shoot!*"

Lea was lifting back up again. "Because you're sweet and considerate, but baby, what is mine is yours."

"And mine too, Andy-boy," Sean rumbled, his free hand finding Lea's breast, stroking her ice-hard nipple.

Andy looked close to crying. "Know. Love... *God...!*" His hands came up and joined Sean's on Lea's breasts. "Want... Sean? Play with my...?"

"With your balls?"

Andy shook his head, biting his lip.

Continuing to move, Lea put her hands over Andy's and Sean's. "Your butt, Andy? You want Sean to play with *your* ass?"

Still biting his lip as if he couldn't say the words, Andy managed a short, emphatic nod.

With a low, rumbling chuckle, Sean withdrew his hand from Lea's breast, from under his lovers' hands. "With pleasure."

As Lea continued to ride Andy exquisitely slowly, just a fraction of an inch or so with each stroke, she heard the *slurp* of lube — *Have to get more of that stuff!* — and then felt Andy tense, pushing up into her despite himself, and she gasped.

"Easy, Andy-boy," Sean said, speaking as if to a frightened animal. "Easy. This is going to feel good, I promise, but you gotta relax."

Andy nodded, lowering his pelvis again, and then groaned — Sean must have found his asshole, must have been circling it as he had with Lea.

They fell back into a rhythm, a slow, small fuck, very different from some of their more athletic endeavors, but no less mind-scrambling for it. "So," Lea said after a little while, "you've never actually had anal sex, Andy?"

He shook his head, face darkening. His brown eyes were open now, and locked on hers. "Always... wanted to."

"But you were saving yourself for Miss Lea, here," said Sean, his mouth suddenly right by Lea's ear, and now it was her turn to tense, and she and Andy both swore.

When Lea's ass had relaxed its grip on his cock again, Andy said — all but sobbed, really — "An'... for you, Sean."

Lea and Sean both stopped. Though Andy's attraction to and affection for Sean was very clear, he never spoke about it. Sean whispered, "You can fuck my ass if you want, Andy. Just like Miss Lea here said, what's mine is yours."

"And mine's... yours." Now Andy was crying, face red and voice thick not just with lust, but with some other emotion.

Still poised mid-stroke, Lea reached out and caressed Andy's cheek beneath the bruised eye. "You want Sean to fuck you, Andy?"

He turned away, scowling his Andy scowl. But after a moment he nodded. "I... Always. Yeah." Then he loosed a groan and his cock head swelled inside of Lea, making her moan as well.

"Sorry," Sean said, chin still on Lea's shoulder. "I should have given you both warning before sliding my finger in like that." Reaching his free hand under Lea's arm, Sean stroked Andy's nipple with his thumb; Lea reached down and began to caress the other. "When Lea here's done taking one kind of ass-fuck virginity from you, Andy-boy, I'd love to take the other."

Their lover turned back to face them, and his expression was full of an un-guarded passion that Lea had never seen there before. "Maybe," he groaned, arch-ing up against his lovers' hands on his chest, so that his cock moved minutely inside of Lea, "maybe you could, you know, do me while I'm, *huh*, doing Lea?"

There was an image that had never occurred to Lea, but that would probably be stamped into her erotic imagination forever. She tried to visualize how such a thing would work, but between her arousal and the fact that she could see dozens of possible ways to put that puzzle together, she found herself just blinking down at Andy.

Sean wasn't feeling quite so overwhelmed. "Man. Holy fuck. I can do that if you... Lea? You up to try this?"

Very aware of Andy's cock inside of her, of his hands on her tits, Lea nodded. "But... how?"

"Know the stretches Cap has had all of us doing, Andy?" Andy nodded, and Sean removed his hand from Andy's chest as well as — apparently — removing his finger from Andy's ass, since Lea could feel the cock inside *her* backside flare again at the same moment that Andy arched again and gasped. "Hamstrings," Sean said, lifting Andy's legs until they were pressing against Lea's back. Next came the familiar sounds of a condom and lube being deployed. Sean grunted, leaning forward until his forehead was on her shoulder.

"Maybe," gasped Andy, "if you get your legs up under my, um?"

"Sure," muttered Sean. "Lea, baby, think you can lift just a bit so I can get Andy's, uh, yeah, off the floor?" Once she'd done so — Sean lifting Andy's legs so that Andy's cock remained in Lea's backside — Sean said, "Okay. I don't know how much I'm gonna be able to control how hard I thrust in, with y'all both pressing down."

"Don't care," Andy panted. *"Please!"*

"Damn," Sean said, and Lea was right there with him. "Okay. Let me just…" He shifted, his hips pressing up against the backs of Andy's thighs, and then suddenly both men tensed… and then relaxed. *"Holy fuck."*

Andy screamed, arching and pushing his own cock deeper into Lea, who echoed his shout.

"Sorry!" grunted Sean. "Sorry. Didn't mean —"

"No." Andy moaned, "God, Sean, no, feels *so fucking good,* oh, *GOD!"*

They lay there for a moment, stunned, catching their breath.

Andy reached up and caressed both Lea's face and Sean's. "Please. Sean." Then he gasped, and Sean's thrust pushed him deeper into Lea once more, and all three of them screamed, *"FUCK!"*

They fell into a rhythm fairly quickly. Lea had the odd, out-of-body feeling that Sean's cock was actually pressing up inside of Andy's, that they were both fucking her ass at the same time. She knew the image was nonsensical, but…

But as the three bodies pressed together, small, rocking motions moving them within and against each other, it really didn't matter much. The sex, the *fuck* — it floated through them as if it were the sentient creature and they merely the conduits through which it flowed.

In slightly less astral moments, Lea was aware that Andy's hands had found her breasts again, that Sean's, which had been gripping her hips, had slid forward, so that one thumb was playing with her clit while the index finger of the other hand had slid inside her. *Come hither,* it beckoned, and she did. Or it did — the feeling, the pleasure, the *orgasm,* surfing the wave between Sean's fingers and the *dark* feeling of Andy's cock moving through her asshole, pushed by Sean.…

Andy was weeping, hands groping, moving. Sean was panting, swearing almost inaudibly into Lea's ear. And that *feeling…!*

Lea felt another finger slide into her pussy — blinked down and saw that Andy's hand had joined Sean's, and that she had one of *each* of them inside of her, and for whatever reason it was that thought as much as the feeling — the feelings, of pussy stretching and clit buzzing and nipples aching and ass *squeezing,* and skin sliding against her and around her and within her, front and back, inside and out…

Come hither, their fingers called to her.

And she *came.*

And they came. All of them, howling a wordless war-cry to the God Love, screaming their claim as his most devoted, most rewarded worshipers.

Lea was not a particularly religious woman. She had grown up in a family that looked at its Jewish heritage as an interesting academic aspect of its own identity. She'd gone through her *bat mitzvah,* had learned enough Hebrew to read the prayer book, had sporadically attended synagogue services, but had never felt any connection to God there.

At that moment, in the temple of her lovers' tangled limbs, Lea felt the presence of the Divine close by, immanent and imminent — everywhere and everywhen — and it was a sublime feeling, one that made her feel infinitely powerful and infinitely small, both at the same time.

A good fuck can make even an agnostic see God — a fact that explained Lea's parents' fascination with Tantra, something about which Lea thought as little as possible.

But this hadn't been a *good* fuck. This had been something else. Something had happened.

Lea just wasn't certain exactly what that something was.

She felt Sean disengaging himself, sliding his hand from her pussy and his chest from her back as a *slurp* announced his departure from Andy's ass. Andy's legs lowered, and his spent cock slid from Lea's backside, sending another tremor through them both.

Andy was still crying. Not crying — *weeping*. Convulsing with tears. Beneath Lea, he rolled onto his side and curled into a ball around her left thigh.

"Andy?" She stroked his back, his heaving shoulder. "Okay?"

He curled tighter around her leg, shaking his head. The answer wasn't necessary. Clearly he *wasn't* okay.

Lea pressed herself against him, kissing his hair, his ear, his black eye. "Love you," she whispered.

"*Why?*" he groaned through gritted teeth. "I'm a faggot! A queer! *A fucking fudgepacker!* Everything Miller said —!"

Sean was kissing Andy's forehead, his nose and Lea's brushing each other. "Miller's a son of a bitch. You're not any of those things. You're Andy. You're the boy Lea and I love."

Fast as thought, Andy turned beneath them, grabbed Sean's face, and kissed him. Nothing sweet or delicate about this kiss: it was desperate and angry, a kiss that couldn't help itself. Then Andy's big hand pulled Lea into the kiss, and their lips met: six lips, sliding around and against each other, impossible and fantastical, but very real.

They kissed for a while, until Andy's sobs had stilled and Lea's lips were raw, but she wouldn't have pulled back from the kiss if they'd been bloody.

"Love you, Lea," Andy whispered. "And dammit, dammit, *dammit*, I love you, Sean. Loved you since we went through training. Every day, wanting to kiss you, and hold you, and suck you, and *fuck you*…!" Another sob wracked Andy's muscular frame. "And that's not how guys are *supposed to feel*, and I didn't want to, but lying in the bunk above you, thinking what would happen if I just climbed down? And then Lea comes, and holy *fuck*, she's so *beautiful*, so *fucking sexy*, and all of the things I feel for you, Sean, I'm finding myself feeling for you, Lea-baby, and watching y'all fuck, and fucking both of y'all and Sean, you sucking on me, and me sucking…. I could sort of pretend, you know, that it was something we were doing for Lea, that I was really just a straight boy sharing my girlfriend with my best friend, but *fuck...!*" Andy was sobbing again, and Lea and Sean just held him.

After another while, they found themselves lying there on the tech booth carpet. Lea was wrapped around Andy's back, while Sean held their lover from the front. Sean murmured, "Andy, I've always felt the same way about you. Don't know that I'd have known what to do about it if we all hadn't ended up in bed together, but you know what? I've loved Lea forever. Longer. And the feelings I have for you don't change the feelings I have for her — they're the same feelings, Andy-baby." He kissed Andy on the lips, that sweet, slow, only-thing-in-the-universe kiss of his.

Andy whimpered into Sean's mouth.

Lea didn't blame him. She knew just how wonderful and terrifying that kiss could be. Kissing the back of Andy's ear, she whispered, "Andrew. I love you. I love *Andy*. I love that he loves me, and that he loves *Sean*. I love that love works that way, that it is infinite: the more I give you both, the more I have to give. The names aren't what's important. The love *is*. And I'll be damned if anyone is going to be able to tell me or either of the men I love that we shouldn't love each other the way that we do. Point Miller out to me the next time I'm at the fire house, and I'll kick him in the balls."

That brought a surprised laugh from Andy and a chuckle from Sean, who added, "I think you'd have to stand in line, Lea-honey."

"But he was *right*," sniffled Andy. "Sean is my, you know...."

"*Who cares?*" asked Lea. "The words he used didn't have anything to do with what you feel for Sean, or for me, or what we feel for you. And the *feelings* he was talking about sure as hell don't. He can go fuck himself, since no one else is likely to take the job."

Now Andy laughed — truly laughed — and Lea hugged him from the back as Sean hugged him from the front, and Lea knew that it was going to be okay.

As they slowly got dressed, her overflowing sense of well-being didn't even diminish when she saw the red light that was still shining at the base of the God mic. Well, it didn't diminish *much*.

At least everyone's gone.

The boys walked her back down to the lobby — all of them walking a bit more gingerly than they had before. They had to go file their report and sign off duty. "We'll meet you back here, and then let's celebrate," Andy said, looking taller and lighter than Lea could remember seeing him. "I'll take you two out to that sushi restaurant you've been telling us so much about, Lea."

Lea was going to ask him if he were sure, but his expression told her not to bother; Andy was happy. He was sure.

She let them out, relocked the front doors, and made her way up to her office. There, on her desk, was a note written with a precise draftsman's hand on heavy sketch paper in purple ink.

Lea,

I need to apologize for listening to you and your lovers today. As soon as I heard that you'd forgotten to shut off the God mic, I turned off the feed everywhere in the theater — except in my office. I found that I couldn't stop listening, and for that invasion of your privacy and your lovers', I am terribly sorry, but it brought back so many memories that I truly couldn't help myself.

I've told you about my beloved wife Sally, and about our boarder Frank. I have never told another soul this, but I think perhaps that you are one of the few who can understand: Frank was not merely our friend and house mate. He was our lover for over twenty years.

In those days, sexuality was a much more black and white thing: you were STRAIGHT or you were QUEER. Now, this was after Masters and Johnson and all of that — the Sexual Revolution should have made distinctions like those irrelevant — but as your lover Andy has found, labels can be terribly hard to avoid.

In any case, I had always been attracted to men. I loved Sally with all of my heart, soul, and body, but had dreamed of making love to another man for as long as I could remember having sexual feelings at all. Sally knew this; for many years, she indulged my fantasies by using a dildo in a harness and pretending to be a man. I believe it excited her nearly as much as it excited me.

When we met Frank at a party, neither Sally nor I had any thought of bringing a third into our marriage, and yet from the moment that he became a member of the household, I think that we all knew that our folie à deux was destined to become a ménage à trois.

Frank was a giant of a man — you noticed that he was much larger than I when you pointed him out in the paintings — and he very much identified as gay. Not that he subscribed to any of the stereotypically flamboyant fashions of gay behavior or dress in those early days of Gay Pride; he was a very masculine, very conservative man. Women loved him. Sally certainly did; and so, to my own shock, did I.

For the first few months after Frank moved in, it was, in fact, very tense among us. Frank, you see, found me extremely attractive — I was small, pretty (in his eyes, I'm happy to say), and, so far as he knew, straight. For him this was a fatal combination. I found him irresistible as well — for the first time the imagined man whom Sally became while we played gained a name: Frank.

Sally was the one who moved things forward. After trying and failing to convince me that here was my chance, at last, to live my fantasy, she told me that if I wasn't going to be a man and seduce our lodger, then she'd have to do it. She got the three of us quite drunk on bourbon — for a tiny woman, Sally truly could hold her liquor —and proceeded to do her own Dance of the Seven Veils. The moment is burned into my mind's eye; it's the third painting on my back wall, the one where Sally is dancing while Frank stares up at her.

And of course, when she was done, she was completely naked except, to my and Frank's mutual astonishment, for the strap-on that she was wearing. She told Frank how much I desired him. She told us both that she was happy to share, facilitate, fuck, be fucked, or just to watch, but that she really, really wanted to see what would happen when her husband got what he wanted.

I'll be honest with you: that first night is very much a blur for me. But it became clear from the first time that Frank kissed me — and then kissed Sally — that we were building something very special.

We had our difficulties. Frank was uncomfortable to discover how attracted he was to Sally, just as I had been uncomfortable with how attracted I was to him. It is funny to think how much the label of being gay constrained him as much as the label of being straight constrained me. And Sally more than once became jealous, because there were times when the intensity of the sexual connection that Frank and I shared threatened her. We each dallied outside the threesome — usually with each others' permission, though not always. We each slept with other men and women — Sally even moved in with a lady for a time — but always we found that our home was in our ménage.

We were lovers for nearly a quarter of a century. I shared a bed with each of them right up to the end. They are with me now in everything that I do, and I miss them both terribly.

I suppose that, aside from apologizing for listening in on the very beautiful love-making that you, Sean, and Andy were engaged in today, what this rather odd, rather dirty old man wants to tell you is this: do not take what you have with these two boys for granted. Even in these times, what you have — what Frank and Sally and I had — is rare. I have already heard how much you all enjoy it, and so I can only urge you to TREASURE it. Even a lifetime is not enough for a wonder such as the three of you are creating.

I will never mention any of this again to you — and certainly never to anyone else. But if you ever need advice, or simply want to talk, I will always be at your service.

I'll make sure that the God mic is off.

Yours,

Gus

The Visitor Takes a Trip

"Mmm," purred Lea, lowering herself onto Sean's straining erection as he sat on one of the kitchen chairs. She gloried in the flare of the head spreading her open. "Feel good, Sean?"

"Damn, Lea-honey," Sean growled into her breast, "you know it does." His big hands pressed gently but insistently down on her hips, pushing her further onto him. His cock pressed past the place where her pussy and her ass was pushed tight by the butt plug that was planted deep inside of her, and now it was Lea's turn to growl.

Then she gasped as his teeth clamped onto her nipple. Her whole body tingled, and she slid the rest of the way onto him — the rest of the way home.

Gazing up into her eyes, Sean sighed, "Love you. Love you so fucking much."

Suddenly the pressure of imminent tears narrowed Lea's vision. "Love you too, Sean."

Behind her came a deep, muffled moan.

Sean's eyes flashed over Lea's shoulder, but she rocked her hips, giving him (and herself) a taste of the delicious fuck that was yet to come.

"Ignore him, Sean."

Blue eyes, lust heavy, floated back up to hers, and Lea smiled. She didn't need to turn around to see Andy, their lover, gagged and handcuffed to another chair, just close enough to hear and smell *everything*. Lea kissed Sean. "Andy's got no one to blame but himself. Isn't that right, Andy?"

Another moan came from behind, but beneath Lea, Sean smiled ferally. "Uh-huh." Sean's cock was pulsing inside of Lea, his fingers twitching where they dug into her hips.

Her lips still against Sean's, Lea murmured — just loudly enough to be sure that Andy could hear — "Fuck me, baby. Show me you love me. Fuck me *hard.*"

It really was Andy's fault. Really.

In the weeks after Andy had finally admitted what had been obvious to Lea for a while — that he was as in love with Sean as he was with Lea — Andy had grown more and more withdrawn.

It wasn't that he didn't seem to love fucking Lea and Sean, or that he didn't love having each of them fuck him. It wasn't that they hadn't tried and enjoyed every sexual permutation that they could think of combining all of their various body parts since that first mind-blowing threeway fuck in the stage manager's booth at the theater where Lea worked.

It wasn't that he didn't seem to love them any less.

It was more that Andy seemed less and less able to talk to them about anything.

Anything.

He became monosyllabic. Sullen. And then his schedule and Sean's at the firehouse, which they'd kept in sync since before Lea had even met Andy, mysteriously changed. Instead of being on duty the same two days a week and off the other five, Andy and Sean had only one day a week at work together.

In some ways, Lea was delighted. It was a treat after all these months to be able to spend some time alone with each of her boys. But while her nights with just Sean were wonderful — a fulfillment of the daydreams (and the more nocturnal ones) that she'd had about being with him since she was in college — Andy seemed closed off to her. Except of course when they were fucking.

And so, one steamy, early summer evening, Lea pressed the issue while Andy's calves were over her shoulders, and she was more literally pressing her strap-on cock deep into his ass. Leaning into him, Lea squeezed his weeping erection, making him gasp. "So. Andy. What's gotten into you?"

For once his answer had two syllables: "*Wedding. . .*"

"*WHAT?*" For a moment Lea thought he might be trying to propose, which she thought would be sweet, but kind of weird timing.

Well, the two times she'd been proposed to before had been even weirder — but only because she'd been trying to break up with the men at the time, not because she was fucking them with a bright purple silicone phallus. "You want to *marry. . .?*"

He shook his head and whimpered, "Naw, naw... But... Don't stop, please, I'll... Promise. I'll... Just... *don't stop,* please, fuck, Lea, fuck me, baby, *FUCK!*"

Lea began long, hard thrusts with her hips, driving her dildo into his ass and driving his cock through her fingers in a way that she knew drove Andy wild.

Fine. He'd promised. He'd keep his promises. He was a Boy Scout, even if he was a mute Boy Scout.

She fucked him hard, both of them screaming, sweating, until her muscles were beginning to burn (*How the hell do they keep going. . .?*) before Andy closed his eyes and arched, his butt clamping around the dildo, and a pearlescent geyser streaming onto his belly and chest.

By that point Lea herself was so excited, the blood pooling around her clit, her nipples buzzing, that she knew she was close. Deciding the answer to her question could wait just a little longer, thanks, she shifted to the smaller, rolling thrusts that pressed the strap-on's nub against her own, and rocked the other, bulbous end of the dildo against her g-spot, bringing her quickly to a small but very satisfying and very well-earned orgasm.

They lay, panting and sweating on Andy's much-neglected bed. "Damn," Andy grunted.

"Uh-huh." agreed Lea. Honestly, that was all she could manage in that moment.

When Andy began to lap at her breast as he unbuckled the strap-on, however, she found the energy to stop him by gently grabbing his ears. Slack-faced, he looked up at her, his brown eyes managing convey both satisfaction and hunger.

"Wedding?"

"Huh?" He blinked at her before shaking his head — not telling her *no,* just trying to remember what they'd been talking about. "Oh. Yeah." He began to look down again, either to kiss her boob or maybe to talk to it, but Lea had gotten tired of him *not talking.* She held onto his ears until his eyes met hers again. "Right," he sighed. "Wedding."

Lea ran a finger down the length of his nose. Really, what she wanted was to be on her belly, him plowing her into the mattress. But he needed to finish this. She needed him to.

"So." He was frowning down at her boobs. A part of her wanted to cover them, to close them away, but she couldn't afford to distract him. He repeated, "So. Wedding. See... My best friend. Prior."

"That's his name? Prior?" Lea just managed to hold back asking if his parents were big Tony Kushner fans.

Andy nodded, brown eyes focussed far away. "Did just about everything together growing up."

This time Lea couldn't hold back the tease: "Everything?"

As she'd known he would, Andy blushed and scowled at her. "Football. Baseball. Fishing. Getting drunk. Getting high and looking for Indian arrowheads in the woods. Everything. Damn, woman. I wasn't *always* a cocksucker."

"Uh-huh."

His scowl twisted, so that Lea wasn't sure if he were fighting off laughter or tears. "Don't give *me* no *uh-huh.*" Then he shook his head. "See. We always promised each other... We'd be each other's best man. You know? I mean, I just had Jessie and Danielle — " His older sisters. " — and Prior, he had nothing but brothers."

"Uh-huh."

"So." He leaned down and kissed her breast. "Wedding. He's getting married. To Cherry." He kissed the other breast. "My old girlfriend. First girl I ever did any of — " He sucked the nipple into his mouth as his fingers traced the spreading lips of her pussy. " — *this* with."

"Uh. Sounds complicated."

"Yup." That was all that Lea got out of him for the next forty-five minutes. Well. That's all that she got out of him about the wedding. She got lots from his hands, and his lips, and she definitely got a goodly amount of his thick, hard cock pounding her into the mattress. On her belly.

It's difficult to complain while you're being fucked magnificently. So she didn't.

Instead, she waited until they'd both stopped gasping for air — he was still blanketing her, his cock slowly weeping its way out of her — before asking once more, "Wedding?"

"Huh," he sighed. "Yeah."

"Best friend marrying old flame?"

"Uh-huh."

"And you're supposed to be the best man?"

"Yeah."

"So, when are we going?"

A huff of wet breath against her neck. "Two weeks."

"Fine. Settled."

"But…"

Ah, Lea thought, *here it is.* "But?" She squeezed *her* butt for emphasis.

He groaned, and then whimpered as his cock finally slid out of Lea. "But, um… See, my ma and pa and all want to meet you. And Prior'nd Cherry do too. See…"

When he didn't finish, she turned beneath him. "What, Andy?"

"See… See, when Prior texted me, he kind was giving me shit, saying Jessie — " The younger of his sisters. " — could be my date, since he knew no woman would ever want to grace my sorry ass with her presence."

"Uh-huh." Jesus, *Lea sighed to herself.* Men. Constantly playing Whose Pecker's Longest.

"So, I told him about you, and see…" He ducked his head against her neck, and for a moment Lea thought Andy was going to say that he'd told his friend about *Sean.* But no. "I kinda told him… we were engaged."

"You WHAT?"

"I… See, I kinda said, you know, *Ha-ha, very funny, it's good you texted, 'cause I was going to ask you to be my best man,* and so then he asked all about you, and I told him — I mean, not about the whole threesome thing or anything, 'cause fuck! But yeah — and he told Cherry, and she told Jessie, and *she* told my folks, and…"

Lea grabbed him by the ears and pulled his face up so that she could see it. She *wanted* to yell at him — what the fuck had he been thinking? — but she was so stunned and he looked so miserable that all that she managed to say was, "Jesus, Andy."

"I know, right?" His brow worked for a moment before he said about the only thing that he could. "I'm so sorry, Lea."

"Uh-huh." Sure. Of course he was sorry. But still… It wasn't as if she had told her family the truth about what she, Andy, and Sean were doing. The only person who knew about *that* was Kirsten, who'd figured out almost immediately what was going on between her best friend, her brother, and her brother's roommate. Well. And Gus, from the theater. Who'd listened to the three of them fucking up in the booth. "Andy. I'm angry with you. I mean, you've set it up so we have to lie to your family the first time I meet them."

"I know. I'm sorry." He looked up at her with the whole puppy-dog eyes routine — it didn't seem to be at all put on, but the sincerity just made Lea want to giggle, which really wasn't what she *wanted* to do right then.

"Yeah. Fine," she huffed, trying to keep a straight face. Not able to manage, she snorted and flopped back onto her belly and lifted her pelvis. "So, Andy, you're going to have to show me *just* how sorry you are."

Like the good boy he was, he dove right in, tongue first. He'd eaten her this way the very first night they'd made love — when Lea hadn't even been sure who the visitor to her pull-out bed was — and it had been the most mind-blowing sexual experience she'd ever had. Until Sean woke her from the ecstatic haze in which Andy had left her and lifted her to another plane entirely.

Lying there once more, ass in the air, face in the pillow, Andy igniting in Lea pleasure that truly made everything else seem unimportant, Lea released thoughts of the wedding for later and focused purely on enjoying the neverending, evanescent moment.

It wasn't, then, until much later — after Andy had licked her to one screaming orgasm and fucked her yet again to some number more — when Lea's mind cleared enough for the one truly awful thought to come clear: "Oh. Fuck. What's *Sean* going to think about this!"

When Sean arrived back at the apartment the next evening, his reaction was absolutely not what Lea (or Andy) had expected. He threw his head back and howled with laughter.

As he stared down at the two of them and wiped tears from his eyes, Lea silently questioned the wisdom of choosing to live with not just one man, but two.

They were both *impossible*.

When at last Sean had stopped snorting and giggling, Lea asked, as calmly as she could, "So, Sean. What are your thoughts on this mess?"

He tittered, then pulled a semblance of a serious face, and said, "Guess I'm wondering, do I get to be the best man, or the bridesmaid?"

Lea gaped up at him, but Andy joined in the sniggering. "Damn, boy. You'd look cute as fuck in a lavender dress."

Which inspired Lea to grab the Braves cap from Sean's head and smack them each with it.

Sean was much more somber, however, when he appeared on the sidewalk as Lea left the theater at the end of the next day.

Part of his sobriety probably had to do with the presence of his mother, who somehow could manage to make just about anyone feel like one of her five-year-old students.

"Hi, Violet," said Lea as she kissed Sean's mom on the cheek. "What a pleasant surprise."

"Oh, honey, I was surprised too, when this boy of mine showed up at as my little geniuses were trouping off this afternoon."

"Hey, Lea-honey," murmured Sean as he leaned in to give Lea a kiss — on the lips.

"So how did I happen to be honored with the presence of not one but *two* O'Connells?" Lea took Sean's hand.

"Well," Violet laughed, "I gather that my son has another surprise in store for you. I, however, took advantage of the opportunity to come and say hello to Gus."

"Oh!" Lea glanced up at Sean's face, which remained stony. "Well, would you like us to walk you back to the shop?"

Violet squeezed Lea's free hand. "Oh, no, honey, he said he'd meet — oh, there he is."

Gus bounced out of the same nondescript side door through which Lea had just exited the bluff-colored concrete-and-glass theater building. "Hello, Violet! Lovely to see you out of uniform, Sean."

At first Lea panicked, thinking that Gus was referring to Sean's naked tryst with her and Andy — but no, she hadn't told the boys that Gus had overheard everything. That he'd apologized and told her that he too had been part of a *ménage à trois* for many years. Which was something she still hadn't quite reconciled her mind to.

"Yeah, nice to be here off-duty." Sean took Gus's tiny hand in his enormous paw and shook it. Whatever the excitable old man had meant, Sean had understood him to mean nothing but the fire marshal inspections that he and Andy had done over the past few months.

"Well, Violet," Gus turned to Sean's mom, bouncing on his toes, "I was so excited when you called. I'd love to show you the new painting — it's almost finished, as much as any painting is ever finished. But I thought perhaps you might join me for dinner?"

When Violet hooked her arm through Gus's elbow, Sean cleared his throat. "Now, Gus, don't you keep this young lady out too late, you hear?"

Violet shot her son a scandalized glare, but Gus laughed. "I promise I'll have her home before curfew, Mr. O'Connell."

"Hmm. She's got school tomorrow, you know. Bye, Mama. Bye, Gus." As the older couple walked off, waving, Sean's smile dissipated.

Lea squeezed his hand. "So, you've got another surprise for me?"

He nodded. "When we get home. Come on. I'm parked just 'round the corner."

He wouldn't talk about whatever it was that he'd cooked up all through the ride home, preferring to sit there, uncharacteristically silent, and so, after she'd run out of things to tell him about the theater, which was just ramping up for the new season, she started talking about her feelings about the mess that Andy had landed them all in. "I mean, it's hard enough to look your mom in the face — but at least she doesn't think you and I are getting *married*, for god's sake!"

"Don't you want to get married?" His eyes didn't stray from the road.

"But…" Lea gaped at him. "Sean, how the hell am I supposed to answer that question? What the hell does marriage… And how could I marry either one of you? I mean, hell, you guys could probably marry *each other* here soon."

"Then *you* could wear the lavender dress."

"*Sean.*"

But that was all that he had to say on the subject for the rest of the ride.

They parked and walked up to their apartment, waving to Lorelle, the downstairs neighbor. (*Oh, god, ANOTHER person who knows what the three of us get up to!*) They entered their home to the familiar smell of fried chicken cooking and the familiar sight of Andy's tapered back at the stove. "Hey, Lea. Hey, Sean-boy."

"Andy," said Sean, slouching over to the kitchen table and sitting. He began to dig in his pants pocket.

If he's going to sit there and fucking play with himself…! Lea fought down two days' worth of frustration and grunted. "Guys, what the hell —?"

Andy, who had turned around with a serious expression on his face held up one hand, begging time. He was staring at Sean, who pulled something from his pocket: a small, lumpy envelope. Sean held it out to Andy, who shook his head.

Sean looked down at the envelope and then up at Lea, who was now not just angry but a bit bewildered — not a good combination. Before she could think of anything to growl at them both, Sean tugged a white gold diamond ring from the envelope, slid down on one knee at her feet, and took her hand. "Will you marry Andy, Lea?"

Lea's jaw dropped.

"Or marry Sean, baby," said Andy. He was suddenly standing behind Sean, his hands on their lover's massive shoulders.

"We don't much care which," Sean said, those blue eyes of his absolutely sucking her in. "Because honestly it doesn't much matter. But will you wear this for… one of us? Or hell, like you said, wear it as a sign of a promise between this country dumb-fuck and me?"

Andy swatted Sean's head. "See, we know that right now what we've got is how it's going to work. And we're both happy with that if you are."

Annoyance giving way to complete bewilderment, Lea shrugged.

Sean squeezed her hand. "But we also know that none of our families are going to be okay with that. At least for right now. And yeah, I know Kirsten, but come on: *Kirsten.*"

Again, Lea shrugged. His point was well taken.

"So what we're, um, proposing is that you take this as a sign of a promise that the three of us are making to each other. And you can decide which of us you want actually to go through the whole ceremony with. Or hell, we can fly off to California and get Andy and me hitched. Whatever. But wear it. And it will... calm down everyone's family a bit."

Still unable to form words, Lea nodded and held out her hand. Sean slid the ring onto her finger.

They all stared at it for a moment.

"It was my mom's. It's been sitting in her jewelry box for as long as I can re-member. I didn't tell her what I meant to do with it, but she was happy to let me have it."

"Oh," rasped Lea. "That explains the twinkly look she was giving me. Do you think she'd understand if I were to tell her it was for Andy to give me?"

Sean shrugged. "Dunno. But in any case, the point is, now y'all can head up to Andy's little backwater of a home and everyone will see this ring, and you won't be lying."

Andy grunted and ran his fingers through Sean's hair. "Won't be telling the whole truth, neither. But no: we won't be lying."

Lea gazed at the sparkles from the diamond. It wasn't big but it was *bright....* "And you aren't coming with us, Sean?"

He blinked up at her, and then at Andy. "Guess. I mean, would it be okay if I came? Would it even be a good idea?"

She leaned down and kissed him. "Wouldn't want to go without my fiancé. Would we, my other fiancé?" She looked up and kissed Andy.

"Nope," said Andy, sounding deeply relieved.

"Good," Sean said, standing between them. "Now, let's eat that deli-cious-smelling chicken, drink some good bourbon, and keep our down-stairs neighbors thoroughly entertained for a few hours, shall we?"

Lea and Andy both concurred that this was an excellent plan.

       Lea: Take a look at this. Sean gave it to me last night. [Pic-ture]

Kirsten: HOLY FUCK!

Kirsten: Wait. I know that ring!

       Lea: Yeah.

Kirsten: So Sean popped the question?????

       Lea: Well. A question, anyway.

       Lea: He asked me if I would marry Andy.

       Lea: It's complicated.

Kirsten: Uh-huh. Sounds like. So did you say yes?

Lea: Maybe? I'm not exactly sure.

Kirsten: How much alcohol was involved?

Lea: None.

Kirsten: Yeah, right. Then how much lube?

Lea: Well. None until AFTER. We used a lot last night actually. Want to hear about it?

Kirsten: **NO.**

Lea: But I love bending your brother over the back of the couch!

Kirsten: NO. STOP.

Kirsten: I can take that strap-on back, you know!

Lea: Just you try.

Kirsten: Then don't make me. God. Yuck. Over the COUCH? Remind me not to sit there. :-p

---

Driving up to the mountains, Lea didn't really know what to expect. First of all, she kept waiting for the *mountains*. Well, there were *peaks*. Peeks of peaks. But everything seemed very gentle and small, not like the mountains she was used to. It felt, she realized, a bit like going to Disneyland as a kid — the Matterhorn rising out of the smog, and looking like a real, snow-capped mountain, but... tiny.

"How high are these mountains?" Lea asked, peering out of the window from her seat behind Andy, who was driving.

Andy said over his shoulder, "I guess some of the mountains up here are four thousand, forty-five hundred feet." It was the first thing he'd said since they'd got in the car.

"Oh," Lea said. "Wow."

Sean turned around. "Don't be disrespecting our mountains now, Lea."

"I'm not!" She felt her eyebrows purse and tried to release them. "It's just..."

"I know," Sean laughed and turned to Andy. "Where she comes from, mountains like these shoot straight out of the ocean."

"Really?" Andy's shoulders looked they were up around his ears.

"Really," said Lea. "They're just... really different." She reached up to rub his shoulders. They were beyond tense. It felt as if the muscles were trying to tear themselves loose from Andy's bones. "Andy...?"

"Listen," he said, looking straight forward, "when we meet my folks... Y'all aren't in Kansas any more, okay?"

"Kansas," said Sean with a smirk, but Andy shot him a look that wiped his face clean.

"Yeah. Up here... My folks are about as conservative as it gets, okay? And I don't just mean politics, though, yeah, we probably don't want to talk about that. Or religion."

This was making Lea distinctly uncomfortable. "I wouldn't do that anyway with anyone I was just meeting, of course not." Then a thought occurred to her. "Andy. Do they know I'm Jewish?" Of all of the things about Lea's life with Andy and Sean, it seemed like the least important, most innocuous detail, but suddenly the fact that she was about to meet people who might *never have met a Jewish person* scared the crap out of her.

"Um," said Andy. "Not really. No. But they've seen your picture."

"I'm not sure I understand," Lea said, trying to stay calm.

Sean intervened. "Um, if I follow what our country boy is saying, most of the folks up hereabouts have about as much pigment as Andy and me do. Are there even many black folks up here?"

"Not many," mumbled Andy. "But… Um… Cherry. And Prior."

Lea waited for more. None came. "They're black? Your ex-girlfriend and your best friend are black?"

Andy nodded.

"Well…" Lea looked to Sean, who shrugged. "Yay?"

Andy grunted. "Sure. Yay. But… I don't want y'all to think my folks are, like, KKK or nothing. But there were only like six black kids in my high school. And Prior, his brothers and Cherry were five of 'em."

Sean's hand came to rest on Andy's shoulder beside Lea's. "How'd that go with the folks?"

"Well… They never said nothin'. But then, my pa never says nothin' anyway. And Ma always said they was welcome in our home, so… But you could kinda see, the idea of me bein' with Cherry, or with… hangin' out with Prior, you could see they wasn't exactly, you know, *comfortable* with it." Andy's accent was thickening with each mile.

"So are you saying they'll see Lea here as an improvement?" Sean said. His tone was light, but his eyes were deadly serious. "'Cause her skin is a few shades paler?"

"*Jesus*, Sean, I have no fuckin' idea, okay?" Andy grabbed both of their hands in one of his. "I have no fuckin' idea how my fuckin' family is gonna react. But I *hope* —" Andy's knuckles whitened as he squeezed their fingers. "— that they're gonna see, like I do, what an amazing *person* you are, Lea, baby."

In spite of her anxiety (or perhaps because of it), Lea tittered, causing Sean to quirk an eyebrow at her. "*Mensch,*" she said, trying to regain her composure. "That's the Yiddish word. *Mensch.*"

"*Mensch,*" the two men said, and then all three of them laughed, though Lea was sure they had no more idea than she did why they were laughing.

When Andy pulled his Yukon into the gravel driveway, a collection of what could only have been Andy's family gathered on the porch.

Andy's father looked like an older, scruffier, slightly weather-worn version of his son — he was even wearing one of Andy's Atlanta Fire & Rescue t-shirts, and his arms were, if anything, even more heavily muscled than Andy's. The older sister Danielle, tall and broad-shouldered like her brother, dwarfed her husband and held a baby; her hair was the same dirty blond as Andy's — the same as their father's had probably been once upon a time. Jessie too was tall, though her hair was brown; her face was rounder than Andy's, but she sported a softer version of his dimpled chin, and they had the same bottomless brown eyes.

The only person there who didn't seem cut out of the same Harris cloth (aside from Danielle's husband Robby, who was skinny and had dark hair) was Andy's mom, who was short, round, and pink-faced, with a massive head of bottle-blonde hair, big green eyes, and a smile that was every bit as bright and as large. "Welcome, welcome!" she called as they got out of the truck. "It's so good to see you, Andrew!" She ran up and gave her son a hug, and then turned to Sean, who was standing at his friend's shoulder. "And you must be Sean. It's a pleasure finally to meet you."

Then everyone's eyes focussed on Lea, and their weight stopped her in her tracks as she walked up to Andy's other side.

Andy reached out and grabbed her hand — the left one, with the engagement ring sparkling in the late-afternoon sun. "Mama, this is —"

"You must be Lea," blurted Andy's mother, grabbing Lea's free hand in both of hers. She pronounced it as one syllable: *Lee.*

Andy cleared his throat. "Um. Le-a, Mama. *Le-a.*"

The woman's smile didn't dim a watt. "Oh, like in the bible, how sweet. Well, it's so nice to meet you, to welcome you into the family. I'm Nadine."

Her husband appeared at her shoulder. His eyes were darker than his son's — they were almost black, and piercing, and made Lea feel very much as if she were being hunted.

Nadine tittered and said, "And Le-*a*, this is my husband Davy Harris. He's been wantin' to meet you."

Jessie appeared over her mother's other shoulder. "We *all* have, mama, c'mon! Hi, Lea. I'm Jessie. The pretty one."

"Hey!" called Danielle with a smirk that told Lea that this was an old family routine, "everyone knows that's *Andy.* Ain't that right, Lea?"

Blushing, trying not to think about all of the things that this family *didn't* know about her relationship with Andy, Lea nodded, and added, "Of course, you're *all* lovely. But yes, I think Andy is gorgeous."

Andy blushed and looked at his feet, squeezing her hand. On his far side, Sean shot Lea a smirk, as if to say, *Nicely done!*

"Mind," said Jessie, "I think Sean here gives lil'Andy a run for his money. Don't you think, Lea?"

Now Sean's smirk said, And how are you going to get out of *this* one, Miss Lea?

"Oh," she said, breathily, "I think Sean is lovely too, yes."

They all laughed at that, and Nadine invited all of them around back for dinner — *supper* — which was (naturally) fried chicken, served with grits, collards, watermelon, lots of lemonade and beer, and Andy's favorite boiled peanuts. Sean proclaimed it "the pinnacle of Georgia cuisine," and Lea hoped that no one heard from his tone how much Georgia cuisine bored him.

No one seemed to notice, except Andy, who took the opportunity of kissing Lea on the cheek to reach across her lap and squeeze their lover's balls. Sean was well-behaved after that.

The meal was lovely. The back yard afforded them a view of the valley that was already lovely, but that became absolutely spectacular as the sun set and the sky turned from blue to scarlet to silver to black. When they were finally done and clearing the plates and platters back to the kitchen, lightning bugs lit their path.

It was magical.

And so Lea was a bit thrown when, after Danielle and her family had said goodnight, Nadine turned to Lea by the sink and asked, "And where does a name like Krakowicz come from?"

"Poland," coughed Lea, and then looked at Andy, who shrugged from behind his father's massive shoulder. "Krakow is a big city there..." She took a deep breath. "It used to be one of the major Jewish centers in Eastern Europe."

Her smile undiminished but noticeably tighter, Nadine just said, "Oh."

Lea nodded. "Yeah. My mom's family were mostly from what's now the Ukraine, though. Not far from where all the fighting's been happening." *Kiev — another Jewish capital*, she refrained from saying.

Lea was very aware of Mr. Harris's predatory gaze, even as Nadine Harris re-established her hostly smile. "Well, that's nice. Poland. Well, you young'uns need to let us old folk go get our rest. Papa's got a big order to finish, and company always leaves me tired. Now, Lea, honey, I hope you don't mind — you'll be sharing Jessie's room. And Sean, I'm sure you'll be fine bunking with Andrew, I know y'all do at the station, so that's all right. Well, good night, all."

"'Night, Mama," said Jessie and Andy in unison.

"Good night, Mrs. Harris," said Lea and Sean.

"Nadine! I told you both to call me Nadine," Nadine laughed as her husband escorted her up the stairs, squinting over his shoulder at Lea.

The four *young'uns* stood quietly until the bedroom door upstairs closed.

"Sorry about that," Andy groaned.

Sean patted him on the shoulder. "Don't worry 'bout it, Andy-boy. I'm sure the lovely Miss Lea can spare you to me for one night."

Andy glared at Sean, which just made Sean and Jessie laugh.

"Hey," Jessie said, "what you say we walk down to Prior'n'Cherry's? I told Cherry you was going to be here tonight, and she said they'd love to see y'all, to meet Lea here. And the lovely Sean as well."

Lea nodded at the idea — less because she wanted more company than that she needed to clear her head — and so the four walked down winding roads past what passed as a town center. Jessie took Sean's elbow and seemed inclined to laugh at everything that he said.

"So what's with your sister's boy-crazy sixteen-year-old act?" muttered Lea.

"Well, she's only been divorced a year or so. I guess the last time she really was on the market, she *was* a boy-crazy sixteen-year-old." Andy turned to her. "Listen, Lea, I'm so sorry about Mama."

She huffed and stared up at him. It was hard to be angry with that face — but she could feel herself working at it. "Andy, what the hell *was* that? I mean, what's she worried about, that I'm going to *infect* you or something?"

"Naw," Andy sighed. "Not that. It's… I'm guessing it's that she's worried that you'll raise the grandkids so's they won't be able to go to church or nothing. That they won't really be part of our family."

"Oh." That actually made sense, but still — "*Children,* Andy? What the fuck?" She said this last in a tone that she hoped Jessie couldn't possibly hear, but Sean turned around. Lea smiled thinly and waved him on. "Andy, sweetheart, you've got to make this right. I don't know how you're going to do that, but please — I can't have you're mom thinking I'm going to snatch her grandkids and your dad staring at me like he's going to grind me up and sprinkle me on his grits. Okay?"

"Aw," Andy sighed, "Papa's not so bad. He —"

"Not so bad? He never said a word, Andy, and he kept *glaring* at me!"

"Naw, Lea-baby, that's just Papa. He don't talk much, but when he does, he sure as hell means it. I know it can make folk uncomfortable sometimes. He ain't *glaring* at you."

"*Ain't* he?" she snapped, and then shook her head. "Sorry, Andy. But yeah — you've got to fix this, or the wedding is *off,* you hear?"

Andy chuckled sadly. "*Which* wedding?"

"Well," said Lea, watching Jessie flounce on Sean's elbow remarkably nimbly for a woman who was nearly six feet tall, "if your sister has anything to say about it, I think we've lost our chance with Mr. O'Connell there for good."

Andy laughed, and Sean shot a nervous glance back at his lovers, which made Andy laugh again.

Prior and Cherry's house sat in its own little valley — *hollow* — and looked as if it were half-way between being rebuilt and falling down out of exhaustion.

"He works in construction. So it's kinda like the shoemaker's kids not having shoes," Jessie said when she saw Lea's expression. "Bought it couple of years back as a fixer-upper, ain't quite fixed it up. But it won't fall down. At least, probably not. Not tonight, anyways."

When they approached the house, the couple were sitting in a glider in the front yard, and something about their body language told Lea that they'd just finished fucking — or were just getting ready to.

Well. Maybe that was just in Lea's own perverted brain.

In any case, when Jessie opened the gate, the woman who must have been Cherry jumped up to greet her and them, while her fiancé stood slowly, rearranging himself before sauntering over. So it probably wasn't just Lea's brain.

"So nice to meet you," said Cherry, whose skin was indeed a few shades less pale than Lea's own — a shade somewhere between *café au lait* and mahogany, if the moonlight could be trusted. She shook Sean's hand and gave Lea a surprisingly warm hug. "I always wondered what kind of woman would finally snag Andy. I should have known."

Lea was about to ask what it was that Cherry thought she should have known when Prior stepped up. "You must be Lea," he said in a surprisingly high, smooth voice. "Pleasure to meet you." If Cherry's skin was *café au lait* there was no other word for Prior's skin tone but *black*. Lea had seen folks so dark their skin almost shown, but not many born in the US.

Prior turned to Sean and shook his hand, greeted Jessie warmly, and then turned to Andy. "So, you pasty-ass pansy. What makes you think you're good enough for a real woman like *this?*" He pointed a thumb at Lea.

Andy narrowed his eyes at Prior. "*Good* enough? I know I'm good enough 'cause she *chose* me — I didn't have to chase her all over the county for two years like your sorry excuse for an ass did, pining after *this* fine example of womanhood." Andy gestured at Cherry.

"Sorry excuse —!" Prior gave a scowl of what Lea assumed was mock indignation. "This *sorry excuse* for an ass can still beat yours into the ground any day of the week, and twice on Sunday, you —!"

But Lea never found out what Andy was, because Andy decided to jump on top of his best friend, knocking him to the ground, where they wailed on each other. It couldn't really be called anything so civilized as *wrestling*; it looked more like they were trying to rip each other's limbs off.

It was… surprisingly sexy. Lea couldn't for the life of her figure out why that might be. "They do this often?" she asked Cherry and Jessie.

"Every time they see each other," Cherry said, and Jessie added, "No idea why."

All three women turned to Sean who held up his hands. "Hey! Don't look at me! I have no idea what this kinda bullshit is about!"

Suddenly Andy and Prior were laughing, still tangled on the ground. "*Pasty ass?*" Andy snorted. "*Twice on Sunday?*"

"Hey!" Prior chortled. "*Pining after this fine example of womanhood?*" He gave Andy's shoulder a wallop just for good measure, and then pulled his friend back up to standing.

"What are you two, ten?" Cherry asked.

"Naw," sighed Jessie, "if they was ten, they'd be more mature about it. Y'all are useless, you know that?"

"Aw, Jessie," said Prior, "you know you love us just the way we are!"

"Him I have to love, 'cause he's kin." She pointed at her brother. "You, Prior, I only tolerate 'cause you're his friend and 'cause I'm getting to wear a fucking brides-maid's dress at your wedding on Saturday. So don't push it. I can find another excuse to wear that dress. Hey, Sean, you getting married any time soon?"

Sean's brow twisted, seeing the trap, but not knowing how to get out of it. "Uh… Not that I'm aware of."

"Good." Jessie grinned at him, then turn to Prior. "Anyway, the point is, you're not worth the dress. So act like a grown man, already."

"Oh," Cherry said, "my baby may be an idiot, but he's definitely a grown man. Ain't that right, baby?" She twined her arms around him.

"Damn straight," he said, and kissed her.

"There," said Jessie, *that's* how a grown man is supposed to act."

"That so, sis?" asked Andy, and pulled Lea to him and kissed her more sound-ly than he had ever done in front of anyone else but Sean.

When they broke apart again, Lea was breathless, her crotch was singing, and she was very glad that it was dark.

"You have to watch that all of the time?" Jessie asked Sean, her arm through his again.

Sean's expression was uncharacteristically blank as he answered, "It has its charms."

Andy chuckled. "Thought that was how a grown man was supposed to act, Jess."

They went inside to the upstairs sitting room and drank until all of them were beginning to get woozy. Cherry turned to Lea at one point and whispered, "I think our men like each other more than they like us."

Lea looked at Prior and Andy, who were laughing, their arms up on the back of the couch over each other's shoulders. Sean was leaning in toward them, smil-ing, but it didn't reach his eyes — though that might have been because Jessie was draped over his back. "You know," Lea mused, "maybe they should marry each other rather than us." When Cherry started, Lea asked, "What?"

"Um. I'll have to know you a hell of a lot better or get a whole lot drunker before I tell you what I was just thinking. But yeah. I've always felt like a third wheel with these two, even if I'm the one they both slept with."

"Lucky you," Lea said, admiring both — all three — of the men. "They don't exactly build them small down here, do they?"

"Well," laughed Cherry, "we have our scrawny boys too, but no, this set is quite the bonus-size package, ain't they?"

"Definitely," Lea agreed, and the two women laughed until they started crying, which made the men — and Jessie — stare at them. "Sorry," Lea snorted, "we were just talking about how Georgia boys don't seem to come in the single-serving size."

"Are you saying we need to lose weight, Miss Lea?" said Sean with a smirk, and it was only then that Lea caught the double meaning in her own words.

"Uh." *Fuckity-fuck-fuck.* The men, Cherry, and Jessie all laughed at Lea's em-barrassment, but she let them laugh, happy that they couldn't see what her perverted, perverted, *sick* mind had served up to her: a vision of herself with Sean and Andy sandwiched around her, making love as they had come to do so well together, with Prior fitting himself in… wherever. And hell, Cherry watching. Why not? "Uh. Lose weight? No."

"Never," snorted Cherry, "We love y'all *just* the way y'all are!"

And the way her skin darkened made Lea wonder just what image the bride-to-be's mind had served up to *her*.

Eventually, the visitors stumbled off with promises to continue the conversation at the bachelor and bachelorette parties the next night. As they stumbled their way out of the ramshackle house — which had indeed managed not to fall — Andy said, "Hey, guys, you think you can find your way back to the house? Sis and I got some catching up to do."

Lea was about to say that, no, she had *no* idea where they were or how to get back to the Harrises' house, but Sean said, "Sure thing, Andy-boy. Cherokee Ridge Road, yeah?"

Andy nodded and led his bemused sister off in the opposite direction.

Lea watched them go and turned to Sean. "What was that about?" she whispered.

"I'm hoping he's trying to warn her to back off of me a bit."

Lea grinned up at Sean. "Aw, poor boy."

"Hey," he muttered, "she's *scary*." Sean led her uphill at slow pace, and Lea could feel the heat pouring out of her into the warm, sticky Georgia night. Moths and lightning bugs played a game of shadow-and-light tag. "Also," he said when they'd gotten a couple of minutes up the road to a place where the winding road passed through a dark copse of pine trees, "I'd like to think that he's trying to make it up to us for all of the entertainment we've provided his family by givin' us a bit of *alone time.*" And before Lea could say a word, he lifted her up onto the split-rail fence, stepped between her surprise-widened legs, and kissed her in that whole-body, nothing-else-in-the-universe way that Sean could kiss.

Within seconds, Lea's libido, which was already at a simmer, went to a full boil. "Oh. God. Sean. Want you. Want you so much…."

"Then by god, honey, you're gonna have me," Sean murmured as he slid his cock out of his jeans and, tugging her panties to one side, slid all of the way home in a single, smooth, pussy-filling, satisfying stroke.

Lea screamed, but it was into Sean's huge palm, which lightly covered her mouth, and her whole body reacted, both to the feeling of him fucking her, and to the realization that they were fucking on the side of a public road. That added a touch of panic to the wild gumbo of sensations and feelings that were chasing around inside of her, but… No one was likely to come along. And even if they did, in that moment Lea couldn't have cared less.

And now the heat was flowing *into* Lea — warm as she already was, the heat of Sean's fabulous cock and of the night were sending her past the boiling point. She felt as if she were turning to steam — to flame — and only the very, very solid point of contact between her body and Sean's kept her rooted in the world.

"Honey," panted Sean. "Baby, wanted… wanted to do this to you all through supper, all through sitting there with Jessie treating me like a damned teddy bear… God, watching your nipples go all… when Andy'n'Prior were down wrassling… Turn you on, Lea-honey? You want to watch me'n'Andy all tangled up at your feet?"

"Uh-huh," she panted, the image now clear in her head — Sean and Andy, sweaty, naked, wrestling, their cocks straining — "Oh, god, god, fuck, *yesss!*"

Somehow, Lea's shirt and bra were up over her tits, and Sean's mouth found one of her nipples and…

Usually, Sean had a devastatingly slow approach to pleasuring Lea — slow, meandering, and insistent, where Andy was usually the more stereotypically passionate of her lovers. But that night Sean's urgency was intoxicating, and now that both of his hands were digging into the flesh of her ass, pulling her close to him, she had to stifle her scream on her own, and so she shoved a hand into her mouth, howling into her own knuckles as Sean suckled, pounding away, groaning into her breast, "Come, gonna, gonna, *aw! —*"

And then he thrust into her so hard that she lifted up off of the fence. He arched back and she arched back, and honestly, it would have been so easy for them to fall, but they didn't — they each released themselves into release in perfect, ecstatic balance.

And then they slowly came down, and uncoupled and rearranged themselves, pulling their clothes back into place and attempting to look like anything but the thoroughly debauched couple that they were. And they stumbled their way back up Cherokee Ridge Road to the Harrises' house. They walked in to find Jessie and Andy waiting for them. Lea had to work hard to pretend that she couldn't feel the residual of the fuck dribbling down her thighs. She could only be thankful that Jessie was, if anything, more drunk than Lea was herself and so didn't seem to notice.

Brother and sister led their guests up to their childhood bedrooms. Andy's room actually had a bunk bed — with a wrought-iron fireman's pole down from the upper bunk. Sean and Jessie waited while Andy kissed Lea good night, whispering into her lips, "Hope he fucked you good enough for both of us, sweetheart."

She nodded, blushing, and then whispered back, "But I bet he's got enough left for you, Fireman Andy."

Which made him sputter and blush right back. Sean winked at her and pulled their lover into their bedroom while Jessie led the way quietly back to her room, which was stuffed with a combination of childhood furniture and what were clearly the leftovers from the home she'd created and left — stuffed animals on top of a glass and chrome liquor cabinet, a leather recliner next to a doll house. A trundle bed with both mattresses made up with satin sheets. "You want to sleep on the inside or the outside?" Jessie asked.

"Whichever," Lea said, "I don't want to take your bed."

Jessie shrugged and took the bed that was against the wall. She didn't bother turning away as she stripped off her skirt, top and underwear, which left Lea to do the same, hoping that the insides of her thighs weren't glistening to much. Lea grabbed a sleeping shirt and waited while Jessie climbed naked into bed, and then slipped under the covers. "Man," Lea said, yawning only partially for effect, "I'm dog-tired."

"Never did understand what that meant," Jessie sighed. "Hey. Um. Can I ask something?"

Uh-oh, thought Lea. "Of course."

"See, Andy, he was trying to tell me…" Jessie flicked off the light, and suddenly Lea could make out glow-in-the-dark stars on the ceiling. "He was saying that Sean's love life is kinda… complicated. Do you know what he was talking about?"

Shitty-shit-shit. "Uh. Yeah. I do. And yeah, it kinda is." Lea lay there, staring up at Orion on Jessie's ceiling. "See, I shouldn't… I think it's not my place to talk about it."

"Yeah. That's what Andy said."

"Yeah." And then Lea had an inspiration. "I don't think Sean wants to talk about it either to be honest."

"Oh." Jessie was quiet long enough that Lea began to fall asleep, but then Jessie sighed. "Yeah. I guess that makes sense, why you'd end up with my twerp of a brother instead of *him.*"

Lea couldn't help but give a nervous laugh. "Well. Um. I've kind of known Sean since I was a kid." Nineteen. That's still a kid, right? "His sister's my best friend. So…" So your brother and I are both in love with him, have been for years, and we all fell into bed together when I moved here, and now we share pleasure in ways that would so not be appropriate for me to tell you. *"So. Yeah."*

"Uh-huh." Jessie sighed again. "'Night."

"Good night," said Lea, and was asleep almost instantly.

The next morning, Lea thought the pounding in her head must be a hangover — though she didn't think she'd drunk *that* much. When she lifted her head, though, she realized that, no, the metallic banging was coming not only from outside her head, but from outside the house.

"Papa's hard at it," sighed Jessie. "Been working on whatever it is for days, won't tell anyone what he's working on. Then again, Papa never tells nobody nothing."

"Quite an alarm clock."

"Yeah. Least he waited until after dawn. That's always my favorite." Jessie slid over, her naked, Harris-scale body suddenly very intimidating to Lea. "Sorry. Gotta pee. Anyway —" Jessie threw on a nylon robe. "—I don't miss much about living with Booger. But not having to wake up to the hammer and anvil, that was nice."

"Must be hard living back with your folks."

"You have *no* idea." Jessie ran a brush through her hair and grabbed mascara from the liquor cabinet, applying it while staring at her reflection in the chrome. "Makes me feel like a damned twelve-year-old again."

"Yeah." Lea was fascinated to watch Jessie continue to apply her makeup — in preparation for going to the bathroom. "Was your ex's name really *Booger?*"

"Yeah," Jessie snorted as she blotted a fresh layer of lipstick, "Robert actually, but everyone called him Booger, he even called himself that. *Booger's home, ba-by-doll!*" Jessie shuddered, and Lea couldn't blame her.

Battle-face on, Jessie smiled at Lea and opened the door, running into Sean. "Why, good morning, Sean!" she said brightly, and Lea suddenly knew *exactly* why Jessie had been so careful before stepping out of her room. Aware of her own disheveled state — feeling the sticky remains of her fuck with Sean — Lea waited until Jessie had stepped into the bathroom, looked carefully down the hall, and kissed both of her boys quickly. She lingered a bit longer with Andy. "So, fiancé, did you and your other fiancé make any boyhood dreams come true last night?"

Sean grinned wolfishly in a manner that made Lea think that indeed, they had debauched the boyhood bunk bed.

"Gawd." Andy chuckled nervously and whispered back, *"No!* That room shares a wall with my folks!" He shook his head. "Can you imagine *what* the heck they'd've thought if we started bangin' the wall last night? Mama has *no* idea what she was doing to torture me when she had the two of us share a room."

"Her loss," said Lea, and licked Andy's ear. "Poor boy." He spluttered, which caused Sean to smile some more.

"C'mon," grumbled Andy, "Mama's making blueberry pancakes."

"Well, damn, boy!" laughed Sean. "Why didn't you say so in the first place!" And so, once Lea had thrown on a robe of her own, the threesome trooped downstairs for breakfast.

The blueberry pancakes were wonderful, but Andy and Jessie's mother wouldn't even look at Lea, let alone talk to her. At least Mr. Harris wasn't there to stare at her.

The day was a long and schizophrenic one.

On the one hand, it was wonderful getting to see where Andy had grown up. He showed them the high school two towns over where he, Prior, Cherry, and the rest had met. He showed them the firehouse where he'd started volunteering at fourteen. ("You do know most boys *stop* wanting to be a fireman at some point, right?" Sean asked, to which Andy responded with a smile, "Uh-huh. So what's *your* excuse.") They saw the honest-to-goodness drive-in where, apparently, all three Harris siblings had lost their virginity — not at the same time, Lea was fairly sure. They even visited Andy's favorite skinny-dipping hole.

Of course, what made everything a bit uncomfortable was that Jessie stuck with them the whole day. Not that Lea could blame her — what else was she supposed to do, since she had the day off work? Lea didn't blame her for wanting to get out of her parents' house. And she wasn't throwing herself at Sean quite the same way, though she was clearly still stalking him.

But when they got to the swimming hole, all that Lea could think was what it would be like to fuck both of her boys in the cool, green water. And then, of course, Jessie suggested they all strip off and jump in, an idea that Sean nixed immediately, and so all four of them walked away a bit grumpy.

They attended the wedding rehearsal at a Baptist church a few towns over in a plain building that actually reminded Lea more than a bit of the synagogue her family had very occasionally attended — except of course for the huge cross over the altar. Cherry looked nervous. Her mother, a generously wide woman with eyes an even more astonishing green than her daughter's, seemed to be spending a lot of time whispering in Cherry's ear while her father stood stoically on the far side. Based on Cherry's grey expression, it was tough to tell whether she was telling Cherry that everything was going to be great, or that it was all going to be crap.

Prior was bouncing on his toes amidst three other big, plum-black men — his brothers, clearly. He grabbed Andy when they walked up and the two men looked as if they were having to restrain themselves from wrestling right there in front of the altar.

Then the minister showed up, and the walk-through took all of fifteen minutes.

Andy and his sister were the only white members of the wedding party.

After what Lea (the former stage manager) could barely consent to calling a rehearsal, everyone trooped over to Prior's family's for a barbecue, which was lovely. Andy and Prior finally got their opportunity to *wrassle,* much to his family's amusement and Cherry's family's dismay. Prior's brothers were hooting the whole time, telling their brother he was a wuss. Well. That wasn't the word they used. But *wuss* basically covers it.

Sean happily helped at the barbecue, working with Cherry's dad and an uncle, flipping enormous racks of ribs and half-chickens and generally ignoring Jessie's chatter.

Lea almost felt bad for the woman. Almost.

Cherry sidled up to Lea as the men all sprinted to form a line when the uncle banged on a battered old gong. The bride-to-be laughed. "No surprise that my man and yours are at the front of the line."

"No," Lea agreed. She looked at Cherry, who seemed to have regained her equilibrium. "You doing okay? You looked a bit overwhelmed at the rehearsal."

"Oh." Cherry shot Lea a furtive glance. "I just got... jitters, you know? Y'all walked in, and I saw Andy and Prior there, and... I don't know. It all seemed... real. You know?"

"Yeah," Lea said. "I mean, I've never been where you are, not yet, but yeah, that makes sense. Hey, can I ask something?"

"Sure."

"Is it… weird for you, having Andy here? I mean, I'm trying to imagine having one of my exes in my wedding party."

Cherry laughed. "Naw. I mean, yeah, a bit. But… Me and Andy, that was a long time ago. We was high school sweethearts, you know? Regular Romeo and Juliet. No one wanted us together — not the other kids, not our parents. Made everyone uncomfortable. Andy just said, fuck them, you know? Oh. Sorry."

Lea shook her head. "Don't worry. I live with Andy *and* Sean. I've heard a hell of a lot worse."

"I bet you have." Cherry's eyebrows lifted. "Is *that* weird? I mean, living with your fiancé and his best buddy — other than my Prior, of course."

"Yeah, it's…" Lea struggled to find a word that expressed the situation without saying to much; she settled on the word that Andy had used with his sister the night before: "It's complicated."

Cherry's look now was appraising. "Uh-huh. I bet. Now, come on, let's go get some food before our boys decide to go back for seconds and there's nothing left."

After the barbecue, the *young'uns* separated out — Prior's brothers dragged Andy and Sean over to one side of the yard with many sideways looks and sniggers that told Lea something really Neanderthal was in the offing for the bachelor bash. Lea walked up to her boys and said, "Listen, guys, I really don't give a shit what goes on as long as no one catches anything and any, uh, performers are treated respectfully. Okay?"

They both promised solemnly that they'd make sure that both of those stipulations were met.

Lea had figured that she'd head on back to the Harrises' and see if she could get Mr. Harris actually to say three words to her, but Jessie and Cherry insisted that she join them and a trio of Cherry's cousins for the bachelorette party. "Nothing very wild, I'm afraid," Cherry said.

"Naw," said one of the cousins, "you got all the *wild* saved up for tomorrow night." That evoked a lot of cackling and speculations about just what Cherry and Prior were going to get up to on their wedding night.

Cherry rounded on them, lips pursed primly. "Tomorrow night, my husband and I are going to *fuck*. It's what newlyweds do. Y'all can snigger about it, but all *I* know is none of *y'all* are going to be getting what *I* do tomorrow night. Now, tonight," she said imperiously, "aren't y'all going to get me drunk and play stupid games or something?"

"Yes, ma'am!" said Jessie. "Your carriage awaits!"

They trooped off on what turned out to be a tour of just about every road house and dive bar in the district — they definitely crossed into Tennessee for a while, and Lea wasn't sure that they didn't spend a little while in North Carolina. Cherry turned out to hold her liquor quite well — much better than her cousins, in fact — but it turned out that she was a *flirty* drunk. She started sidling up to men in each bar, and Lea and Jessie had to fend off some of the more aggressive men from taking advantage of her. "She's gettin' married tomorrow,"

Jessie told one would-be suitor who barely came to Jessie's shoulder, "and it ain't to you."

Some time after midnight, Lea convinced them all it was time to head back to Cherry and Prior's and play whatever silly games they could think up.

Lea — who was the most sober of them — drove the whole way back, hoping that Sean and Andy were okay. And that they weren't doing anything too stupid.

When they got back to the house, bottles of booze magically appeared, and Lea finally felt like she could partake now that she wasn't driving, and the cousins, who were already pretty well gone, started getting sloppy. When they were trying to come up with something suitably embarrassing to do, one of them turned Cherry and said, "Naw. Nah g'na play Truth or Dare'th you. Y'always asking us to kiss each other or get all nekkid or something. Naw." That brought an indignant look from Cherry, but everyone agreed: no Truth or Dare.

"How about Never Have I Ever?" asked Lea as she sipped a very smooth rye whiskey.

"W'zat?" asked the drunkest of the cousins.

"Well, haven't any of you guys played this?"

They all shook their heads.

"Oh. Simple. So, we take turns. And whoever is It says something they've never done. Like, if it were me, I could say, 'Never have I ever walked on the moon.' So after I say that, if any of you *have* walked on the moon, which I'm guessing you haven't, you have to drink. Okay? And, um, if only one of us *does* have to drink, she has to tell all."

All of the eyes in the room were now focused on Lea. She licked her lips. "So, shall I start?" When everyone nodded, Lea said, "Okay. So... Never have I ever kissed another girl."

"*Really*," gasped Jessie. "I thought you was from San Francisco!"

"I am," Lea said. "Even so. Never."

Cherry turned to two of the cousins and raised an eyebrow.

The cousins were indignant. "No fair! 'S only 'cause *you* dared us!"

But the others all started chanting, "Drink!"

And so they did.

Jessie went next. "Um. Never have I ever... I dunno. Never have I ever given a blow job to a guy while he was driving."

Everyone looked around the room; no one drank, which sparked a round of relieved laughter. "It's a good thing!" Cherry said. "That's a good way to get yourself killed! And maybe *he's* gonna die happy, but..."

Another round of laughter.

Cherry said, "Anyway, my turn. Let's see. Um. Never have I ever let a guy tie me up."

Fifty Shades strikes again, thought Lea, and lifted the rye to her lips. It was only when she lowered the glass that she realized that the whole circle was staring at her open-mouthed. *"Really?"* said Jessie. "I mean, *please* tell me that wasn't my brother!"

"NO!" said Lea. "God, no! I mean, Andy may have, you know, *things* that he likes —" *Like having me take him up the ass, or licking at me and Sean while we're fucking, and I did handcuff myself to the table once, but he didn't tie me...* "God no." The circle waited. "Oh. God. Yeah. So this was my ex-boyfriend John, who was kind of a dick, actually. He liked to tie me up and keep me just on the edge of... you know, for as long as he could before he'd let me, um, you know." Eyes glistened. "Come. Before he'd let me come. And it felt really good, but honestly, he was a controlling bastard."

"Wow," said Jessie.

"Tell me about it," Lea agreed.

The game went on as the game always did — raucous laughter, embarrassment, surprises. Lea got to know more about this group of strangers than she did about some of her close friends.

Well. Not Kirsten. Kirsten told Lea *everything*. Almost everything. It had taken Kirsten seven years to tell Lea she was bi. But yeah.

Eventually, the cousins, who lived the next county over, decided they needed to head home if they were going to make the wedding. One of them had actually stopped drinking a couple of hours before, so she offered to drive. When they were gone, Jessie, Cherry, and Lea looked at each other. "So," Lea asked, "you guys want to turn in?"

"Nah," sighed Cherry. "To be honest, I'm worried about the boys. I'd love the company, if y'all don't mind."

Lea agreed, and Jessie did too. She picked up her glass and gave Cherry an evil grin. "Never have I ever slept with a black man."

Cherry was about to say something — probably that it was unfair — but she stopped when she saw that Lea had taken a drink and downed one herself. "So?" she asked Lea.

Lea shrugged. "Yeah. Dated a black guy for a little while. Also a couple of Asian guys. Never a Hispanic guy." She shrugged again. "Okay, my turn. Let's see. Never have I ever... been on a honeymoon." She smiled at Jessie, who glared back.

"Fine," Jessie said, and drank. "I mean, what is there to tell you? I spent a week in Orlando with Booger. We both got sick and if we fucked, I can't remember it, because, I mean, sex with Booger was so quick anyway it was more like a sneeze than a passionate love-making session or anything. So fine. I was on a honeymoon."

"Ouch. Sorry." Lea turned to Cherry. "Hope you and Prior have something nice planned."

"We're heading down to New Orleans. It's supposed to be beautiful."

"That's what I hear," Lea agreed. "I've never been. The food's supposed to be amazing."

"Uh-huh," Cherry said, but she had that mischievous, flirty look she'd gotten at the bars, and Lea felt suddenly nervous. Cherry smiled and said, "Never have I ever slept with two men at once."

Jessie laughed and said, "I wish," but Lea's stomach went cold. Cherry was looking at Lea like she *knew*; but Lea couldn't just *admit* that she slept with Sean and Andy — not in front of Andy's *sister!*

At that moment, the front door opened and Sean's blessedly welcome voice called out, "Y'all here? The house hasn't fallen on anyone?"

Cherry rolled her eyes. "Naw, we're upstairs in the sitting room. Is my man with you?"

"Yeah, he'll be here in a bit. He and Andy are both trying to hold the other up. It's not working very well." Sean's head appeared at the stairwell. "Hey, now. You guys look cozy."

Lea had to stifle an urge to kiss him. Instead she reached out and took his hand. "So. Anyone going to be too sorry tomorrow?"

Sean shrugged. "Well, not Prior, not me, not Andy."

"So I'm hoping," Cherry said, "that Prior's brothers didn't drag him down to some so-called *massage parlor* down in Chattanooga."

"Naw," Sean said, running his fingers through his hair. "They'd just arranged for a dancer-lady. Who was... Well, she moved real nice, I guess I can say that. And Prior's brothers kinda tried to get her to take things beyond the, um, entertainment level, but your man's a gentleman — very respectful of the young lady. So. You guys. Nice bachelorette soirée?"

"Great," Cherry said, "We hit about every bar in about four counties in three states. And we've been playing Never Have I Ever."

"That so?" Sean winked at Lea.

Jessie, who suddenly seemed much drunker than she had a few minutes before, stood and leaned her whole body against Sean's. "You ever play, Sean?"

"Uh, no, Jessie, I can't say as I have."

"Well," Jessie sighed, throwing her arms around Sean's neck, "never have I ever kissed —"

Sean tried to back up, but she held him tight. "Hey, now!"

"Jessie," said Lea, "remember — complicated."

"Fuck that!" Jessie growled. "What does that even mean?"

"It means," said Sean, grasping Jessie's face, "that I like guys. I like men."

Jessie froze. "What?"

"I have a... boyfriend, Jessie." Sean relaxed his grip, cupping her face in his hands.

Jessie flinched from him as if his fingers were on fire, stepping back and staring.

"I'm sorry." Sean shot her a sympathetic smile.

Jessie gave a groan so low that it seemed to come from her knees. Her face a mask of abject humiliation, she ran down the stairs.

Sean started to move after her but Lea grabbed his hand. "No."

Cherry nodded as the door slammed below. "I think she's just embarrassed. Haven't seen her throw herself at a guy like that since high school." She moved to the window where they could see her fleeing across the porch and into the front yard. "She'll be okay. So. Sean. You like guys."

Sean shrugged.

Cherry looked from him to Lea. "'Cause it sure looked like you liked Lea here well enough last night in the pines."

Suddenly, Sean's face went ghostly pale.

Cherry smiled, however, and raised the tumbler of rye in her hand. "Never have I ever slept with two men at once. Lucky bitch."

"Uh." Lea didn't know how to feel — embarrassed to have been seen fucking on the fence, terrified that Cherry would tell Andy's family, amused that the whole farce of pretending to be engaged to Andy had been pointless. She looked out the window to see that Jessie was stock-still in the middle of the front yard, staring at the glider. "What the hell?"

Sean grunted. "Looks like Prior'n'Andy passed out in the swing-seat."

Cherry gasped and said, "I don't think they're passed out."

Sure enough, the two friends were moving, tangled in each other. But instead of *wrassling*, they were… "They're *kissing*."

Jessie shot a look up at the house — Lea couldn't tell if she saw the three of them at the window or not, but in any case, she ran out the gate and into the night.

Oh, thought Lea, *damn*.

But then Cherry and Sean both hissed and Lea looked at the two friends making out on the glider. Andy, who was on top, had started grinding his crotch against Prior's. "Frotting," sighed Lea.

Sean grunted. "Uh-huh."

Lea grabbed his bicep, which was rippling with tension. "You okay, Sean?"

He grimaced. "I dunno if I should be angry… or really turned on."

"I know what you mean," sighed Cherry. Then she held her hand in front of her mouth. "I mean…"

"We know what you mean," Lea said. The other woman's nipples looked as if they were getting ready to take off. It was mesmerizing, in a disconcerting way.

Cherry nodded and they all turned back to watch the two men dry-hump on the glider. "What you call that there? Sean?"

"*Frotting*," said Sean. He flashed a look at Lea and managed a small grin. "Andy-boy's mighty fond of frotting. Two girls, it's called *tribbing*, ain't that right, Lea?"

"Yup."

"Oh." Cherry shuddered. "I guess… Every time the two of them idiots started wailing on each other, rolling around on each other… Every time they do that, all I can think about is what it would look like if they was naked. You know."

Lea and Sean both nodded. Lea *did* know, had had exactly the same fantasy watching her boy and Cherry's wrestle. Maybe Sean had too.

Out in the moonlight, Andy reached between them and Sean swore quietly. "I think we're about to see it for real." As Andy yanked open his fly and Prior's, Sean groaned and swore again. "Should I stop them?"

Lea couldn't think how to answer other than to ask, "Do you want to?"

Sean came up behind Lea and embraced her. "Dunno. I really don't know."

"No," said Cherry, reaching back and grabbing Lea's hand. "I mean, I kind of want to kill them both, but I kinda think they've both wanted to do this for a while."

"Uh-huh," agreed Lea and Sean. His erection was pressing against her back.

Cherry groaned. "I guess... Better they get this out of their systems now, right?" Her hand clutched Lea's.

"Sure, yeah," Sean said.

Lea stared down at her boyfriend — her lover, her fiancé — fucking his best friend. "I guess."

As Andy ground away, his jeans slid down his tight ass, revealing a flash of pale skin.

"Damn, I've missed that. That boy of y'all's has a truly beautiful backside, don't he?" said Cherry.

"Uh-huh," they agreed again.

Cherry moaned again and unselfconsciously pulled Lea's hand against her chest; the feeling of those bullet-like nipples rising and falling against Lea's knuckles was *really* disconcerting. Especially in contrast with Sean's fingers, which were clenching and unclenching at the waist of Lea's skirt — as if he were having to work very consciously not to let them stray higher. Or lower. Lea let her free hand rest on one of his. Just to reassure him. Or, maybe, to encourage him. To encourage him *down...*

Sean gurgled into the back of Lea's head when *his* knuckles found forbidden territory through her light summer skirt: Lea's crotch, which was humming with need.

"Don't know about y'all," Cherry said, "but the sight of the two of them grinding together like that is getting me all tingly. You know?" Then she glanced down at where Sean's thumb had begun to insinuate itself between Lea's legs. "I guess y'all do know."

"Fuck yeah," Lea found herself gasping.

"Definitely," Sean groaned, sliding his crotch against the small of Lea's back.

"Well, then," Cherry said, lancing the pair with an intent stare before turning back to look at the two men outside, "I say we enjoy the show and kill them both later. Okay?"

"Okay," Lea and Sean agreed.

Down on the glider, Andy slid down between Prior's thighs. In the dark, Lea couldn't see Prior's cock, but she watched as Andy lowered his head down into the space where it must have been.

"Oh," said Cherry. "Oh, my." She pulled Lea's hand harder against her chest. And Lea never knew why she did it, but she turned her hand and cupped the other women's breast. *"Oh,"* Cherry sighed and shuddered. "That's… Oh. My."

Lea's fingers trembled. She watched the pale flash of Andy's face bobbing up and down like a flame at the end of a black candle.

"Yeah," agreed Sean into the top of Lea's head. "My, my, my." And as he began to stroke her with one hand, with the other he pulled up the back of Lea's skirt and opened up his jeans.

It was an indication of how wild the whole situation had gotten and how quickly that only a small part of Lea's brain panicked at the thought of Sean taking her from behind right next to a woman whom Lea had only met the day before. Most of her brain, however, was sending out a very clear *PLEASE!* signal, and that was the part that leaned her forward, put her free hand on the window sill, and tilted her pelvis so that, once Sean had shoved her panties down, he was able to slide into her in one smooth, long stroke.

Lea groaned, naturally, which caused Cherry to look down at them and gasp.

"Sorry," Sean grunted. "We can —"

"Naw," Cherry sighed. "G'wan." And then she slid her hand across Lea's back and began stroking ribs and the side of her tit.

Lea obviously wasn't new to the sensations sparked by having two people pleasure her at the same time — had had two people pleasure her quite thoroughly, lucky bitch that she indeed was. But she was very aware of the edges of Cherry's long, manicured nails through the fabric of her top and bra. Her breath caught, and her hand slid from Cherry's breast and grabbed the sill, less to keep her balance that to hold onto something solid.

Down in the yard, Prior arched and twisted as Andy sucked him.

"Damn," said Cherry. "Looks like Andy has got real good at that."

"Oh, yeah," Sean panted. "Hell, yes."

One long finger nail traced the outline of Lea's nipple, and she could feel her eyes cross. "So, you like boys, Sean?" Cherry asked.

"I love Andy," said Sean.

"Huh." A rustle made Lea turn her head, and she saw Cherry pull up the hem of her dress and slip the fingers of the hand that wasn't tantalizing Lea's boob down the front of her panties, bright red to match Cherry's name.

About six inches from Lea's face.

"And," Cherry continued, voice even breathier, "I guess you like girls."

"Oh, yeah." Sean hissed, slowing his thrusts. "Would you like…? If it's okay with you, Lea, would you like me to… Can I help you, Miss Cherry?"

"Oh. Sweet Jesus. Please."

Sean swore, but Lea recognized this profanity: it told her just how turned on he was. But Sean was Sean — he always wanted to do the thing *right*. Instead of simply grabbing at Cherry's pussy or her tits, he reached up and unzipped the slinky purple dress.

Cherry let it slide off, along with her panties, and leaned next to Lea against the windowsill. She let out a gasp; Lea assumed that Sean had begun to tantalize her with his hand — he would never go straight to the finish line, not Sean. At least not usually.

Lea turned her head and saw in fact that, while he was fucking Lea very, very nicely, he was letting his hand float over Cherry's ass, *just* touching it. Lea smiled, knowing how amazing that feeling could be.

"This boy of yours's got nice hands," Cherry sighed, confirming Lea's assumption. An army of goose pimples appeared on Cherry's ass, her back — down the arm that led to the hand with which she was playing with herself.

"Yes," Lea said, "yes, indeed he does."

"I aim to please," said Sean, sounding, in fact, very pleased with himself. "And you, Miss Cherry, you…" He slid his cock out of Lea so that just the tip of the head split her labia, then slid all of the way back in. "You have a very nice ass."

Lea reached between her legs and squeezed his balls, making Sean gasp, which made Lea and Cherry both laugh. Lea became very aware of the green of Cherry's eyes, which was startling amidst the dark skin of her face.

"Bet he's got a nice cock too," Cherry said with a smile.

"Oh, yes," Lea answered, smiling back. "Yes, indeed he does." Weird as this was, it was kind of nice, being fucked fabulously, all while chatting with a girl-friend. Surreal. Nice.

"Does it do that bendy thing Andy's does?" Her eyes crinkled.

"You mean…?"

Cherry pulled the hand from her panties and demonstrated the downward bend of Andy's erection. "Prior's always wondered why I love getting it, you know, like you are."

Her eyebrows flying up, Lea blinked at the other woman. Truly, this was without a doubt the *weirdest*… Again, Lea giggled and Cherry followed, and it all felt so wild and so weird and so *good* that Lea didn't notice that Sean had stopped his steady thrusts.

"I think Andy-boy's about to give Prior an introduction," he murmured, "to that, uh, bendy thing."

Lea and Cherry both looked out the window, and saw what Sean meant. Apparently, Andy had finished Prior off, since Andy was now the one sitting on the glider — lying on it, staring up at his friend, who was straddling Andy's waist, reaching back and holding…

"Sweet Jesus, what is Prior *doing*?" Cherry gasped.

Once again, Lea felt anxious. "Um, are you guys sure we shouldn't stop them?"

Sean leaned down and kissed Lea's back, doing something with his hand that made Cherry gasp again — higher this time. "I think… I mean, sex is sex, right?" he murmured.

Below, Prior was lowering himself onto Andy's cock; he let out an audible cry. Andy's hands flowed over Prior's body, soothing, calming.

"Sweet Jesus," said Cherry.

"It's another thing Andy does really, really well, Miss Cherry." Sean began to fuck Lea again; his voice sounded calm, easy, in spite of the fact that his lover was introducing Cherry's fiancé to anal sex down on the swing. He gave a grunt as he slid home again — making Lea kind of forget about Prior and Andy, forget about *everything.* "Y'all had to get blood tests and all, right, for the wedding?"

Cherry, who was biting her lip, nodded. "Tests for everything known to man, I swear. Stupid. We only slept with each other, last three years. What we gonna catch? But— *Oh!*" Cherry's eyes crossed as Sean once again did *something* with his hand that clearly made her feel very good indeed.

"See, me and Andy, we get screened every three months; don't want us picking up something — home or work — and passing it along to someone else when we're trying to rescue'em and all. So we're clean. And Miss Lea —"

"I had myself tested too as soon as I got here," she gasped. She didn't want to be talking about STDs. She wanted to be *fucking.*

Sean's hand had worked under Lea's skirt and his thumb began tracing the insides of her thighs.

Prior called out again — Lea couldn't quite make out what he said, but she could see the white length of Andy's erection disappearing inch by inch into Prior's backside.

"Damn," Cherry said, staring down at the men. Lea assumed that the other woman was as turned on as Lea herself by what they were seeing, an assumption that was confirmed when she arched back into Sean's hand, her own hand grasping at Lea's shoulder.

"You can say that again," Lea sighed. Sean had picked up the pace slightly, and it felt *soooo good...* "Oh, God, Sean."

Sean just let out a long, steadying breath, as if he were preparing to jump out of an airplane, and then began plunging deep and hard, pressing the breath out of Lea.

"Damn," repeated Cherry staring back to where his hips had slapped against Lea's ass. As Sean withdrew painstakingly slowly, her green eyes widened. "Oh, my."

"Uh-huh," Lea panted. "Nice, right?"

Cherry licked her lips. "Um. Can I...? I mean," she said, her eyes flashing back to the window and her man and Lea's fucking, "I mean, I don't wanna do, um, but, Lea, can I *touch* that?"

Lea found laughter bubbling up again. "Don't you think you aught to ask Sean? *Huh!*"

Sean slammed home again. "If it's okay with Lea here, how could I say no?" He slid back out until, once more, only the tip of his cock remained inside of Lea, and her toes and fingers curled.

Cherry reached back over Lea's ass, her breasts sliding along Lea's back — again, short-circuiting Lea's brain — and her hand sliding over Lea's ass, fingers closing around Sean's cock.

Sean gurgled and thrust through Cherry's fingers, pressing back into Lea and... "*Oooo...*" she sighed.

"Ooo," echoed Cherry. "My, my, my..." Fingers were pushed against Lea's pussy by Sean's thrusts — Lea was not even having to work hard not to think about whose fingers those were, because it felt *sooo* good.

"Jesus, God," groaned Sean, and his hand in Lea's crotch pulled her hard back against him, trapping Cherry's fingers, and now Lea and Cherry both groaned with him.

Gripping the battered window sill with both hands, Lea looked over her shoulder. Cherry's cherry-colored panties where just inches away. Sean's hand curled around beneath them from the back, while Lea could see Cherry's hand working at the front.

Prior and Andy were groaning loudly enough to be heard from this distance; the glider outside groaned beneath them.

"Oh, say, now," Cherry sighed, "could I, maybe...? I have kind of a fantasy. And if my boyfriend's gettin' *his*," — And getting it *hard*, by the sound of it, Lea thought. — "maybe, you know, I could kinda get mine?"

"Sure," Lea said, lost on the feeling of the fuck.

Sean just panted.

"'Kay." Cherry's voice was suddenly rising in pitch. She stood, and for a second Lea thought she was going to kiss Sean, which Lea wasn't sure she was okay with. Instead, when Sean was once again barely inside of Lea, Cherry swung her leg over his cock, facing Lea. Her legs were longer, and so although Lea knew logically the other women was standing astride Sean's erection, it suddenly felt weirdly as if the cock that split Lea's labia were Cherry's.

"Um," Lea began, but then Sean thrust in, his thumb pressing against Lea's clit, and honestly? The bounce of Cherry's boobs against Lea's back, the whir of Cherry's knuckles, covered in silk, pushing against Lea's butt — Lea couldn't have cared less. "Oh. God."

"Jesus," Cherry and Sean answered together.

As Sean once again fell into a steady rhythm, Lea lifted her head. Down in the yard, she could just see the pale blur that was Andy; his rhythm seemed to be matching Sean's. "So Sean," Lea sighed, "you like fucking two women at the same time?"

"Fuck, yeah," he grunted. His left hand, sticky, grasped Lea's breast firmly. "You... like fucking two guys at the same time?"

Lea laughed, setting all three of them shivering. "Fuck... yeah."

"Y'all talk too much," said Cherry, and they all laughed and shivered again. Cherry lay her forehead on Lea's shoulder. "Always... wanted... to have a cock..."

And from in between Cherry's legs thrusts *Sean's*, not as deeply as usual, perhaps, but deep enough, and Sean's thumb against her clit, and his fingers on her breast, and Cherry moaning and Sean growling and Lea —

Coming.

Lea would have thought that she was an old pro at having an orgasm brought on in close proximity to not one but two other people. She would have thought that coming while one person was pounding away at her pussy and another moaned ecstatically into her shoulder was a familiar, almost everyday occurrence.

Of course, *everyday* didn't include the person doing the moaning being a woman, and a woman whom Lea liked, but had certainly never thought about sharing a lover with. It wasn't that the orgasm was any less wonderful — it was just that, where Lea so often felt as if she had left her body when she came, now she was very aware of her body: of the feeling of her pussy pulsing around Sean's cock, of the sweat on her nose, of the trembling whir of Cherry's fingers against Lea's ass.

Cherry came next, a high sigh and a shudder.

Sean, astonishingly, kept going.

"Damn," gasped Cherry, shuddering again.

Lea would have reached back and fondled his balls, knowing that would most likely set him off, but she wasn't sure that she would be able to stay upright if she let go of the windowsill, and so she looked over her shoulder. "Hey… Cherry… *You* ever… kissed another… woman?"

Startling green eyes blinked. "Never… have I ever." Then she took the hint, leaning forward and capturing Lea's lips between her own.

It wasn't weird or unpleasant. It wasn't a turn-on either.

When Lea had been in college, while she was still acting, one of her teachers had challenged the class to choose scenes that forced them to do something that they would never do in their own lives. Lea and Helen Kim had decided to work on a scene from play called *Stop Kiss* in which two women who think of themselves as straight find themselves extremely attracted to each other and after a long back-and-forth share a kiss (and are subsequently assaulted — but that happens off stage).

The scene had been Helen's idea, but she had been incredibly uncomfortable with the idea of actually kissing. She kept stopping the scene before they got there.

Finally, the night before they were supposed to present the scene, Lea had come to Helen's dorm room with a bottle of wine and refused to start rehearsing or leave until they'd finished the bottle off. They'd talked about their boyfriends, they'd talked about their politics (Helen was from a very conservative family), and they'd talked about how they felt about the idea of kissing each other. Where Lea was moderately uncomfortable with it, Helen was frankly terrified. Lea had tried a dozen ways to see if they could just touch their lips together — no emotional content, no nothing — but Helen finally simply freaked out and asked Lea to leave. It had left Lea feeling frustrated as hell, though not in a sexual way.

The last time Lea had seen her, Helen had been waving a rainbow flag while marching down Market Street in the Gay Freedom Day parade.

Kissing Cherry was fine — just lips touching lips, no big deal, no turn-on. At least not for Lea. Cherry really seemed to be getting into it. And Sean…

As Lea had suspected, the sight of his girlfriend making out with another woman — while he fucked his girlfriend between the other woman's legs — sent Sean over the edge. "Aw, damn, fuck, *shit, holy* —!" He pulled hard with both hands (at Lea's breast and crotch) and thrust as deep as Cherry's presence would allow.

And then, as Lea felt aftershocks of orgasm ripple through the three of them, she heard a shout and loud crash from below.

"Oh, damn," Cherry sighed into Lea's lips. "I think they just broke the swing."

Once they'd disentangled themselves and looked out the window, Lea could see that, yes, indeed, the glider had collapsed. Prior and Andy were fighting their way out of the tangled mass of wood and stumbling toward the house.

Sean and Lea followed Cherry downstairs — Lea distracted by the line of cum that Sean had splattered across the back of Cherry's panties and up her back when he'd pulled out of Lea.

When they reached the front door, Cherry opened it, revealing her boyfriend and Lea's standing unsteadily, kissing.

"Gentlemen," said Cherry, and the two men broke and blinked through the door. "You had fun tonight?"

"Um," muttered Andy.

"Yeah," sighed Prior, staring at his fiancée's half-mast red undies.

"Well, good. We had ourselves a nice time too." Cherry crossed her arms. "But Prior Isaac Lawrence, after tomorrow, if you *ever* touch another man — or woman — without *telling me first*, I am going to cut off your *thang* with a rusty pair of shears and use it for fish bait. *Do you hear me?*"

"Yes, Cherry," said Prior, staring now at his own feet.

Cherry leaned over and gave Lea a kiss — once again on the lips. "Lea. Sean. It has been lovely *entertaining* you while our boys *had fun* out here in the yard. We look forward to seeing you tomorrow at the wedding."

Andy wouldn't talk, the whole way home.

And when Lea finally slid into the trundle bed, trying not to wake Jessie, Andy's sister spat, "*Complicated*. Like fuck."

Shitty-shit-shit. *"Sorry."*

"Are you and Andy even engaged, or is that all just some bullshit smoke screen?"

Lea tried to think how to answer that. "We are. And Sean. Too."

"What?"

"All three of us, Jessie. It's —"

"That's…!" Jessie growled. *"Disgusting."*

Lea lay there, heart beating. *What the fuck do you say to that?* "Sorry, Jessie."

At breakfast the next morning, none of the Harrises — not even Andy — would look Lea in the eye, let alone talk to her.

Fuckity-fuck-fuck.

Mr. Harris got up from the awkward table first, tapping Andy on the shoulder and muttering something about *Delivering the present*, and they disappeared.

Sean tried to start a conversation about the wedding, and another about the weather — faced with the silent antipathy of Andy's mother and sister, however, he muttered something about going for a ride and dragged Lea out to Andy's truck.

They drove up to an abandoned fire tower that Andy had shown them. Where the silence at the table had been smothering, stifling, the quiet in the car was a relief. When they reached the lookout, Sean parked, sighing, "Well, it could be worse."

"How?"

"A hundred years ago, they'd have tarred and feathered me'n'Andy, stoned you'n'Cherry just because, and lynched Prior on principle."

"Oh."

They looked out at the valleys spread out beneath them.

"God, it's pretty," sighed Lea.

"Uh-huh."

"Wanna fuck?"

"Sure."

And so Lea and Sean made love there, overlooking three states' worth of the Blue Ridge Mountains in the front of their lover's SUV — their lover who was feeling less like their lover every day.

It was lovely, and it was a relief from the oppressive dread that was crashing down on Lea.

For a while, at least.

When they arrived back at the Harrises', Nadine, Jessie, Andy and Mr. Harris were sitting at the table. The men were silent and sweaty. The women were just silent.

"Hey, there," Sean said, flashing his sunniest smile.

As Sean later put it, "I might as well have been peeing in a thunderstorm for all the good it did."

Trying to keep from wringing her hands, Lea took a deep breath. "So. I guess it's time to get ready for the wedding?" She hadn't meant to ask it as a question, but the Harrises' stony expressions made it difficult to state as a fact.

Nadine smiled a brittle approximation of her usual grin. "I don't think we will be going to the... wedding, Miss Krakowicz." Jessie nodded in affirmation.

Lea's heart plummeted.

"Ma!" whined Andy.

Mr. Harris merely rumbled, his dark eyes boring into Lea.

Mrs. Harris cleared invisible dust from the linoleum table. "I do not think that I can, in good conscience, celebrate what is so clearly a sham of a sacred sacrament. A sham perpetrated by the couple themselves, my *son* —" Her voice and face both bespoke acid distaste, and her eyes too slashed toward Lea. "— by his *so-called* fiancée, and by their... *boy-toy*."

"*Ma!*" Andy was crying. Lea had never seen him cry — except during sex.

She felt as if she might be closer to vomiting than to tears.

Jessie didn't look any happier, but she was nodding solemnly, her eyes too locked on Lea.

Nadine Harris stood, imperious. "You may do things very differently in California, Miss Krakowicz, and I am not surprised to find that perversion has found its way into a cesspool like Atlanta, but that is *not* how we behave here!" She began to turn to make a dramatic exit.

Before she could clear the table, however, her husband's enormous hand grasped Nadine's elbow. "*SIDDOWN.*"

Eyebrows disappearing into her teased, bleached hair, Nadine sat down.

Davy Harris's eyes flicked back from his wife to Lea, and any urge she might have had to speak disappeared. After a moment, he said, "You love my boy, Lea?"

Now she felt like crying. She nodded.

"You love my boy, Sean?"

Eyes enormous, Sean nodded as well.

"You love these two, boy?"

Still blubbering in a manner that broke Lea's heart, Andy nodded as well.

"Well, then." Davy added his own gruff nod. "Least none of 'em likes to fuck animals like my uncle Billy." When Nadine started to speak, he turned his intent gaze on her. Her mouth slammed shut. "And least none of 'em likes to beat up little black girls and rape 'em like your grandpa, Nadine. We got plenty of perversion around here, and it's always been pretty darned *mean*, 'cause can't no one talk about it." He turned from his wife, who was bright red, to Andy. "That's why we's uncomfortable about you'n'Cherry, son. Not 'cause she's black, though, *dang*, my pa woulda been sure it was the 'Poccalpse if he'd seed his grandson with a... black girl. No. Her ma and your'n is sisters. You's cousins."

Oh, mouthed Andy.

Jessie's mouth was hanging open, and Lea thought hers was too.

Davy stood, towering over the table. "Preacher al's talks about *love*. How it heals all things. Well, I can see that the three of y'all love each other. And I can't think how the Lord would see that as a bad thing." He surveyed the five stunned people around him. "Now let's get dressed for the danged wedding."

Later, Lea could barely remember the wedding service itself. Shock, probably. Well. Certainly.

Cherry and Prior made a beautiful couple. There had been singing. That's about all she could remember.

At the reception, Lea did see Cherry's mother and Andy's talking very politely. *The same green eyes. Oh, my god.*

Jessie got good and drunk and disappeared with one of Prior's brothers. Lea wished her well.

Sean danced with just about every woman at the reception, and he kept grinning at Lea in a way that reminded her that the ring on her finger was *his*, whatever everyone else thought.

Andy was very quiet, but he held her close when they danced. Lea wasn't surprised to find that he danced quite well.

As the reception began to spin out of control, Cherry bounced over to Lea and Andy and whispered, "We're getting ready to leave. Come back with us, okay?"

Before Lea or Andy could answer, she'd shimmied her way back over to her husband.

And so about a half an hour later they strode down into the *holler* where Prior and Cherry's house still improbably stood. Sean was giving Andy grief, saying as the only person who'd slept with both the bride and the groom, *he* should have been the minister.

Prior was laughing. Andy was glowering, but there was a bit of a smile there.

Lea had her arm hooked through Cherry's. "So... you said last night you'd always wanted a cock?"

Cherry's face darkened, but she laughed.

"Well," Lea whispered, "I think I might have a wedding present for you." And she held her finger in front of her mouth — *secret!* — and both women dissolved into giggles.

The Georgia evening was thick and sweet. As they turned into the front yard, lightning bugs lit the path, revealing....

"Holy fuck!" Prior barked.

"It was my present for y'all," Andy said. "Pa made it and we delivered it this afternoon. Didn't realize how badly you'd need it."

An iron glider stood where Prior and Andy had destroyed the old one the night before. The black beams were bedecked in ribbons and flowers.

Cherry ran to Andy and threw her arms around him. "Oh, Andy, baby, that's so beautiful!"

Prior laughed, joining her, "And it ain't fallin' down like the rest of this damned house!"

They all laughed, even Andy.

Cherry's green eyes caught Lea's and then flicked up to her husbands. He nodded.

Cherry's voice which was usual self-assured, quavered slightly. "Would you three... like to join us tonight?"

Andy blinked, flushing, though Lea didn't think it was due to embarrass-ment. He looked back to Lea and Sean who both shrugged the decision back to him. He looked at his first lover and his most recent, licked his lips, and shook his head. "Naw. It's y'all's wedding night. This is a night for you two." He leaned forward and kissed the bride. And then the groom.

"Maybe a raincheck, then," Prior murmured into Andy's lips.

They were all happy with that idea.

The next morning, the whole Harris clan was gathered on the gravel drive again. Danielle and her family seemed to have missed the previous day's storm, but even Jessie showed up to say goodbye.

Davy Harris said not a word, of course — Lea was sure he'd used up a year's supply — but Nadine made a point of kissing Sean and Lea each on the cheek and telling them they were always welcome in her home.

Back in Atlanta, everything returned to something like normal. Andy's shift and Sean's mysteriously shifted back into sync. The three of them went back to sharing a bed and employing it fully.

As she'd promised, Lea sent a strap-on to Cherry (and Prior) as a present. It was the same model as Lea's, only in Cherry's namesake color instead of purple.

Cherry informed Lea that she and her husband had *both* enjoyed it enormously.

The one thing that didn't change was Andy's distance.

Nothing that Lea or Sean could think of seemed to make their lover *himself* again. No laughter. He seemed to have been infected by his father's reticence. In bed, where Andy had always given as good as he got, he became passive and much less assertive.

And Sean, thrown off balance, became uncertain as well.

It was putting quite a damper on the life they shared — not just sexually, but in every aspect.

It got to the point where Lorelle from downstairs asked if something were wrong. And Lea didn't know what to tell her.

Finally, at her wits' end, worried that Andy's funk would destroy not just the threesome but her relationship with Sean, did the thing she's sworn she'd never do: she went to Gus, the septuagenarian tech director who was the only other person she knew who had created a successful *ménage à trois*.

Sitting in Gus's office high above the theater's shop, Lea found herself apol-ogizing, but Gus would have none of it. "I told you that I'd be happy to help, Lea, dear!"

She sighed, staring at the newest of Gus's oil-and-canvas tributes to his wife. It showed Sally — recognizable because of her brilliant red hair — laughing with a slight blonde woman while the large, dark figure of Gus and Sally's lover Frank loomed behind them. "Is that… Violet O'Connell?" She pointed to the blonde.

"Oh, yes," Gus said, smiling as always. "Violet. Sally was very, very fond of her." He blinked and looked back toward Lea. "But it sounds to me as if your young man Andy is wracked with guilt."

"*Guilt?*" Lea snorted, shaking her head. It seemed like such a Jewish reaction from such a *non*-Jewish boy. "You really think so?"

Gus steepled his fingers in front of his mouth and nodded. "Hmm. Sally was a Catholic — not a very observant one, of course, but once a Catholic… In any case, I told you that she once left me and Frank… for a woman. For nearly a year. It destroyed the woman's home life, but Sally finally found that she belonged with us. But when she returned, she was so crippled with guilt — guilt at having made a mess of the young lady's marriage, at having abandoned me and Frank. It didn't matter that the woman was happy to be out of a loveless marriage. It didn't matter that Frank and I were ecstatic to see her back. She couldn't give herself to us fully until she had… atoned for her sins."

"That sounds more Jewish than Catholic."

"Hmm. Nonetheless." Gus looked back to the painting.

Staring at the piece of art too, Lea puzzled at what he was saying. "So… we need to find some way for Andy to find… absolution?"

Gus simply nodded and patted Lea's hand. Then they both stared at the painting for some time.

"Oh, god, Sean, baby, fuck me, fuck me *hard!*"

Sean was answering Lea as best he could, pounding up into her as she straddled him on the kitchen chair.

Behind her, Lea heard a long, high, keening moan. "Tell me, *huh!* Is… Andy crying?"

"Looks… like."

She turned her head, which bounced as Sean continued to pound away. Tears were indeed flowing down Andy's cheeks. And his cock, bending away from his body as always, seemed to be straining to reach Lea and Sean. "You… sorry… Andy?"

Blinking the tears out of his eyes, he nodded.

"You *sure?*" Lea found that she was quite enjoying the role of the dominatrix, but she wasn't sure she could hold out much longer.

Andy screamed into his gag, nodding harder so that some of his tears crossed the gap landing on Lea's bouncing ass.

"Sean," Lea said, "why don't you walk us over there. I'd like to hear Andy tell us what he's sorry for."

Sean stood, still planted deep inside of her; she had a momentary flash of feeling very small next to her two lovers. Still, she was the one in charge, for all that they out-weighed her together by much more than three times.

When they were next to Andy, Lea said, "Look at Sean's cock, how it's spreading me. Don't you wish you were inside of me like that? Or that he were inside of *you?*"

Andy howled into his gag.

Lea leaned back and undid the bandana.

Andy's breath was raspy and labored. "Gawd, Lea. *Gawd....*"

"What are you sorry for, Andy?"

He sobbed, "Sorry I embarrassed you with my family. Sorry my family treated you both so crappy. Sorry I fucked Prior without askin' either of y'all.... *I'm so, so sorry, Lea, Sean!*"

He was wailing in earnest now.

"Do you apologize?"

"YES!"

"Will you ever do it again?"

"NO!"

"And if you do, sweetheart, because we all break promises sometimes, will you simply tell us, instead of bottling it up and punishing yourself, which is much less fun than having us to it?"

"YES!"

Lea turned back to Sean, who had managed to keep his steady rhythm going. "What do you think, Sean?"

"Sounds... huh... like he means it."

"Hmm," Lea said. "*Do* you mean it, Andy? Are you heartily sorry?"

"*Yesss!*" he sniveled. "Please, Lea, Sean, I'm so, so, so, sorry!"

Nodding, Lea whispered to Sean, who bit back a chuckled. Lea looked back at their bound lover. "Okay, Andy, we believe you. Open your mouth."

Blinking, he did.

Sean backed Lea up so that the end of the butt plug protruding from Lea's ass was between Andy's teeth. "Take it out," Lea ordered. "Gently."

Andy's mouth clamped down on the plug. He tried to pull his head back enough to move it, but couldn't, bound as he was, as so Sean helped, pulling Lea in the opposite direction. Lea felt the plastic plumb-bob stretch her asshole and then slide through. She swore.

A *clunk* let her know that Andy had let the butt-plug slide out of his mouth to the ground. Lea could feel his breath against her open asshole, and it made her shiver, contracting around Sean, which made him groan. "Kiss it," she sighed, "and we will release you. Kiss my ass, Andy."

Andy leaned forward, and his lips found the quivering flesh of her anus. And his tongue.

That got Lea swearing again. Which got Sean swearing.

When they'd caught their breath, Lea gasped, "Well, Sean? Should Andy be released?"

"Fuck, yeah."

"And has he earned his reward?"

Andy whimpered. Sean just chuckled.

And so Lea pronounced, "Yes. He has earned his reward."

And Sean — ridiculously strong Sean — slid himself onto Andy's knees, so that the head of Andy's cock bounced against Lea's backside. Steady now between her lovers — where she belonged — Lea reached back, held Andy's erection steady, and let Sean lower her onto it, so that, for the very first time, Lea had one of them in her cunt at the same time that the other was in her ass, and she felt as if she were finally complete.

"You're… forgiven, Andy," she moaned. "Now fuck me. Fuck me, *both of you. Fuck me* **hard!**"

The Visitor Has Company

"Let me see," sighed Lea, licking the index finger of her right hand as she ran the left one up Sean's bicep and down Andy's. "However shall I choose which of you I should marry?"

Both men moaned. Lea giggled. She didn't giggle very often, but this called for it.

They were back to back, sitting, each handcuffed to the legs of the other's chair. Naked. Each sporting a dark red erection, the tip of which glistened with pre-cum.

"Oh, gentlemen, you can't hurry a lady. And after all," she said, letting both hands flow down over their chests, stopping *just* short of their very emphatic hard-ons, "you did ask for this."

Both men whimpered.

Well, they hadn't exactly asked for *this* — they'd asked her to decide which side of their triangle would be the one to become official. And gay marriage wasn't legal in Georgia yet (though it was clearly just a matter of time), and so it was up to Lea to choose: Andy or Sean?

Only Lea didn't want to choose. Didn't see why they had to choose. And so she'd agreed to consider it only if they made themselves completely available for her delight. Which they'd done.

And so, for the past two hours, she'd been slowly teasing them — with her fingers, with her mouth, with the strapon they each loved her to use on him. All while slowly discussing the relative merits of each choice.

Which really wasn't a choice. She wanted them both, always. When they'd originally proposed to her, back at the beginning of the summer, it had been a way to keep Andy's family from finding out just what the three of them were up to. Sean had gotten down on one knee and asked her to marry *Andy*, for fuck's sake. Andy had asked her to marry Sean. Or to wear the diamond ring as a sign of a promise between the two men.

But Andy's family had seen through the charade quickly enough. Lea could still barely talk to Andy's mom, Nadine, or to his sister Jessie.

The whole getting married thing — what was the point?

She got down on her own knees, letting her fingertips brush the insides of their thighs. Andy twitched; Sean moaned.

Lea's Tantra-loving, West Coast parents would probably be more concerned with the idea of Lea staying in Georgia than with the idea of her shacking up with two guys. Probably.

And Kirsten—Sean's sister already knew all about it. Well, most about it.

Lea's fingers traced lines up the insides of the far legs, evoking twin shivers.

Not Violet. Not Sean and Kirsten's mother, whose ring Lea was wearing on her left hand. Lea loved Violet; her disappointment was actually the thing that Lea was most afraid of — that the very proper, very traditional Atlanta kindergarten teacher would be disgusted by the choices that her son and his lovers had made. That Violet would blame the whole thing on Lea. Which struck Lea as not just terrifying but blatantly unfair. It wasn't like she'd *asked* for things to turn out the way that they had. Exactly.

Shitty-shit-shit.

Tilting her head to one side and then the other, Lea admired the two lovely penises that were at her beck and call. She let her fingers run over their balls, which jumped, and then, for the first time since she had closed the handcuffs on them two hours before, she circled the bases of those two lovely penises, squeezing every so slightly as she let her hands stroke up — "I'll tell you what, boys." — and down.

Sean sounded as if he were trying to say *What?*, while Andy simply gibbered.

"I'll tell you what," she said again — again with an up-stroke. "The one of you who can keep from coming the longest is the one I'll marry."

They both gasped; both set their jaws in determination, closing their eyes.

Okay, thought Lea with grin, *this might be fun.* And she began to give them the lightest, slowest handjob that she could. She leaned forward to lick the crevice between their elbows and —

And the doorbell rang.

Shitty-shit-shit! *"Um. Hold on a minute! Be right there!"* Could it be Lorelle from downstairs, requesting that we be *less* quiet?

Lea stood, grabbing her silk robe from where she'd let it pool to the floor.

The bell rang again.

The two men — firemen, after all — had managed to uncuff themselves and were pulling jeans up over their still-dripping erections.

"Sorry, guys," she whispered, giving each cock a quick tug and then pulling her robe shut. *"Coming!"*

"I wish," one of the guys muttered, which unfortunately struck Lea as amusing, and so she was giggling again as she opened the door and —

And was greeted by a weeping Kirsten. "Oh, Lea!"

"Kirsten! What...? You're here." It was a stupid thing to say but as much as Lea could manage. The last time they'd talked, just a few days before, Kirsten had been in San Francisco.

"Gianna got m-married," sobbed Kirsten, face blotchy, "*and it wasn't to me!*"

"Aw, shit," sighed Sean as his sister threw her arms around Lea and wailed. Andy just grunted. Like Lea they knew that Gianna had been vacillating between her ex-boyfriend and Kirsten. Like Lea, they'd seen this coming for months.

Kirsten clearly hadn't, though.

Lea patted her best friend on the back. "I'm so sorry, Kirsten."

"Feel stupid."

"I bet."

Sean put a big hand on his sister's shoulder. "Want me'n'Andy to go beat her up?"

Lifting her head, Kirsten blinked up at her brother and then snorted. "No beating up Gianna!" She turned in Lea's hug and threw her arms around Sean and then Andy. "Gawd! The two of y'all make *me* look like a fucking midget. You'd crush Gianna like a grape!"

"For making you cry like that?" said Andy, patting Kirsten on the back awkwardly. "Least we could do."

Kirsten pushed up on her tiptoes, kissing Andy's cheek, when her stomach growled.

"You eat anything at all today, Kiki?" Sean asked, running his fingers through his sister's hair.

Kirsten shot him an embarrassed smirk. "Naw. Been kind of upset." Her stomach gurgled again.

"Yeah," laughed Sean. "I guess. Want some eggs or something?"

When Kirsten nodded, Sean and Andy wandered over to the kitchen and began preparing a meal for her. Lea was admiring their shapes, admiring the way they worked so smoothly together, when her friend sighed, "Sorry, Lea-honey."

"Sorry?"

"Y'all were... *playing*, weren't you."

Lea blinked at her friend and then at the room — the two chairs, still back-to-back, each with a pair of handcuffs dangling... The strap-on hanging from a cupboard handle. Lube. Condoms. "Um. No big deal."

"Uh-huh, right." It was reassuring to see Kirsten's habitual smirk back in place.

"We'll survive. So Giannaa and what's-his-name got married?"

The smirk melted. Kirsten nodded and pulled out her phone. On it was a text from that morning that read, "K, we're in Reno. We eloped. Forgive me." There was a picture of Gianna and man who resembled her brother than anything — dark, small, slight. They were standing in front what looked like a motel, but bore a heart-shaped neon sign reading *Temple of Venus Tatoo Parlor and Wedding Chapel*. Both were smiling maniacally.

"Well... Fuck." The end of Kirsten and Gianna's relationship had been looming for months, but this seemed needlessly cruel. "Sure you don't want Sean and Andy to go break their kneecaps?"

Kirsten's smirk returned — a bit soggier, but back, at least. "Naw. Well. Not tonight, anyways." She rested her head on Lea's shoulder. "Thing is, I knew she was leaving — was gone already, really. Still. Kind of kicked me in the tits, you know?"

Lea gave her a hug.

"Don't blame you, Kiki," said Sean, carrying to the table a steaming plate of scrambled eggs and some of the home fries they'd had left over from dinner.

Andy carried a bottle of Jack Daniels and four glasses. "I'd've wanted to get out of there too."

"Yeah," sighed Kirsten, sitting down and tucking in. "But I bet you wouldn't've hung around so long. I feel so fucking stupid."

"Hey," said Sean, "no one gets to call my sister stupid. Except me."

Kirsten flicked a bit of fried onion at him, and he snickered, picking up one of the tumblers that Andy had set out. He lifted it in a toast: "To the return of the Prodigal Sister — who is not stupid, no matter what anyone says."

They all laughed and raised their glasses.

After she'd eaten a bit — and drunk a bit — Kirsten shook her head. "I guess... I feel stupid 'cause this managed to catch me by surprise. But also 'cause I jumped on a plane and only thought about the fact that I couldn't exactly go home and cry on Mama's shoulder when I was half-way here."

"I wondered why we'd rated a cross-country visit," Lea said, swirling her whiskey in her glass. "I mean, it's wonderful to see you and you're always welcome, and we're glad to help, but, yeah. I guess I'd have expected you to head home, if anywhere."

Sean reached out and took his sister's hand. "And you could've talked to Mama."

"Uh-huh. And have *you* been discussing the details of y'alls sleeping arrangements with her?" With her glass, Kirsten indicated Lea, Andy, and the never-closed pull-out the three of them had been making such energetic use of since the spring. When Sean shook his head a bit sheepishly, Kirsten grumbled, "Didn't think so."

"Don't blame you," Andy chuckled. "I mean, my folks finding out was pretty awful. But your ma? She's scary."

That made Lea laugh. "Violet isn't scary!" When that statement was met by three skeptical faces, Lea shrugged. "I mean, I can see that you wouldn't want to... disappoint her."

"Yeah," smirked Kristen. "Lea-honey, I bet you haven't exactly been looking forward to explaining to her just what you and your *fiancé* here have been getting up to with Mama's Sir Galahad of a son."

"*Galahad?*" said Sean, a look of outrage on his face. "Wasn't he, like, a *virgin* and shit? Nuh-uh. No. Not even Mama thinks I'm *that*. Besides, Lea's my fiancée too. So's Andy." He grabbed both of their hands, and Lea found her middle warming for reasons other than the bourbon.

"Exactly," said Kirsten, glowering. "House we grew up in was so fucking straight, we never even *heard* of such a thing as being queer. Let alone AC/DC like me and you turned out, Sean. Mama'd blow a gasket."

Brows bowed, Sean murmured, "I think Papa'd be the one who'd really blow."

"Don't remember. Just remember when he'd left." Kirsten frowned and Lea reached out and squeezed her friend's hand with her free one, linking the four of them. "Anyway, Sean, Mama had no clue. Remember her favorite bands?"

Sean gave a surprised snort. "Queen. And Village People."

"Yeah, ain't that something," chuckled Kirsten. "She thought the Village People were *such nice men!*" She said this last in such a demure, Violet-like drawl that all four of them burst out laughing. Well. The accent was part of it; the image of Violet O'Connell, Kindergarten Teacher and Southern Matron, watching those under-dressed men performing "YMCA" or "Macho Man" was more than even Lea's fairly broad mind could encompass.

After they'd laughed and drunk some more (and then talked some more, and drunk some more), and Kirsten had finished her "breakfast," Sean stood and kissed his sister on the top of her head. "You okay, Sis?"

"Okay, Big Bro." Kirsten squeezed his hand. "Why don't you guys go, uh, finish what I interrupted. Or, you know, I can go for a — "

"No, I'll stay out here with you, K," Lea said. "These guys are tired, aren't you, boys?"

Sean and Andy glanced quickly at each other, then back to Lea and Kirsten. Together they both nodded, and Sean gave a not-very-convincing yawn. "Uh-huh."

"Yeah," said Andy, "we've got work tomorrow. Tomorrow evening."

"G'night, Sis," said Sean, ruffling her hair with another kiss. The two men shuffled back to Andy's bedroom.

Lea watched them wistfully. The boys hadn't had a night alone in the apartment since the theater season had closed the previous spring. She wished...

Kirsten sniffled, and Lea put her arms around her friend. With a sigh, Kirsten said, "They're gonna boff, aren't they."

"Probably."

"That's... gonna take some getting used to." Kirsten made a face that caused the silvery tracks of salt down her cheeks to catch the light. "I mean, Lea-honey, you could go back there. Or I could, you know, go for a walk."

"No, K, honest —"

Now Kirsten's face was in a more typical mode: skeptical. "Sweetie, I interrupted y'alls... fun."

Lea was about to deny it, but Kirsten pointed to the chairs, still back-to-back, handcuffs still dangling. Then she pointed over to the counter, where the strap-on and lube were waiting. Lea shot her friend a sad smile. "Well, yeah. But we'd been going for quite a while, and honestly, I can do without for a night. I'm... very satisfied in that department."

Kirsten gave a sour snort. "Bitch."

There was a grunt from Andy's room at the back, and then another, followed by the rhythmic sound of the bed hitting the wall.

"Oh, damn," sighed Kirsten, and then held up her hands. "I'm trying not to visualize any of this too much, but... I mean, how do those two not, like, *crush* you?"

"Well," Lea answered, trying to think how to say anything that wasn't going to make her friend want to puke, "they kind of... do. But in a very nice way."

"Damn." Pouting, Kirsten looked down the hallway, where the *thump* of the headboard was growing stronger. "Gotta be Andy on top, right?"

"Well, actually, it's probably Sean. Andy likes... Yeah. Though we all sometimes take —"

Kirsten held her hands up. "Sweet Jesus. Here I always figured you and Sean for straight vanilla. Thought I was the kinky one. Damn."

One of the men — Lea was pretty sure it was her friend's brother — screamed. Kirsten blanched.

"Come on, K," said Lea, taking her friend by the hand and leading her back to the table. "I think we should grab another drink. And you need to tell me all about Gianna."

They sat and drank, both pretending not to listen to the increasing sounds of passion coming from the back room. Kirsten told Lea the whole story — most of which Lea already knew — of how Kirsten and Gianna's relationship had disintegrated once Gianna's ex, Frankie, had reappeared in her life. "I mean," Kirsten sniffled, "it's not like I didn't see it comin'. I feel like such a..." Kirsten blinked and shook her head. "Am I really drunk, or is the wallbangin' happenin' in stereo?"

Lea, who was a bit woozy herself, had to listening for a moment before she heard the echo from downstairs. "Oh. Um. That's Lorelle and Freddy. I guess the boys kind of... inspired them."

Kirsten gawked at Lea, and then, though her eyes were still red-rimmed, she began to laugh, snorting until tears were flowing again — tears of laughter.

At that point — as Lea had begun to giggle along — their laughter was interrupted by a series of bellows (Lea was able to identify them as Lorelle, then Freddy, then Sean, and finally Andy). And then Lea and Kirsten truly couldn't do *anything* but laugh.

What else was there to do?

Waking up the next morning, Lea was discombobulated. She was in her bed, sure. There was an O'Connell wrapped around her, murmuring amorously though (blessedly) unintelligibly into Lea's ear. These things were not unusual.

What *was* unusual was that the O'Connell in question was Kirsten, who was (again, blessedly) still asleep.

Lea gingerly detached herself from Kirsten's full-body embrace and tip-toed off to the shower.

By the time that she'd rendered herself more or less human again and returned to the main room, Andy, Sean, and Kirsten were all seated at the table nibbling on toast. None of them seemed to be able to meet any of the others' eyes.

"Good morning," chirped Lea as cheerfully as she could.

The three Georgians muttered "Morning" back, but still none of the three of them looked up.

Well.

Shit.

Shitty-shit-shit.

Lea had learned as a stage manager and director to face awkwardness: to name it and move on. Nothing was going to get done after an opening had bombed until someone said, "Well, we sure sucked last night. How are we going to do better?" And so Lea faced the elephants in the room and addressed them. "Kirsten, Andy and Sean are in love. They are also, apparently, in love with me. We all fuck, but they like to fuck all on their lonesome when I'm not available. Being large guys, sometimes they fuck pretty loudly."

Now all three sets of eyes were wide, and focussed on her.

"Sean, Andy: Kirsten and I could absolutely hear you last night. That's fine. We could also hear Freddy and Lorelle from downstairs, which was hilarious. Kirsten, does it bother you that Sean and Andy have sex?"

Kirsten shook her head.

"Sean, Andy: like you, Kirsten is bisexual. Does it bother you that she likes women as well as men?"

Both men shook their heads. Sean reached out and took his sister's bright pink hand.

"Good," Lea said. "Does it bother you that she was in bed with me last night?"

Both men now blinked. Andy's eyebrows shot up.

Kirsten turned bright red, which told Lea she was on the right track. "Not *in-bed* in bed. We just snoozed on the same matress. Any problem?"

The men once again shook their heads.

Lea took a deep breath; she was about to head out into deeper water. "Kirsten: when you woke up this morning, were you dreaming about Gianna — or were you dreaming about me?"

Kirsten threw her hands over her face. Sean petted at her head, but Andy — mortified as he still clearly was — snickered. "She was moanin' *your* name, Lea-baby."

Sean backhanded Andy none too gently, and then whispered to Kirsten, "I don't blame you, Sis. I've dreamed about Lea here for years."

"Thank you," Lea said, choking a bit on a sudden upsurge of emotion. This was *beyond* complicated. But she needed to say the last bit. She reached out and urged her friend's hands down from her face. "Kirsten, I need you to look at me, okay?"

Kirsten unwillingly lowered her hands as Sean continued to stroke her hair. She was once again crying, not that Lea blamed her. She looked as if she were waiting for Lea to scratch her eyes out, but she met Lea's gaze.

"Thank you." Another upsurge. Another breath. "Kirsten, my BFF, I really, really don't mind. You can dream about doing whatever you want to me. I'm... I'm honored, I guess."

Kirsten's eyes widened.

Now it was Lea's turn to reach out and take her friend's hand. "Just so long as you understand I am *not* bisexual, and that it's your brother and this eternal twelve-year-old —" She flicked her head toward Andy. "— that I am in love with and planning on spending the rest of my life with. Though God alone knows how *that* is going to work out. Okay, K?"

Kirsten shot her a bleary, off-center smile and nodded. "God. Now *I* feel twelve."

Sean kissed the top of his sister's head. "Long as you don't start sighing about **Bobby** Wang."

"*Wong*, shithead. His name was Bobby *Wong*. And if I hear that name again, I'm going to tell your *fiancés* here all about a certain Giselle —"

"Yeah. No." Sean held up his hands in surrender, but he was grinning. "Listen, Sis, we'll get a real breakfast together. Why don't you go and clean off the plane dust."

Kirsten got up, gave her brother a hug back, and then shuffled off to the bathroom, while Andy got up and walked over to the kitchen.

When the door closed behind Kirsten, Lea turned to Sean, ready to tease him about this Giselle, whoever she was, but Sean was staring at Lea, his expression as serious as Lea could remember seeing it.

"What, Sean?"

He bit his lip, but his gaze remained knife-edged.

Suddenly nervous again, Lea frowned at him. "Sean?"

That night, after the boys had driven into work, Lea and Kirsten were on the pull-out watching *Clueless,* working on their second bottle of Pinot Gris, and getting very silly."Gawd, I wanted those clothes when I was a kid," Kirsten tittered.

Snorting, Lea leaned against the body pillow she was propped up against and said, "You did have a thing for plaid when I met you."

Kirsten poked her. "And *you* had a thing for wearing all black."

"I was in mourning for my life. I was unhappy." Lea tried to say it with a straight face, but couldn't even begin to manage it.

"Yeah, right."

"I got over it. You never went through a goth phase?"

While Alicia Silverstone applied makeup in a mirror, Kirsten actually considered this. "Naw. Well, maybe for a week or two. To try to impress Bobby that Sean was teasing me about." She gave a nostalgic smirk.

"Bobby *Wang*?"

Kirsten's eyes narrowed. "*Wong.*"

Lea grinned. "Same name, you know. Chinese doesn't have a long A sound."

"Well, I know that *now*. When I was in eighth grade, all I knew was Bobby was cute, and always wore eyeliner and black Green Day shirts, and that Sean wouldn't stop givin' me shit about him."

"How in the hell did you find a boy named Wong to get a crush on?"

"Hey! You've lived here. Atlanta ain't San Fran, but it ain't just black and white. First girl I ever wanted to kiss was Tracy Rodriguez." Kirsten's eyes flicked to Lea and then back to the screen. "Guess I always kind of liked people who had more pigment than me. Which is, you know, anyone with any pigment at all."

"You have pigment. Just, you know, in spots." Lea almost touched a freckle on her friend's arm — would have done it a year before — but instead fell back into watching the silly movie, watching Alicia Silverstone's Cher banter with her black best friend Dionne. Who reminded Lea of a less curvy, younger Cherry. Cherry. "So Stacy Rodriguez. How old were you?"

"Gawd. Twelve, thirteen maybe? Freaked me the fuck out. I mean, it was okay that I thought she was cute, 'cause, you know, she *was*, but I started having all of these *thoughts*, you know?"

"Yeah. I know. Being thirteen is hard for *anyone*." Lea looked at her friend. Kirsten was sitting with her knees pulled to her chest. Lea could ask about the first time Kirsten actually kissed a girl, or when Kirsten realized that she had a crush on Lea, but that was probably too direct. So she took a completely different tack. "So Sean. Who was this Giselle?"

That got Kirsten to laugh. "Giselle Beauchamp!" She took a swig of wine. "So there I was, crushing on Tracy and Bobby, and Sean being an asshole about it — about Bobby, 'cause I didn't tell no one about Tracy, ever — and there's this girl in his freshman class that he keeps talking about. And one night I'm coming back from the bathroom and I hear this, um, *groaning* from Sean's bedroom; he's moaning her name. *Well*, I thought, *time for me to pay you back for all the* Bobby Wang *shit*. So I shove open his door and..." Kirsten laughed and turned bright red.

"And?" Lea asked. "And... *what?*"

"And there's my damned brother's naked white ass. He's on his bed, on his pillow, humping away at it, groaning, 'Oh, Giselle, Giselle.'"

"Oh, man."

"Right? So I walked back out, wanted to puke, but the next morning, I told him if I ever heard another word about Bobby *Wang*, I'd tell Giselle he fucked his pillow and pretended it was her."

"Wow. Bet he never said another word."

Kirsten gave a pleased grin. "Nope."

Lea clicked her glass to her friend's. "So what was this Giselle like?"

"Don't know. Never did meet her." Kirsten turned toward Lea. "Bet she looked like you. I think Sean's been in love with you since before he even knew you."

Better, thought Lea and lapsed back into watching the movie.

After a while, when the movie had gotten to a part that she and Kirsten both hated — where Cher and Dionne decide to give a girl a makeover to make her more "popular" — Lea asked, "So you ever do that? Hump a pillow?"

"Say *what?*"

"You know. Use a pillow to masturbate. I used to do that all of the time before I discovered vibrators. Still do sometimes." *Not that I've needed to masturbate....*

"What in God's name —?" Kirsten's expression was dubious and a little embarrassed, but Lea could see the curiosity fighting to come out.

"You know," Lea said, grabbing the body pillow she'd been leaning against, "like this." She threw her leg over the pillow and began to rock her pelvis against the cushion. She cocked her head and looked toward Kirsten.

Kirsten, whose mouth and eyes were open wide. "Uh. Lea? What the fuck?"

"You never did this?"

"No." Kirsten, whose face was turning a pink that Lea didn't think was entirely due to embarrassment.

"It feels good."

"Uh. I bet."

Continuing to grind her crotch against the pillow, Lea pulled her nightshirt over her head.

"Lea. Sweetie. What the fuck are you doing?"

Lea ran her hands over her breasts, tweaking her nipples. "What does it look like I'm doing?"

"Driving your poor friend crazy."

"Well, that's kind of the idea." A shiver passed through Lea. She turned her upper body toward her friend; her pelvis kept moving on its own. "K, I'm trying to make sure that my best friend, who has just had an awful couple of days, gets what she's dreamed of. She deserves it."

Kirsten licked her lips. She was having to work hard to keep her eyes from floating down to where Lea continued to hump away at the pillow. "You... You don't want this. You're not... You don't have to —"

"Let me tell you a story," Lea said, smiling. "Remember when I told you about us going up to the mountains for the wedding?"

Kirsten nodded. Her fingers were clenched in the legs of her pajama bottoms. "Andy's friend. His ex."

"Prior and Cherry. Yes." Holding up her left breast with one hand, she circled the nipple with the fingers of the other, keeping her eyes on Kirsten's, which slowly widened. "The night before the wedding, Andy and Prior... hooked up. Really energetically. And Cherry, Sean, and I could see them. Frotting. Sucking. Fucking."

"Damn."

"Uh-huh. We couldn't decide —" She switched her hands to begin teasing the other nipple. "—whether we wanted to kill them, or whether we were really, really turned on. Both, I guess, but mostly turned on." As the memory flowed back, the raw excitement of it flowed back as well, and Lea felt her labia spreading as she slid them over the satin-covered body pillow. "Sean bent me over, right there in front of the window where we were watching, and he fucked me and fingered Cherry, both at the same time. Cherry started playing with my tits, but then she wanted to feel Sean's cock pushing into me, so she wrapped her fingers around that big, long, cock as it was plowing into me, those fingers of hers pressing up against my pussy, and *fuck,* Kirsten, it felt so good. And then we kissed, me and Cherry...."

Kirsten whimpered. Her nipples were pushing out against her silk PJ top, wide as old silver dollars. She was biting her lower lip.

"I realized, K, that no, I wasn't attracted to Cherry. But that didn't mean that I didn't enjoy having sex with her. I don't know what that makes me, but I know it means that I would be more than happy to give my best friend, who I love with all of my heart, anything she wants. *Anything.*" Lea lifted both of her modest breasts, offering them. Offering herself.

"Sean —?"

"Suggested this. Thought you needed it."

"A-andy —?"

"Said he'd be stroking himself at the thought until he came home tomorrow."

Kirsten gave another whimper, her own, much less modest breasts dancing beneath the blue silk. Her hands raised as if against Kirsten's will, fingers reaching toward Lea's offered breasts, and —

And Lea's phone screamed — a fire truck siren.

A text. An *urgent* text. From Andy. Lea pulled back, though it was not what she wanted to do to poor Kirsten. "Um. That's actually an emergency. I need to get that."

Kirsten fell forward, catching at the air.

"I'm so, so sorry K." Lea was already off the bed, grabbing at her pocketbook. She pulled out the phone and gasped. "Sean's been hurt. Andy needs us to meet him at the hospital."

Any sign of lust evaporated from Kirsten's face. "*Hurt?*"

"That's all it says." Lea pulled on the sweats that she had stripped off earlier that evening. *Oh, God. Oh, God, please let him be —*

"C'mon." Kirsten had thrown a sweater over her PJs and stood, stony-faced, by the door. "Let's go."

Grabbing her keys and her bag, Lea ran over to her friend and gave her a kiss on the lips. "I'm so sorry, Kirsten."

"I know."

Looking up into Kirsten's face, into the grim-set blue eyes and the clenched jaw, Lea was struck by how much she looked like her brother. "Yeah," said Lea. "Let's go."

There is no car ride so long or so short as a ride to the hospital.

Since her own birth, Lea had only been in a hospital twice — both times to visit friends who'd just had babies. This didn't seem anywhere nearly as exciting. It was, in fact, frankly terrifying. Driving well above the speed limit, not knowing whether Sean was even *alive*. Terrifying.

Andy did text once: *Surgery*.

Well. That implied that Sean was still alive.

Lea felt so fucking stupid. Why was she upset? How could she not have seen this coming? She knew her boys bargained with death every day. They danced through burning buildings. They doused overturned tankers. They unstitched tangled metal and stripped away wood and soothed down flame, but death was always nearby. How could Lea ever, *ever* forget that?

Later Lea would swear that the ride lasted five minutes, though even on a quiet night it was a half-hour drive from their apartment to the stocky eight-story building that was Atlanta Medical. The hospital was, incongruously, lit in a lurid rainbow of color.

Neither Lea nor Kirsten paid the bizarre decor any mind. Holding hands, the friends sprinted in through the hospital door. At the front desk, a middle-aged black woman — she reminded Lea of the lady she'd flown out to Atlanta next to, the one who'd been gleefully reading *Fifty Shades* the whole way across the country — directed them to toward the ICU.

There, in the waiting room off of the Trauma ward, Lea and Kirsten encountered a surreal tableau.

Violet O'Connell sat in one of the plastic hospital chairs, her face streaked with tears, her expression indomitable. In her lap, she was stroking Andy's large head while he sobbed. Around her stood three firefighters, still in their turnout gear, their faces stoic and begrimed. Ignoring their nods, Lea slid to her knees and hugged Andy from behind. "You're okay," she found herself crying. "Oh, God, Andy, you're okay."

"Sean!" Andy howled into Violet's knees.

"Shh," said Violet, and Lea found herself echoing Sean and Kirsten's mother, though it was as much to calm herself as to calm Andy. Perhaps Violet was doing it for the same reason.

"Sean's out of surgery," said Joanie, the one female firefighter at the station, "but they won't let anyone in yet."

"What happened?" Kirsten asked.

"Floor gave way," moaned Andy. "Pushed me."

"They were up on the fifth floor of an empty office building on Poplar," Billings said. He was young and black and looked terrified. He'd joined the department only a few months before. "Squatter's cigarette started it."

Captain Olson put his hand on Billings's shoulder. "Fire started on the floor below. If they'd both fallen together, their weight might have carried them all of the way through. Sean probably saved both their lives."

Andy trembled and Lea hugged him harder. Violet's hand trembled in Andy's short hair.

Kirsten gave a shuddering breath. "What happened? To Sean."

"Broken leg, compound," answered Joanie. She blinked at Kirsten. "Banged his head hard. He's been unconscious since Andy here carried him out."

"Thank you, Andy," whispered Lea.

Kirsten echoed, "Thank you, Andy."

"Kirsten?" said Violet. Clearly disoriented, she blinked up at her daughter. "What are you...? Did you...?"

It was frightening to see the preternaturally self-possessed Violet so shaken.

"Surprise visit," Kirsten answered, and Lea could hear a sad attempt at a cheerful tone that made it sound even more miserable. "Was gonna come by the school tomorrow but..."

"Wow," said Billings. The fireman stared at Kirsten.

The captain cleared his throat. "You must be O'Connell's... Sean's sister."

"Yeah," Kirsten said. "Just flew in from California. I'm his younger sister —"

"Kirsten?" The gravel-voiced question hung in the air. Lea looked up to see a man in his sixties — a shock of white hair and denim-blue eyes wide in wonder. "My God, girl. I haven't... You're... beautiful."

Kirsten grabbed Lea's shoulder. "Papa?" She sounded as if she were speaking to a ghost.

"Thank you for coming, Rob," Violet said, barely audible.

The man — Kirsten and Sean's father, whom they hadn't seen since they were children — suddenly grew cold. "Of course I came." He said this without turning to Violet.

"Mr. O'Connell, Mrs. O'Connell," said Captain Olson, "we need to get back on duty. No, Andy, you stay. I think you're needed here more than at the station." Billings and Joanie fell in behind the captain, who said to the room, "Sean's a brave man. A fighter. I know he'll pull through. Good night."

"Good night," answered Lea and Kirsten. Andy was quietly crying again, and the elder O'Connell's seemed to be locked in some silent argument — an argument they'd clearly been fighting for a quarter century.

Trying to break the already strained mood, Lea stood and extended her hand. She was struck that Robert O'Connell was nowhere nearly as tall as his son — was barely taller than his daughter — and was narrow-shouldered, unlike either of them. But those eyes, and the square chin: those proclaimed him as their father. "Mr. O'Connell, it's a pleasure to meet you. I'm Lea. I'm... I'm Sean's fiancée." The last word seemed to weigh down Lea's tongue as it left her mouth.

Those pale blue eyes widened and that look of wonder returned. "His...?" He took her hand. "The pleasure is mine —" He stopped, staring at the ring on Lea's finger. The ring that he had given Violet for their engagement. He continued to shake Lea's hand, but he shot an arctic look toward his estranged wife.

"We... haven't exactly announced it," Lea whispered.

Robert O'Connell left his hand in hers, but it was if she had ceased to exist. "You are my wife, damn it, Violet. I gave *you* this ring. How could you?"

Violet looked up at her husband, a portion of her usual dignity back in place. "You are my husband, Rob, and always will be, no matter what the court said today. But you and I both know that ours has always been a marriage in name only."

"Violet." He said the name like a curse. His hand tightened on Lea's. "I don't give a good God damn what the Supreme Court has to say. Nothing they say will change the fact that you offended me *and* the Lord when you —"

"Supreme Court?" Lea mostly wanted to derail the argument, but she honestly had no idea what they were talking about.

"Mama?" Kirsten asked.

"I'm a lesbian, dear. I have always loved women, though I wouldn't allow myself to see what that meant until your father and I were nearly ten years married. I'm sorry —"

"Violet, damn it!"

"—that I didn't tell you and your brother long ago." She took a shaky breath. "Lea, dear, the Supreme Court ruled same-sex marriage legal today. It is... the law of the land."

Suddenly, Andy was standing behind Violet, his hand on her shoulder. His wide brown eyes caught Lea's.

She slipped her hand out of Robert's grip, but he didn't seem to notice. "Violet," he said, his voice trembling, "don't you dare try to share your —"

"Papa," Kirsten said, standing now next to Andy behind her mother. Robert scowled. "I'm bisexual. So is Sean. If you cared so much about how we turned out, I think you should have been more a part of our lives than a card at our birthdays and Christmas, and a card with a check on my graduation." When her father gaped at her, open-mouthed, Kirsten squeezed her mother's shoulder. "Mama, I'm so sorry I didn't tell you sooner. Sean and I didn't even come out to each other until this year. But I'm so glad you told me. And I know Sean —"

"Excuse me." A very tired looking woman at the entrance to the ICU stood in a white coat, a clipboard dangling from her fingers. "Are you all here for Sean O'Connell?"

Any emotion that might have been washing through the waiting room was swept away by the doctor's thin voice. The five of them all nodded.

"Well, I've got the best news possible at this point, which is no real news. We've just done an MRI on Mr. O'Connell, and there doesn't seem to be any sign of cerebral hemorrhage. He has had a severe concussion, however, and so we are keeping him in an induced coma. Hopefully, once the swelling has gone down, we'll be able to take him off the sedative. We won't know anything for certain until he's woken, but for right now, there doesn't seem to be anything to indicate that Sean is in imminent danger."

The five gave a collective sigh.

"Now, we've got a bit of a full house tonight, and so I'm afraid I can only bring one of you back there. Perhaps one of Sean's parents?"

Lea could feel Violet and Robert both begin to bristle, but before they could say anything, Andy said, "I... don't think Mr. and Mrs. O'Connell would be comfortable with that. Miss Lea here is... Sean's fiancée. Would you mind going back with the doctor, Lea-honey?"

"I..." Lea blinked at the three O'Connells, who stared, square-jawed back at her. "If that's okay with everyone else?"

Robert and Violet gave stiff nods. Kirsten mirrored them, shooting Lea a pleading look that reminded her disconcertingly of earlier in the evening.

Lea walked over to the doctor, who said, "We'll be right back."

The doctor led the way through the door, into a room that seemed to contain more monitors and cables than air. There were beds, each bearing an occupant, each wreathed in a rainbow of —

"Oh, the lights out front," Lea found herself muttering. When the doctor turned her head toward Lea, Lea said, "Sorry. The front of the building. Was that because of the Supreme Court?"

The doctor's eyes, red-rimmed as they were, sharpened their focus. "Yes." She leaned toward Lea, bringing a whiff of a medicinal scent that momentarily returned Lea to the office of her childhood pediatrician. "Hmm. So Mr. and Mrs. O'Connell are divorced?"

"Uh, no. Separated. For twenty-five years or so."

"Hmm." The doctor led Lea to a bed that looked like all the others, but the occupant was larger.

Sean. With a tube down his throat. One leg elevated, splinted, and heavily bandaged. Looking very pale, what little of him wasn't covered in gauze, plastic, or bruises.

Lea felt her knees begin to go; the doctor's surprisingly firm grip held her up.

"Well," the doctor said, "that answers that."

"What?"

"Do Sean's parents know he's queer?"

"*What?*" Though it was difficult to stop looking at Sean, trapped there on the bed, Lea couldn't help but snap her head around to look at the doctor. There was no judgement on her face, just the same air of knowing fatigue. Lea scratched her ear. "Um. Bi. They do now. I think they don't exactly agree about it."

"I bet," the doctor said, giving a sad shake of her head. "Coming out to your folks is hard enough — having it happen like this isn't fun. My folks found out I was a lesbian because me and my..." The woman shook her head and wrote down some notes on Sean's chart. "My wife. Wow. It's going to be nice actually being able to *say* that down here. Anyway, the night I graduated from med school, we went out to celebrate, kind of tested our own limits and things got a bit out of hand. Had to call home for bail. Hard to explain what we were doing at a place that called itself a Bar and Girl." She replaced Sean's chart and gave Lea a weary smile. "So, Lea, I had assumed, based on some physical evidence and on the behavior of the young man who brought Sean here in —"

"Andy."

"Yes. He had to be dragged out of here, wouldn't let go of Sean. Anyway, I had assumed that Sean was gay. But you're his fiancée?"

"It's..." The regular path of Sean's heartbeat on the monitor was mesmerizing: reassuring and terrifying, both at once. "It's complicated."

"I bet. Look, it's none of my business one way or another, but I need one person I can list here as the responsible party. And it sounds as if going to his parents would be a mess. And Andy seemed a bit distraught."

Lea nodded, still watching Sean's pulse on the monitor because it somehow seemed more real than his very still body.

"I don't think there's going to be any need, but Lea, if there are any decisions that have to be made about Sean's care, are you comfortable making them?"

The enormity of that question made Lea's own pulse skip a beat, but she nodded again.

"Thank you. I'll need you to sign a bunch of forms before you leave."

"Sure." Lea's hand reached out of its own accord and touched Sean's shoulder. It was one of the few parts of him that wasn't swathed in bandages or medical equipment. "Is he...? I mean, I know you can't tell me, but is he going to be okay?" By the time she got to the end of the sentence, she was snivelling. Tears flowing. Snot flowing.

The doctor held out a tissue. "Good job. I don't think I could have made it this far without turning into an absolute mess. Look, I don't know. And like you said, it would be wrong of me to pretend that I did. But he's a healthy, strong man. He'll hurt like hell when he wakes up, but there's nothing to make me think he won't be waking up. That's as much as I can say. Okay?"

"Okay." She stroked Sean's shoulder again. "You hear that, Sean? You're going to wake up. We need that, me and Andy. And Kirsten. And your mom and dad. Your dad came. So you need to come back to us. Okay?" She placed a kiss on the small patch of his cheek that was showing. It was frighteningly cool.

They walked back to the waiting room to find Andy, Kirsten, and Violet sitting together, hands clasped and heads bowed. Lea might have thought they were praying, but for Kirsten muttering "Son of a bitch" over and over.

"Where's your dad, K?" Lea asked.

Violet answered, "Robert had to go. He didn't feel terribly comfortable staying."

"Son of a bitch."

"Don't say that, Kirsten, dear. Your grandmother was a very lovely lady."

Improbably, the doctor snorted, which made Lea laugh through her tears.

Once the laughter had settled, the doctor said, "Well, I need Lea here to sign some forms. But then I'd like all of you to head home. Sean's stable and we've made sure he won't be waking up. There really isn't anything for you to do here, and he's going to need your help for quite a while."

"Children," said Violet, "I doubt very much that I am going to sleep tonight, so I am going to stay here. Why don't you head home and I'll call you if anything changes."

Kirsten and Andy both began to object, but Lea could see the logic in what both the doctor and Violet had said. "Come on guys, I'll sign the damned forms, and then let's get home. We'll be back here soon enough."

When they got back to the apartment, Lea looked at Kirsten and Andy, both of whom stood, hollow-eyed, in the kitchen. "Do you guys want a drink?"

They both gazed at her owlishly and shook their heads.

"You want to take a shower, Andy?"

He looked up, and Lea felt as if she could truly see his eyes for the first time that night — desperate, feral, frightened.

Lea ran over and threw her arms around him.

Startled for a second, Andy gasped her name, and then began once more to sob, as Lea held him tight.

Out of the corner of her eye, Lea saw Kirsten shift, saw her begin to move away. Lea was about to tell her to stay, but Andy's huge hand reached out and pulled Kirsten into the embrace. "Please don't go," he blubbed. "All in this together."

And so Kirsten folded herself into the embrace, and for a good, long time, the three of them just stood there together, vibrating. Nothing sexual — just three people trying to reassure themselves that they were alive, and Sean was alive, and that things were going to be, if not okay, at least not absolutely horrific.

Of course, twenty or thirty minutes in, Lea wasn't exactly surprised when two hands found her breasts: one with long fingers and short nails, the other with shorter fingers but long, purple nails.

She looked up at the two of them, very aware of the four-inch difference between her own height and Kirsten's, which somehow made Andy seem even taller.

They were both looking down at her, blue eyes and brown, and as soon as she saw them she knew that what she needed — what they all needed — was touch. Lots and lots and lots of touch. "Guys?"

Their eyes were wide, brown and sky blue, and focussed on her. It was her call. Her lead. Lea's California Jewish roots made her want to talk first, to hem in whatever they were about to do with words.

But Lea wasn't up for *words*. She unzipped the hoodie she'd thrown on and pulled it aside so that those fingers closed around her naked breasts.

Fuck it. Sean had asked Lea to sleep with his sister. Andy had said how much the idea of that turned him on. Sean would understand why they needed this.

Sean...

Desperate to shut out the image of Sean — big, strong, invincible Sean — with a tube down his throat, wrapped in gauze and plastic, his skin so pale that the freckles on his visible cheek seemed to have been picked out in pen... Desperate to shut out the ghostly feeling of his cool flesh on her lips...

Lea pressed herself against them, trapping their trembling hands against her tits, and pushed up on her toes to kiss Andy.

As soon as their lips touched, it felt as if they had broken some cold film that was covering the world like ice on a pond. Heat flowed between them. Andy moaned and Lea, relieved, answered him.

Then, before Kirsten could pull away, Lea turned and pressed her lips to her friend's, and it was Kirsten's turn to moan.

Not the same as kissing Andy, exactly, but not the same as the quick smooch Lea had given her friend before they drove to the hospital, nor the same as the play-make-out kiss Lea had shared with Cherry that very weird night before Prior and Cherry's wedding. There was heat here too, and it made Lea feel a bit drunk, though she was as sober as she could ever be on a night like tonight.

Then Kirsten slipped her tongue into Lea's mouth, bringing out goose pimples, and Andy moaned again; not a moan of longing this time — a moan of pure lust.

It was a sound that Lea knew intimately. Her body was apparently conditioned to meet that sound with a state of absolute readiness. Her nipples hardened. Her pussy lips spread, quickly becoming moist.

Andy's hand slid from Lea's breast, and Lea whimpered in disappointment, but then Kirsten's free hand took its place and Andy's hand slipped down to Lea's ass, encouraging her to turn to her girlfriend.

Well. He did say the idea of Lea and Kirsten making love turned him on. Clearly the idea of seeing it set him on fire. Lea could feel the head of his cock pressing against her bottom rib even through the thick fire-proof pants.

Then Kirsten's fingers closed on Lea's stiffening nipples, and Lea forgot all about Andy for the moment. He would be just fine.

Lea's hands flowed under Kirsten's sweater, under the silk pajama top, finding the soft swell of Kirsten's boobs.

In all honesty, Lea had always been fascinated by Kirsten's boobs. They were bigger than Lea's, there was that (everything about Kirsten was bigger than Lea), and the nipples were wide and pale — though not as pale as the flesh around them. It had never been a sexual thing, not at all. But there was something glorious, truly womanly about them.

And it turned out that touching them was a lot of fun. Soft yet substantial. And the nipples: bigger than a man's, obviously, and slower to rise, but responsive, insistent...

Kirsten bit Lea's lip, and thought disappeared for a while.

After that while had passed, Lea found herself breaking the kiss and staring up into her best friend's eyes — the eyes that were so much like Sean's. They were filled with a familiar cool blue flame.

Andy's hands moved, pulling Lea's hoodie the rest of the way off, yanking the sweater over Kirsten's head. At the same time Lea found that her hands were unbuttoning Kirsten's top and sliding it to the ground.

Growling, Kirsten pulled Lea back up into a kiss, their breasts flowing over each other. In a way that was the thing that drove it home: the feeling of Kirsten's tits sliding against her smaller ones wasn't like anything she'd ever felt with any man. Kissing was kissing — Kirsten, Cherry, Andy, Sean. But *this*...

A small, clear part of her mind congratulated her on being okay with this. On not being freaked out.

Well. Maybe a little freaked out. But more turned on and full of need, and full of the desire to give something to her best friend. And to her fiancé. Her fiancés.

And hell, it wasn't as if this were exactly unpleasant. As far from that as possible.

Now it was Kirsten who broke the kiss, panting, wide-eyed. Pupils dilated. Dark pink from her hairline down to below her nipples. (*Breath quick; bouncing...*) Kirsten started to back away again, but screw that. Lea reached up and ran her fingers along her friend's lips. Kirsten shivered, but didn't back away any further.

Looking at Andy, Lea saw that his pupils too were wide, and the bruised, haunted expression was gone, replaced by one that she knew well: raw desire. She smiled, squeezed the hard-on at the front of his trousers, and led them both over toward the bed, which was still set up for watching *Clueless*.

She positioned them both next to the bed. When they both reached out to her, Lea swatted their hands away and turned them toward each other. She could feel uncertainty from them both, but this was silly; each of them had told her that the other was attractive. She nudged them together until at last they gave in and kissed.

It was amazing how much it seemed as if Andy were kissing a female version of Sean. Lea wouldn't have thought of Kirsten as looking much like her brother, coloration aside; at the very least, Kirsten was very curvy where Sean was *not*. But watching her, Lea realized that Kirsten kissed just like Sean: the same full-body embrace, the same straight-on, un-flinching, nothing-here-but-us kiss. Lea wondered as she knelt beside them whether Sean and Kirsten had ever practiced on each other. She'd have to ask. But not just now: she didn't want to kill the mood. They all needed this.

Gazing up at them, she ran her fingers up their legs, onto their very different asses: Andy's high and muscled, Kirsten's round and gloriously sensuous through the silk PJ bottoms. Lea slipped the hand that had been fondling Andy's bum between his tented trousers and Kirsten's smooth belly. She ripped open the Velcro fly, unzipped the pants and began tugging them down.

Andy shrugged off the suspenders, and down came the heavy turn-out pants. The dark red head of his cock was poking Kirsten damply in the solar plexus.

Kirsten's eyes flew wide and she broke the kiss, staring down. "Jee-SUS!"

Andy growled and pulled her back in for another kiss.

Good boy, thought Lea with a grin, yanking down his boxer-briefs and Kirsten's silk bottoms. Glorying in their shared shiver, Lea reached up, took Kirsten's hand (which had drifted down to Andy's now naked ass) and wrapped her friend's fingers around Andy's erection.

That evoked another shiver, one that Lea shared with them.

Lea had a moment of panic — not about them, they were clearly caught up in the moment — but about herself. A twinge fluttered through her that she was afraid might be jealousy. If it were, that might kill the whole evening, forcing them to confront what was happening to Sean without the drug that was keeping them all sane.

She watched her friend's fingers stroke her fiancé's cock for a moment before realizing that the twinge wasn't jealousy: it was envy. With a smile, Lea leaned forward and gave the head of Andy's cock a lick. As she did, her hands found their way up the backs of their legs. As she'd done a hundred times, she stretched her fingers under their asses to fondle their...

Balls.

Andy had balls, sure. Balls that Lea loved to play with.

Kirsten, obviously, didn't, and Lea gasped when her fingertips slid along Kirsten's slick, fleshy lips.

Kirsten gurgled into Andy's mouth.

Lea hadn't really meant to dive into the whole *playing-with-my-best-friend's-pussy* thing quite so soon. To be honest, when she'd begun her seduction of Kirsten earlier that night, Lea had managed to work her courage up just to the point of feeling okay about Kirsten touching *her* privates. She'd figured that in order for K to get off she'd have to provide some help, but...

But here she was, her thumb on her BFF's asshole, and two fingers thrust along the full length of Kirsten's labia, and a stiff protrusion of flesh quivering between the tips.

Well. In for a dime...

Licking at Andy's glans again as she juggled his testicles, Lea reached out her other fingers just a *bit* further and squeezed Kirsten's clit between the tips.

Kirsten gurgled once more. Andy moaned in chorus.

Lea discovered that, as long as she didn't over-think it, exploring just how to get her friend off was actually kind of fun. Well. A lot of fun. Lea discovered, for example, that Kirsten's clit was much more sensitive than her own. Lea barely had to tickle the little jewel to get Kirsten's thighs clenching and her fingers twitching around Andy's rod.

Just beginning to consider what to do with the thumbs that were had slid into her lovers' backsides, Lea was caught totally by surprise when Andy broke from them. Kirsten too was surprised, apparently, because she began to whine...

Andy, however, was very clear that no one was going to be left out here. He strode behind Lea, picked her up under the armpits, and lifted her until his cock slid between her legs from behind. Startled, off-balance and falling forward, Lea reached out.

Kirsten was there. Lea should have known. She let her legs wrap back around Andy's waist, and her arms locked around Kirsten's neck. It felt a little like the yoga pose her teacher called *Shiva's Dance* — only instead of one leg, both were in the air.

Also, a *lingam* was lodged very emphatically in her *yoni*. It occured to Lea, based on what little she knew about Shiva, that this was probably incredibly appropriate. The grey-skinned god would probably approve.

Lea sure did.

Two pairs of hands were holding her in the air. Andy's were clamped onto Lea's boobs, providing a kind of cantilever, while simultaneously making her nipples hum. Kirsten's hands slid down Lea's belly, so that Kirsten's forearms supported Lea as Andy began to thrust into Lea's pussy.

Also, coincidentally, pushing Lea's mons over Kirsten's searching fingers.

Kirsten, Lea quickly realized, had a very good working knowledge of what to do with another woman's pussy. As Andy slid into Lea, his cock plowing her G-spot as always, Kirsten's strong fingers began pinching and caressing Lea's stretched labia and her vibrating clit.

Lea found herself staring into her friend's eyes in shock.

Kirsten grinned, leaning forward to kiss Lea. Their mouths still locked, Kirsten murmured, "I think I can see the attraction of this whole threesome thing."

Lea wanted to make some witty, smart-ass riposte, but "Uh-huh" was about all she could manage.

Based on the volume of his grunts and the way that his arms were quivering, Andy wasn't going to last long — which was probably a good thing. He began thrusting even harder, slamming Lea against Kirsten, and then, arching back, gave a bellow.

Lea was lifted into the air — it felt almost like flying, though she was still firmly rooted to the earth by Andy's cock and those powerful legs of his. Lea could feel his cockhead pulse deep inside of her, could feel a flood of semen spill out of her around his shaft.

Then, slowly, the flight ended. Andy knelt, panting, until Lea's feet hit the floor once more, and he withdrew from her, splattering all over the backs of Lea's thighs and calves. He stumbled over toward the pull-out.

Kirsten kept hold of Lea, keeping her from falling. "Hey, Leelee."

"Hey, K," Lea gasped, collapsing against her friend, their breasts slipping around each other.

"You guys always so athletic?"

Andy grunted from bed, "Fuck no."

"Good thing," gasped Lea. "We'd probably all be dead."

"Happy, though," Kirsten said. She kissed Lea, walking them over to the bed. When they reached it, Kirsten let Lea pour onto the mattress and stared down. "Um."

"Anything you want, K." Lea smiled up at her friend, knowing it was true. Anything Kirsten wanted — for tonight at least — Lea was happy to give her.

Kirsten's expression grew serious — it was not entirely unlike Sean's I'm-going-to-fuck-you-so-hard look.

Still smiling, Lea looped her legs around Kirsten's waist and pulled Kirsten forward until she toppled onto Lea's sweat-slick body.

"Um." Kirsten gulped. "Okay. Can I...?" She bit her lip.

"Anything. You. Want."

A fierce grin spread across Kirsten's face. "Turn over."

Well. That wasn't something Lea had expected. But sure. Anything. She began to pull her her knees beneath her, opening herself up, dripping pussy and ass...

"Sweet Jesus." Kirsten and Andy said that together. Kirsten took a breath and grabbed the body pillow from the other side of the bed. "Um. Maybe later. I had something a bit... Yeah."

Still on her knees, Lea peeked over her shoulder, over her raised ass.

Kirsten's skin was dark, her eyes wide. "Just... lie on your belly across the pillow."

Grinning, Lea rolled onto the pillow and began humping it, just as she had earlier. Well. Not just. Now she was naked and already fully aroused. The satin felt... *Mmm.*

Kirsten and Andy swore together. "Um, yeah, Jesus, Leelee, just... rest on the damned thing with it under your hips so your ass is in the air. Okay?"

"'Kay, K." Feeling as if she were made of syrup and smoke, Lea rolled onto her belly.

"Damn." Kirsten reached out and ran a hand over Lea's backside. "You do have a gorgeous ass."

"Thank you," Lea said. "And it's all yours for tonight. Well. And all Andy's too." She winked up at him.

He winked back, but he wasn't smiling.

Kirsten placed a reverent kiss on each of Lea's cheeks.

"So, K," Lea murmured. "What do you have in mind?"

"Was thinking of tribbing." Kirsten kissed her way up Lea's back.

"Tribbing?" Andy coughed. "Don't you have to be...?" He demonstrated a vaguely scissors-y pose with his fingers.

Kirsten lay on Lea's back, her full breasts sliding over Lea's shoulderblades. She placed a kiss on Lea's earlobe. "Mmm. I'm glad you haven't neglected their education, Lea."

"Welcome," Lea answered.

"But Andy," Kirsten purred, "there's lots of ways for two women to bump uglies." She pushed up until she was on her knees, straddling Lea's butt. "I have wanted to do this for so long, sweetie..." And then she began to hump Lea's backside, groaning, "You do have a gorgeous..."

Lea would be fine with this — Kirsten sliding her pussy against Lea's ass until Kirsten came. But that wasn't all that Kirsten had in mind. She leaned back, catching herself with her hands and letting her crotch slip just a little further down...

If Lea had thought about what tribbing might feel like (which she hadn't, really), she'd have guessed it was kind of like dry-humping together — not unlike what Lea had been doing with the pillow. Rubbing her clit against something that felt nice.

It *was* that, obviously — though Kirsten was doing all of the rubbing. But the feeling of Kirsten's pussy sliding against Lea's, it wasn't at all like humping a pillow, or fingers or even dry-humping Sam, her high-school boyfriend. It was warm, and slippery, and when Kirsten's clit bounced against Lea's, it felt as if lightning had set her crotch alight.

Also, it was Kirsten. There was something mind-scrambling about that, for sure.

It was a gentle climb to bliss — from Lea's perspective at least. She could feel the orgasm meandering up her spine as Kirsten ground their clits together.

Andy, serious as always, still looked a bit like... Well, like a man who's woken up in the middle of a sexual fantasy. He was stroking his cock back toward full erection.

Lea looked over her shoulder. Kirsten was arched back, her breasts shiny with sweat, rippling as her pelvis rocked against Lea's ass. This was her fantasy too. *Nice.*

And Lea was certainly enjoying herself. Enjoying herself immensely, feeling the blood build up in her pussy. And all she had to do was lie there. Relaxing. *Nice.*

So relaxed was she, in fact, that it took her a second to notice when Kirsten slowed and then disengaged, leaning back over Lea's back and panting Lea's name.

"Hmm?"

"Can I lick you, Leelee, baby? I've always wanted to do that too."

"Sure."

"Only, I've already come twice, and as amazing as that felt, its kinda exhausting."

"Sorry." Lea reached a hand back and squeezed her friend's butt. "I'd love you to eat me." As Kirsten began to slither back down the length of Lea's back, kissing each vertebra, Lea looked up at her boy. "Hey, K. You want Andy to fuck you while you eat me?" When Andy's jaw dropped, Lea winked at him again.

It was fun to reach those rare moments when Kirsten was speechless. After lying there for a moment, her breath tickling Lea's open pussy, Kirsten stammered, "Um, y-yes? If you —?"

As she'd known he would, Andy streaked over to Kirsten on his hands and knees. "Want to," he grunted. "Please. Gawd, please."

Kirsten nodded, and Andy whipped out a condom, rolling it on.

Lea grinned and let her head fall back onto her hands. "You on your belly, K?"

"Yup."

"Then I think you're about to get a really nice surprise."

Andy thrust into Kirsten with a low growl of lust.

Kirsten answered him with a shocked *"Ohhh!"* followed by a very content *"Oooooo."*

The first time Andy had fucked Lea from behind — the first time they'd fucked — the feeling of that down-curved erection of his on the sensitive front wall off Lea's pussy had been a revelation. "Feels good, doesn't it?" she sighed.

"Fuck... yes!" groaned Kirsten, and then lowered her mouth to Lea's bottom and...

And Lea got a quick blast of just how talented her best friend was with her tongue.

Sean and Andy were both great at licking Lea to climax. Brilliant. To be honest, she'd never been patient enough to keep dating a man who couldn't get her off with his mouth. Even Asshole John had been very proficient, even if he'd been a complete jerk about it, teasing her on the edge of orgasm until she was weeping for release. Even her first boyfriend, Sam, had gotten pretty good at it.

But Kirsten...

Part of it was the simple fact that she was smaller than most of the guys that Lea had dated. The flamelike dance of Kirsten's tongue was a much more fine, delicate feeling than any of her boys had ever evoked — even Kirby Takahashi, who was smaller even than Kirsten, when it came to that, and who was the most proficient cunnilingist Lea'd ever met...

Even he...

Lea found that her fists were clutching spastically at the comforter cover, and that very, very loud sounds were erupting from deep inside of Lea — from the point where Kirsten's unbelievable tongue had set Lea's already aroused pussy aflame. The movement of that *tongue*, combined with the rhythmic pulse of Andy's pounding moving Kirsten's face against Lea's bottom, it was all...

Lea had become a connoisseur of mind-blowing orgasms since she'd moved in with Andy and Sean. She'd grown to recognize dozens of different ways that their ministrations unleashed the bliss inside of her.

This... This was a new one.

It felt as if Kirsten were a glassblower, and Lea the molten lump of goop at the end of the pipe — well, Kirsten's lips — and the licking and nibbling was slowly inflating Lea, making her awareness expand and begin to clarify, until suddenly a final kiss from Kirsten's lips transformed Lea's consciousness in to a perfect, transparent, infinitely fragile globe. She was aware of everything. She understood everything.

And then, as is the way of such things — both orgasms and glass — the bubble burst, and Lea was plunged into darkness.

When she came to herself, Lea was on her side. Her pussy was still wet and pulsing.

She watched the two faces: Kirsten on the body pillow, Andy's tilted up toward the ceiling. Their eyes were open but focussed *elsewhere*, their mouths slack. Lea found herself smiling at the pure, esthetic beauty of it.

And she found herself grateful that they seemed, like her, to have lost themselves in the oblivion of the fuck, to have let go of worrying, for the moment, about the one person who wasn't there.

Sean. Sean should be here.

Taking and releasing a deep breath, Lea kissed the two as they continued to groan away, rolled off the pull-out and walked on rubbery knees over toward the kitchen.

She wanted to grab a glass and have some water. but the strap-on hanging by its harness from the cabinet pull... That got her thinking again.

Sean. You should be here. I love your sister, but I wish...

Feeling a pulse of agreement — knowing it was her imagination — she took down the strap-on.

Maybe...

She snorted and shook her head, but still stepped into the harness and began to pull it up.

Sean needed to be here. (She gasped as the back of the double dildo slid into her.) And maybe she could bring him here for a bit.

Fuck it. A degree in theater with a psych minor had to be good for something, right? She grabbed some lube from the counter. (*Should buy stock in the company...*)

As she walked back toward the bed, her purple dong wobbling in front of her, Lea had the very odd feeling of being much larger and heavier. She sauntered behind Andy, who was straddling Kirsten's thighs, pounding into her her raised pussy for all that he was worth.

She loved watching Andy's butt while he was fucking. It was a true piece of art. And something she'd never have seen if they hadn't been in a *ménage à trois*.

Lea reached out and touched that beautiful, bright red ass and said, "Hey now, Andy-boy. Slow down there or there won't be any left for me."

Andy and Kirsten both gasped — at her voice? at her touch? — and froze.

It was eerie; she'd meant it as a kind of joke, but the voice that had come out of her mouth had truly sounded like Sean's. The same cadence, the same timbre — though a couple of octaves higher. Andy and Kirsten both looked around, eyes wide.

Trying to smile at them, though she had goose pimples all over, Lea sidled up behind Andy, her legs outside of Kirsten's. "Hush," she murmured, still in that Sean voice. "I'll bring y'all on home."

She squirted some lube into Andy's ass and slowly, gently pressed in.

Panting, trying to stay relaxed, Andy still gave a wordless cry when the head of her cock pushed through the ring of muscle. He arched — not enough to disengage, but enough to thrust harder into Kirsten, and now it was her turn to groan.

"This is going to feel good, Kirsten," said Lea (and it was her own voice now). "Shh." She continued to push in, her hands gripping Kirsten's hips for balance.

She, Andy, and Sean loved to fuck this way. Well, they loved to fuck just about every way. But this was a wonderful, intimate, gentle position, one that they all loved after they'd spent their energy on more fanciful, athletic configurations. A sandwich. And it didn't matter which position you were in — the one on the top, providing all of the thrusting necessary for both cocks; the one in the middle, fucking and being fucked, or the one on the bottom, feeling both of your lovers pour themselves into you — it was always a magical experience.

It was this time too.

As Lea began to pump into Andy's backside, pushing his cock deep into Kirsten, Lea watched those goose pimples march from her skin to theirs. She reached around and began to play with Andy's tiny nipples.

Panting, he reached down and began to do the same with Kirsten's, but Lea had a thought. She knew that Andy's fingers could be unbelievable, magical while he was fucking, and so she urged his hands down toward Kirsten's crotch.

When Kirsten began to whimper at the absence from her breasts, Lea reached one hand past Andy and took his place, playing with her friend's gently rippling breasts.

"*Oh, Jesus!*" Kirsten gasped. "Jesus, Jesus, *fuck me!*"

"Yes, ma'am," Lea answered, and picked up her pace just a bit.

Andy threw his head back onto Lea's shoulder. "God! Aw, *GOD!*"

Well, it's always nice to get your lovers calling out to God. But that wasn't the person Lea wanted them screaming for — not Andy, any way. She carefully sank her teeth into Andy's neck as she'd seen and felt Sean do hundreds of times — not trying to draw blood, just letting you know that someone else was fully in control.

Andy tensed, but Lea kept fucking him, harder now, hard enough that Kirsten was pushing back, her own fuse clearly lit. Lea could feel a tremor roll through Andy's chest as his breathing lost its rhythm, could feel his arms clenching as he continued to diddle away at Kirsten, the good boy.

Kirsten was arching against him, her breasts bouncing against Lea's fingers. "*JESUS. FUCK. JEEEEESUS!*" She let loose a throaty, high shout that Lea had heard many times — though never from the same room

And that was all it took: Andy arched too, trying to push as deep into Kirsten as he could, and he screamed to the ceiling, "*SEAN!*"

And then Lea released her teeth from Andy's throat, and both of them collapsed, panting, onto the bed.

Thanks, Sean, thought Lea, panting too. And she was about to slide on top of them both, kiss them both, and —

And Lea's phone rang. Again.

The sirens. Again.

She stumbled off of the bed and pulled her phone out of her bag. "'*Lo!*"

"Lea, honey," said Violet O'Connell's calm, cultured voice. "I'm so sorry I woke you. But Sean's waking up."

Looking over at Kirsten and Andy, who were gaping at her, still panting, Lea shot them a hopeful smile. "We'll be right there."

As quick and as long as the drive had seemed on their first trip into the hospital, it seemed infinitely quicker and longer now. As the three of them stumbled through the rainbow-lit facade of Atlanta Medical, Lea was aware that they were even more disreputable looking now than they had been the first time. She could only be thankful that the hospital smelled like a — well, like a hospital. Because otherwise, she knew that she, Kirsten, and Andy would be very fragrant indeed.

As they ran out of the elevator into the Trauma unit waiting area, they found Violet and the same doctor standing, looking much more animated than they had earlier that evening. "We took him off the thiopental about an hour ago," the doctor said, almost bouncing on her sneaker-clad feet. "Sean's EEG showed signs of increased activity even with the drug, and those have only gone up since we took him off. Your Sean is strong as an ox."

"Yes, ma'am," said Andy, eyes tearing up again. Lea and Kirsten both hugged him.

The doctor strode back into the ICU, promising to let them know if anything changed, looking somehow less tired than she had when Lea had first seen her.

Violet was crying too, but smiling.

"You okay, Mama?" asked Kirsten.

"Never better," said Violet, but then looked down.

Lea's breath caught. "Violet?"

Sean and Kirsten's mother squared her shoulders and looked back up — looking much more like herself. "I feel," she said, "as if I'm walking around without any clothes on. I've spent my whole adult life afraid that my children would find out that I am, you know..." A brief sigh, squelched with determination. "And now everyone knows, and the only person who seems to care is you're father, Kirsten. And he already knew."

"Son of a bitch," muttered Kirsten.

Her mother shushed her, but she was laughing.

Seeing that made Lea think for some reason of Gus's painting of Violet — of Violet and Sally, his wife. Laughing. "Sally."

Violet's eyes widened and her laughter stopped.

Seeing the confusion in Kirsten and Andy's faces, Lea spluttered, "Um, Gus's wife Sally left him and... And their lover Frank. She lived with a woman for almost a year. Broke up the woman's...!"

Violet nodded. "Yes. Sally."

"Aunt Sally?" Kirsten's eyes too were wide, now. "I remember her! She was real funny, and had all that *red* red hair. Didn't she stay with us after Papa...?"

Violet seemed to be fighting the urge to look down again. "Sally was the *reason* that your father left, Kirsten, honey. She was the first woman I was ever..."

Violet blushed. Violently. "Well. Ever *intimate* with. First woman who understood what was happening to me. The only woman I've ever been with, to be honest."

"But... Mama, *why*? You were only, what, forty?"

"Because I was still married. Because I was a mother first. And because by the time you and Sean had grown, it felt... selfish."

"Mama." Kirsten stood tall, giving a very good Violet O'Connell impression, though she was already far taller than her mother. "Mama. It's time for you to be selfish."

They all stood there, contemplative. After a while, the doctor came back in. "He's awake. Groggy, but awake. And he'd like to see you." She held up her hands to ward off the stampede that the visitors were already starting. "We've taken away some of the gear, but I can still only have two of you back there at a time. Okay?"

The four of them all looked around, blinking.

Violet, whose color was still high, said, "Perhaps Miss Lea —"

"No, Violet," Lea said. "Andy and I can wait. I think he needs to see his mom and his sister."

Mother and daughter looked at Lea, then at each other, and then they followed the doctor into the ICU.

Andy and Lea stood there. He fidgeted, eyes locked on the door.

"Andy, what?" Lea wrapped her arms around him. "Are you really worried that he's going to be angry with you or something?"

Andy sighed. "Yeah."

"What, about letting him fall?"

"Nah. He'll just be happy he got me out of the way. Asshole."

"Like you'd feel any diffently."

"Well... Yeah. I guess." He kissed the top of her head. "It's just... I fucked his sister."

Lea looked up into his face. He seemed to be serious. "Uh, so did I, remember?"

"Fuck, yeah, I sure as hell remember that. But, see, you'n'Kirsten, that's a fucking wet dream —"

"Not for Sean!"

"I guess."

"Andy. Baby. Sean asked me to let Kirsten sleep with me because it was what she needed. Do you think he'll be upset with you because you did the same?"

He grimaced. "Yeah. I guess not. But... It was what *I* needed.... What I *wanted*, anyway. Gettin' my rocks off while he's lying here — feels selfish, you know?"

"Stop sounding like Violet, Andy." When he pouted down at her, she laughed, pushed up on her toes, and kissed him. "It'll be okay. If he's upset, I'll just keep knocking him out until he forgets the whole thing."

"Hey!" Now he was laughing too.

The door opened. Kirsten and Violet came through, holding each other and sniffling, but smiling.

From the doorway, the doctor said, "He asked to see you two."

They followed the doctor, who was looking a bit tired again, back to Sean's bed. The breathing tube was gone, and some of the monitoring equipment was folded away. Sean's leg was still elevated, his head bandaged. But his blue eyes were open, and his raw lips bent up as they approached. "Hey," he rasped.

Andy let out a sob, leaned forward, and kissed Sean on the mouth.

"Ow," said Sean, but he kissed Andy back.

The doctor turned away, making notes on her clipboard.

Then Andy stood back and it was Lea's turn — she touched her lips to Sean's chapped ones as gently but as gratefully as she could.

"So," Sean whispered when she too stood back, gazing down at him, "smells like y'all kept Kiki busy. Thanks."

Lea and Andy both shuffled there.

Sean. Sean was okay. Lea felt tears finally beginning to come again. Andy sniffled.

"Hey," Sean rasped. "None of that."

Lea wiped her nose. "We're happy you're going to be okay."

"Me too." He smiled again, but his eyes were drooping. "Hey, guys, know what?"

"What?" they answered together.

"Once I'm outta here? What you say... we have a wedding?" And then he closed his eyes, though he was still smiling, and drifted back into sleep.

Seven weeks later, Lea woke up in the big pull-out alone.

That was fine. She'd had plenty of company over the past few months — more than her share, even she was ready to admit.

But the day was going to be a long and difficult one — an exciting one, but still, Lea would have loved...

"Hey, Leelee," croaked Kirsten, stumbling out of the room that had been Andy's, her blonde hair tangled in a spectacular bedhead. "You ready to get those boys hitched?"

Stretching, Lea smiled. Her boys were getting married. "Yup. Let's go do it."

When they arrived at City Hall and took the elevator all of the way up to the roof, where the ceremony would be taking place, Lea was shocked at the crowd that had already assembled.

Kirsten chuckled at her friend's gasp. "Yeah. No one wanted to miss it." Then she gave a small sigh. "Well, almost no one."

Lea had expected just the two grooms, herself and Kirsten as witnesses, and Sean's mom — oh, and Lea's parents, who were waving to her from the crowd assembled around the flower-bedecked arbor at the far end of the beautiful roof-top garden. But it looked as if at least a dozen of the firefighters from the station had turned up in their dress uniforms — many with their significant others. Prior and Cherry too were waving at Lea, and next to them stood Andy's whole family. Actually smiling and waving as well. (Not Danielle and her family, though. Interestingly, Andy's oldest sister seemed to be having the hardest time of his relatives reconciling herself to the whole idea of her brother marrying another man.) And standing next to Violet were Sassy and Gus. They too were waving, Sassy sardonically as ever, Gus with his usual brilliant smile.

Lea was stunned.

"Hey, baby," said a low voice in Lea's ear, making her jump.

"Sean!" She spun around.

Sean and Andy were standing there in matching morning coats and white ties. They looked gorgeous. Then again, Lea thought they always looked gorgeous. Sean smiled crookedly at her, so that the now-barely visible scar above his left eyebrow winked in the sunlight. "Yup."

Andy grinned. "Just texted Ms. Carter to let her know we're all here. She should be up in a minute."

"I can't believe the crowd!"

The men both nodded. Andy said, "Yeah. Thought maybe later, but not now."

"Nervous?" Kirsten asked.

"A bit," her brother answered, to which Andy added, "Fuck yeah."

Behind them, the elevator door opened behind the boys and Ms. Carter, the officiant from the clerk's office, stepped out. "Oh, my!"

"Quite a crowd," agreed Sean, smiling but pale.

"Well, how wonderful," the clerk said. "Are you ready, gentlemen?"

They both nodded very seriously.

"Then let's not keep your fans waiting!" For a very bland-looking, grey-faced woman, Ms. Carter was apparently someone who thrived on having an audience. She strode down the aisle toward the arbor, waving and shaking hands with the babbling crowd.

As soon as the five of them reached the front of the crowd however, everyone became suddenly very serious.

Ms. Carter nodded to them and they took their places, with Sean and Andy facing her, Kirsten at Sean's side and Lea next to Andy.

The crowd behind them grew silent. Lea could here the traffic in the street eleven stories down.

"We are gathered together here in the presence of these witnesses," said Ms. Carter with a nod to Kirsten and Lea, "to join these men in matrimony, which is an honorable estate, and is not to be entered into unadvisedly or lightly, but reverently and discreetly. If anyone can show just cause why these men may not lawfully be joined together, let them speak now or hereafter remain silent."

This silence was rich and full. Lea had to work not to turn around and look at Nadine Harris — but was pleased that, whatever she may have been thinking, Andy's mother kept it to herself.

The clerk continued, her thin voice carrying far better than it should have, "Sean, do you take this man to be your wedded husband, to live together in the estate of matrimony? Will you love, honor and keep him, in sickness and in health, as long as you both shall live?"

Taking a deep breath, Sean said, "I do."

"Andy, do you take this man to be your wedded husband, to live together in the estate of matrimony? Will you love, honor and keep him, in sickness and in health, as long as you both shall live?"

"I do." Andy was fighting back tears.

The clerk then led them through their vows — all of the usual stuff, no New-Age-y flourishes for these boys: *for better and for worse, for richer and for poorer, in sickness and in health.*

No more sickness for a while, please, *the agnostic Lea prayed.*

Andy began openly to cry.

"Take hands, gentlemen," said Ms. Carter, and they did. "For as much as Sean and Andy have consented together in wedlock and have witnessed the same before this company, and thereto have given and pledged their troth, each to the other, and have declared the same by joining hands."

Tears were dribbling down Sean's cheek too. He and Andy gripped their huge hands together as if they were getting ready to arm wrestle.

"Now, by the authority vested in me by the State of Georgia and the Office of Mayor of the City of Atlanta, I pronounce you to be married and extend to you my best wishes for a successful and happy married life together."

Oh. Damn. *Now Lea was crying.* Why do people cry at weddings?

"A personal thanks for granting me the honor and privilege of extending the marriage rites to you on this wonderful day. Ladies and gentlemen... may I present Misters Sean and Andy... Krakowicz."

Already weeping, Lea felt her jaw and stomach drop. They'd taken *her* name?

"You may kiss."

The audience cheered.

As they drove to Sean's childhood home, Lea laughed, "Mr. and Mr. *Krako-wicz?*"

"Thought you'd like that," said Andy, still sniffling.

"Didn't want to leave you out," said Sean, tears dry, nose still pink, but crooked grin firmly in place.

"Yeah," laughed Kirsten, who was driving, "like the two of y'all would *ever* leave Leelee out."

Sean tugged on his sister's carefully coifed hair. "No making fun of me, my husband, and the woman we love."

Andy blew his nose and said, "Actually, we're thinking about kids. So's there's never any question."

"Oh." Lea hadn't even gotten that far in her brain. "Thank you, guys."

"Hey. It's *your* name," laughed Sean. "Thank *you*."

They pulled up in front of the O'Connells'. Kirsten chuckled. "Y'all ready for act two?"

As they walked through into the back yard, Lea fought down what she recognized as stage fright. Silly. She knew how this turned out. She took off the grey jacket she'd worn to the boys' wedding, leaving her in the strapless white dress that Kirsten had helped her buy — that Kirsten insisted on calling her Marilyn Monroe dress, though Lea was very aware she was no Marilyn Monroe, and, anyway, there weren't any subway gratings nearby to push the skirts of the dress up.

The whole crowd was streaming into the back yard: everyone from the rooftop wedding, plus a couple of Lea's and Kirsten's friends from college, a couple of Lea's cousins, and a few family friends of the O'Connells. Kirsten whispered into Lea's ear, "Ready?"

When Lea nodded, Kirsten kissed her on the cheek and waved at Lea's mother, pointing at the *chuppah* that they'd set up on the back lawn.

Lea's mother started clapping rhythmically, and many in the crowd took it up, gathering around the ceremonial canopy.

Then Sean stepped into the *chuppah* next to Lea's mom, wearing a white *yarmulke* and prayer shawl, and Lea's breath left her body completely.

Lea's father chuckled into her ear, "No passing out. You don't want to keep Sean waiting."

Lea shook her head. *Also,* she thought, *grass stains would be a bitch to get out of this dress.* "Daddy?" she whispered, "you're okay with this?"

"Sweetheart," her father sighed, placing a kiss on her brow, "I've never seen you so happy. How could I not be okay with that?"

And then a solo flute — played by a former girlfriend of Kirsten's — played the wedding march, and Lea's father walked her up the aisle toward Sean.

As she walked around him seven times under the *chuppah*, what Lea was thinking about was how many times she'd dreamed about this bit — how many times, after one of Sean's visits to California (once she'd diddled away the sexual tension) she'd day-dreamed about marrying him. Sometimes she'd visualize a city hall wedding (though nothing as beautiful as Andy and Sean's), sometimes in a vaguely imagined church service, but usually under the sky. Under a canopy.

Lea's mom, the tantric JewBu, had begged to officiate, since a rabbi isn't required in a Jewish wedding. Most of what she did was — at Lea's insistence — traditional: the seven blessings, mostly. She'd insisted on reading the racier bits from the Song of Songs and singing "Sunrise, Sunset." Mostly on-key.

At least she'd kept her clothes on. Lea still shuddered, thinking of her mother's version of a coming-of-age ceremony, which had been part *bat mitzvah*, part Native American spirit quest, a lot of talking about the Goddess and the power of the feminine divine, and all of them — Lea and a bunch of middle-aged women — running around the woods naked.

Lea looked up into Sean's deep, deep, pale blue eyes. *Oh, yes*, she found herself thinking. *I could look into those for the rest of my life.*

Another sexy bit from the Song of Songs (*Let him kiss me with the kisses of his mouth!/For your love is better than wine./Your name is like ointment poured forth;/ Therefore the virgins love you*) and suddenly Lea's father was kneeling, placing a knapkin-wrapped wine glass at her and Sean's feet.

Holding her hand, Sean grinned at her and mouthed, *One, two, three!*

They stomped on the glass and the crowd — the Jewish ones, at least — cried "Mozel tov!"

Sean pulled Lea off her feet and gave her a kiss that left her breathless and made her wish everyone would just go away for a half an hour.

Everyone but Andy, who was cheering on Sean's far side as Kirsten cheered on Lea's. Andy she wanted to stay.

Eventually, Sean put her down and grinned down at her, his *yarmulke* tipped far to one side. "Mrs. Krakowicz."

She grinned up at him, panting. "Mr. Krakowicz."

Violet came up and kissed Lea only a little less fiercely than her son. Kirsten settled for a kiss on the cheek, but her wink let Lea know that Kirsten had been thinking of kissing Lea every *bit* as fiercely as Sean.

Andy, however, pulled Lea up into a fiery — though brief — smooch that raised a couple of the guests' eyebrows. The ones who weren't aware of just how complex a wedding this was.

Lea's parents, who were both beaming, had provided a light kosher lunch — none of that pickled fish crap, Lea had insisted and gotten: felafel, hummus, tabouleh, and pita chips; chicken and egg salad finger sandwiches; baklava for dessert. The crowd milled happily, eating, chatting, and wishing Sean and Lea well. She decided that *mazel tov* should always be spoken in a Georgian drawl.

The whole fire house contingent were very boisterous, sipping California wine (and passing around a flask or two, Lea was pretty sure), slapping both Sean and Andy on the back, telling them they were very lucky men.

Joanie, in a lovely dress — the only firefighter not in a Class A dress uniform — gave Lea a hug and whispered to her that she was a lucky bitch.

Lea could only laugh and agree.

Even Jack Miller, the asshole, made a point of congratulating the three of them. Sean whispered to her as Miller walked away that Miller's wife had left him the previous, and he was a wounded puppy.

"No one deserves it more," muttered Andy, and Lea couldn't in good conscience disagree.

Lea's parents circulated, but a knot of the older crowd eventually congregated around them: Violet, the Harrises, Gus, and Sassy, who Lea could swear was just about to break out in something like a smile at any moment.

The only person who didn't seem to be having a good time was Jessie, Andy's middle sister, who picked glumly at her hummus, standing behind the *chuppah*.

"You okay?" Lea asked.

Jessie shrugged and then gave Lea a smirk that reminded Lea very much of her brother. "Weddings," she sighed. "Since I left Booger, they make me feel all... funny."

"Oh. I bet." Lea pointed surreptitiously at Andy and Sean, who were talking to their fellow firefighters, and then to herself. "Are you okay with *this*?"

The smirk soured, but then Jessie shook her head as if to straighten it again. "Would it matter if I wasn't? Andrew's... happy." Now she began to sniffle. "Like Pa said, a blind man could see he loves the both of y'all... and that y'all love him."

"Yeah," agreed Lea, and then handed her one tissue after another as Jessie began to cry.

Wish I could help, *Lea thought.* Wish I could make you as happy as I am.

Eventually, the crowd started to thin. Most of Sean's childhood friends and Lea's classmates gave them hugs and kisses. A couple of her own distant cousins handed Lea envelopes that she would later discover had checks in them.

Once the only remaining guests were those who had been at the morning's wedding as well, Prior tapped his glass. "As the best man for the *next* wedding, could I ask all of y'all who are coming to the last stop in this progressive weddin' party to get going?"

In the car on the way up to Andy's Blue Ridge Mountain home, Lea noticed that Sean was pensive. "Something wrong?"

Andy laughed. "Wrong? What could possibly be wrong? He's *married* our asses!"

Lea and Kirsten laughed with him, but Sean just smiled. "Just wish... I know it's stupid, but I wish Papa could at least have come to *one* of the ceremonies."

Lea expected Kirsten to mutter "son of a bitch" again — but instead she drew an envelope from her bag.

Sean snorted. "A *check*?"

"Hey," said Kirsten, somber for her, "it's a bigger one than I got for graduation. But there's a letter too."

Sean gawked. "You're shitting me. I thought that was against his religion."

"Apparently not. He asked me to give it to you after you'd married them both," Kirsten said, and held it out to her brother, even though he was driving.

Shaking his head, Sean said, "Read it."

"You sure?"

When he nodded, she unfolded the letter, handing the check to Lea. "*Dear Sean,*" she read:

> Thank you so much for inviting me to your wedding
> services. I hope you understand that I cannot in good
> conscience attend, not because I disapprove of you or of
> the choices that you have made, or because I disapprove

either of Lea or of Andy (who both seem lovely and clearly love you very much), or that I do not care about you or your happiness, but because as a man who has done his best to follow those precepts laid out by his faith as good, proper, and moral, I know that I could not attend without blackening a day that I hope will be the brightest of your life. I cannot do that to you, any more than I can endure myself the moral distress.

The day of my wedding to your mother was the third happiest day of my life, after the days of your and your sister's births. I know that this may not seem possible to you, but I love your mother still. I left because as angry as I was (and am) with her for turning her back on her vows to me and to God, I did not want to abuse her, either by venting my fury, or by forcing her to continue to live in a manner that she assured me was nothing but a lie.

When I came to the hospital after you were hurt, your sister, who seems to have my temper rather than your mother's, told me in no uncertain terms that I should have been more present in your lives. I can see that that is true. Please, Sean, forgive me. As I said, I stayed away not because I did not care, but because, in a way, I cared too much. For me, my absence from your lives has felt like a form of penance. Nonetheless, I have been thinking about this, and have come to realize staying away from you is one of the more shameful things I have ever done.

I know I cannot ever make up for two decades of my non-presence in your life, and Kirsten's. However, once you, Lea, and Andy have gone through your weddings, I hope that I may come and speak with you, and come to know you at least a little. I spoke with your mother about this. She grants that it would be a good thing, even now.

You are probably very angry with me, and with good reason. I have spent much of my adult life lost in wrath. It is self-serving, then, to say this, but trust me: do not waste your love on anger. Our Savior teaches us to love our neighbor as ourself, to turn the other cheek. I thought that I understood these precepts; I am discovering only now how very difficult but how very important they are.

In any case, I wish you nothing but joy on your wedding day, and hope that my letter has done only a little to darken it.

Please give my best good wishes to your wife and your

husband.

Love,

Robert F. O'Connell, Jr.

"Holy fuck," gasped Andy.

The rest of the car ride they passed in silence.

At the Harrises' house, the moveable feast was increased by the presence of Andy's friends and family. They all gathered in the back yard as the Indian summer sun began to dip toward the ridge across the valley, bathing the proceedings in golden light.

This service was a much more traditional one in every respect except that it was performed by Captain Olson, who turned out to have been a mail-order reverend and had officiated a number of his colleagues' weddings, and who, once he understood just how complicated Sean and Andy's situation was, said that it would be his honor to preside over the wedding of Andy and Lea.

It was a beautiful service — a beautiful day for it. There were bridesmaids (Andy and Sean's sisters and Cherry) and groomsmen (Prior, Sean, who'd changed into his Class A's, and two of the other firemen), a flower girl (a cousin), and an old Hammond organ played by another cousin (one with a mullet and an axe-like face that he tried to hide behind a scraggly beard). Both of Lea's parents walked her down the aisle this time. She wore her mother's old veil and carried a bouquet gathered by Davy and Nadine.

Prior (who Sean had insisted be Andy's best man) read Lea's favorite passage from scripture, from the Book of Ruth, and Jessie (who Lea had asked to be her maid of honor) read another bit from the Song of Songs — one of the less racy bits, this time (*Set me as a seal on your heart,/as a seal on your arm;/For stern as death is love*).

And Captain Olson gave a sermon on the sanctity of marriage, on how it was something larger than the individuals who entered it — and on how marriages, like snowflakes, are unique. That it is up to the participants to discover how best to serve their marriage.

He then led Lea and Andy through the exchange of vows — they were old pros at this point — and (for the first time that day), in the exchange of rings.

"You may kiss the bride," Captain Olson proclaimed, just as the sun set fully, and Andy gave Lea a smooch that was every bit as scorching as Sean's had been earlier that day.

"Mrs. Krakowicz," he murmured into her lips.

"Mr. Krakowicz," she murmured back.

The party began in earnest then.

The organ player turned out to be a kick-ass musician and a gravel-voiced, bluesy singer, serenading them with old R&B classics as tables and chairs and enormous amounts of food began to appear as if by magic.

As everyone helped set up the feast, Lea, Andy, and Sean snuck into the house, up to Andy's room, with its bunk bed and fire pole. Andy pulled the third ring from his vest pocket, and, together with Lea, placed it on Sean's finger. Then the three of them engaged in a passionate three-way kiss.

Lea had begun unzipping both men's flies as they were lifting her dress — revealing the very lacy, very almost-not-there undies she'd bought just for them — she was working at finding somewhere in her body to stuff the two erections she could feel growing against her belly, and —

And Nadine's cheery voice called up the stairs: "A-a-andrew! Le-e-ea! Your guests are looking for you!"

"Coming, Ma," Andy said through gritted teeth. They all fumbled their clothing back into something like presentable condition.

"Fuck," grumbled Lea.

"I wish," one of the guys muttered, which unfortunately struck all three of them as hysterical, so that — even though they carefully re-entered the back yard seperately — Lea was fairly sure that most everyone was sure that the bride and groom had snuck off for a quickie, in the grand old traditions of weddings.

If they only knew.

Evening was beginning to fall; even this late in the year, some lightning bugs cast their glamour around the edges of the crowd.

The organist had gained a band at some point, and continued to lay down an impressive medley of scorching old rock and blues. It was the perfect soundtrack for a Southern sunset.

Conservative Nadine Harris may have been, but it was clear that she knew how to throw a party. The music and the food were hot, the beer was cold, and all were plentiful. Dancing, drinking, and eating fed off of each other. Everyone seemed to be having a blast — everyone except Jessie, who moped at the head table, which was the one facing the darkening twilight, and Miller, who was getting quietly drunk amid the increasingly rowdy crowd of firefighters.

Lea was blissfully sweaty, just having surrendered her husbands to their sisters (Kirsten and Danielle) on the dance floor, when Captain Olson appeared before her, chest bedecked in medals, silver-and-black hair just slightly mussed. "Captain!"

"May I have this dance?" he asked, extending his hand.

When the band shifted to a slow ballad, she curtsied and allowed him to sweep her back into the dance area.

He was a really good dancer.

"Thank you, Captain. It was a beautiful ceremony."

"You're very welcome, Lea. And please, you're married to not one but two of my boys. Call me Pat."

"Of course. Pat." She smiled up at him.

He smiled back. "And thank you, Lea. You're very, very good for those two. At the very least, I don't think they'd have ever done anything about their feelings for each other without your help."

"You were aware...?"

He smiled at her. "Please. I work with this boys. I live with these boys. I'd have had to be stupid not to. Not that I was going to be as much of a dick about it as Miller. But yes, I knew. So, yes, it was my honor to come to all three these lovely services. And my pleasure to officiate this evening. I owe you, Lea. If there's ever anything I can do for you..."

Staring at the rest of the firefighters, a deliciously nasty thought occured to her. "Capt... Pat. Do you see Andy's sister Jessie up at the head table?"

"The one who looks like someone peed in her beer?"

"Yup. Um. I know that a couple of the guys came without dates — Billings, Miller —"

"Me for that matter," said the captain.

"Really? I thought the blonde —?" With her chin, Lea gestured to a woman in a low-cut blue dress who was sitting at the firefighter table.

"She's a friend of Joanie's. *Really* a friend — Joanie has been very clear about that. Giselle's got a thing for firemen, apparently."

"So does Jess... Did you say her name was *Giselle?* Is it by any chance Giselle Beauchamp?"

"I think so, yes."

"Wow." Lea laughed and shook her head. "Well, Jessie. She's a bit blue — she got divorced last year — and she kind of had a thing for Sean. Which I feel badly about. And. Um. I happen to know that her fantasy is... Um. Being with two guys. Two firemen."

Pat laughed. "God. She must hate you."

"Well, I think she's working on trying not to. Which is why I kind of was hoping..."

"You'd like to make her fantasy come true."

Lea nodded sheepishly.

"Hmm. You're a very nice sister-in-law."

"Thank you."

They danced for a moment. Pat's eyes never strayed from the head table.

"I think," he said, "that I can make that happen. In fact, I'll see to it. Personally."

"Really?!" She blinked up at him. "Lucky Jessie."

"Well," he laughed, "lucky me. We'll see, but I may still owe you that favor, Lea."

The song ended and he bowed to her formally. Still staring at Jessie, he meandered over toward the firefighters' table where he chatted with Joanie and Giselle, who laughed at something he said. Then he turned (*Oh, God, not Miller!*) to Billings, who had also just stepped off the dance floor and was looking much less *young* than he had at the hospital. Billings's eyes flew wide, and he glanced up at the head table.

Oh, yes, thought Lea, *lucky Jessie for sure.* Grinning now, Lea began to make her way to her sister-in-law, but was waylaid by another sister-in-law — in all honesty, her *favorite* sister-in-law.

Kirsten threw her arms around Lea from behind, so that Kirsten's ample bosom bounced against the backs of Lea's shoulders and Lea's own, less ample bosom was nearly squeeze out of the strapless dress. "Where the hell do you think *you're* going, Leelee!"

"I was —"

"Well, whatever it was can wait. You are gonna dance with Kiki!" And with that she pulled Lea back out to the mosh pit — not a slow dance this time, it was something that sounded as if the guitarist had taken a chainsaw to his instrument.

They bounced up and down together, waving their arms (Lea trying to remember not to lift them too far; she didn't want to flash all of her new relatives) before Lea screamed up into her best friend's ear, "Want me to tell you a secret?"

"Sure!" Kirsten looked manically, wildly happy in a way that Lea hadn't seen her since Kirsten had shown up from California.

"See that blonde over at the firefighters' table, the one next to the captain?"

"Uh-huh!"

"Guess what her name is." When Kirsten simply gawked at Lea, Lea laughed and whispered loudly into her friend's ear, "Giselle. Giselle Beauchamp."

Kirsten grabbed Lea's arms. "YOU. ARE. FUCKING. KIDDING. ME!"

"Nope. And see Billings and the captain talking?"

Kirsten's face took on a wide-eyed *What next?* expression.

"They're going to show Jessie a good time."

Kirsten's jaw dropped.

"That's what I do for sisters-in-law that I like."

"Yeah? Well... What are you gonna do for *me?*"

Looking at her skeptically, Lea *hmm*'ed. "I *guess* I like you." When Kirsten started to huff, Lea laughed. "I love you, K. You know that. So. What do want? Two men? Two women? One of each?"

Kirsten kept blinking. "I...? I get to *choose?*"

Lea nodded.

A goofy smile spread across her friend's face. "Uh. The one of each thing was kind of amazing."

Lea pulled Kirsten into a tight hug and giggled into her ear, "Well, that's 'cause one of them was *me,* silly."

Kirsten squealed in a way that told Lea she was blushing like a beacon. "Well, yeah. But having your *husband* bang me from behind, licking away at your juicy —"

"Cherry! Prior! Have you met Sean's sister Kirsten?" Lea spun her friend around to face the couple, who froze in the middle of some sort of dance that looked like it would have been a *lot* more fun with clothes off.

Prior stared at Lea, his dark face slack and gleaming. Cherry smiled as if they were chatting at a tea party — though her nipples looked as if they might jump off of her chest — and said, "Only in passing. Lovely to meet you, Kirsten."

Lea glanced up at her friend, who was gawking at the attractive black couple. Cherry was curvier than Gianna or than Lea — nearly as curvy as Kirsten herself — but Kirsten *had* said she liked folks with more pigment than she had, and Cherry and Prior certainly fell into that category. As the music soared to yet another cacophonous crescendo, Lea said, "Kirsten's my very best friend, and hasn't got a date tonight. I was thinking maybe you guys could entertain her."

"Entertain?" asked Cherry.

"Uh-huh. Remember the game we played the night before your wedding, Cherry?"

Cherry snorted. "Never Have I Ever?"

"No," Lea said, smiling. "The one after that." The one where you, Sean and I boffed while our then-fiancés fucked down in the garden.

Now Cherry's jaw too dropped. "Uh..." She whispered something in her husband ear. Grinning, he nodded.

"K, do you think Mr. and Mrs. Lawrence could show you a good time?" When Kirsten just stared, Lea goosed her.

Snapping out of her reverie, Kirsten said, "Um. Cherry. Prior. I think Lea here has told me a bit about this, um, game, and I would *love* to play it with you."

The three of them looked for a moment as if they might go at it right there. Lea laughed and did an internal victory dance, feeling like the Fairy Godmother of Threesomes. "Now, guys, don't disappear on us just yet."

"No," said Prior, who was grinning at Kirsten. "We got to drive you and your *husbands* to y'alls honeymoon suite."

Lea quirked an eyebrow. "Honeymoon suite?"

Cherry batted her husband on the shoulder. "Hush. It's a surprise, Lea-honey. Don't you worry, we ain't going nowhere."

"And," Prior added, "we would love to entertain Miss Kirsten here in the meantime."

Lea left the three of them dancing — Kirsten shot Lea a wide smile and a thumbs-up — and made her way over to where her parents were laughing with the Harrises. It was a bit disconcerting to see Davy Harris laugh at all, but Lea's mother was chatting away, touching Andy's father's blacksmith shoulders, telling some sort of joke that probably made no sense at all in the mountains of Georgia.

Oh, fuck. She's flirting with him. Panicked, Lea shot a glance at Nadine Harris — she too was smiling brightly, however — not the pained, exaggerated smile that Lea had gotten to know so well earlier in the summer, but a genuine grin. Her hand was resting on Lea's dad's forearm. *Oh. FUCK.*

Lea forced a bright, bridely smile. "Hey, guys!"

Nadine's smile broadened. She turned and kissed Lea on the cheek. "*Mazel tov!*" She mispronounced it, but honestly, Lea was deeply touched that Mrs. Harris would say it at all.

"Thank you." She kissed her mother-in-law back. "And thank you for the wonderful reception. It's fabulous."

Davy Harris grunted a *You're welcome*, his eyes glistening. It was an eloquent statement for him.

"Hey, Daddy, can I ask you something?" Lea said, pulling her father to a quiet spot near the kitchen window.

"Congratulations, Lea-leh." Her father kissed her. "I always told you you'd find the man for you."

"Thanks," Lea said, pleased but unwilling to be deterred. "Daddy, you and Mom are *not* going to have an orgy with my in-laws."

Michael Krakowicz grinned. "Now, honey, that's certainly not anything we're planning. But Nadine, Davy, your mother, and I are grown-ups, the last time I looked."

"And they're *really* traditional. I'm still amazed that they've let me, Sean, and Andy back into their home, let alone have one of our weddings here."

"I think they'd surprise you," said her father with a smug grin. "And Nadine has been asking all about *those wild California wife-swapping parties* she's heard about."

"Oh. Daddy. God." Lea knew she was being hypocritical — that she had become even more of a poster child for non-traditional marriage than her parents. But still... "Just don't... I have to look these people in the face."

"Well, if Violet, Nadine, Davy, your mother and I can look at our children and not think about how you spend your evenings, I think it's fair to ask the same of you."

Lea scowled. "Oh, fine." She could see the fairness in that. Still... "Just. Yeah. Try not to leave them feeling like they need to keep their grandchildren out of the State of California."

"Grandchildren?"

It was a pleasure to get her unflappable father off balance. "Hypothetical grandchildren."

"God, Lea, don't give an old man a heart attack."

"Uh-huh. Then don't start making out with Nadine Harris while anyone can see it."

Lea's father, the professional arbitrator, got his negotiating grimace on. "Fine," he said, finally. "Deal."

She kissed him, releasing him back to the fluttery attentions of Andy's mom, and walked over to where Sean's mother was talking with Sassy and Gus. "You guys having fun?"

"Oh, yes," said Sassy, who was indeed smiling, much to Lea's astonishment.

"We have been discussing the unusual nature of your marriage," said Violet, "and Gus has been telling us about his own... *ménage.*"

"Of course," Gus burbled, squeezing Violet's hand, "we couldn't formalize it, not even in the ingenious manner you and your gentlemen devised."

"Well," Lea sighed, "it's still not as if we're all legally married. And it's not as if most of the folks here have any idea that this was the third wedding of the day, or that they wouldn't run screaming into the night if they did know."

"No," Violet said, "but we have a *very* clear idea of just how real it is."

"And just how wonderful," added Sassy, taking Violet's hand.

Oh, thought Lea. *Oh, wow.* "Thanks. I think I'm going to go find my husbands." Lea wasn't quite sure what she was seeing here, but she wished them well with whatever it was.

Sean and Andy were over drinking at the firefighters' table. Their collars were undone, their color was high, and they looked absolutely edible. Lea walked behind them, threw her arms around their necks, and kissed each of them on the cheek.

"Lucky bitch," Joanie said, but she was grinning.

"Where's the captain?" asked Miller, who looked thoroughly drunk. "Gotta drink a toast to the married... uh... yeah."

"He's out dancing," Lea said, pointing out to where Captain Olson and Billings were sandwiched around a bright-faced, grinning Jessie.

"Huh," said Andy.

Lea kissed his ear, and then whispered, "I asked Pat and Billings to show your sister just how lucky a bitch I am."

Andy huffed. *"Damn."*

Sean raised an eyebrow, which reminded Lea of something. "Hey, Joanie, have you introduced your friend to my boys?"

Joanie looked at Lea as if trying to figure out what angle she was playing and then shrugged. "Sean, Andy, this is my college friend Giselle."

Sean choked on his beer. "Giselle?" He stared at the woman. "Giselle *Beauchamp?*"

Giselle, who had been looking a bit bored, perked up. "Yes?"

Lea laughed. "Sean here apparently had quite a crush on you in high school." She shot a wicked smile at her husband. "Kirsten was telling me *all* about it."

Sean turned bright red.

"You *did?*" asked Giselle. "God, I wish I'd... Wait! Sean O'Connell? We had Math and Spanish together?"

Still blushing furiously, Sean nodded. Andy and the other men laughed.

"I remember!" Giselle was beaming. "You were always staring at my tits and I kept wishing... Well... *damn,* Sean. You filled out real nice!" Now it was Giselle's turn to blush.

Joanie grinned and patted her friend on the arm. "Gigi here has always had a thing for firemen."

"She has?" Miller sat up.

"Yes, Jack, she has." Joanie shook her head. "God knows why."

"Oh, Giselle," Lea said with a snort, "I *totally* get that one!"

They all laughed and gave a toast to women who had a thing for firemen.

The band took a break not long after — they'd been playing non-stop for hours, and the crowd all settled for a bit.

Lea found herself looking at her husbands and wondering just how long they had to stay. And where this *honeymoon suite* might be.

When she asked the boys, they smiled at each other and then at her in a manner that stoked the little flame in Lea's middle up to a low boil. "You got something you want to do?" Sean asked, grinning lazily.

"Uh-huh."

"Well," said Andy, his smile more evil than their husband's, "your carriage awaits. Let me go tell Prior."

"Prior?" Lea wasn't sure what Prior had to do with anything — but then remembered that he'd said he was going to drive them.

A few minutes later, Prior tumbled into a chair next to Lea. Cherry and Kirsten both stood behind him, already looking thoroughly debauched from the dancing. "Y'all ready to leave?" he asked.

Lea and her men nodded.

"Well, then!" Prior stood and, as he had done that afternoon, began tapping a glass."Ladies and gentlemen. The bride and groom are going to be leaving." Prior squeezed Sean on the shoulder apologetically. "Appreciate it if y'all could gather in the driveway to see them off."

Everyone stood, some of them clapping, and began to make their way out around the side of the house. Andy held one of her hands. Sean had his hand placed subtly around Andy's shoulders.

A warm hand grabbed Lea's free one. It was Jessie, face glowing with excitement.

"Hey, Jessie!" Lea squeezed her new sister-in-law's hand. "You having a good time?"

Lea didn't need to see Jessie's emphatic nod to know she was, but it was nice to see. "Lea-honey, did you set this up for me? 'Cause if you did —"

Lea shook her head — a small white lie. "Pat just asked me what you'd think of some... company. The rest of it is just you." Well. Maybe not so small. But one Lea didn't mind telling.

Jessie narrowed her eyes, "Uh-huh. Well, I take back every awful thing I ever said or thought about you, Lea." She shot a look to the two firemen who were walking beside her, looking very happy to be there. Jessie leaned closer to Lea. "It's just... I don't know..."

"Nervous?"

Jessie shrugged and shot the two men a smile. She whispered, "It's just... I ain't had nothing 'tween my legs in over a year that didn't run on batteries." She giggled — a disconcerting sight in a six-foot-tall, broad-shouldered thirty-year-old. "I don't know if I... if they're gonna..." She ran out of steam, settling for a pleading look.

"You'll do just fine, Jessie. Let them make you feel good. Make them feel good. Trust me," Lea said into Jessie's ear, "the reality will be even better than the fantasy." When Jessie just stifled another giggle, Lea squeezed her hand again. "And I didn't know you were a *Firefly* fan!"

Now Jessie just frowned. "Firefly? Like... lightning bugs?"

Lea laughed. "Never mind."

They rounded the corner of the house. There, standing ready, was in fact a carriage — well, a horse cart, decorated with flowers.

"Wow!" Lea gasped. "I guess you weren't kidding about the whole *carriage awaits* thing!"

"Nope," said Andy, stepping up into the cart and holding out a hand to Lea. "Wasn't kidding."

As Lea joined Andy among the flower-bedecked hay bails, Prior slid up onto the driver's seat and called out, "Time for the tossing of the bouquet and the garter!"

The crowd whooped; Kirsten handed up Lea's bouquet. "You gonna try to catch this, K?"

"Abso-fucking-lutely!"

"Then get ready!" When Kirsten leapt off the running board, Lea turned her back to the crowd.

"Ready! All the single ladies," Prior sang. "Lea — one, two, *three!*"

Lea heaved the flowers back over her head and heard what sounded like a war break out behind her. When she turned around, she saw that she'd sent the bouquet off to the side. A disgruntled scrum of twenty- and thirty-something women parted to reveal...

To reveal Sassy, holding the flowers with a look of such astonishment on her face that Lea couldn't help but laugh.

"Now, all the guys!" called Prior — and as she lifted her foot onto one of the hay bails, Lea noticed that most (though not all) of the men shrunk toward the sidelines.

"If you guys don't have more balls than that," Andy crowed, "y'all don't deserve the chance to see up my wife's dress!" He lifted the skirts of the Marilyn Monroe dress, which had managed to hold up remarkably well. Wide-eyed, some of the more prurient males scooted back front and center.

Sniggering, Andy lifted the hem of the dress to reveal the blue garter on Lea's left thigh — borrowed from Cherry, so it covered two of the *something borrowed* items (the dress was new and the veil she'd worn had been her mother's). Pulling down the garter with one set of strong fingers, Andy began to stroke the other hand up toward Lea's pussy.

She'd known he was going to do something like that. "Andy," she whispered in her sultriest voice before his fingers found pay dirt, "keep going and everyone here — your folks, my folks, the kids — is going to get a first-hand view of what a screaming orgasm looks like. Go ahead. If that's what you want."

He stopped, his mouth open, his eyes wide in a look of absolute wonder. "God, I love you."

Behind him, Sean and his sister laughed.

Andy glared at his husband before standing up. "Ready?" he called, and before the gawkers had turned their faces away from the inside of Lea's thigh, he shot the garter like a rubberband out over the crowd. A couple of the younger guys scattered, laughing, but not Miller, who was facing away, trying to chat up Giselle. He felt the lace hit his head, grabbed at it with his hand, and then gawked when the whole crowd began to cheer him.

"Hey, Sassy!" Lea called, "shall I introduce you to Jack Miller?"

The whole crowd broke up in laughter.

Sassy answered, "I don't think that will be necessary, Lea, dear," and they all laughed again.

Miller stood sheepishly, holding the garter as if he were afraid it would bite. Then Giselle said something to him that turned him bright red and made Joanie throw her head back and laugh.

Andy said, "Sorry, Jack. Guess you're on your own."

And with that, they waved goodbye, and Prior clucked the horse to a walk.

Once they'd rounded the bend and were headed away from what Lea knew to be the center of town, she asked, "So, where are we going, husbands mine?"

"Told you!" Cherry called from the seat beside her husband, "it's a surprise!"

Then Sean climbed back and gave first Lea and then Andy a smooch. From his jacket, he pulled out a length of thick, white silk and held it up in front of Lea's eyes. "Trust us?"

Suddenly speechless, Lea nodded, and he tied the blindfold on.

They rode for what felt like an hour, chatting and laughing — though Lea found that she was very quiet. Eventually, her boys began kissing her, their hands wandering intoxicatingly over her skin — her chest, up her skirt, down her arms, but never quite touching anything that might actually light her fuse. She began gasping and moaning into their mouths before she understood — the day she'd locked them up. The day Kirsten showed up. "Payback?" she whispered into one of their mouths.

"Uh-huh."

"Yup."

"I... don't mind," she sighed. "Take your time."

As they continued to tantalize, Lea tried to listen to the night around them, just to keep from going insane. Birds and crickets sang. There was kissing going on in the front of the cart — Lea thought it was Kirsten and Cherry, but she was sure Prior was involved in there somewhere.

After an eternity of teasing bliss, the cart rumbled to a stop.

"Holy —!" said Sean. "It looks *amazing!*"

"Thanks," Cherry said.

Prior continued, "Thought maybe gettin' married might be a good time to finish the danged thing."

"Is this... your house?" Lea gasped as one of the boys' fingers brushed the seam of her tiny panties. "Can I — *huh!* — see it?"

"Later," Sean said. "The surprise isn't done."

"Oh."

They helped her down off of the cart, Sean holding one arm and Andy the other. Lea heard the gate squeak open, and they walked her forward, but not all of the way to the house. After a dozen steps they stopped.

"Put out your hands," Andy said, and when she did, they snapped a pair of handcuffs around her wrists.

She gasped.

"If you want to stop —" Sean said.

"No," Lea gasped. "Please."

"Huh," grunted Sean, and gave her one of his universe-encompassing kisses, replacing all of the air from her lungs with flame.

They turned her, and walked her off of the path. *Where* —? But then they had her step up and lifted her arms, snapping the handcuffs to something above her head, something metal. That's when she understood. Wrought iron. "The glider?"

"Uh-huh," said Andy, kissing her quickly before they both stepped off the glider and left her swinging there.

"Guys?" She knew she was safe, but it was hard not to feel —

"We'll be right back. Gotta get... ready for you."

"Oh. Okay."

And she heard them stride off toward the house. There was a burst of laughter from the others, and then the door closed, and she was alone with the crickets. Alone with her crotch and her nipples buzzing with need, her hands cuffed above her head. She fought the urge to rub her thighs together to try to get her off.

John the Controlling Asshole had done this kind of thing to Lea all of the time: tying her up in his bedroom or her bedroom or once the office that he shared with two other programmers. He'd leave her there until she was actually frightened that he might leave her there all night, might leave her there for Kirsten or his officemates to walk in on her. He'd wait until she was weeping before returning, nibbling her until she was just on the edge of coming, fucking her, and then finally releasing her.

This didn't feel anything like that.

Lea was filled not with anxiety but with anticipation.

She trusted Andy and Sean.

She loved them.

She just wanted them to come back and fuck the hell out of her.

She heard the front door of the house open and close. Steps crunched up the gravel. "S-sean? Andy?"

The steps grew closer.

"Guys?"

Two very low, very feminine voices recited together:

We will rejoice in you and be glad;

We will extol your love more than wine.

Rightly do they love you.

"Cherry?" gasped Lea, and the glider rocked as she twisted toward them. "Kirsten?"

It rocked again as the two women stepped onto the swing. "We're your hand-maidens," murmured Cherry, stepping behind Lea.

Kirsten's voice was breathy, though she seemed as always to be holding in a laugh. "We're getting you ready for your *men*." Her fingers brushed Lea's ribs through the bodice of the Marilyn Monroe dress, and Lea shuddered.

Cherry unzipped the back of the dress, which slid down Lea's body, pooling at her feet. "No bra?" Cherry asked.

"Nope," Kirsten murmured. "But don't you love the undies?"

"Sure do."

"I helped her pick them out." Kirsten's voice was coming from somewhere around Lea's bellybutton.

"Nice." Cherry's came not far from Lea's ass. "Why don't we take'em off."

In response, Kirsten purred and began to pull the lace thong down.

Lea gasped, twisting in her chains so that she was now facing the other way.

"Mmm," said Cherry. "Waxed and everything. What a sweet little cookie you got, Lea." And she tasted the cookie in question, making Lea gasp again.

"I helped her with that, too," Kirsten said, "lucky girl that I am. But I got to say, I'm mighty happy to get another chance to taste this amazing backside." And she began to apply her flamelike tongue to pleasuring said backside very, very thoroughly.

Sean and Andy had gone down on her together many times, and Lea would have gone to her grave swearing that the feeling of their tongues on her pussy, her ass were unlike anything else she'd ever experienced — and she still would have sworn that. But the feel of Cherry's tongue tentatively but thoroughly exploring her clit while Kirsten's much more confident, amazing tongue danced tarantellas of flame around the sensitive flesh of Lea's asshole — it wasn't *better* than having Sean and Andy eat her, that was for damned sure, but it sure as hell was mind-bending.

Four hands found Lea's breasts, and any thought of comparison disappeared.

Some timeless time later, footsteps sounded on the gravel and Lea bucked in surprise, shocked to find her legs around Cherry's neck.

Sean? Andy?

"Y'all got her nice and ready? Sure looks like it." It was Prior's high, smooth voice.

"Hnh," Lea answered, and her tormenters laughed.

Cherry asked tartly, "You want to check our work?"

"Don't mind if I do," chuckled Prior, stepping onto the glider so that it swayed with his weight. His big, strong hands touched Lea's belly and the small of her back. "You mind, Lea, ma'am, if I check how well they done?"

Lea tried to say something like *No, thank you for asking, that would be just fine,* but it came out as an incoherent string of consonants.

Prior clearly understood, because his hands slid down to both her slits, front and rear, slipping through the saliva and juices they were slick with and finding with remarkable quickness her clit and her asshole. His hands were calloused, but smooth and *big,* and the feeling of them stroking the sensitive spots that Cherry and Kirsten had been teasing so exquisitely — it was almost more than she could take. She screamed, and it was only her leg-lock on Cherry's neck and Prior's grasp on her pelvis that kept Lea from flailing completely out of control.

"You know, Lea," growled Prior, "if it's okay with my wife and your husbands, I'd sure like to see if I can get you to make that sound a hell of a lot more. What you say?"

"I... say... *fuck yes!"*

Prior kissed Lea on the ear, squeezing her cunt lips between his fingers, evoking another scream. Lea could smell the unimistakable scent of her men's cum wafting from Prior's chin.

"So, Prior," Cherry said, lowering Lea's legs from her shoulders, "you get the *grooms* all ready, or are they gonna pop like corks at the sight of this sexy lady."

"Oh," said Prior, unaccountably shy, "I made sure they're ready to give Lea here all she needs. Why don't y'all go in and send them out here, and I'll keep Lea here company."

With a swish of satin and silk, the women stood, causing the glider to rock again. Lea could hear their feet crunching back up the path to the house. "No dippin' your wick, Prior Lawrence," called Cherry. "Lea there belongs to Sean and Andy. And *you* belong to me. And to Miss Kirsten here."

That brought Kirsten's distinctive cackle.

"Yes, dear," answered Prior, and Cherry's laugh joined Kirsten's.

Prior moved around behind Lea, his fingers still moving over her cunt, but his long, thick cock taking the other hand's place between her butt cheeks. "I will take you up on that promise, though, Lea," he whispered in her ear, letting his erection slide up and down her crack. "Some day soon, I'm gonna fuck you till you scream."

"P-promise?"

"Promise." He let go of Lea, and she couldn't help but whimper.

But then she heard two heavy sets of footsteps coming from the house.

"Andy? Sean?" she called, out loud this time, and this time they both answered, "Here, baby."

"Thanks, Prior," Andy said. Lea heard them kiss.

"Oh, my pleasure, man. Really. My pleasure. Now, you folks have yourself a ball. No one to listen for a mile or more but me, my wife, and Kirsten, and I think we're gonna be inside making our own noise."

"Yeah," Sean laughed. "I'm not thinking about that. But thanks, all the same."

Prior laughed too, and then Lea could hear him walk back to the house, closing the door.

Still Lea was alone, strung up on the glider, a sacrifice for the taking.

Still they did not join her.

"Guys?"

"Do you have any idea," sighed Sean, "just how amazing you look there, all slick and wet, like some river sex goddess?"

"You know," Andy added, "I usually hate it when you get all poetic, Sean. But this time, I got to agree with you."

They both stepped onto the glider, and it began to rock. One man took Lea's right hand, and the other took her left, moving the cuffs binding them apart on the metal bar overhead so that she was facing the front of the swing, rather than the side. It made her stand on tip-toe.

They moved around her; she could *just* feel their cocks, stiff and wet-tipped, brushing her belly, her back.

Sean groaned, and Andy answered him. Sean said, "We meant to tease you as long as we could — get you begging for it, you know?"

"But I don't think you should have to wait no more," Andy said, his fingers flowing over her belly, her breasts.

"And I don't know that we can stand to wait either," added Sean. "So, Mrs. Krakowicz. You ready for us to consummate this marriage?"

"Please."

Sean stepped into her, lowering his mouth to hers, letting his hands move down below her butt cheeks, so that he could help her lift her legs around his waist. Andy helped steady them, holding Sean's cock in place as Lea lowered onto it with an open-throated howl that echoed through the surrounding pines.

Sean began to thrust — but slowly. It was only after a minute that Lea was aware that their thrusts were causing the swing to glide back and forth.

It felt like she was fucking the ocean.

Lea turned her head back, and Andy's mouth too found hers. Impatient, she began flexing her ass against his cock, but he just said, "Shh," and began to let his fingers play with her asshole.

That was pretty okay too.

"Behold, thou art fair, my love, behold thou art fair," Andy murmured in one ear, while in the other Sean sighed, *"Until the day break, and the shadows flee away, I will get me to the mountain of myrrh —"* He squeezed her ass with one hand. *"— and to the hill of frankincense."* The thumb on the other hand slid down over her smooth, hairless mons and began to circle her clit.

Lea arched, opening herself to them, so that Andy's finger pressed into her anus.

Their marriage was about much, much more than amazing sex.

But it was awfully nice that it had that too.

A *slurp* of lube announced that Andy was preparing his cock to join Sean's inside of her.

Amazing sex. All through these hills, there was lots of it going on. Jessie Harris was hopefully getting the fuck of her life from two hunky firemen — not as hunky as *Lea's,* but more than hunky enough. A muffled giggle told Lea that Kirsten was trading pleasure with Prior and Cherry, and Lea had enough personal knowledge of all three of them to be certain that their night would be epic. Lea's folks and Andy's were probably playing games that neither she nor he would want to think about. Lea had a good idea that Sean's mom and Lea's boss were up to something — possibly in the company of sweet old Gus, though that was another scene Lea wouldn't want to spend too much time imagining.

Hell, Lea even had a pretty good idea that Joanie and Giselle had been planning to help Jack Miller, recovering asshole, get very lucky indeed. Though Lea was also pretty sure that it would be part play, and part object lesson in how to treat women.

Cousins. Friends. Co-workers. People were fucking gleefully all over these mountains, screaming and grunting and sighing and swearing and crying and laughing. And —

And Andy slid into Lea's ass, filling her completely — making her feel truly complete — and she knew that as much pleasure as all of these people were experiencing (and she hoped that they were feeling a hell of a lot of it), none could come close to the joy that she and her husbands were feeling.

The boys kissed over Lea's shoulder, and then kissed her. They found a slow, steady rhythm with their thrusts in time with the rocking of the glider — small, unrelenting. Titanic.

Neither of the men showed any signs of being in a hurry, thanks, Prior. (*Did he suck them both into his mouth at the same —?*) The rolling, two-beat fuck moved through Lea, setting her slowly aflame, the heat spreading out from her pussy, her ass, her breasts, her lips, her...

As was often the case, the pleasure made Lea begin to weep, to feel as if she were becoming wholly liquid. *"Awake, O north wind; and come, thou south,"* she murmured, *"blow upon my garden, that the spices thereof may flow out. Let my beloved come into his garden, and eat his pleasant fruits."*

"Oh, Jesus, Lea-baby," groaned Andy as his cock thrust at last all of the way in and his balls danced with Andy's against Lea's bottom.

Fighting to maintain the steady swing, Sean grunted, "We'll eat... your pleasant fruits."

Still crying, Lea laughed now, feeling the still-distant orgasm peeking over the horizon, filling the sky. And as her sightless eyes filled with the immeasurable light, Lea knew that this moment was eternity. Heaven on earth.

Many waters cannot quench love, neither can the floods drown it.

Listening to the rising sounds of passion issuing from her loves' throats and from her own, to the satiny sound of skin sliding against skin, Lea knew without any shadow of a doubt that she was no visitor to this place.

Wherever Andy and Sean were — that was her home.

THE END

(for now!)

Goddess: The Visitor's Wedding

Jessie waved at Andy and her new sister-in-law as they rode away in the flower-decked cart, and she found herself trying not to think about the men at her elbows. Jessie hadn't ever been exactly overburdened when it came to male companionship. Booger barely counted, and they'd been divorced for over a year — all but for forever before that — and besides him…

Beside her, two men — men — in dress uniforms stepped forward, each taking a hand.

Jessie's middle flipped, then flipped again.

The horse cart bearing Jessie's brother and his bride — and their husband, for God's sake, and his sister, not to mention Cherry and Prior — turned the corner, and as it disappeared, Jessie could just make out Andy's teeth closing on Lea's ear, and that did funny things to Jessie's middle too.

"So, Jessie," said the older one, Pat, the captain, who looked more like George Clooney than any man Jessie had any right to be near. "You're looking a lot happier than you did this afternoon."

Smiling at him, Jessie tried to say something cute or clever but all that came out was a kind of wobbly Hmmmm!

On her other side, Billings, young, black, and sweet as honey, squeezed her hand. "Nice wedding. Easy to be happy."

"Three nice weddings." Jessie laughed, fighting down the panic brought on by the two very different hands holding hers. "God." Not even thinking about it, Jessie began to lead the two men back toward Pa's shed, where she'd led Booger so many times back when they were kids — away from the house, from prying eyes.

But tonight there were dozens of Harris cousins and guests laughing and drinking. Prior's brothers, passing a blunt around. Deacon…

Something stronger than panic began to grip Jessie's middle.

The men didn't seem to notice. Pat was chuckling. "Well, three nice weddings. And unique. Can't say I've ever seen anything like it."

"You okay with it, Jessie?" Billings whispered.

"Okay?" Jessie was struggling with the image of Deacon Lawrence after Prior and Cherry's wedding. Him passed out on her bed upstairs, dead drunk with his pants halfway down. And her, kneeling there between his knees, ready and raring to go, left to take care of herself. Again. Humiliating.

Deacon hadn't said a word to her since.

Not that she could look him in the face.

The other guests were laughing and her cousin Billy had started playing "Devil with the Blue Dress," but Billings continued, still whispering, "Okay with Andy, and Lea, and… You know."

Sean.

Andy and Lea and Sean.

"Oh, yeah" said Jessie, not sure at all how she felt about it, but only having enough room in her head for Jessie and Pat and… She turned to Billings. "Um. You got a first name?"

Pat snorted and Billings scowled.

"What?" Jessie asked, hoping she hadn't just fucked the whole thing up. But it seemed like asking a boy's first name when you were about to do whatever it was they were about to do was kind of a reasonable question.

Billings's annoyance softened as he looked at her. "It's okay. I just don't use it a lot. It's… Mario."

"Super Mario!" chuckled the captain.

Billings growled at him, but Jessie recognized this: two boys giving each other shit. She laughed, feeling slightly less out of control, and squeezed their hands. They both laughed along.

Then, as they rounded the back of Pa's shed, Pat leaned over and kissed her, his lips finding hers without hesitation but without too much force.

Billings's — Mario's lips touched her bare shoulder, and began to work their way up toward her neck.

Now she was feeling out of control.

Jessie turned between the two men, falling back against the corrugated steel of the shed wall so that the whole wall shook, unleashing a low roll of thunder that seemed to pass over them. Thank god cousin Billy is playing like the crazy man he is and nobody can hear that. She meant to ask them were they sure, but they seemed pretty damned sure. Before anything like a question could form itself, Mario captured her mouth in his, and Pat's teeth closed around her earlobe, and holy fuck…

She and Booger had made out so many times back here, back before they were married. Hell, after they were married. That'd stopped pretty early on. When Jessie had figured out that no matter how hot he got, once Booger shot his load, he was done for the night, and it was Jessie and her magic fingers again.

Somehow, Jessie didn't think that would be a problem this time.

Mario's lips were cool and full — not as wide as Deacon's, but softer than Pat's, and plusher than Booger's by a long shot, and they sent a steady flow of sex down her spine.

Billy's band segued straight into some scorching, bluesy something that was all bass and backbeat, and Pat was nibbling his way down her neck while Mario's tongue began to slide between Jessie's teeth and Pat's tongue slipped into Jessie's ear, and that flow of sex passed all of the way through her and good Lord!

Jessie's sex life had been mostly a lot of desire and not a lot of satisfaction. Booger hadn't been her first lover — he'd been one of four boys she'd regularly jumped into the back seat with at the town's crappy old drive-in theater. Thank Jesus for Pa's old Cutlass — Jessie was 6' in her stocking feet (Andy liked to joke that she was 5'12"), but that old boat had been wide enough for her to do all sorts of fun things without sticking her feet out the window...

But nothing like this.

Pat began to kiss his way down the side of her neck and that sent a bolt of forked lightning down to her nipples and her pussy, and she moaned into Mario's lush, luscious mouth. Two hands began to pull down the bodice of her black cock-tail dress (Bless you, Lea, a bridesmaid's dress I might actually wear again — if it survives the night) revealing her breasts to searching fingers, and two other hands began to pull up the skirt, and Jessie didn't know which hands belonged to who — didn't know, didn't care — but as a mouth closed around a nipple and fingers found and traced the weeping length of her pussy, Jessie screamed, and a flare of terrifying heat pulsed through her, and in spite of herself, in spite of how fucking good she felt, she pushed the two boys away.

They stood there for a moment, staring at her, and she stared back. Jessie found that she was panting, and that she was crying, and she couldn't account for either, but she didn't really care. "God," she gasped, "wanna fuck you two fuckin' dry." Then she put a hand in front her mouth, stunned that she'd actually said that.

Mario grinned like a man who's been given a hundred dollars change for a ten dollar bill. Pat smirked. "Fine with us," he grunted, and both men reached out to her bare breasts again, and that heat almost immediately began to rise again in Jessie. "But not where anyone could see us," she gasped.

"Okay," her men said, their hands still searching, distracting.... Mario flicked his head toward the shed door. "In there?"

"Oh, God, no!" Jessie giggled. "Not unless your idea of comfy is an anvil and a pile of scrap iron."

Pat smiled, less smirky now, "No, can't say that it does. Anywhere in the house?"

Jessie shook her head. "Only room with any privacy is Ma and Pa's, and... Um..." Even at age thirty, the idea of fucking on her parents' bed made Jessie queasy.

"Yeah," laughed Mario, "I bet." He leaned forward and kissed her again, gently pressing Pat's fingers and his own against her aching nipples.

"I think," said Pat, "I know where we can go." His voice was low, rumbling, and full of something that made her moan into Mario's lips again. "Come on, Bill-ings," he continued, suddenly full of command. "Let's get my truck and take this young lady where she can fuck us fuckin' dry with nobody watching." His fingers gave her nipple a gentle squeeze, and, together with Mario, he pulled Jessie's dress back up over her boobs.

When Mario pouted, Jessie said, "It's okay, baby. You can play with 'em all you want, later." Then she leaned forward and kissed Pat. "You too, Captain."

"Good." Pat grinned and held out and took one of Jessie's hands, while Mario took the other.

Cousin Billy was wailing through some old Bruce Springsteen number that had the remaining partiers jumping up and down and screaming. Jessie could see her sister Danielle writhing against her wimpy husband in a manner that should have made Jessie uncomfortable, but tonight didn't bother her at all.

As they walked off toward the road, Jessie realized that the sight of Danielle and Robby grinding like a couple of teenagers didn't bother her because, in fact, she felt like the sexiest bitch in Georgia, there between her two gorgeous men. Hell yes! Reaching out with her fingers, she stroked the front of each fireman's dress uniform pants, and confirmed that each was sporting what felt like a healthy hard-on. Damn.

As they passed the house, a departing car's headlights revealed the silhouette of what Jessie thought for a second was a small tree where no tree ought to have been. As the glare swept on, she realized that it was in fact three silhouettes in close embrace: two girls, Robby's kin from across in Tennessee, and the one person Jessie least wanted to see: Deacon Lawrence. He had his arms around both girls and his lips attached to the smaller one, the redhead. "Hey, Deacon."

Deacon broke the kiss and stood up straight, his eyes flashing up to Jessie's wide with guilt. "Uh. Hey, Jess." But then he took in the two men beside her, and his eyebrows shot up. "Damn, girl!"

"Damn, yourself," she countered, standing tall as she so rarely did. Pat and Mario squeezed her hands. Holy fuck. "You gonna treat these young ladies right?" No passing out, leaving them to get themselves off?

The redhead turned tomato-colored and burrowed into Deacon's armpit. The blonde covered her face and looked at her lavender shoes. But Deacon kept his eyes locked to Jessie's, answering in a low, measured voice that told her he know exactly what she was asking, "Yes, Jess. I am." Then he smiled. "You gonna treat these young men right?"

Jessie glanced at Mario, whose skin was darkening, and at Pat, who had a huge grin on, and smiled herself. "Oh, yeah, Deacon. I sure as fucking hell am."

They all laughed, a sound echoed from all over the Harris property. Deacon took the two girls and led them off up the road toward where his car must have been parked. "Have fun," he called over his shoulder.

"You too," she called back, feeling somehow drunker and happier than she had even two minutes before.

Pat started leading her down the road in the opposite direction. "Shouldn't that be, You three?" he chuckled, and Jessie laughed with him.

"Jessie?" Mario said. "What was that about?"

"Oh." Suddenly she felt just as drunk, but not as happy. "Can I...? Can I tell you after we get to the car?"

"Sure," both men answered.

As they walked down the long line of pickups and SUVs that lined the road, Jessie's eyes adjusted to the dark. She could make out the stars — Pegasus rising — and lightning bugs dancing in the grass.

"Here it—" Pat started, pulling out his keys as they came even with a shining black Suburban, but stopped when a woman's groan came from the other side of the road.

There, another big, shiny SUV had its back gate up. A woman Jessie recognized as the one woman firefighter from Andy's company was kneeling behind another firefighter—a man. His face was invisible, hidden between another woman's pale thighs.

"Hey, Captain!" said the woman firefighter. Her far arm seemed to be pumping up and down at... something.

"Joanie," said Pat. "Is that...?"

"Jack Miller," said the kneeling woman. "Me and Giselle're giving him a lesson in how to treat a lady." She leaned forward and bit the man's ear, making him groan and making the woman whose legs were over his shoulders call out again. "This round, I'm providing... positive reinforcement."

"Uh, carry on," said Pat, sounding off balance for the first time that night.

"Yessir," said Joanie. "Practice makes perfect, sir." She did something with her hand that made Miller pull up his head. "Now, Jack, what have we talked about?"

"Better to give..." gasped the fireman, and then swore and dove back in.

Jessie felt her jaw drop. What the fuck is happening tonight? Did Lea put something in the beer?

"Have fun, Captain!" Joanie called. "You too, Super Mario." She winked at Jessie. "And I don't even have to tell you to have fun."

"Um. Thanks," Jessie said, and pulled Mario Billings to the passenger side of the car, away from the increasing sounds of the woman's moans of arousal — something Jessie had never heard, at least not without a wall or a car window to make it a bit less....

The locks clicked open, and Pat called, "Why don't you two get in back. I'll play chauffeur."

Mario opened the rear door for Jessie. He was standing at attention, and it was tummy-meltingly sweet and gentleman-like — though the tent at the front of his dress pants kind of spoiled the effect a bit.

She stepped in, and started to sit behind Pat, but he said, "Why don't you to stretch out in the back row."

Shrugging, Jessie moved to the way-back, and Mario slid in beside her.

She kissed him, and then felt funny—she didn't want Pat to feel left out.

Mario gazed into her eyes. His, she realized, were a hazel that seemed to light up his whole face. Strong jaw, full lips… Gorgeous. Oh, God…

"So," he said, taking her hand, "what was that about with what's-his-name by the house? You said you'd tell us." He ran fingers up the inside of her arm.

"Oh." Jessie shivered. "Deacon. Him and me, we… Um… We hooked up once, at his brother's wedding — Prior, he was Andy's best man."

"Oh?" His eyes were warm and solemn.

Jessie licked her lips. "Um. Yeah." She shivered again, goose pimples breaking out on her arms, her chest. "Hooked up. Sort of. Only—"

Mario raised Jessie's arm and kissed her wrist, and (Oh, God!) Jessie was in the back seat of a big old boat of a car again, and all she wanted to do was —

"Only?" Mario asked.

"Only, um, Deacon, he passed out before anything really… happened."

"Ah." He kissed the inside of her elbow. "He left you hanging."

Unable to speak, Jessie nodded and looked out the window, away from Mario. It was pitch black outside. The Suburban was winding uphill through the woods — but since the town was surrounded by hills and woods, Jessie had no idea where they were going.

"So that's why you were telling him to treat those girls right," called the captain from the front seat. "You let us know if he doesn't. We'll sic Joannie on him."

Trying not to get lost in the feeling of Mario's lips against her bare shoulder, Jessie panted, "Wouldn't you, uh, rather — hnhh —wouldn't y'all rather be with her and that Giselle girl? Or that blonde and that little redhead?"

"Nope," answered Pat. In the rear view mirror, Jessie could just see his mouth, turned up in a grin.

Mario lifted his lips from her neck and stared into her eyes, those hazel eyes of his looking other-worldly. "Why would we want that, when we get to be with a goddess like you?" And then his mouth found hers, and Jessie was lost.

Goddess. And there hadn't been even a bit of a tease or a sneer in his eyes. Why in God's name would anyone—?

Kenny, Jessie's first boyfriend — well, the first boy Jessie'd slept with — had called her Jessie the Giant. She'd been about six inches taller than him, had outweighed him, but he'd been the first boy she'd let between her legs in the back seat of the old Cutlass. What had been showing at the drive-in that night — Grease? Jessie couldn't remember. But she could remember him being fascinated by how big she was. Big ass. Big tits. Big everything. Definitely not a goddess.

Little runt.

Joined the Marines after graduation. He was Jessie's height by then, and dating Christy Palmer, who was 5'2" and a 32A. Went off to Iraq. Never came back.

Poor Kenny.

As the Suburban rolled through the Georgia night, for the first time in her life, Jessie felt herself being adored. Worshipped. It was an amazing feeling. Overwhelming. Amazing.

Mario kissed his way down her neck, along her collarbone. Somehow, the top of Jessie's dress was back below her tits, and so as she arched into the touch of his lips, her breasts lifted, big, soft, and pale, but he worshipped them just the same, kissing, licking, nibbling around the edge of one nipple with mind-scrambling slowness, as if to make sure he'd kissed every single bump, before latching his teeth onto the aching, insistent flesh at the center.

Clutching the headrests on either side to keep from exploding, Jessie found herself staring at the review mirror.

Pat's blue eyes flicked up and met hers. He winked.

Mario had moved on from the other breast, and was kissing his way down Jessie's trembling belly. She gaped down at him, kneeling between her thighs, but his eyes held the same steady adoration. Without breaking eye contact, he pushed the dress up, so that it was now more of a belt: breasts bare, nothing below but the pink undies she'd put on that morning dreaming that someone would tear them off of her. Mario kissed the inside of one thigh, and then the other. "Can I eat you?"

Jessie gaped at him, wanting to say Fuck yes! or Please do! or If you insist! or something clever or cute, but all she could do was nod like an idiot.

Smiling, he hitched his thumbs under the strip of dental floss that ran over each of Jessie's hips. When she didn't move, he mouthed Lift up. His breath whispered along the inside of her thigh.

Feeling as if she might pass out soon, but thinking that letting him remove her panties first might be a good idea, Jessie did.

He pulled off the tiny swatch of lace and laid it on the seat, then gazed at Jessie's pussy.

"You… you don't have to."

He shot her a wild, wicked grin, leaned forward, and pressed his lips against her, and flame blossomed inside of Jessie, leaving her blind, breathless, and more alive than she had ever felt. Mario's hands slid up and found Jessie's breasts, sparking more flame.

Booger had licked at her a few times, but he'd had a look on his face like he was going to catch cooties or something, and Jessie had had to fake an orgasm to get him to stop. Hank Miller, her boss at the hardware store, had done much better, getting her good and wet before flipping her, fucking her bent over the ledgers on her desk. That had lasted a few months, till Jessie had mentioned as they lay that she was thinking of leaving Booger, and then the son of a bitch had fired her.

But neither of them had made her feel like this. Neither of them had done it like they'd actually wanted to do anything but get her ready for the main event.

This… This was the main event. The only event. For now.

Now .

The day that Jessamyn "Jessie" Harris had married Robert "Booger" Jenkins, the preacher had told them, "Eternity isn't later. Eternity has nothing to do with time. Eternity is now and always. Your life together is part of and of a whole with the eternal reward you wish to attain."

Well, marriage to Booger hadn't been any kind of reward. But now....

Jessie was aware of the pressure of Mario's tongue, of the heat and slide of his lips and teeth, but she wasn't really aware of herself at all.

And so when fingers ran along her cheek and into her hair, she was confused — her own? Mario's — but he had both working at her breasts, so how...?

"So fucking sexy," growled Pat, and leaned forward to kiss her throat.

Jessie hadn't ever wondered what a power cord felt like when the switch turned on and the electricity flowed. She didn't need to wonder now.

Trying to keep from losing herself in the feeling of two mouths teasing eternity out of her flesh, she panted, "Shouldn't... you be... drivin'?"

Pat chuckled and kissed her way up her throat to her ear. "We're here." His voice seemed to hum through her, meeting up with the edgeless flame of Mario's tongue, and Jessie was lost in the vibration, her whole body drowned in a feeling that was too big, too scary to be called pleasure. She felt herself lift off of the chair, so that her only points of contact with the world were the two men's mouths, which lifted her up — like the paper-bag hot-air balloons she'd made with Andy once — and let her fly.

# #

Tears. She remembered feeling so damned good, then why were there tears?

A hand brushed through her hair, which was tangled. Another rubbed her naked thigh like it was a colicky baby. And another...

Another hand covered her pussy, a fourth her breast.

"Hey, Jessie," said Pat, the one up near her head.

"You okay, baby?" asked Mario, from the other end.

"Okay?" she laughed through the tears. "Okay? Sweet Jesus with a hard-on!"

They laughed with her, though neither of them sounded certain they should.

Jessie sat up, her legs slipping off of Mario's shoulders. She leaned forward and kissed him. "Thank you."

"Welcome."

She turned and kissed Pat. "Thank you, too."

"Welcome." She could feel him grinning into her lips. "So. We done for the night?"

She blinked at him. "Aw, fuck no!"

"Good." He stood and held out his hand to her. "Come on. Unless you want to fuck us fuckin' dry in here."

"Nah." She peered out the window, but the outside was black. "Where we at?" Mario stood behind her, his hands on her hips, where her dress was slowly working its way back down.

Slipping out the door, Pat gave a grunt of a laugh. "A place where we can make all the noise we want, and nobody's going to hear us."

Curious, nervous, Jessie followed Pat out the door and was confronted by smell of pine and, overhead, the bright river of light that was the Milky Way.

They were on a mountain top. There were plenty of those around the town — but this one looked familiar. Turning her head, Jessie saw a dark shape thrusting up into the dark night. "Oh!"

"Yup." Pat squeezed her hand.

Stepping out out of the car, Mario took the other. "A fire spotting tower?"

"Yeah," sighed Jessie. They were on the same sides they'd been on walking to the car. It was... sweet. "Andy volunteered up here when he was in school."

"Me too, for a couple of months," murmured Pat. "Forestry Commission. Summer before my senior year of college and I thought it would be fun. Spent most of the time reading the same four books over and over and whacking off, dreaming about getting a visit from a six-foot blonde goddess of a full-blown woman with her dress falling off."

Pleased and embarrassed, Jessie tried to cover her bare boobs, but of course only managed to pull her two boys' hands to them. They didn't seem to mind.

When they began to caress her — Mario gently, Pat more aggressively — she sure as hell didn't mind either.

But as the fire started to catch again, Jessie decided that it was time for her to take control. Or at least try. She peeled their hands away from her and stepped toward the stairs that led up to the tower. As she walked, she pushed her dress down over her hips and let it fall to the pine-needle-covered ground. (It's black. I can clean it later. Fuck it.) Stepping out of it, she turned and leaned back against the metal i-beam holding up the tower at the corner next to the stairs. For a moment, feeling the moonlight splashing over her body, taking in their stunned expressions, she did feel like a goddess. A bit. "Either of y'all gonna join me?"

For a moment, she stood there, buck-naked in her low pumps, there at the top of King Mountain; the air flowed over her flowering pussy, still warm, but cooler than down in the valley, and Jessie felt her skin erupt in goose pimples.

The two men sauntered toward her, shedding their uniforms as they came. With the moon behind them, it looked like they were shedding layers of themselves — jackets first, shirts.... Mario's silhouette was a bit taller and leaner; Pat was broad-shouldered...

But when their bare chests pressed against her bare chest and their mouths latched onto her throat, her ears, the differences blurred into a haze of moonwashed sensation, and heat and wet and sound flowed through Jessie, and she was blind.

Ma and Danielle liked to read those god-awful Harlequins and Mills & Boons, with their throbbing manhoods and their weeping womanhoods. Fuck that shit. Somewhere around five years into Jessie's marriage to Booger, one of the girls at the store had turned her onto smut: to stories featuring cocks and cunts and lots and lots of FUCKING. Just what she wasn't getting in real life. She'd bought herself a Kindle for Booger to give her as a birthday present and nobody had any idea what she was reading that was keeping her so happy.

Or kept her sneaking off to the girls' room so often.

And she'd discovered that her favorite stories always involved a woman with a man in uniform. Well, in uniform for a while. Cop. Military. Firefighter, like her snot-nosed little brother. Even better, two men in uniform. For a while.

And here she was: living the story.

And holy FUCK, it was better than the fucking books.

Two very different mouths latched onto her tits at the same moment that two very different hands slid up between her goose-pimply thighs and began to stroke her pussy lips.

Much better than the fucking books.

Not wanting to lose herself completely, not wanting all of this to end, to turn out to be some sort of bizarre dream or something, Jessie decided she wouldn't be like the girls in most of her stories — lying back and enjoying themselves, letting themselves get carried away on the waves of feeling — Jessie ran her hands down the men's rippling, bare ribs to their still-uniformed hips. To their crotches.

A long, thin pair of fingers pushed themselves up into her slick, welcoming cunt while a muscled thumb began to whir over her clit, and a sound exploded from Jessie that she was pretty sure they'd heard all the way down in the valley. All the way down in fucking Atlanta.

And she really didn't fucking care.

But she did want...

Sliding her unsteady hands up to the tops of the two flies, she popped the buttons, unzipped the trousers, and yanked out two....

Two throbbing manhoods. Two rods of velvet-wrapped steel. Two massive, moist-tipped members.

She grabbed the two cocks, glorying in their size: both big — one long enough that the head bounced against the bottom of her tit, the other thick enough that her not-tiny hand just closed around it at the root.

They groaned into her breasts, and she gloried in that too. Gloried in the feeling of their hands twitching, even as they continued to pleasure her.

Throbbing . She was beginning to throb now, her cunt — her weeping womanhood — beginning to tighten involuntarily around Mario's fabulously invasive fingers, her clit beginning to pulse against Pat's thumb.

No. No.

She'd already come once — hell, twice really, once when they'd had her against Pa's shed, and once in the back seat, and she wanted a cock inside of her. Cocks inside of her.

She was the goddess, damn it, and the goddess wanted to be fucked.

She pushed their pelvises, still gripping their cocks, and they both stumbled back and blinked at her. Jessie's body grumbled at the disappearance of all those amazing fingers, but fuck it. Her body was gonna get what it wanted.

Steering Mario so that he had to sit on the wide staircase up the tower, Jessie turned toward him and knelt between his knees. She gave Pat's thick erection a squeeze and let go; she trusted that he'd know what to do with it.

Mario's eyes were wide. It made Jessie's heart flutter, somehow, and she leaned forward and kissed him. "Can I eat you?" She stroked the length of him. "Pretty baby?"

He nodded, his wide eyes still locked on hers, his mouth open wide. Funny: he didn't look at all like an idiot.

As she began to lower her mouth to him, she waggled her ass and whispered over her shoulder, "Consider yourself welcome, Captain. Make yourself at home." Then, holding Mario's long, dark cock steady, she sucked him into her mouth.

Mario hissed.

Pat grunted. "Jesus Christ." There was a rustling sound. "I appreciate the invitation. You shaking your beautiful ass at me seemed like a good hint, but it's good to know." Jessie heard his trousers fall to his feet, heard the sound of latex unrolling over his cock.

Yeah, Jessie thought with a full-mouthed grin, this is gonna be GOOD. And she focussed on sucking at Mario's cock head, tracing the edges with her tongue. She was holding him up with one of her ridiculous, man-like hands, but her lips still couldn't quite reach her fingers. Damn.

Deacon's cock had been maybe as long, but it hadn't ever gotten all of the way hard like this. She wasn't sure she could take all of this into her body — anywhere in her body — but she was damned sure looking forward to trying. For now, she enjoyed the soft smoothness of him. Velvet on steel.

And then she felt two strong hands run up the flesh of her thighs, her hips. Felt Pat's lips touch surprisingly gently against the base of her spine, and then kiss their way up until she felt his belly sliding against her back, his muscled thighs against the backs of hers, and his cock sliding up against her open pussy. "You ready to get it from both ends, Jessie?" he whispered, tickling the back of her neck. The head of his cock spread her already wide lips even further.

She moaned and nodded atop Mario's cock, which made Mario hiss again.

"You okay me going first, Billings?"

Mario gave a high, breathy laugh. "Age... before beauty, Cap." Then Jessie sucked more of him into her mouth. "I ain't... complaining."

"I bet. Age into beauty, that's what I think." And then Pat grabbed hold of Jessie's fluffy hips and pressed himself into her.

Full. He didn't push all of the way in — couldn't have on the first go, wide as he was — but a wonderful, overwhelming feeling of fullness flooded her senses. The pressure of Pat sliding relentlessly into her drove her mouth further onto Mario's rod, and it felt like all of Jessie's insides were overflowing with cock.

Cocks.

Two.

It had been so long since Jessie's had one cock inside of her — Deacon's barely passed her lips before he spurted and passed out. And that last time with Booger was almost two years ago, and his wasn't even as thick as her thumb, but this...

Pat grunted, pushing further into her, spreading Jessie's hymn-singing pussy, making her mouth open wider in sympathy, and driving Mario deeper into her mouth.

"Jessie!" moaned the man in front of her, stroking her hair like he was petting a scared cat, while the man behind panted, pulled his beautiful, gorgeous, fabulous tree trunk of throbbing manhood back out of her just enough to make Jessie whimper at the loss, and then thrust into her again, beginning a steady rhythm that made Jessie literally see stars spinning around Mario's belly button, which was a lot closer than it had been.

Without stopping his thrusts, Pat grunted, "Feel... okay... Jessie?"

She wanted to scream Fuck, yes! or sing Gospel or something, but her mouth was blessedly full, and all she could do was moan and nod.

Mario, who was whispering Jessie's name over and over, reached out and took her breasts in those amazing, long fingers. At the same moment, Pat let go of one of her hips and let his hand slide around to her clit.

If she'd ever been proud of anything, Jessie had always been proud of her ability to multi-task. To balance three spreadsheets while handling email and talking to Danielle about little RJ's colic. To cook four different dishes in two pots, a pan, and a slow-cooker while cleaning the kitchen and doing her nails. To give Booger a blowjob that had him taking the Lord's name seriously in vain while planning out the next day's shopping and getting herself off (since no one else would bother).

Okay: she was proud of her blowjobs, too.

But she was barely aware of this one, though the swelling head of Mario's cock was well past her molars and spit was pouring out around it. Here she was, having an experience she really, really hoped she'd remember for the rest of her life, and the sensation was literally short-circuiting her. She couldn't keep the sensations straight, let alone her own actions. It was as if all of the pleasure she'd been so desperate for over the last year — rubbing herself up against Sean like an idiot, pulling Deacon back up to her house, lying there night after night with her Kindle in one hand while the other worked away at her pussy — all of the sex she had ever wanted had come crashing down on her all at once and she couldn't remember whose hand was whose, or who was making what sound or where they were or...

And then one of them — Mario — screamed "JESSIE!" and clutched at her tits, and a flood of heat poured down her throat, and amazing as that felt too, Jessie considered for a moment that she might drown up there on the top of King Mountain. And considered that dying that way wouldn't be all that bad a way to go.

But Mario pulled out of her mouth, and semen and saliva spilled out onto her neck and chest as he lifted her up — Pat still pounding into her — and she coughed and spit, but she was breathing, and screaming, and there was still a big, thick cock driving up into her, and fingers on her clit, and fingers on her tits, and Mario was kissing her and eternity beckoned and —

And Pat growled and thrust hard into her, lifting her to her toes, and fingers on her clit and on her tits and her tongue in Mario's mouth, his cum, and —

And eternity was now, after all. Just like the preacher said.

And Jessie stayed standing, but it was just because her men were holding her up. She was boneless. Muscle-less. A cloud of satisfaction floating between them. YES.

The captain, steam rising from his back, picked up all of their clothes and led the way up the tower.

Mario picked up Jessie, and began to climb. Not fireman's carry, either: one arm under her knees, the other supporting her shoulders, her head tucked against his neck. She felt safe and warm and...

He brought her up seven flights of stairs without complaint — Booger, the wimp, had nearly dropped her just getting her across the threshold to their hotel room. Though Mario's boner was making itself known against her backside, this man wasn't even breathing hard.

Jessie thought that was a bit of a shame, so as they reached the observation deck she whispered, "You gonna fuck me, pretty baby? You gonna take that gorgeous thing of yours and stick it —"

With a cry that set Jessie's nerves buzzing, Mario poured her against the railing, there, a hundred feet above the top of the mountain, above the trees, among the stars, and thrust up into her.

Pat said something, but Jessie couldn't hear it, couldn't help but cry in harmony with Mario and grab onto the rail as he began to fuck her — sliding slowly into her... and into her...

She was wide and wet from the pounding that Pat had given her, but sweet Jesus, Mario was sliding up into a part of her that no one had ever reached. Fingers clutching at the wooden rail, Jessie her head back and howled at the moon.

The moon.

As Mario began to move against her — his legs tensing against the backs of hers, his chest against her back, his long fingers curling over hers — Jessie stared up at the full moon and began to laugh. Not surprised laughter. Not embarrassed laughter. Really, honest-to-god laughter like Jessie remembered doing with Danielle and Andy.

"What you laughing about, Jessie?" called Pat, his voice muffled.

"I AM A FUCKING GODDESS!" she screamed out into the night. "I got two beautiful men making me fucking scream and I'm standing on top of the fucking world, and I feel... like a fucking... goddess." She pushed back against Mario until something slap against her clit, making her jump. His balls.

"Holy fuck," he groaned into her ear. "That's 'cause... you are a goddess, Jessie."

She laughed again, and she felt herself tighten around the glorious, pulsing length of him.

"Ah!" Mario clenched around her. "Gonna... I'm gonna..."

"Cum for me, baby," sighed Jessie, and tightened around him again.

That was all it took: Mario bellowed, pressing his whole body as close to hers as possible before collapsing, panting, against her back. His head fell onto her shoulder.

Breathing heavily herself, Jessie gazed out over her domain. The black forest that fell away below her feet. The stars dancing for her entertainment above. The distant bubble of light on the horizon that marked Chattanooga, an hour and a half off to the west.

"Shit!" Mario gasped.

"It's okay, baby," said Jessie, squeezing his softening hard-on with her pussy once more. "I don't mind."

"No!" He backed out of her, releasing a flood of her juices and his spooge, and Jessie whimpered at the loss. "I... I didn't wear... I wasn't —"

Jessie turned and kissed him silent, then looked into his deep, warm eyes. "It's okay, baby."

"No!" His eyes were wide, the white flaring between his brown skin and his brown-green eyes . "I didn't... I'm so sorry."

After another kiss had calmed him again, she hugged him. "Tried for eight years to have a kid with Booger. I... I ain't very... fertile. Doc says." It was about the last, least goddess-like thing she wanted to say to this man. But she could see his panic and remorse, and she felt as if she owed him that. Into his ear she whispered. "Wasn't the plan. But if you just got me pregnant, I would... I would be fine. I would be... really happy."

Pat cleared his throat. "Not sure I'm going to let him off so easy. A man under my command should know always to use the proper safety gear."

Mario spun around. "Sorry. Captain."

Pat smirked. "At ease. Just be glad it didn't bite you in the ass this time."

"Yessir."

"Now, if you don't mind, Billings, I think our goddess has some more worshipping in store." When Jessie's eyebrows twitched, he smiled and waved his hand down at a mattress and blanket that he seemed to have materialized on the observation deck. "Your altar awaits, your divine-ness."

Jessie found herself floating toward him. "Where'd you find that?"

"Inside." Pat grinned. "They hadn't changed where they hid the key." He held out a hand.

Jessie took it, stepped close, and nipped at his chin. "What you got in mind, Mr. Captain? Do I need to be disciplined for leading one of your men astray?"

"No, ma'am." He grabbed her ass in both hands and pulled her close. "Even a captain doesn't outrank a deity." And then he kissed her — a deep, full-body kiss that sucked the air out of Jessie's body and replaced it with heat.

Ma always said boys don't give a damn for something they can get for free. What she'd meant was don't dress like a slut. But also don't be too easy. It was a lesson that Jessie had always felt like she'd failed at her whole adult life. Yet here she was: she hadn't played coy with these men, hadn't teased or pulled out the Southern belle act, like Danielle. When they'd come over to her and asked her to dance — Jessie sitting there moping in her beer — Jessie had all but thrown herself at them. Had reveled in the feeling of being on the dance floor with the two handsomest men there — excepting maybe Sean, but fuck him anyway. Had thrilled at the feeling of their bodies moving against hers, of her body moving against theirs. When they'd all walked over to send Andy and Lea (and Sean) off on their honeymoon, they'd held her hands and it had never occurred to her to say no to what they seemed to be suggesting. Which was this: Jessie, gloriously naked on the top of King Mountain with one man's spunk flowing down her leg, and hungry for the other man's cock, which was pressing against her belly. She was probably going to be walking crooked for days — if she could walk at all — but damn right, she'd given herself to Pat and Mario for free, and damn right, she was going to keep doing it until she couldn't any more. And they seemed eager for more.

"Wanna fuck me again, baby?" she murmured into Pat's mouth. Taking his hands from her ass — hoping they'd be back there soon — she stepped back and lay down on the mattress. Her altar here above the world, beneath the moon and stars.

He followed her, a grin like a dog in a butcher shop on his face. But as he knelt between her spread thighs, he pulled a packet out of a pile of clothes and began to open it.

"You can go bareback too, if you want."

Pat's eyes narrowed and then closed. "As nice an offer as that is... I've had other... partners recently." He met her gaze again, and when she nodded began to put the rubber over that thick cock of his. For a moment, Jessie considered offering to help, but the sight of him rolling the latex over his straining erection...

It was one thing to feel it through his trousers, to feel it even in her pussy. Seeing its thickness made Jessie's tummy flutter — even knowing that it fit fabulously inside of her. "That's... I guess you get the extra-large size." She blinked and turned to Mario, who was leaning against the railing with the moon behind him, the silhouette of his semi-hard dick hanging between his legs. "Both of y'all."

Mario gave a huff of laughter. "Yes, ma'am."

Then she felt Pat moving between her legs, felt the tip of his cock nestle between her pussy lips. She looked up.

His eyes were dark. "I like the extra-large size," he whispered, and pushed just the plum-sized head of his cock into her. Then he withdrew, and in spite of herself Jessie whimpered.

"Don't worry, Jessie," Pat said, his grin broad now, and his eyes full of dark fire. "I'll give you all you want. I just thought this time you might like it if I gave it to you —" He pressed the head into her again — no further than the previous time — and withdrew. Again. "— a little at a time." (Out. And in.) "You just let me know if you want more." Out. And in.

The feeling was... Jessie had a hard time thinking straight, let alone finding the right word, but...

Exquisite.

To keep from turning into a gibbering mess immediately, Jessie looked over at Mario — at his backlit outline. "Want to join us?" She held out one limp hand.

Mario's shadow shook its head.

A trickle of old, familiar anxiety seeped down Jessie's spine, dulling even the exquisite feeling of Pat's cock spreading her just wide enough... Had she fucked up like usual? Had she hurt his feelings somehow?

Mario shook his head. A puff of steam showed that he'd laughed. "Captain's turn. You tired me out."

"Not for good I hope."

"Oh, no. Never."

And with that warmth flowed back into Jessie, and Pat's invasion-and-retreat began slowly scrambling her nerves again.

"Besides," Mario continued, shifting. "I... I mean, it's kind of amazing watching you."

Pat gave a grunt as he pulled out of her. "You're not one of Joanie's peeping toms, are you?" (In. And out.) "She's noticed somebody's been trying to watch her in the shower," he added for Jessie's benefit.

"No, sir!" Mario stood almost at attention before leaning back against the railing. "Um. I think she found the culprit. I think she's got him... um... in hand."

Jessie had no idea what Mario meant by that, until she remembered the woman firefighter jerking the man off while he was eating her friend in the car. "Oh!"

"You mean —" (In. And out.) "Miller?"

"I think so, sir."

(And in.) "Jesus. Lucky bastard. I'm surprised she didn't kill him." (And out.) "I am sure she'll... discipline him. But I probably should make sure she doesn't want to file a complaint." (And in.)

"Yessir."

"Uh, Billings?" And out.

"Yessir?"

"Please call me Pat. I mean," he grunted (and out), "This isn't exactly a formal occasion."

"I would have thought worshipping a goddess would be a very formal occasion."

"Fair enough," Pat laughed, so that his cock slipped free of Jessie's pussy, making them both groan at the loss. "Still." (And in.) "Please. Pat."

"Okay," Mario laughed, and it was like music, like the stars sparkle. "Pat." He walked over and sat on the edge of the mattress just above Jessie's head. "I love the way you glow when you get excited." He ran a finger across her forehead, across her lips.

"Hmm."

"So," he said, running that finger along her chin, around the edge of her ear, "you're divorced?"

Shy, overwhelmed, Jessie nodded.

"Well," panted Pat, "he's an idiot." (And in.) "His name's really Booger?"

She nodded again. "Robert really. But yeah." Booger's home, baby-doll!

Billings's magic finger traced Jessie's left collarbone, which she hadn't thought about since she'd broken it playing volleyball sophomore year of high school. But she was thinking about it now. (And not Booger. Definitely not.)

(And out.) "Jessie. I've been divorced three times. Trust me. This wasn't your fault." (And in.)

"I..." Jessie wanted to look away, but couldn't take her eyes off of Pat's. Off his lust-dark face. "It was."

"Bullshit." (And in.) "Who filed for divorce?" (And out.)

"Um. He did. But we both... It was, you know, irreconcilable differences."

"Did you fuck around on him?" When she didn't answer, his brows shot up and his slow, relentless in-out paused. "Really?"

"Um. Once." Over the desk. "For about a year."

"Huh. And did Snot-boy every find out?"

She shook her head, wanting to smile at the nickname.

(And in.) "So that wasn't it."

When she shook her head, Mario whispered, "It was the baby thing, wasn't it."

She looked up into his face now, which was in shadow. His eyes, however, were bright and warm. Feeling as if Pat's slow, insistent invasion were pushing the emotion up into her throat, as if opening her mouth would let all of it come spilling out, she nodded, her lower lip trembling in spite of herself.

"Well," growled Pat, "that sure as hell isn't your fault." (And out. And in.)

"After we found out, he... he didn't want to touch me, 'cause I was..." A rocky place where his seed could find no purchase.

(And in. And out.) "Said he was an idiot."

Drowning in the feeling, she reached up and touched both men's warm, strong faces. "Don't... Don't wanna talk right now." She gave Mario's face a squeeze, then brought the hand up so that both cupped Pat's chin. Looping her legs around Pat's ribs, she pulled the captain to her. "Wanna fuck."

"Yes, ma'am." (And IN.)

Booger had stopped fucking her like this — missionary — after the bad news had come. After that, when they fucked (when they fucked) she'd been on her hands and knees. Kenny, the shrimp, had loved to have her on top, had loved to watch all her bits jiggle. Nick had wanted her to straddle his lap while he sat there, the one time they'd boffed in the back of the old Cutlass, so he could keep watching Batman. Buster, who she'd dated for a month or two just before she and Booger had finally hooked up — he had loved to do it standing up, had loved the fact that Jessie's pussy was the right height for him to pull her panties to the side and slip into her in line at the snack shack with no one the wiser. (Actually, Jessie had kind of liked that too.) And Hank, the motherfucker, had loved bending her over her desk.

Mind, she'd enjoyed the hell out of all of those, even doggy-style with Booger. When that happened.

But honestly? This was Jessie's favorite position. By far. Her on her back, her legs around her man, kissing, touching, feeling him so deep...

It made time stop. It made all of the noise stop. That was almost as amazing as the feeling of him moving inside of her.

Time.

Time was no fun. Time wasn't eternity.

Now was eternity. Definitely.

"So beautiful, so beautiful," Pat whispered over and over into her lips, and it was going to make Jessie cry, it really was, but then his breathing got shallow and his thrusts shaky and time kicked back into gear. "Gonna, gonna cum, gonna, aw, shit. Baby, Jessie, gonna —"

"Shh," she said, feeling that goddess-flame burning inside of her again, and pulled him as close to her, as far into her as she could, and then she squeezed.

Jessie was no slip of a thing. She was a big girl, and so men's grunts and hollers and twitches didn't usually impress her much. She liked the fact that she could get them feeling so good. But Pat — he was a big man, and he seemed to swell as he came, inside and outside, it was like getting caught up in whitewater, like that time she'd fallen out of the raft with Andy, and she'd thought she'd die — she had no power, no control, but somehow that had made her feel even more alive, every part of her.

A religious experience. Sort of.

And just like she'd come up out of the water that day on the river, she came up for air as Pat's last spasms faded.

"Took me to heaven, baby," she panted in his ear, and squeezed again.

Pat let out a strangled series of words that Jessie's mom would have definitely disapproved of, groaned "Goddess" — and rolled off of her, gasping for air. After a moment, he barked out a laugh and stood a bit shakily. "Well, Jessie, I think you have officially fucked me fucking dry." When she pouted he laughed again. "For now. I need to use the john. Billings, you gonna keep our goddess company?"

"Yes. Yes I will."

Jessie had almost forgotten Mario. Almost. She turned to him, and was stunned by the fire burning in those hazel eyes.

He kissed her, and Jessie felt the flood begin to suck her down again. He pressed up against her side, that long erection standing proud once more. "Jessie... I... can... do you...?"

"Get that beautiful thing in me. Now." Then, hearing herself, she snorted. "Your goddess commands it."

A sound bubbled out of him that sounded a bit like a mountain cat purring. "Yes, oh queen of the night." Then instead of sliding on top of her, he lifted her right leg with his, sliding it so that it was beneath her right thigh, but over the left one. And his erection slid smoothly, blessedly, fabulously into her, and they both gasped. "Holy... Holy fuck, you're wet."

She couldn't help laughing, She wanted to say something smartass like, Well, if I'm gonna fuck y'all dry, it has to go someplace, don't it? But instead, she smiled, pulling him closer. "You make me that way."

"Lucky me." He kissed her again, his hand roaming over her front. At the same time, he began to move inside of her — not the mind-scrambling pussy-pounding he'd given her over the observation railing, and not the just-inside-her torture Pat had given her just now. Just a wonderful, gentle fuck.

"Lucky me... too," she sighed, falling into a sea of hazel before leaning closer and capturing his lush lips in hers. After a couple of minutes (an hour?) she murmured into his mouth, "What you call this?" She squeezed his leg between her two.

He groaned and then returned to the slow, spark-inducing fuck. "Dunno if there's a name. Side scissors? Dunno. I just... I like being able to see you. Touch you. And... most of the girls I've been with couldn't take as much me as you, so it's a way I can be deep inside you without hurting you."

"Huh." She squeezed her legs around his again, and gloried in the feeling of her pussy tightening around him. "How old are you."

He tensed for a moment. "Twenty-five." His left arm, which had slid under her back, found her far breast.

"Huh."

"Thought I was younger?" When she didn't say anything, he slid his right hand down her belly and between his thigh and her pussy. "Lot of people do." His long fingers brushed to either side of her electrified clit.

She gasped, "God. Don't care. Don't care." And she didn't. The fact was, since her divorce — for months before — she'd been feeling incredibly old and incredibly young both at the same time. Now she felt like Jessie. For the first time in years. She felt like who she was and who she wanted to be, and that feeling was even sweeter than the two cocks and the two mouths, and all of the sensations they'd filled her with.

"You're so beautiful."

"Don't." It came out as half a laugh, half a sob. "I'm not."

"Yes you fucking are," said Pat from somewhere below her feet, his voice rumbling through her. "I've seen my share of women, Jessie. Seen them fucking. You are absolutely... radiant." He walked around to the head of the mattress and sat.

Again, the sob-laugh burst out of her. "So this is... hnh... old hat for you?"

"No. Believe me. No." Pat shifted, his hand stroking the ear that Mario wasn't nibbling on. "But threesomes, yeah. I've done a few of those. Wife #3 and another guy, a friend of mine. Wife #2 with a guy and a couple of times with other women.

Hell. She and I did a threeway with the woman who eventually became Wife #3. And trust me: you're beautiful. And right now, you're fucking gorgeous." He gave her earlobe a soft pinch.

"Damn straight," muttered Mario into her other ear, sending shivers all the way down to Jessie's toes. Then he chuckled.

"What?" Mostly, Jessie didn't want to hear them tell her how beautiful she was, when nobody ever told her that but her Ma and Pa, and they weren't who she wanted to hear it from. "What's funny?"

Before Mario could answer, Pat grumbled, "Wife #2. She's... She's kind of unique." He gave her lobe another pinch, and then circled the outline of the ear. "All my exes tell me I make a much better ex than a husband. But she still likes to... Um. We still, sometimes..." He sounded off-balance for the first time since she'd met him. "You saw her tonight. Giving a hand job to —"

Jessie gasped, partly because of the feelings they were sparking in her, and partly in recognition. "To... that Miller asshole? In the back of the car?" Miller's face buried between the other woman's thighs. When Pat grunted a yup, another image flashed across her mental movie screen. "You were gonna do a threesome with her and that blonde?"

"Giselle, the one who's fireman crazy, yeah," sighed Pat. "Yeah. Joanie thought it would be fun."

"Fun," chuckled Mario into her ear, sending another flight of goosebumps across Jessie's flesh.

Fun. "Can't tell me you wouldn't rather —"

"No." Pat's finger slid down across Jessie's lips. "I'm right where I want to be. Jessie. I mean being with a couple of women is fun. Even straight women like Joanie. And Mario, I hope you'll understand when I say that it isn't your ass I'll be dreaming about tomorrow."

"No problem, Captain. Pat. Understood."

"Jessie..." Pat sighed. "When I was up here all those years ago — you were probably still in junior high, if that even — I watched a forest fire catch. It'd been a really dry summer, and one night, right around sundown, a valley about five miles that way —" He pointed with his free hand. "— went from nothing to firestorm in about five minutes. And don't get me wrong, it was scary as hell. But it was also beautiful."

"I remember that," Jessie sighed. Smoke turning the sunset cherry red. "I was... Yeah. Young."

Pat gave a sad laugh. "Yeah. Cradle-robber, me. Anyway, that's you, Jessie, babe. I knew from Andy you'd had a rough year, and Sean had said, from when they were up here —"

Shame doused Jessie like cold water. "Oh. God. Sean. I —"

"Don't, baby," whispered Mario. "Sean felt bad he had to turn you down like that. Felt like he'd made a bad situation worse."

"My point is," said Pat before Jessie could say anything, "is that when we brought you behind your dad's shed, I did it 'cause it seemed like me and Billings here could give you something nice. Do right by you. And to be honest, I owe Lea for making not one but two of my men really happy, so when she suggested me and Mario show you some fun, I wouldn't have said no even if I hadn't wanted to."

"Lea!" huffed Jessie. "I knew she was behind this!"

"You complaining?" Mario asked, squeezing her clit and he plunged into her. "God... no."

"Good," said Pat. "But what I was trying to say was, the minute we started to kiss, it was like that woman under all of that sadness just burst out. It was just like that fire. Kind of scary. But absolutely breathtakingly beautiful."

Now the sob had almost no laughter in it.

"And the sex... Sex always feels good, Jessie," Pat continued. "But this? I mean, don't get me wrong, not many women can take all of me like you."

"Damn straight," said Mario, pushing so deep that Jessie saw stars.

"But it's you. I don't usually have these, like, serious conversations mid-fuck, believe me."

"Damn straight."

She laughed, tightening around Mario's leg and cock.

Mario bit her ear, turning the laugh into a moan. "Some people are just unhappy. You can't do a thing about it. You..." He squeezed her clit again, turning the moan into a full-on howl. "You happy now, Jessie?"

"FUCK YES!"

They stopped talking for a while and Jessie let herself float back into that eternal present of ecstasy. Four hands, two mouths, one cock. One very happy Jessie.

She came, but instead of stopping, they continued, and Jessie felt that whitewater feeling again, only instead of being caught up in the river, she was the river. She roared and seethed and burst, flung herself up into the stars and landed right there, back in the bank between her demon lovers, and roared again.

"Wanna make you happy," whispered Mario, and the gentle power of it flung her up once more, and again... "AH!" And then he drove himself into her, and they exploded.

And they settled. Panting.

"Happy." Jessie was weeping, but yes, she was: happy as she had not been, possibly ever.

Mario kissed her, and kissed her again.

"Shooting star," Pat said.

Jessie and Mario looked up. This wasn't a momentary needle of light — this was a silent, silver, slowmotion fireball, rolling across the sky.

"Make a wish, baby," panted Mario.

Jessie grinned.

And they lived happily ever after.

About K.D. West

The Amazon best-selling author of the *Erotic Tales: Letters to Allison* and *Juliet Takes Flight* story cycles as well as the up-coming novel *A Joy Forever: An Erotic Education*, **K.D. West** is a teacher, writer and performer living in a small suburb of a big city: "Not a huge amount to say — I'm an author of steamy stories who happens to be a teacher; these things don't mix well in public, so I tend to be fairly quiet about real life in my blogging. I am, however, interested in all sorts of things — books, writing, theater, mythology, and, obviously, erotica! I'm a huge reader of genre fiction — mostly mysteries and fantasy, but also science fiction and historical romance."

West is working on two intertwined series involving a young woman and her older lover (the *Juliet Takes Flight* and *Erotic Tales: Letters to Allison* stories), a series of stories about friends discovering that they can become much more (*Friendly Ménage Tales*), and a series of the kinds of fairytales that the Brothers Grimm might have written if they'd been interested in stories where the heroine got the princess (*Sapphic Fairytales*). Also on the way: *By the Numbers,* an erotic paranormal/urban fantasy novel involving a long-lost friend coming all-but-literally back from the dead, and showing a happily married couple just what they'd been missing.

You can follow K.D. West on WordPress, Twitter (@KDWestWrites), Facebook, Pinterest, Google+, Tumblr, or even LinkedIn.

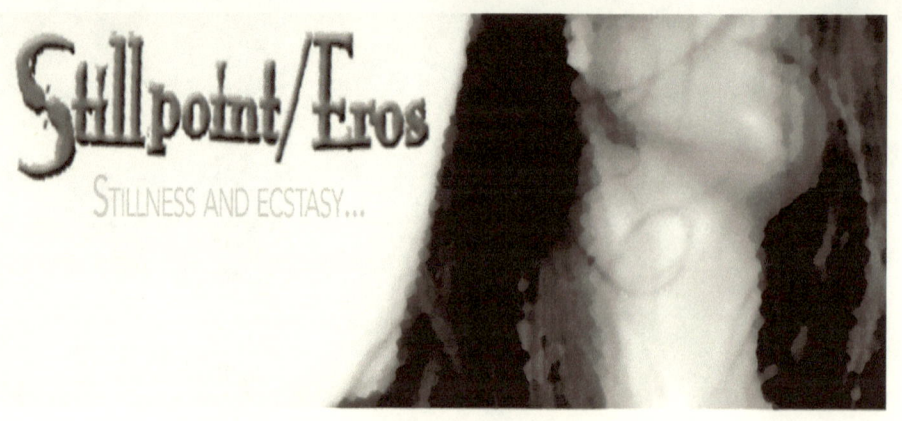

Stillpoint/Eros
STILLNESS AND ECSTASY...

Erotica to feed the mind, the spirit…

and, oh, yes, the body.

Fine erotica for the discerning individual,

available as ebooks, print books, and audio-books!

Stillpoint/Eros

Sign up for our newsletter and download for free stories!

StillpointEros.com/Free-Download

FOLLOW US:

Twitter: @StillpointEros • Facebook: StillpointEros
Google+: +StillpointErosBooks